THE QUIET BEYOND THE WELL

1

CW WREN

To everyone who broke themselves trying to fix everything else. Go take a nap and drink some water, lovies.

CONTENTS

NOTE FROM THE AUTHOR

The Quiet Beyond the Well is a dark fantasy novel that contains material that some readers may find distressing including: terminal illness, death of a parent, violence, attempted abduction, attempted assault, murder, profanity, grief, substance use and self harm.

One of the key themes of this story is healing and it is the author's hope that many will find that within its pages, however, if while reading you find something you feel should be included in the above list please don't hesitate to contact the author.

Uncharted North
Lunochy
The Bleeding Trees
Belwarie
Caillie Sea
Invengarry
Murdoch
Arborlynn
Obanes
Ember's Meadow
The Ash Woods
The Isle of Rest
Isle Basalt

PRONUNCIATION GUIDE

Emer: eh-m er*
Calder: kol-der
Danu: dan-oo
Aven: ī-ven
Bás: bahs
Caillte: kīl-chuh
Mian: mee-un
Neamhní: nyæv-nee
Teárlach: chahr-lukh

æ - pronounced like the 'a' in the English "cat".

kh - pronounced gutturally, like the 'ch' in German "Bach".

ah - pronounced like the 'a' in the English 'father'.

u/uh - pronounced like the 'u' in the English 'cup'.

ī - pronounced like the 'i' in English "write".

---

* this is a break from the traditional pronunciation which is ev-ir.

There are no beautiful surfaces without a terrible depth.
Nietzsche

There was quiet.
Then chaos.
Then nothing.

PROLOGUE

It was quiet as she fell.

The only sound was Lachlan's voice in her head.

"We can save him," he had said. *"If you come with me, we can save your father."*

All evidence of the fight around her seemed to fall away. A riot of emotions—known and unknown—hung between them. Emer's eyes snapped closed and the breath was stolen from her lungs as her body crashed into the frigid water.

Slipping beneath the surface was like crossing the Array into a foreign realm of calm and quiet. It was a deceptive and eerie contrast from the battle that raged above the surface, and the girl who now sank beneath the flaming ship welcomed the lie. The heat of the flames could not touch her with the cold water hugging her close. The deep refused to let the fire's light corrupt it, diffusing it across the surface and bathing her in shadows.

Her head lolled back and the hair that escaped her braid danced across her face. Saltwater burned her eyes, but she watched and waited, expecting him to have jumped in after her.

As she sank further into the depths, she grew weightless and her arms rose ready to embrace him. He had promised to stay with her. How quickly promises seemed to wither these days. When she closed her eyes, she could still see the flames, the arrows, the blood, and the look in Lachlan's eyes as he threw her free of the burning ship. It had been to protect her, to hide her in the deep darkness, but the plunge into the void hurt her all the same.

A tingling sensation bloomed in her chest and fueled the burning in her lungs. She assumed that the grip of death would be cold, but it was more like a warm caress. The warmth spread from her center and down her arms, dripping from her fingertips.

Dying. This is dying.

The thought rang loudly, but she felt no fear. The idea of facing the evils above was far more terrifying, and despite the consequences, the temptation to stay below the waves overwhelmed her. If it was only her fate at stake, she might have succumbed. The words of her promise echoed in her mind, matching the progressively slowing pace of her pulse as she fought against the seductive call of the sea.

Upon meeting the night air, she coveted the deep, painful breath that filled her lungs. Secondary to the need for air was the need to create as much distance between herself and the monsters intent on slaughtering her friend and his men. She spared a glance at the ship, ravaged by flames. The cries of the crew ceased, and the deafening silence caused bile to rise in her throat. She had not seen the ship that ambushed them; only the flaming arrows that mercilessly descended upon them were proof that it was not the night itself that had attacked.

Her movements through the water grew lax and slow as exhaustion took hold of her limbs. A wave swept past, causing her to choke on the water that invaded her mouth and slipped down her throat. Driftwood collided against her shoulder, but Emer was grateful for its intrusion despite the pain. Perhaps the Elders didn't hate her as much as it seemed.

The thick fabric of her dress became an anchor, forcing her to grip the splintered wood until her cold and wrinkled hands bled.

With the night's bite against her face and back, the chill and wariness set deep in her bones. Soon, she relented and began to drift wherever the sea wished, hoping it would make better choices than the ones that had led her to this moment. Dropping her forehead to the damp and swollen wood, she spoke to no one in particular.

"Help."

A wave stole the word from her lips; the tide collected her tears; the night and all its stars ignored her cries.

And then there was nothing.

CHAPTER I

A heaviness wrapped her body. Dull aches began to grow and spread as the brackish taste of salt coated her mouth. Amongst the sea of harsh sensations, Emer felt a gentle tug on her braid.

Not dead then?

The hiss of rolling waves drowned out the thought, which was banished entirely by the cold water that caressed her lower body. The chill forced her eyes open to confront the reality of her situation. Her father once said the dark side of the truth was that once your eyes are open to it, you cannot return to the blissful ignorance of before.

"*Things cannot be un-seen or un-known,*" he would say.

The truth was her world had gone from vibrant to varying shades of gray. Part of her knew that had little to do with the bleak surroundings she was beginning to take in and more to do with the circumstances that brought her to this moment.

Equally unfortunate that they were.

Once her eyes adjusted to the shore, she realized the land was not actually leeched of color. It was early morning, and the colors slumbered, waiting for the sun to kiss them awake. How often she wished for the same. To sleep and not wake until life was vibrant once again.

As her consciousness seeped back in, she winced. Her cheek felt raw against the sand and rocks below her. Each stone mocked her with a sharp jab, and each grimace only encouraged the sting. Exhausted and weighed down by her sea-soaked clothes, she struggled as she rolled onto her back. Clutching at her middle, her hand searched for the small pouch tied around her waist. Her fingers brushed the rune her brother had etched into the leather.

Courage.

It was the same rune she drew at the bottom of the letter she had left for him—the only clue to what she had done.

Emer felt anything but courageous as her cold fingers delved beneath the flap in search of the small piece of fabric within it. For without it, she would truly be without hope.

Like her, it was soggy and worn, but it was still there, and she dropped her head back into the stones. Emer gripped the fabric tighter, causing her fingers to hurt and seawater to seep from between them. She did not know it was possible to feel this defeated, this alone. She also did not realize that, depending on the company, sometimes being alone was better.

Another tug at her braid signaled that she was not entirely on her own after all. She turned her tired gaze to the side, moving her aching body the bare minimum required, and found a curious set of eyes staring back at her. Pale blue and belonging to a surprisingly large white bird.

Any other day, she would count herself lucky to happen upon such a creature. It was strikingly beautiful and just peculiar enough that it seemed magical. She could not be bothered by any of those things today, though.

If her limbs had cooperated, she would have shooed him away. When she found she lacked the strength, she instead murmured, "Kindly, fuck off." The words came out cracked and hoarse, the rawness making them sound less convincing.

The bird cocked its head. She stared blankly at it for a moment, and when it did not move, she assumed they had reached a truce. It would politely let her die before bothering her further—a small kindness.

The sun fought to break through the scattered clouds, but one of the beams found passage, and its warmth cascaded over her. For a moment, she dreamt she was home.

Home was reading in her meadow.

Home was the sounds of her brother sparring nearby—Finn never far from his sister.

Home was following their mother's voice calling for supper and finding their father by the fire in his favorite chair.

Her daydream was dispersed by the sound of the next wave and the accompanying tug on her braid. This time, the creature tugged harder.

"Impatient bastard. Just go," she cursed. It was a whisper, her voice still too tender for use.

The bird began hopping excitedly, the rocks shuffling beneath his talons, then silence. She exhaled but internally knew better than to show the Elders signs of her relief.

"Merrow or Selkie?" a deep voice rumbled from far too close.

There would be no meadow.

No family supper.

No fire next to her father's favorite chair.

She knew that the moment she looked into his eyes—the stormy blue of the unforgiving sea and keen with suspicion.

A sharp burst of air crashed against her face, and when she opened her eyes once more, she saw the man—a knight if his leathers were any indication—tracking the retreating bird. Apparently, she was not worth facing off against this new opponent.

Traitor.

When those piercing blue eyes returned to her, she withered under his stare.

Alarm coursed through her as he continued to watch her,

waiting expectantly for the answer to a question she could not recall. Her hands fought for purchase in the rocks as she attempted to force herself up, her body shaking in protest. He stared down at her with his head tilted, not unlike the bird, a predator admiring his prey.

Lethal and curious.

Unlike the bird, however, there was no brilliant white. He was clothed head-to-toe in black.

Her eyes darted around her surroundings as if she hoped to find her voice.

Nothing. She recognized nothing.

The knight cleared his throat to pull her attention back

"It is not common to find a maiden emerging from the sea, and I know some silly little girl from the Isle of Rest did not just wish herself here. So, I'll ask again... Merrow or Selkie?"

Distracted by his voice, Emer did not dwell on the slight. The unfamiliar lilting brogue signaled that this shore was not a sanctuary after all. She had been far safer at the mercy of the sea and its monsters than the one looming over her now.

While the cloak hid the length to which violence had refined his body, it only drew attention to his tall frame and broad shoulders. His features were severe for a man of his age. He was young in years, only a few more than Emer, but they were clearly harsh. With eyes that spoke of the beasts he had battled, and scarless, cruel features that were proof he had won.

He did not approach her as a man intent on rescuing her, or attempt to pull her from the hard ground she prostrated herself on. He did not even give her reprieve from the water still greedily reaching for her.

While it was growing increasingly clear that he was not there as her hero, it remained to be seen if he would be her villain instead. The uncertainty sent another spike of fear through her blood, which felt sluggish and chilled.

The knight's full lips pursed together, and his dark brows

pinched. He evaluated each movement, feature, and wound. A strategist trying to piece together her story.

Emer's brother once told her that it was okay for her heart to falter as long as her glare didn't. She bit back her fear as she shifted her weight and lifted her hand to him.

She was not beautiful in the traditional sense but in the same wild way that the sea is beautiful. Despite its beauty, the sea was also deadly and, just like a Merrow, could devour him without a second thought if it pleased.

"Mortal," she forced out the word as she met his eyes.

The knight's lip twitched as he assessed her glare, though it was unclear if he was hiding a smile or a snarl—she would not ask, and he would not tell.

He extended his hand to her. A foreboding rune inked in the center of his palm, waiting for her to take notice. But Emer did not look at his hand, denying him the recognition that would have flashed in her eyes if she managed to pull her gaze away from his.

One look was all it would take to draw out her fear, just as it only took one look at her to conjure his suspicion.

Overreaching, he slipped his long fingers under the cold, green fabric of her sleeve and over her icy skin, allowing his calloused fingertips to rest over her pulse point. The beat was rapid, which was not entirely surprising given that the sea had swallowed her and then spat her back out.

Pain radiated through Emer as she shifted her weight and tested her muscles. The knight held her firmly, making no attempts to acknowledge her struggle as he guided her out of the reach of the waves.

"While you certainly curse like one, I suppose you are not seductive enough to be a Merrow." He paused to study her with a raised brow. "Nor are you naked enough to be a Selkie."

"Excuse me!" Her lips stuck together and stung as she forced them to form the words, but her shock dulled the pain of her outburst.

Despite not being able to stand independently, she tried to pull her arm free of his grip.

"I did not write the legends, Bonnie," he explained. He tested the way the pet name felt on his lips and then shrugged. "That's just how the lore goes."

Her muscles tensed beneath his fingers.

"The legend is wildly inappropriate," she countered.

He shrugged again. "That may be true, but not as *wildly* inappropriate as being so captivated by you that I stole your seal skin so that you would be mine forever, which is the fate of most Selkies caught lounging on the shore. Again, according to legend," he said, clearly intent on keeping her off balance.

Dazed and unwilling to grant the stranger any further reaction, she stared blankly ahead. There was nothing to indicate why he was there or where he came from, and it enraged her to think she was so unlucky that he would have stumbled upon her in a remote location.

The Elders are assholes.

Emer collapsed into the lush growth, running her wrinkled fingers through the clovers that swept across the space, starkly contrasting the rocky shore that greeted her.

"I'm curious how you found yourself on my shore?" He grunted as he lowered himself onto the grass beside her, holding the panels of his cloak closed. Tossing his dark curls from his eyes, he looked at her once more.

"I was not aware that anyone could just claim an entire shoreline," she murmured.

Although he did not correct her, there was a slight shift of his expression, an added smugness, that told her she was wrong.

His tone was flat when he spoke next. "Ignorance does not excuse the offense." Tilting his head back, he studied the clouds. "Basking, perhaps?" he asked.

"Basking requires the sun, does it not?" Her words came out heated despite the fact that there was frost forming on her bones.

He plucked a clover from the ground and examined it before tossing it over his shoulder. "Can't say. I'm not well-versed in the practice. If you were not basking, can you explain why I found you amongst the waves?" There was a subtle edge to his voice that betrayed his feigned disinterest. His words were growing sharper. All the better to carve out the truth.

As if slipping back into a nightmare, the images of the night before flashed through her mind.

The sounds of the screams.

The feeling of falling.

The silence that followed as the sea stole her away.

A tentative pull against her fingers brought her back to her senses. Her gaze dropped to see him uncurling her fingers and inspecting her hand. Red half-moons lined the pale skin of her palm from where her nails had dug too deeply. Emer ripped her hand from him and pulled it close to her chest. The knight's eyes narrowed.

She was under no illusions that interlopers were welcomed on Isle Basalt, and his attention was certain to prove problematic. The details of how she came to be in her current state would endanger her and any of the men who managed to survive the ambush. *If any of them made it to shore, it was not this one.* She silently prayed to the Elder of Endings that he had spared them, that there was still hope for a cure—hope for her father.

To make matters worse, there was no way to know if the man next to her or his brethren was responsible for the attack.

"I don't know what happened," she whispered.

Lie.

His eyes grew cold before his attention shifted to the abrasion across her cheekbone, and her fingertips moved to where his eyes came to rest. "You've been in an accident." It was an observation rather than a question.

Her unease grew with every passing moment she was subjected to his scrutiny, and instinct told her that if she did not leave soon, there was a strong chance she would not be leaving at all.

Emer rose to her feet, stumbling back when the knight followed, only saved from falling by his firm grip on her wrist. There was a warning in how he looked at her then, releasing her from his bruising hold one finger at a time.

"Off so soon?" His tone was pleased, drinking in the desperation of her features like nectar. Sweet and stolen.

"Yes," she answered, stepping back and collecting clovers in the skirt of her dress.

He watched as she took several more steps away with an excitement in his eyes that had her fighting the urge to run for fear that was exactly what he wanted.

"Thank you for that... and for coming to my aid earlier, but I must be going," she said, giving him her back once more.

He cocked his head, amusement rather than rage creasing his brow.

"Where?" His warm breath was on her neck, having quickly and silently closed the distance between them. She reeled from his proximity as she turned back to face him. Her height brought her gaze level with the clasp of his cloak, and she was forced to tilt her head to meet his stare.

"I am on my way north for... my family," she muttered.

"And how far north will you go, little Merrow?" He decided the earlier name had not suited her.

"That is none of your concern, *and* that is not my name," she barked, deflecting his question.

"You've given me no name. What is it that I shall call you then?" His voice was thick and dark.

"Also, none of your concern."

Her glare slowly left his eyes and down to the now visible knife sheathed at his side. Her hand twitched almost imperceptibly. It had not escaped him that rather than fearing he had a weapon, she immediately considered how she would take it from him. This time, he did not even fight the corner of his lip as it curled up.

"Merrow it is," he remarked smugly.

"I'm sorry?" she questioned.

"There seems to be some disagreement regarding what is and is not my concern." He stepped forward, asserting both his size and authority. "*You*, for example, are very much my concern. It's not wise for a helpless maiden to wander alone."

Both knew the deception of his response. She didn't believe he was concerned. He didn't believe she was helpless.

Regardless of what lay beyond the shore, Emer was certain it had to be safer than this.

"I will be sure to send word if I encounter one." Her smile as she spoke the words was painted on with practiced strokes.

He laughed. It was a deep chuckle that surprised even him.

Emer stiffened at the sound, recognizing it for what it was—a warning.

"Do you know the easiest way to tell if someone is being deceitful?" His tone was mirthful, yet she knew she would find little humor in his musing. He stalked around her and it took a conscious effort not to follow his movement. "Some will say it is in the person's voice; others will swear by the eyes. Do you know how I know you are lying, *Merrow?*" he exaggerated the last word in a teasing and honeyed voice.

Determined to deprive him of her attention as he circled her, Emer made herself stare at a single cloud in the distance. It looked like a skull, and it was entirely unhelpful in keeping her nerves. She hated this place.

Leaning forward, he tilted his head next to hers.

"Your neck," he whispered against the shell of her ear, prompting her to take a hurried step forward. "More specifically, the pulse of your heart, which I can see in your neck." He ghosted his finger up her throat.

"In case you have not noticed, I am having a bit of a day. Have you considered my elevated pulse is simply a sign of annoyance? Or do you just *think* you are that charming?"

"Oh, I have noticed many things. Since you refuse to be honest, allow me to be brutally so." Brutality was one of his finer qualities, so it seemed like a fitting place for his pause. "You've been in an accident, which you allude to not remembering. You're visibly injured either from attacking someone or being attacked."

"I didn't—" he interrupted her protest by raising his finger to his lips.

Her eyes flared with indignation.

What. An. Ass.

"You are nearly frozen. You have clearly spent the night in the water and are most certainly not from here. Despite all those observations, do you know what I find the most curious about you?" he asked.

She stood there, stunned, unable to understand how things had gone wrong so fast and how she could escape this situation. Escape *him*.

"It would be more fun if you tried to guess," he teased, and there was a playfulness in his voice.

As Emer watched his delight at her defiance, she knew she was the toy.

Scowling, she bit down so hard, she thought her teeth might crack. "I have no interest in your games," she said sternly.

His eyebrow tipped up.

"You have not asked for my aid. Not. Once. That is what I find quite curious."

The accusation caused her stomach to sink into her boots. Anyone else in her position would have asked for help, but she was only focused on getting away.

"The role of victim doesn't suit you, so why don't you tell me why you are *really* here," he sneered.

She dropped her eyes to her feet, the knight still standing at her back, and she knew it was time to decide. Emer's heels dug into the earth below, and she ran.

The sound of a sword being unsheathed caused her blood to run cold, and she cursed as she prepared to meet its even colder blade. Her feet kicked at the heavy skirt of her dress, but rather than moving forward, she stumbled. Falling to her knees, her fingers again embedding themselves deep into the clovers. Confusion swelled as she lunged forward, and the bodice of her dress acted like a net, tethering her in place.

Reeling around, she found his sword driven through the skirt of her dress and deep into the hillside. Despite the cries of the fabric as she worked to tug herself free, the sword remained in place.

Although he released the hilt, his arm casually draped over his bent leg, he remained on one knee as he watched her. A smug grin pulled at his lips as he shook his head from side to side slowly. "We were not finished," he chimed.

Enraged, Emer lunged for the sword.

Counter to what she had expected, he did not flinch or withdraw as she advanced, and the distance between them reduced to nearly nothing.

"You have gold in your eyes," he observed aloud.

Flecks within the green that seemed to illuminate, to burn brighter, as her frustration flared and a faint pink taunted her cheeks.

He winked.

She snarled.

Fueled with an anger she had never known, Emer freed the sword and leveled it at its owner.

Slowly, he rose to a standing position, allowing the tip of the blade to drag down the fabric of his cloak as he stood. Despite willing her hands to steady, he ran his thumb over his lip as though he could taste her fear.

Bravery is something rooted deep within the bones of those

with no fear. Courage is in the marrow of those whose bones shake with fear, but they force their bodies to keep moving despite it. While she was not brave, she was courageous.

His smile widened like he could taste that too.

Taking an unhurried step back, he raised his hands, revealing the thick black lines of the tattoos in the center of his palms— runes, the language of the Elders' magic.

The Elders, being neither malevolent nor benevolent, required some form of payment, offering, or sacrifice to call upon their magic. While the meaning of the tattoo inked on the left palm was obscured, Emer was certain of two things about the one on his right. The rune represented death, and his preferred currency was blood.

Though her arms were tired from clinging to the debris, her hands screamed at her for gripping the hilt so tightly, and her legs shook with fear. He would not get to see the pain on her face or the satisfaction of drinking in her terror. She would only allow him to see the rage churning inside her. He did not let her run, so she would fight.

Emer caught her reflection in the blade's steel for the briefest moment. She did not recognize the fierce creature staring back at her, but she was grateful for her. The girl from the meadow would not have fought him, but the one who emerged from the sea was going to draw blood.

The knight nodded to himself, seeing her expression harden with resolve.

"Truly, I cannot decide if I am delighted or annoyed," he mused. His thumb rubbed across his lip as he pondered her. It was the *why* that made her dangerous and the *why* that prevented him from letting her go.

He stepped forward, his eyes fixed on her, no longer bothering to look at the sword she wielded. "Do you know one of the most important rules of sparring, Merrow?" He watched her intently as he tilted his chin up and unclasped his cloak. The fabric slid down his body, revealing the muscled form wrapped in dark leather, a black tunic, and weapons fixed to various limbs. "Know your opponent."

Emer's lips parted as she surveyed the additional weapons hidden beneath his cloak—a sight that would cause most to stand down. She did not.

Either because she believed she could beat him.

Dangerous.

Or she had a secret worth dying for.

More dangerous.

"You'll fight me?" His voice was softer but threatening all the same.

She readied her stance and secured her grip on the sword.

"While you may be the most beautiful creature to wield a weapon on this Isle, I promise you, I am the deadliest. This is not wise." His words were a startling mixture of threat and flirtation. In the same breath, he unsheathed the other sword he carried. "Last chance," he offered.

When she did not answer, he brought his sword down in a thunderous crash as it met her guard. The collision traveled the length of the blade and through her bones. It was violent enough that she feared her limbs would shatter, and she let out an unintentional groan.

Despite the ringing in her ears, she heard him huff. He was not fighting her... he was mocking her. Her blood began to boil, fusing and hardening her insides. Pride was a dangerous thing and something she intended to use against him. He made another half-hearted movement to engage her, and instead of blocking, she spun out to the side, carrying her weight through the spin and swinging towards his side.

Reckless.

He had been reckless in underestimating her. As he silently cursed for allowing himself to be distracted, he darted back. He almost managed to escape the path of the blade completely. Shifting his weight, he lowered his sword in another powerful arc and disarmed her.

With a dull thud, the sword fell unceremoniously to the grass, and she recoiled at the fire that radiated up her arms. His lethal gaze fell on her, watching as she panted through her grin.

"Do you always smile when you lose?" It sounded more curious than haughty.

"You were never going to let me leave. I only wanted to make you regret it." Her chest heaved as she spoke.

It was as though her words triggered awareness of the pain he had not yet registered.

Elders' tits...

His hand traveled to his side, finding torn fabric and a sticky warmth. A deep, guttural sound crawled up his throat. The wound was too shallow to put him in any real peril, but it would scar—a reminder that he should not have mocked her. On top of that, it was damned inconvenient. He pulled his finger back and studied the blood that painted them. For a brief moment, he almost smiled back.

"Does your achievement somehow overshadow the fact that I may now kill you?" he asked with a raised brow.

Her smile faltered, but only slightly.

"That was as much a possibility before as it is now," she argued.

"You may have tipped the odds, sweetheart. You see, you proved me right. You aren't nearly as innocent as you pretend to be," he countered. Emphasizing his point by waving his sword in her direction.

"Then perhaps you will think twice about trying to keep me," she said, raising her chin higher.

"I assure you, I want that more than before." His grin was unmistakable now.

A captive was better than a corpse. At least the fate of the former could be changed.

Her task was to reach the Well and beseech the Elders' magic to heal her father, and while she had failed, she could at least ensure the knight did not learn of the others who were sent for it. If he was preoccupied for long enough, then any survivors would have a chance to disappear further inland. She gathered all the confidence she could muster.

"Perhaps some dry clothes and food would aid in my recollection," she suggested.

He smirked.

"Do you always lie so sweetly?"

He motioned his head, instructing her to walk, and she scowled. His eyes narrowed in warning. Not seeing how this situation could get much worse, Emer asked with a saccharine smile, "Do women always heed your every command without question?"

"No," he said quickly. "*Everyone* does."

CHAPTER 2

An incredulous scoff escaped her, eyes almost rolling out of habit, but the movement halted at the seriousness of his expression. Gone was the arrogance she saw earlier, replaced by cold boredom—making her call into question who exactly she had just stabbed.

She could feel the atmosphere around her shift as he drew closer—just like it does immediately before a lightning strike. He would be her keeper, but with fire thrumming in her eyes, she made it clear she would not be easily kept. Like daring to catch the aforementioned lightning with nothing but a bottle.

"Shall we?" he asked her with a sarcastic bow.

Her shoulders shifted in agitation, fighting against the truth that she was coming to accept. She was left with no choice but to follow him. Within a few steps, she realized she had been wrong before, the situation could get far worse. The gravestones that came into view were the proof. Her eyes darted across the markers that emerged from the ground like mournful wildflowers.

He stepped in close at her side, tilting his head to better view her horror at realizing she had washed up to a graveyard. "The Elders must have deemed this a convenient place to discard you," he mocked, and whether he realized it or not, his words met their mark.

They had abandoned her in her short-lived quest, and she wondered if they decided to before she even left the shore. She wrapped her arms around herself, pulling tightly in hopes it would keep the tears that threatened to fall at bay. The confidence she had forged began to crack and was at risk of shattering entirely.

From behind, a heavy fur cloak came to rest around her shoulders.

"While I wouldn't normally keep my charges warm, it hardly seems appropriate when they are, in fact, a helpless maiden. Besides, I've found myself... indisposed," he said, glancing down at the tear in his tunic.

"Yes, because this thing has never seen blood," she groaned under her breath with a grimace.

"Not mine," he said with a sharp smile before turning around and heading into the field of granite in front of them.

If the significant disparity between their sizes was not apparent before, it became painfully evident as the cloak swallowed Emer whole. She had deemed him tall earlier, but suddenly, she felt so small—something he no doubt intended. When he looked over his shoulder to watch her trailing behind him, it banished any warmth she found under the cloak. The weight of it pressing on her shoulders became claustrophobic; the soft fur that lined it became too sharp against her cold skin. The earthy scent of it hung in the cold air around her, a mockery of warmer memories. Of oak barrels of whiskey and salt water.

Emer contemplatively strode behind him. If she attempted to run, it would be gambling with his patience. If she continued to follow him, it would be a gamble with his humanity. She never had the constitution for games of chance. Given the suspicions he clearly held and the fact that she had already raised a sword against him, she could hardly believe there was an outcome that didn't end in a cell. She reminded herself again that a captive was better than a corpse.

The wind blew hard at their backs, pressing the knight's thin tunic to his frame and revealing muscles sculpted from years of wielding a weapon. If they were not evidence enough of his battle-hardened nature, the fact that he was entirely unfazed by the wound she inflicted was. She continued to read his body like a book. His hair was as black as a raven's feathers, his eyes were a piercing blue, and his accent left no doubt that she had arrived on Isle Basalt. Though what shore, in particular, eluded her. Regardless, she would not be welcomed.

The war between their two isles may have long been over, but the spilled blood that seeped into the soil cultivated deep roots of bitterness and hate.

The cause of the strife and lingering tension was always unclear to Emer. She often wondered if perhaps the Elder of War sought entertainment or the Elder of Endings company. The reason seemed to vary depending on who she asked and how much they'd had to drink.

Lachlan, only ten years Emer's senior, was too young to have fought in the war himself but once told her that those who had returned no longer found comfort in the quiet meadows of their land. It was in the silence that their ghosts were the loudest.

Although minor forms of violence had never particularly bothered Emer, the thought of the lives lost in battle or the act of sending a soul across the Array was something she could not stomach. It was not an affliction her brother had, and when raids and disappearances began to plague their quiet corner of the realm shortly before their father's health began to decline, he took up his sword like the warrior he was at heart—possessing a fearlessness she had always admired.

Fear was Emer's constant companion, although she had not understood that was what it was at first. When she was young, she thought it was butterflies that stirred in her chest. As she grew older, the butterflies grew more restless and became a hum beneath her skin. A hum that occasionally felt so intense, she thought she might burst. Eventually, her fear became a part of her. A thick black thread woven through her spine that when pulled without warning, would draw her taught like a bowstring. When that happened, she found herself shuddering and tugging against the imaginary thread and the wrongness it stitched into every part of her.

The ever-watchful big brother, Finn, was all too aware of her twitchiness—a descriptor he used to describe the state that she seemed to be able to hide from everyone but him. It was one of the reasons why he taught her to fight all those years earlier. He knew it would be rather difficult for her to be lost in her mind if she was busy dodging his fists.

It became their routine. If Emer began to spiral, she and Finn would escape to the meadow and spar. Given the frequency of the episodes, the ritual resulted in her becoming quite proficient in hand-to-hand combat. She also learned how to wield a knife—something only her brother and a handful of overly touchy men knew.

As running away to the meadow with Finn was not always possible, she also became talented at painting her nervousness as something else... something acceptable.

Lies. Emer painted pretty lies.

It was remarkable how often her manner of coping with her internal turmoil was praised.

How mature she was.

How driven she was.

How accomplished she was.

But the reality was, she was scared, tired, and a little broken. Everyone saw the pearl, not the layers of toil and crushing weight that formed it. So, she continued to craft her nervous energy into more attractive things, doing everything she could to keep her nervousness at bay.

She was not brave like her brother, but she had pretended to be many things, and if she could deceive an entire village into thinking she was something she was not, surely she could trick one knight.

As if he managed to stalk her through the thoughts she wandered to, the knight turned to glare at her over his shoulder. Given that she was currently in a land famed for its abundant magic, it was within the realm of possibilities. She waited for the knight to turn his back once more, then she thought every foul thing her imagination could muster and married them with the types of curses that could make the Elders blush.

Nothing.

She released a breath.

The incline of the hill continued to increase, and soon, they were deep within the landscape's lush green trees. The scene around them was a far cry from the land of fierce warriors and brutality from the stories. It almost reminded her of home. The sun cascaded through the leaves, creating a light show as the wind danced through the branches. A performance that had her thoroughly distracted. She could hardly reconcile how a place so pure and peaceful could exist in a land known only for its cruelty.

Her attention was snatched back by the sharp cry of a bird above. Shaking her head, she focused on the much more important task at hand. She needed to concoct a convincing story before they arrived to wherever it was that she was being led. There had been no signs of a port, merchants, or homes from the shore, and she hoped that the distance would work in her favor. A plausible explanation to satisfy the knight's questions would need time. As would her plan to escape if her story failed. Almost as if the Elders caught on to her glimmer of hope, the trees began to clear, revealing the turrets and battlements of a keep.

High atop the rocky hill, the keep was an intimidating sight. What little sun there was bathed the pale stones of the otherwise cold structure, softening its harsh edges with a warm haze. Emer imagined its location offered a breathtaking view of the sea. A view that she was growing less confident she would ever see with each step.

Lost in thought, she had not seen the knight unsheathe the small throwing knife that was secured at his chest. The cold metal of that knife now twirled across his long fingers—a display blocked from view by his broad shoulders. His eyes ahead, but his attention on her.

Her feet halted, and she turned back to the woods. Before she even took a step, a strong hand gripped her wrist. Whirling her back to face him, she saw the blade of his knife tapping against his lips.

"I think not," his voice rumbled.

The corner of his mouth tipped up only enough to reveal a sharp canine behind the blade. Turning the knife in his palm, he brought his hands to her shoulders. The movement caused her to startle back, but he held the cloak firmly in his hands, anchoring her in place. Glaring, he pulled the hood up and secured her hair from view.

He had been searching for answers that had been lost on the Isle of Rest for too long to let her slip through his grasp, but he could not simply walk her into the keep. Her copper hair was too red, and her eyes too bright. It took one look to know where she was from, and the men at the keep who had lived to see the war with her people would be far too eager to send her back home in pieces. Getting his answers meant keeping her to himself, which also meant keeping her hidden.

"Keep this up. Keep your eyes down. And, *Elders above,* do not decide to become chatty because I think you will find my company far more pleasant than *theirs,*" he said, tipping his head towards the keep.

"Doubtful," she hissed.

The knight rolled his head between his shoulders to assuage his frustration. He opened his eyes after a long blink, only to once again meet her defiant gaze. "You want to test me?" His stare intensified, and he bent his head low to meet hers. "Go ahead, Merrow... *scream*. But you alone will have to deal with what answers your call." His words sent a chill across her skin that rivaled the waves she had emerged from.

While she was under no illusion that she was safe in his charge, he had not harmed her despite having ample opportunity. Discretion could work in her favor. No one could be bothered to hunt a ghost. She pressed her lips closed and stood in silent agreement.

"Come," he commanded.

With her eyes turned to the ground, she followed. The stones of the keep's courtyard were uneven beneath her already unsteady feet. The smell of smoke filled her lungs. It was not the scent she recognized from the hearth at home—this smoke was heavier and almost acidic. Soon, the smell was accompanied by the sharp sound of metal striking metal.

A forge.

Beyond the noise of the smith, she could hear the murmuring of conversations. Gruff and throaty voices grew louder with each step.

Fear gnawed at Emer who knew the men around her would likely not take kindly to her presence, let alone the fact that she was only there because her attempts at stealth had failed. A crime they would all gladly see her ashes scattered in the wind for.

She jumped at a sudden sharp hiss from nearby and it took her a moment to realize it was the sound of molten metal being plunged into cold water—not the terrible beast she had created in her mind.

The atmosphere felt charged by unstable energy and yet colder than it was outside. Despite the chilled air filling her lungs, her skin felt scorched and her palms damp. She could hardly focus her thoughts on anything but the unpleasant hum in her veins, ringing like the heated metal of the forge.

"Calder, it appears you have a shadow," a deep voice sounded.

The knight stopped, and she slammed into his back. The impact was solid, but he did not stumble or acknowledge it apart from a breathy exhale before he greeted the man who spoke.

Calder... his name is Calder.

She silently formed the word, unable to decide if it suited him, and then quickly dismissing the thought as it hardly seemed relevant given the circumstances.

"Have we begun recruiting children?" the man asked.

Calder's hands were crossed behind his back, and one of them twitched as if he felt she needed a reminder not to speak. As though the insult to her height were cause enough to correct the man and instead offer her candidacy for torture and imprisonment.

"An informant and potential witness that I have brought to the keep for questioning. I would like to avoid whispers of their contributions, given that they have valuable information regarding some of the recent raids," he said in a hushed tone meant only for the man who had stopped them.

He lied.

"They experienced some hardship on their journey and will likely need to remain for a time," Calder continued.

She couldn't hear the man's response over the beating of her own heart. His charming tone poured from his lips with unbelievable sincerity, but she knew them for what they were—wholly and beautifully fabricated. His own pretty lies. She suddenly took little comfort in being his secret, and the urge to run, to scream, to do something became overwhelming. However, the understanding that she was outnumbered and unwelcome had her paralyzed with indecision.

Calder seized a moment of his peers' distraction to step closer to Emer. His hands, having been clasped behind his back, quickly found her wrist through the slit in the cloak.

"Don't," he growled over his shoulder.

His grip was firm with warning but not painful. Clearing his throat, he returned his attention to the other man but did not remove his hand.

Shortly after, they exchanged goodbyes. He tugged against her wrist, leading her toward a set of stairs at the end of a hall. Emer tried to remain focused, to orient herself on the layout of the keep, but her mind kept returning to the same question.

Why did he lie?

As was typical, the uncertainty led the way to a spiraling torrent of thoughts. Her mind betrayed her, for when she shook free from the fog of fear, she could no longer remember how many corners they rounded nor how many sets of stairs they climbed. She needed to focus. As far as everyone else was concerned, she was not a threat, and that meant she didn't have to take down all the knights of the keep.

Just Calder.

They approached a door, which opened with a haunting creak.

"Go," he demanded.

CHAPTER 3

Emer raised her head for the first time since entering the keep and met his gaze as she walked into the room. Scanning the space, she noted the various personal items. This was not a room... it was *his* room. Unease surged through her as she searched for anything she might be able to use to defend herself.

Her eyes narrowed on a knife—similar to the one he taunted her with earlier—situated atop a stack of letters on the desk across the room. It called to her like a song, and she had to force her steps to slow as she made her way closer. The thought that its owner might use it to open up correspondences or men's throats, depending on the day, caused her to flinch involuntarily. As she gripped the hilt, the door closed, and she spun around, the knife concealed beneath her cloak.

He grabbed a chair, placed it by the fire, and motioned for her to sit, but Emer didn't move. She had no intention of closing the distance between them and knew that she could easily be overpowered in a seated position. The muscle in his jaw flexed because, as she suspected, not many people defied him when he gave an order.

Cracking his head from one side to the other, he growled and walked to a small chest. He proceeded to retrieve a light tunic and dark brown breeches before unceremoniously tossing them onto the bed at Emer's left.

She eyed the garments suspiciously.

"I've decided not to divulge the details of how our paths crossed... yet. I imagine you know that if you attempt to leave this room, I will raise the alarm that an intruder has breached the perimeter. As you can imagine, we do not entertain guests, so you would be quickly spotted and treated as an intruder would be." He chuckled humorlessly. "I can promise you that you wouldn't find it pleasant."

Emer might have been impressed by how bored he could sound while threatening someone, if it were not directed towards her.

He returned to the chest, this time, throwing his selection over one shoulder. The tunic he wore clung to his skin, sticky with blood concealed by the dark color of the fabric. Reaching for the hem, he raised it just enough to see the shallow wound that ran across the base of his ribs. He grunted as he studied the thin line of angry flesh, an imperfection on an otherwise blemish free torso.

Emer suspected the number of people who had managed to scar him were few and the number of people who did so and still breathed were far fewer.

Calder's fingers surveyed the damage, fresh blood wept from the wound and streaked passed thicker clots of crimson.

Grimacing, Emer tightened her grip around the knife. Perhaps if she stabbed him again while he was distracted, the combined wounds would grant her enough time to exit the keep before he sounded the alarm. She was confident she would need to vomit but had grown accustomed to multitasking. She lifted her heel to move forward when the knight unsheathed one of his swords.

"You know what I love about scars?" he asked. His tone held genuine curiosity.

She placed her heel silently back to the floor, momentarily

disoriented by his question. Over by the fire, he leaned against the stone wall, leaving one hand stretched high above him. Although his back was to her, she learned earlier that the position made him no less aware or dangerous. Rather than answer his question, she continued to watch him warily from the other side of the room.

"Their stories. The best scars have the most interesting ones," he explained.

With his back still to her, he pulled his tunic up once more and then positioned the heated blade to his side. It wasn't until she heard the hiss of the hot metal against his cool blood and smelled the searing of his flesh that she realized what he was doing. She almost dropped the knife to cover her mouth in horror as she watched him cauterize his wound.

His head tipped back as a low, feral sound spilled from his chest. His other fist clenched so tightly that she swore she heard bones crack. Calder dropped his tunic, and his shoulders rose and fell with several deep breaths.

"I think this one will be *very* interesting," he said with a rasp.

He straightened, testing the movements. Satisfied, he stepped away from the fire and turned to meet her shocked stare.

With a knowing smirk he added, "Don't forget to breathe, sweetheart."

Rather than releasing the shaky breath she felt quivering within her, Emer let her lungs burn, closing herself off from her fear and the nauseating scent.

"It seems we are both in need of..." his words trailed off as his eyes washed over her. "Self-care," he continued, making his way to the door.

Before he exited the room, he paused to turn around—an undeniable smirk painted across his face. His earlier annoyance was replaced by a searing satisfaction that resulted from the fact that he was winning, and she knew it.

"While you appear to be an intelligent little thing, I suspect you may also have a mischievous side. This door will be locked the moment I leave in case you were entertaining the idea of doing something spectacularly stupid."

The instant the door closed, Emer stumbled back into the desk. She refused to allow him to witness her mask slip, but its weight had become too heavy. She felt like she was free-falling into an abyss. A gaping chasm of anger and grief that had her sight blurring with tears and her hands shaking with rage.

This is not how it was meant to be.

She had been good; she had done what was asked of her, and yet her father was sick. She had been brave and left her home to fix things, and yet she was now a captive.

Emer swallowed her scream but felt its impact rattle her bones. She could not fill her lungs with enough air to quell the tightness in her chest, consumed with the same overwhelming nausea she had when her father first became ill. When his waking hours grew non-existent and he became a silhouette of what he was—tangible and present but ever-fading. She recalled the collective desperation she felt when the healer had proven utterly useless. His efforts were like trying to stifle the flames of a burning meadow with a thimble. Despite his attempts, she and everyone she loved were still burning, and she could not feign any gratitude for his labors.

She thought she knew what it meant to be broken. She had been wrong because, at least then, there was hope. Hope that roared to life when Lachlan told her of the Well. When he spoke of the Guardian and the need to petition the being tasked with keeping the Well, Emer had not hesitated. She would beseech the Guardian, she would gain access to the Well, and she would save her father from whatever was ravaging his body. But just like the village healer before her, she failed him before the sun even rose to shine light on the promise she'd made.

Her father was going to die.

She was going to die.

Her mother and brother would be alone, and she didn't even

get to say goodbye. Those words ricocheted in her heart, leaving bruises with each collision.

The numbness that eventually swept over her was a small kindness. In that numbness and darkness, she stayed. Her hands trembled with a mixture of fear and fury. Her head throbbed and her teeth hummed from how hard she had gritted them.

Slowly, she felt the thick black thread of dread through her center begin to give. Each breath caused it to loosen a bit more. With sobering clarity, she realized that with every fear of hers having come to pass, there was nothing left to be afraid of. She had fallen to the bottom of the abyss, and here, not even the monsters could find her. It was there that she found the will to climb.

Emer hoisted herself off the floor, the knife still in her hand. She straightened her spine and turned to the garments on the bed. Whatever came next, she intended to face it wearing pants.

Unlacing her boots, she removed her leather pouch and slipped off her dress. After quickly dressing in the tunic and breeches, she slid the knife into her boot. Knowing he could return at any moment, she used the time alone to get to know her opponent as he suggested. Starting with the map above his desk.

Her eyes grew wide as they darted across the various landmarks and notations. It was vital that she determine where on Isle Basalt she had found herself, so she turned her attention to the letters. She was highly aware of the rustling that radiated from the thick parchment as she scanned letter after letter, taking breaks to occasionally peer over her shoulder. After the earlier demonstration of his ability to move in behind her without so much as a sound, she was convinced she could feel his breath against her neck sporadically as she snooped.

Some of the letters were of no consequence, providing very little insight into the man who currently kept her locked away. Other letters were quite tedious. Reports being sent to indicate the status of various keeps and their men. One to the east appeared to be running low on ale and was quite adept in expressing concern for the *"unfortunate situation they found themselves subjected to."*

By the fourth letter, she was fairly certain she was being held in Obanes, something she confirmed after cross-referencing against the map. She was struck by the vastness of the Caillte Sea. It was a small miracle she ever made it to land. Cursed as it may be.

While she could not identify Calder's rank or importance, it was quickly apparent that many sought his guidance. Some had requested a ruling over some manner of dispute. Others were simply seeking his favor and support regarding a particular decision.

It was also clear that he was well versed in war—both in the strategizing and in the killing.

Terrific.

The rustling of the papers grew still as she heard the faint creak of wood and carefully watched the door for Calder to appear. When it remained closed, she returned to the search with renewed vigor.

At present, his skills were being leveraged to train knights in hopes of replicating his "abilities" during an extended time of service. She could take some solace that he had not been leading the raids against her home.

One of the letters seemed more personal than the others. It was from someone named Lina and, although the words were practical, the tone was affectionate. The author was clearly fond of the brute. While it felt wrong to read such a sensitive correspondence, Emer knew any amount of information could save her, and lack thereof could seal her fate.

She prowled through the rest of the letter, but the vague text divulged very little. In addition to the letters was a small stack of books.

The Law of Armys.
Unsurprising
The Order of Tides.

Odious.

Tam Lin. The same story Emer's father once gifted her.

Curious.

A heavy ache settled in her chest as she ran her fingers over the spine—a sensation as familiar as the contents of its pages. A ballad of adventure, magic, and love. She pulled the thin book free from its companions and studied the aged cover, worn with time and frayed from use. Turning the book over, she could see the page edges were wrinkled and bent—features she always felt were signs a book was well-loved.

As she opened it, a metal object connected with the desk below. Her eyes fell on the necklace lying on the desk beneath her. The iron had been manipulated into the shape of a butterfly. She rubbed her thumb over the rough edges of the metal as she placed it back into the book and in line with the others.

A piece of parchment concealed between the books caught her attention. Tugging at the corner, a letter slowly came into view. The thick black scrawl of the name *Muireann* stood out starkly against the parchment, yellowed from the time it spent waiting to be sent. Flipping over the letter, she froze, her eyes narrowing on the image embossed in the wax seal. A sun, a moon, and a raven in between. She dropped the letter as if it would somehow sprout fangs and bite her.

Death and darkness ride on the wings of the raven.

Ravens had long been considered an omen and messengers of the Otherworld as one of the few able to cross the Array while still living. Like the ravens, the clan associated with them were seers and senders of death.

An icy fear seeped into her at the realization that Calder was no ordinary knight. He belonged to the Morvran clan—a Sea Raven, born for bloodshed and battle. The people he hailed from were mercenaries, unstoppable on land and unbeatable on the sea. With a law of their own, those unfortunate enough to earn their attention lost their lives and she could still feel the weight of his storm-cloud eyes.

CHAPTER 4

The quiet of the room was broken by the crackle of the fireplace, startling Emer's tired nerves and causing her to turn. Her eyes did not fall on the whispering fire, but on the knight who sat silently before it and the devious smirk he wore.

Legs outstretched and hands intertwined in his lap, Calder was the picture of ease. "Oh, please, don't stop on my account," he said with a nonchalant wave of his hand.

Emer stumbled back into the desk, her hand clutching her chest and eyes wide.

With a pointed look and an arched brow he said, "I'm sorry, was that rude?"

"You can't just... do that to people!" she barked.

"Keeper. Captive," he crooned, pointing his finger at the respective party. She opened her mouth but could not get any words to leave her lips. Calder's expression shifted as he took in her appearance and the way her petite frame drowned in his clothes.

"You are smaller than you seem," he confessed.

It was a compliment—a testament to how she carried herself. Emer, however, mistook it for criticism. Her eyes settled on the single plate on the floor next to his chair.

"Indulge me," he said with a tip of his head, beckoning her to approach. "Given that you have been so reluctant to tell me about yourself, please enlighten me on what you think I am."

She wondered if his choice of wording was intentionally designed to unsettle her. "*What*" rather than "*who.*"

"Sit," he said with his lips.

Play he said with his eyes.

It was a command, not a request but Emer remained unmoved and silent.

"I've been told I have a pleasing voice, but I must confess, I dislike repeating myself. Don't make me ask again."

His stare intensified, and she thought back to the letters on the desk as she made her way across the room and sat in the chair opposite him.

"So?" he prompted.

"You are a knight," she replied, still resisting his game.

He let out a disapproving click.

"Merrow, you disappoint me... you can do better than that," he chided as he reached down to pick up the plate from the floor.

Her eyes followed the movement and came to rest on the steaming food, despite her best efforts to ignore the alluring smell.

"Someone named Lina cares very much about you, although her reasons are beyond me," she spat.

"She does," he confirmed, but then paused greedily, awaiting another observation.

"People seem to value your opinion, which I assume is why you are quite impossible."

He let out a low chuckle, which caught her by surprise. "Yes, there are those that either desire or require my approval." His stare urged her to react to the power he alluded to possessing but Emer consciously masked her expression from revealing any of her interest or fear.

"You are simply repeating what you read from the correspondences you rifled through. Are you not able to deduce anything that isn't explicitly stated? I thought you were smarter than that," he goaded.

"You're a Sea Raven," she barked out in frustration, despite everything rational in her screaming not to take the bait, not to play his game.

He leaned forward, resting his chin on the "L" made by his index finger and thumb. The act once again revealed the rune that was tattooed on his palm. Black ink with an even darker meaning.

"Very good, Merrow, and tell me… what is a Sea Raven?"

Eyes fixed on the tattoo—its implications weighed heavily on her chest. The knight let out a sharp whistle to regain her attention.

"A harbinger of death," she replied with as little emotion as possible.

The corner of his lip turned up, and his heated gaze fell to her neck. Despite the neutrality she forced into her features, her rapid heartbeat betrayed her. He hummed in agreement and then his expression became thoughtful.

"I realized something…" He paused, soaking in the silence while Emer held her breath. "Is it that you are not curious or have you already determined what it is that I have come to realize?"

Initially, she was confused by his question, but as he took a bite of bread from the plate his meaning became clear.

She watched him consume another bite of the food. *Her* food.

"I admit that I admire your boldness, but I cannot encourage it. So, you can answer my questions or go hungry. It's your choice," he stipulated.

There was no smile present as he lifted his chin and waited for her response. She turned her gaze from him, unwilling to let him see the hurt in her eyes as she took measure of the hollowness in her stomach. A forced choice was not a choice, and while the hunger aches would grow stronger, it would not overcome the strength of her will.

"You do realize, the more you resist speaking to me, the more suspicious you become." His candor struck her with surprise but it was quickly replaced by annoyance.

"Do your actions not hold the same weight?" she hissed.

He laughed. It was empty and cold.

"If there is not a knife currently in your boot, I will sincerely apologize for my *actions*," his voice dripped with pride as her eyes widened.

He clicked his tongue in admonishment as he leaned forward. "Did you think I would leave you in a room with a weapon if I didn't think I could easily disarm you?" he taunted.

For fuck's sake!

"Why even leave it at all?" she sneered.

"Curiosity." He shrugged. "You're not the first of your people to mask ruthless intent with fabricated distress. Though you are, perhaps, the first to attempt it in a dress."

Her face contorted in anger and her lips twisted to prevent herself from saying something she might regret.

"Now that you have proven my point and will be receiving no apology, I would like to have my knife back."

He held out his hand and Emer fantasized about all the ways she could wipe that grin off his face, but ultimately, she knew it would end poorly for her.

Holding his stare, she pulled the knife from her boot.

"Careful," he warned.

The seven Elders themselves could have appeared in that room and demanded she hand it over and she still would not have given him the satisfaction. Raising the dagger, she swiftly threw it to her right, piercing the map fastened to the wall and embedding it deep into the wood, ensuring it struck straight through Obanes. Finn would have been proud and that thought made Emer smirk. When she looked back to Calder, her smile fell.

He rose from his chair with preternatural grace, allowing his arm to brush hers as he passed. The contact was so brief and yet so charged with menace that it seared into her skin. She felt each footfall of his boots in her bones and could not hide her startle at the sound of him freeing the knife from the wall. Everything inside her screamed for her to run from the predator that stalked forward. When he returned to stand in front, she turned away, driven by obstinance and fear.

The press of cold metal beneath her jaw was featherlight, the blade only a kiss.

"Eyes on me, Merrow." His words were like smoke, warm against the side of her face, and she choked on the breath that lodged in her throat.

He slowly redirected her gaze back to his, careful not to break the skin. He lowered his face until their noses almost touched. "Don't *ever* look away from me like that. Understand?" he cautioned.

The intimate distance kept her silent as she stared back into the heated pools of his eyes. When she didn't answer, he raised his brow in warning. She nodded, noticing that he pulled back the blade slightly to allow the movement. Even as she watched him step away, he did not seem to make a sound. A wraith of a man sent only to haunt her. The door creaked as he opened it, and he paused in the doorway.

"You will find you'll not like me as an enemy," he warned.

The strangled cry of the lock falling into place was all the encouragement she needed to fold into herself. Standing against the intensity of his scrutiny made her and what little energy she had remaining feel insufficient. She knew she needed to continue searching the room as she would need to strategize how to escape, but she allowed herself another private moment to be afraid.

CHAPTER 5

As soon as he was in the sanctuary of the hall, Calder released a whispered string of curses. Raking his hands through his hair, he fought the urge to drive his fist into the stone walls of the passage. He needed a drink far more than a broken hand—the promise of the former led him down the corridor and toward the banquet hall.

In the courtyard, he could already hear the shouts of the men's revelry echoing through the keep. Noise and the scent of musk slammed against him as he swung open the heavy door of the hall. It was not often that he found himself down here and drinking with the other men. He was brought to the keep for his expertise, not his likability, and preferred to keep his alcohol consumption separate from his work. The physical pain in his side and the metaphorical pain in his ass caused him to break that rule. What was one more, given that he had already broken several?

Dozens of men crowded around the long tables littered with coins, stones, and ale. While outside of the keep, the debaucherous atmosphere would be a welcomed distraction, the rowdy energy in the room only tugged at his fraying nerves. It was peace he craved because that reduced the likelihood that he would rip into anyone who crossed him in his current agitated state. Grabbing a mug, he dipped into the barrel of ale and retreated to a table in the far corner of the room. He took a deep drink, holding the liquid in his mouth as if it would wash away the bitterness of the day, and closed his eyes.

The air around him stirred just a moment before he heard a body drop into the chair across from him and he did not need to open his eyes to know who it was that imposed on his respite. He could smell him.

Fucking figures.

"Dempsey," Calder said to the inside of his mug just before taking another deep draw.

"Calder," Dempsey acknowledged in return.

While Dempsey possessed charm, when weighed and measured by Calder's standards, he had been found wanting. Calder, not being one to mince his words, did not make it a secret that he thought the man was a cretin. Being a cretin, Dempsey developed an unhealthy obsession—one rooted in disdain rather than desire.

"Exhaustion doesn't look good on you, old man," Dempsey observed as he took a sip of his ale.

It was a common slight despite Calder hardly being older than Dempsey. However, if Dempsey counted time in achievements rather than sunsets, the discrepancy between them would have been notable indeed.

"Nor does envy on you," Calder remarked in a humorless tone.

Dempsey scowled. "You weren't sparring today... I merely wanted to make sure you were in good health."

His observation was true, even if the other half of the statement wasn't.

Given the present circumstances, it was less than ideal for anyone to be watching Calder's movements too closely. The fact that it was Dempsey drawing attention to it made the unfortunate timing that much more problematic.

If Calder had something, Dempsey wanted to take it. Hence,

of all the available seats in the hall, he chose the one Calder intended to put his feet on. It was a venture met with little success and usually nothing more than an annoyance. However at present, what Calder had was a castaway he failed to extract information from hidden away in his room. His thoughts flickered to the green-eyed girl, likely cursing him from somewhere in the keep before returning to the problem at hand.

"The last I checked, I didn't report to you or anyone in this keep, for that matter. But I'm delighted my absence wounded you," he responded with a slight smirk before taking another sip.

Dempsey's eyes were hungry, a scavenger scenting blood, so much so that Calder was tempted to check if the wound in his side had given him away. Ironically, Calder's blood was one of the main reasons why Dempsey despised him. Instead, he leaned back in his chair, knees spread wide and taking up space, ensuring his face remained impassive despite the pain admonishing his arrogant posture.

"Does it bother you?" he asked with a sigh.

Dempsey straightened.

"That despite your name and your coin, it is *my* approval you need here, and it is the one thing you cannot buy?"

"One day, you will fall from your pedestal," Dempsey warned as he stood from the chair.

"Good thing I've got wings," he retorted, a click of his tongue and a wink further punctuating his defiance. Though the wings he spoke of were figurative, a tattoo worn by members of his clan, their meaning remained the same.

Ravens do not fall.

Dempsey's lips curled in a feral sneer. It was far too easy to get a rise from the man, and perhaps Calder shouldn't make it a habit to do so, or maybe Dempsey should not make it a habit to approach him. Having been unsuccessful in achieving whatever he had come for, Dempsey spat a curse under his breath and stormed back into the crowd.

Why he was being subjected to everyone else's tantrums today, only the Elders knew.

Although his outward expression remained unbothered, internally, Calder began to wonder if Dempsey knew more than he let on. He could have seen the girl and that would be problematic. Despite the fact that the solitude of his corner was restored, his agitation remained. If the growing nuisance had been following him, he could have seen the altercation on the shore. Slamming his mug on the table, Calder stood and exited the hall.

By the time he returned to his room, the sun had dropped from the sky. He found his newly acquired problem seated by the fire when he opened the door and had no doubt that she halted rummaging through his things to race across the room at the sound of his approach.

He shot her an incredulous glare and shook his head, not bothering to hide his exhaustion from her. To his surprise rather than challenging it, she seemed relieved she would not have to rise to the occasion.

"I'm not in the mood to be stabbed in my sleep and I am tired. Be a good girl and allow me to escort you to your cell. As a *non-helpless* maiden, I'm sure that won't be problematic," his mocking tone paired well with the mischief in his eyes.

He remained in the doorway, motioning for her to exit the room. She followed his instruction, but not before grabbing her dress and the cloak he had offered earlier, intending to use the latter as a blanket. Stopping in front of him, she donned her most disingenuous smile and curtsied. Her smile grew more natural as she saw his features pinch in annoyance.

She left the room and began down the long hallway.

"Merrow," he called from further behind her.

Emer turned to find him standing at the room across from his. Taking a key out of his pocket, he unlocked the door and pushed it open. The sight had her alternating between surprise, relief, and suspicion.

Aside from the lack of personal items and burning fire, the room was similar to his. Hardly a cell.

"You are quite honestly exhausting, and the cells are a fair distance from here. I have no interest in making that journey to determine whether or not you have done something spectacularly stupid throughout the night," he said.

While his reasoning was suspect at best, she did not argue. Sleep deprivation would not help her cause, and a bed was the preferable choice over the damp floor of a cell.

"So, you were just trying to scare me?"

Calder tilted his head in that slow and feral manner. "I don't *try* anything. If I want something, it happens."

His wolfish grin revealed dazzling canines as he backed into the darkened corridor and closed the door—locking her away from the Isle and her purpose that lay further inland.

Her eyes welled with tears, but they were not the same unruly tears of sadness she had wept earlier. They were the hot and bitter tears of unbridled rage. It tore through her with a force that reduced her soul to ribbons. She threw the cloak and the dress as she fell forward, her knees colliding with the stone floor. Emer pressed her face against the bed to smother her scream. She screamed until her throat felt raw.

Once the intense ringing that flooded her ears receded, she slowly blinked her eyes. She had been so focused on the things missing from the room that she hadn't noticed the one significant thing the room did possess.

A window.

She scrambled onto the bed and ran her fingers over its edges. Pressing against the glass, she felt hope begin to give under her palm.

CHAPTER 6

Calder stood frozen in the hall, struck still by the familiar and muted sound that came from the other side of the door he had locked. It was not the meek cry of a broken girl. It was the stifled roar of someone with rage to spare and nothing to lose. It was the battle cry of a woman who would ruin his life if he gave her a chance.

He tensed his jaw and narrowed his eyes. She would not be kept, and he would not be sleeping. For the first time in recent memory, Calder didn't know what to do.

Exhaustion gnawed on his bones and frustration clawed at his flesh. He twisted, feeling the bite of pain from the newly cauterized wound on his side. It was a welcomed distraction from the uncertainty threatening to unravel the carefully crafted order he established to keep his own monsters at bay. While answers were elusive, he knew exactly where he could find pain. Following the sounds of the bustling keep, he made his way down the corridors to do just that.

With the sub-tenant and tenant-in-chief handling business in a nearby town, the men of the keep relocated to what they affectionately came to call the Den. An attractive name for an ugly place in the bowels of the keep, where they gathered to beat the absolute shit out of each other. Something that recent events made increasingly more appealing to Calder.

He made his way down the stairs, whose edges had been rounded by the countless men before him. The air was thick with the iron-rich scent of the bars below, the acidic aroma of the smoke from the torches, and a musty odor that he could never be certain was attributed to the keep or the men. The temperature dropped for a time as he continued his descent, but soon, the body heat of the waiting crowd below and their accompanying shouts chased the cold away.

A wall of shadowy figures appeared in the corridor at the base of the stairs, the light from the torches bursting through the spaces between them and revealing brief flashes of the bodies battling on the other side. Anticipation danced down Calder's spine like a streak of lightning.

Surprised by his presence, hushed murmurs were exchanged as Calder pushed his way through the crowd. He wasn't there to disrupt their game, he merely came in search of the same thing they did.

Release.

As he broke to the front of the crowd, he could see the two men currently locked in an intense match. Blood and sweat glistened over their darting forms. It was unclear if they had drawn blood from each other or if it was the product of previous rounds.

In the Den, the weapons varied night by night, and upon seeing tonight's weapon of choice was knives, Calder's smile grew sharp.

He watched the men tussle, their blades glinting in the torchlight. One of the men disarmed his opponent, pausing with his knife pressed firmly to his throat. Quickly, their expression shifted, and the man who lost kneeled. The victor let out a deep chuckle as the blade retreated before he slapped the man on the back and helped him to his feet. They congratulated each other on a well-fought match and then rejoined the crowd.

Most would not sign up to be beaten, broken, and bloodied, but pain reminded them they were alive. Brutality sang in their blood, and the chains on the back wall were a reminder that brutality was what this space was built for, just like them. A deep voice boomed, calling for the next fighter, and the crowd cheered.

Calder looked around at the many faces that were free of damage. With a smirk and confident stride, he walked into the center.

The crowd grew quiet as the men looked at each other. All those present were knights, but that did not mean they would willingly fight a Sea Raven. They were a different kind of monster.

A chuckle rang from the quiet crowd and they parted as the source of the amusement made their way to the front.

Banner fucking Kinkaid.

It didn't take long for him to meet Calder's gaze, given that he was a head and shoulders larger than the average man.

The torchlight caught the decorative rings and beads threaded through the braids on the sides of his head, which joined the rest of his dirty blonde hair tied back with a leather strap. The shadow of the feather he twirled between his fingers danced across his olive skin as he approached. He tucked the feather into one of his meticulous braids when he reached the center.

"Tomorrow, I will either be able to boast of beating the infamous Sea Raven or that I at least had the spine to try. Something none of you clearly do," he shouted to the crowd.

"For good reason," Calder shot back.

Though Calder did not make friendships as a rule, Banner had a habit of ignoring rules.

"At least buy me a drink after you kick my ass?" he asked with a smirk.

When paired with a charming smile, many mistook Banner's

roguish nature and the mischievous glint in his eyes as traits mutually exclusive with bloodlust.

Many people are also fools.

Many of those fools are also dead, courtesy of the poison-filled hollow of his feather and the sharp gilded edge at the base that delivered it.

While Banner opted for a strategic approach rather than overt strength, having been trained by Calder, he was more than capable in a fight.

Calder nodded as Banner grabbed the knives from the man who shouted earlier, tossing one to his opponent.

The crowd cheered as the men squared off.

"Not often I see you down here. To what do we owe the honor?" Banner teased in a hushed voice.

Rather than answer, Calder twirled the knife in his fingers and allowed the hunger in his eyes to speak for him.

"So, someone pissed you off... great." Banner rolled his eyes and lunged, swiping the blade level with Calder's chest.

A hiss threatened to escape between Calder's gritted teeth as he leaned out of the path of the blade. A trickle of warmth skated down the muscles of his abdomen from the newly angered wound. He righted himself and then dropped his forearm on Banner's elbow, knocking away the arm. Calder brought around his knife, but Banner blocked the strike. Sliding his boot between Banner's spread stance, Calder hooked his heel and pulled his leg out from underneath him.

As Banner fell to his right knee, he swung his left foot, forcing Calder to jump back. Using the momentum, Banner spun and rose with gravitas.

"Cute," Calder offered drolly.

Banner gave him a wink, and they began to prowl towards each other once more.

"Hmmm, you've got crazy eyes. Is it a paramour, mayhaps?" he asked Calder with a raised brow.

An observation that received only a growl.

"Not one to kiss and tell?" Banner teased with a knowing smile.

Calder decided two things in that moment.

The first was that the tumultuous events of the day clearly had an impact on his normally stoic features. The second was that, friend or not, he was most definitely going to kick Banner's ass.

They began to circle each other, and Banner stepped back closer to the wall. Strategically, it was a poor decision as the position left him vulnerable, and Calder almost chastised him but realized too late that it was he who had made the mistake.

Banner slipped his foot under one of the chains, and with a swift kick, launched it outward.

The kiss of the metal against Calder's cheek drew another growl from deep in his chest and he stumbled back, shaking off the impact. The crowd erupted in shouts and whistles. Banner bowed to his admirers before readying himself for Calder's retaliation.

Banner laughed.

Calder snarled.

They both charged.

The pair became a blur, slowing only when their limbs were tangled. Their knives shook, suspended between them, ready to strike, held back only by the strength of the other. Calder's lips pulled back in a feral manner and his opponent's eyes darted briefly to the exposed teeth inching closer. Banner's jaw clenched from exertion as he fought to hold his guard against Calder's brute strength.

"You know," he grunted. "You seem a little tense, boss..." With each word Banner spoke, Calder exerted more of his strength. "More than usual... wanna talk about it?"

Calder answered by throwing his head forward, savoring the satisfying crack of Banner's nose and the blood that followed. Knocking Banner's arm away, Calder planted a powerful punch in the center of his chest.

Before Banner recovered, Calder kicked the knife from his hand, the metal clattering across the stone, and pressed his own to Banner's throat.

Banner vibrated with laughter beneath Calder's grip, crimson staining his amused smile. If people were not afraid of Banner, they were not paying attention.

Calder shook his head at the madman, who sucked in his bloody bottom lip as if trying to hold back another snarky comment. He released him and then began to walk away.

Banner spat out a mouth full of blood. "Don't forget about my drink, Raven! Remember, I know where you live!" his shout was teasing and not the temperament of a man who just had his face bashed in.

The haunting echoes of laughter filled the corridor as Calder made his way topside.

Reaching the courtyard, he tipped his head back and took in a deep breath, savoring the crisp cool air entering his lungs and the tension that seemed to expel from his muscles along with his exhale. When he opened his eyes, however, every muscle in his body locked up as his blood ran cold. His gaze narrowed to where Emer's room would be located and the open window that mocked him.

"There's no fucking way," Calder doubted, certain the scared creature he had left locked in the room wouldn't have jumped out of a second-floor window.

As if in answer, a raven cried in the night and Calder began to run.

As the knight ran through the halls, Emer stumbled through the night.

There was nothing in the keep that she trusted—not the quiet, the darkness that settled, the stones of the walls, or the birds in the sky.

As she ran, sweat streaked down her neck, searing into the wounds in her shoulder from where the bark of the ash tree had torn into her exposed skin, courtesy of the too-large-tunic. It was unclear if the slickness of her palms was from fear of being caught or if the scraps of her dress that she used to wrap her hands and forearms had failed. Those were problems for a new day. Tonight, her only concern was to become a ghost to haunt the only person who knew she existed. Given that Calder would be held responsible for not only his lie but for losing her if he confessed, she doubted he would raise the alarm now that she was out of the keep.

If he intended to hunt her down, he would do it without the help of his brethren. That thought kept her feet moving despite the exhaustion that was setting in.

There was a moment before she jumped from her window to the tree in the courtyard that her doubt had become a tangible being. The tendrils of darkness below her crept up from the shadows and grew closer with each moment she hesitated. She promised her father that she would do *anything*.

So, she jumped.

Now, racing along the outer edge of the keep, her chest heaved and her muscles screamed. Despite the pain, she felt a smile tug at her lips.

Calder had seen her broken on the shore, but what he failed to understand was that she had been broken long before he found her and she knew how to put herself back together. She only wished she could see the look on his face when he realized his mistake.

CHAPTER 7

"Elders bless me," a male voice rumbled.

Emer searched the darkness before her but found nothing. She knew the lack of response was not because she was alone but because whatever it was enjoyed her panic. As she peered into the void, she wondered if even the night was a malevolent entity here.

A soft glow appeared in the distance, accompanied by the rasp of a deep inhale. The flickering embers drew closer, giving shape to the man who stalked towards her. Only the outline of the cloak that masked the man and the soft glow as he took greedy draws from his pipe were visible.

She stiffened.

The air around him felt wrong, his presence was an oily sensation on her skin. As she moved to run, his hand lashed out and planted against the wall of the keep, blocking her path. His other hand, strong and calloused, slammed against her nose and mouth as she began screaming. The impact of her head against the stones caused her vision to spot.

"Careful, lovely, don't you know there are monsters in these woods?" he purred as he moved closer, pressing his chest against hers.

Blinking away the blur from her collision, she looked at her attacker but found the shadows of his hood still obscured his features.

Even without seeing him, she could feel his leering gaze sweeping over whatever the moonlight revealed.

The hum beneath her skin roared to life.

"All sorts of creatures lurk in the dark here. Witches and Fae folk, Sluagh, nameless creatures, and beasts unknown," he said, drawing his nose up the side of her throat as he spoke.

She struggled against his hand, her airways blocked, and her panic was rising with each stolen breath. Each gasp she fought to capture was laced with the scent of the herbs he had packed into his pipe. The aroma churned her stomach, and she strained to turn her head.

Clawing at his wrist, Emer felt herself growing faint. With her last bit of strength, she released a strangled cry.

When he finally removed his hand, she drew in the desperately sought air. Smoke quickly swept into her lungs, and she realized too late that he had only released her to blow the toxic cloud between her gasping lips.

Her body protested the invasion and she coughed violently in his grasp.

A deep chuckle radiated from under the darkness of his hood.

"What mischief have you caused for the Elders to place you in my path? It is certainly not a reward for my behavior. So, I can only assume it is a punishment for yours," he whispered.

Her eyes burnt and her mouth grew wet. His face was next to hers, pressed against her hair. He drew in another deep breath but this time it was not from his pipe.

He was breathing in *her*.

The horror of it caused another scream to tear through her. He gripped her hair in his fist and pulled it as an angry snarl rumbled from his chest.

"What did you just say?" he demanded.

Emer's tongue felt thick, and she tried to shake her head in confusion, but his grip on her braid kept her still.

What had she said?

It was only a moment before, but it already seemed far away. She remembered screaming. A scream in the shape of the only name she knew. Calder was many things, but his threats were far less terrifying than the promises that dripped from this man's lips. Promises that seemed to grow fainter as her dizziness grew.

The man's hand slipped to her throat and he hummed.

"Fortunate, indeed. I do so love breaking his things."

A whistle pierced the night and he took a startled step back to scan the sky above them. Emer used the temporary distraction as an opportunity to thrust her knee between his legs. Curling forward, he released his grip in addition to several hoarse curses.

Willing her legs to carry her far and fast, Emer fled. Even as disoriented as she was, she recognized that the much taller man would have no difficulty catching up to her once he recovered, and she cursed her inefficient and unsteady steps. She turned back, expecting to see the man lurking behind but found only darkness.

All manner of relief shattered as she collided with a solid wall, the impact sending her stumbling backward. Pain shot through one of her wrists as her fall halted.

"The sea is the other way, Merrow. Or did you already miss me?"

Calder's voice should not have given her relief, and yet Emer found herself crumbling before him.

This man who had not laid a hand on her.

This man who had a Lina who loved him.

This man who read Tam Lin.

He was not like the man behind her.

She blinked wildly. Her lids were heavy and her thoughts fragmented.

In her confusion, Calder's eyes first appeared to be as black as onyx. A heartbeat later, she found them as she remembered—a stormy blue.

They searched hers, the fury in them quickly dissolving into an expression she had not seen him wear before.

Concern.

Calder leaned in, angling his face and bringing his nose to hover near her jaw. The scent of the Aisling root coated his tongue and he jerked back. Gently, he pressed his fingers under Emer's chin and studied her fearful expression. His jaw worked and he turned his attention to the darkness behind her.

While it was not uncommon for men at the keep to indulge in inhalants, Calder included, there was only one person who smoked Aisling root and only two possible explanations for why her lips reeked of him.

Mother. Fucker.

"What happened?" The concern he felt was entirely absent from his voice.

Emer shook, her fingers curling into his cloak confirming that whatever transpired led her to decide that she was safer with him. It caused a strange ache in Calder's chest as he watched her process what had just occurred, the extent of which he was still unaware. He suddenly felt responsible for the dull and distant look in her eyes, the same ones that had been full of fire just that morning. It ignited a rage that would only be doused by blood, but the broken way she collapsed into him held him in place.

Dempsey would have to wait.

He moved to reach for her but paused, unsure if his touch would cause more harm. Slowly, he brought his hands to either side of her, wrapping them warmly around her elbows. For the first time, she relaxed into his touch.

"Come," he said softly, leading her back to the keep.

Although the journey was short, he noted each and every time she turned to look behind her, carefully tallying them. He did not know who the castaway was, but she was a daughter, a sister from what he could tell, a person... and he would break one of Dempsey's fingers for each time she looked back.

At the entrance to the keep, he hesitated, scolding himself for only then noticing she was not wearing a cloak. He was not ready for his little shadow to be in the light, even if it was only the moon. Removing his own for the second time that day, he thew it over Emer. She would need to remain his shadow until he figured out what to do with her. She swayed from the weight and he groaned.

When she was finally deposited on the edge of the bed, Emer sighed in relief.

She was so very tired.

Calder stepped away until his back met his closed door and just stared at her.

"You." He paused. "Jumped out the window."

Emer did not look at him—she did not acknowledge his fury or even the faint hint of surprise in his voice. Instead, she looked around the room, blinking slowly several times as if the scene would change when she opened them next.

"This isn't my room," she observed. The effects of the smoke she inhaled still addled her mind and weighed heavy in her body. Someone larger or more familiar with the root would not have been affected so dramatically, but to Emer, the impact was almost immediate.

Calder scrubbed his hands down his face. "How much did you breathe?"

"Dunno... blew it into my mouth." She shrugged, wincing at the pain the movement caused.

When Calder rolled his neck to the side in irritation, an audible crack echoed through the space. Unable to remain still, he crossed the room and reached past Emer to a mug on his desk. Emer did not startle at his movement or his nearness, but instead, slowly drew her gaze up until it met his. The gold of her eyes more akin to that of a dying star. Again she blinked slowly as if she was once more looking at something that didn't make sense.

"Drink this," he said, pushing the mug of water towards her.

She wrinkled her face and turned away, "I don't have to listen to you."

"Want to bet on that?" he asked with a quirked brow.

Emer lifted her chin in defiance.

Leaning down and bringing his nose to hers, he growled, "You need to sober up. So, you can either drink it or you can wear it." He punctuated his warning by bringing the mug in front of her lips.

"Asshole," Emer spat as she leaned away from him and snatched the drink.

"Brat," he hissed back.

Emer brought the mug to her lips and drained the contents, though, at one point, she forgot to breathe and began to cough. Rubbing her temple, she attempted to soothe the sudden ache but her hand was snatched away.

"What the..." Calder croaked.

The sticky warmth that she had noted earlier was not sweat but blood. He tugged at the bloodied strips, and while she tried to pull away, she could not free herself from his grip. Her muscles were too weary and his hold too firm. She turned her face away but winced. The fabric of the cloak was a hot poker against her damaged skin and she fidgeted beneath it.

Shifting his attention from the damage on her hands to her neck he said, "Oh, Merrow, what have you done?"

He unhooked the clasp allowing the cloak to fall to the bed and reveal the wound he could only partially see before. Calder's nostrils flared at the sight of her shoulder. Brushing her hair back, he slipped his hand beneath the collar and peeled back the fabric, revealing several deep gouges over the curve of her shoulder and collarbone.

Emer flinched, pulling the damp fabric back over her exposed flesh.

"Did he—" he began to speak, but she stopped him.

She hated the concern in his eyes.

She hated how something about his features was soft and hard all at once. It was his fault she was in the keep, that she had to escape in the middle of the night, and he had no right to feel whatever it was that swam through his eyes.

"It was the tree," she barked, pulling at the cloak and tossing it at his feet.

She didn't look at him when she heard his boots move across the floor, nor when he returned and placed a container on the table at her side.

"It's yarrow. It will fight any infection," he offered.

Emer eyed the jar with contempt, and while the aches in her body began to grow as the effects of the herb wore off, she could not bring herself to accept the offering.

"I should go to my room," she said quietly.

When she moved to stand, Calder's hand came to her uninjured shoulder holding her in place. Still intoxicated, she would have been terrified at how powerless she was if she didn't feel so heavy.

"You keep saying *your* room. Nothing here belongs to you, little Merrow. Everything here is *mine*. And you are going to stay right where you are until that shit is out of your system."

Emer could only muster a pathetic glare before finally admitting, "I'm so tired."

Calder crossed his arms as he sat back in the chair by the fire.

"Then sleep."

"I am not sleeping with you in the room," she argued. Though, the way her body began to lean made her words less convincing.

Calder let out a derisive snort. This time when his eyes surveyed her, it was not her injuries that held his attention.

"Lovely to know how little you think of me, but I promise, I have a particular taste in the women I bed and one *key* trait is that they are conscious."

Heat flushed Emer's cheeks as she considered all the particular tastes he might have. She laid down, turning so that her back was to Calder and she closed her eyes, willing the room to stop spinning.

After a moment of silence, Calder heard her murmuring something and rose from his chair, leaning over to find Emer's eyes closed and her breathing slow.

"What was that?" he asked quietly.

"You said, not naked enough for a Selkie. Not seductive enough to be Merrow," she mumbled.

His eyebrows shot up in surprise.

"I did," he confirmed.

Emer murmured something else and Calder leaned in closer to make out what she said.

"Say it again, Merrow," he urged, curious what her unguarded mind might reveal.

A sleepy smile pulled at her lips as she sighed the word once more.

"Liar."

Only when he was certain Emer was asleep and would not wake did Calder slip from his room.

It had been a long time since he tasted failure. Tonight was a reminder of that failure, which caused a tightness in his throat and bitterness on his tongue.

There were plenty of reasons why he should stay in his room to either get some sleep or watch over his ward. None of those reasons were louder than his need to expel the energy coursing through him. The desperate desire to replace the bitterness with something else.

In the courtyard, he stood quietly against the cold stone. Aside from the men already engaged in their nightly entertainment, the space was quiet. He returned to where he had found Emer outside the keep, backtracking her steps. There was a narrow path of exposed earth along the edge of the wall, and while remaining close had kept her out of sight, it also captured footprints. He quickly found her small boots running along the shadows. Her steps were fast but the footfalls themselves were unsteady, pained from the injuries sustained in the jump.

When the air became thick with the scent of Aisling root, Calder stopped. Bending down, he studied a section of the ground darkened by the burnt herb. His face twisted with disgust, realizing that this must have been where their paths crossed. He could see Emer's footprints eclipsed by much larger ones that crossed the space to her in only a few strides. When his gaze rose to the wall, his body stiffened.

For a long moment, he denied what he saw. Kneeling down, he lined his hand up to the five crimson smudges. A tiny hand, pressing bloody fingers into the stone; the dirt disturbed from where she had struggled.

Anger ripped through him once more as the scene of what had taken place became clearer.

He was her keeper. She was *his* to protect. No one should have been able to touch her, and the person who did would need to learn not to reach for what did not belong to them.

He strode back to the keep, winged by darkness and rage.

This was far from over.

CHAPTER 8

Emer's hands ached. Her shoulders ached. Her very soul itself ached.

When darkness finally claimed her, it was not a restful slumber but merely her body's inability to remain conscious. While her escape had been short-lived, its consequences certainly were not.

The rough material of the blanket caught on her shoulder wound, pain ripping her from sleep like a fish from the sea. She swallowed her scream as she took in gulps of air. Her hand hovered above the throbbing as she fought her instinct to grip her afflicted shoulder. She glared toward the chair by the fire, prepared to make a sharp remark to defend her vulnerable state, but Calder was not there.

With a pinched brow, she turned to scowl at the jar of salve, but her eyes snapped shut from the pain. With Calder no longer in the room, she rationalized that she could use it now and he would likely never even know she accepted his help. Making herself a martyr for the sake of pride was not an honorable hill to die on. At best, it was a foolish, stubborn, and slightly elevated patch of dirt.

Begrudgingly, she reached for the concoction, coughing at the potent smell. Profanity filled the air along with the bitter and astringent notes of the remedy. She spread the viscous balm over her shoulder with shaky fingers. While the mixture had a cooling effect, the pain that woke her was only heightened after it was applied.

Sitting in the bed, she braced herself against the window, allowing the cool air to fill her lungs and soothe the nausea that churned her stomach. The window in Calder's room faced the sea and Emer dropped her head to rest on the sill as she watched the sun slowly begin to rise, painting the sky red.

She faintly recalled a rhyme about the meaning of a red sky being either warning or delight. Before she could remember which was associated with morning, the door began to open, disrupting her thoughts.

Calder carried two bowls, one in his hand and the other balanced on his forearm. With the other hand, he held the door ajar, only allowing enough space to enter the room and close it softly behind him.

The silence between them persisted as he made his way further into the room. Given all that had transpired the night before, his lack of acknowledgement only made Emer's scowl deepen. She picked up one of her boots—which she did not recall taking off—from the floor next to the bed and threw it at his head.

Calder snatched the boot before it could make contact, without spilling a drop of the bowls' contents. "Are you ready to be civil?" he asked, having the audacity to sound bored.

She responded with a vulgar gesture she had seen Finn use in the past that had proven quite effective in expressing his displeasure.

"Well, isn't that attractive. Are you always this lovely in the morning?" he queried.

Emer did not answer and he shifted his attention to the boot still clutched in his hand, turning it and inspecting its sole. "You are quite tiny, you know that?" he observed before throwing the boot into the corner of the room.

Calder placed the bowls on the desk near the bed. "What is going on? You look like a púca crawled from under your bed and terrorized you all night," he teased.

She had, in fact, been terrorized all night.

By pain.

By nightmares.

By the scent of him clinging to his bed.

Worst of all, the thought that this was all *him*. That he had used this mysterious man to shake her, to make her compliant.

"Did you send him after me?" Even though her tone was harsh, the lack of volume betrayed her exhaustion.

"The... púca?" Calder took a half-step back to stare at the bed he now stood in front of. Distracted, he missed the wild look that flamed in her eyes as she glowered.

She kicked her foot out and caught one of his shins.

"Fuck!" he grunted as he stumbled away.

"The man from last night!"

Calder took another step back and his expression turned sour. Eyes fixed to hers and hands in tight fists he said, "I may not trust you. I may not even like you all that much. But I would never have orchestrated or allowed what happened last night."

Although it was not the first time she offended him, she was surprised she had. It was evident that there was more he wanted to say but he didn't utter a word. The longer he watched her, allowed her the silence if she chose it, the more convinced she became that he had nothing to do with the man from the shadows.

"What exactly did happen?" he asked.

She was not ready to absolve him yet. Even if he did not direct the man's actions, he had given him the opportunity. Calder was the reason she was trapped and unable to defend herself. For that reason, she decided that he was just as worthy of her bitterness.

"You happened," she murmured.

A raven who put her in a cage to see if she would sing. Instead she tried to fly and learned she only knew how to fall in the right direction.

She closed her eyes and planted her head against the wall, the last of her fight leaving her.

He nodded.

"I intended to apologize to you this morning," he began and Emer cracked one eye open.

"But?" she questioned, expecting him to comment about her sharp tongue and multiple attempts to assault him from the comfort of *his* bed.

"But," he echoed. "I don't even know your name and I would like to address my apology properly. So, a deal. Breakfast in exchange for your name."

She turned to him, wary as she considered his offer. Her name seemed harmless enough. It was not as if it would reveal more about her than he already knew, and it required minimal compromise.

"My name is Emer. Em to my family."

Heat rushed to her face as she scolded herself for offering a nickname that she did not want him to know or use.

"Emer," he repeated back.

She expected him to say it like a curse but found the lilt of his voice rolled it over his tongue like a wave.

"Named after the wife of the great leader of the Painted Legion, perhaps? And a symbol of wit, fairness, and ferocity if I recall correctly. Hence why she captured the eye of one of the most brutal men in the history of the Isles." He recited the origins of her name as if reading it from one of his books.

That lore was not part of his people's history, yet he knew it as well as Emer did, and she couldn't decide if that intrigued her or made her even more suspicious.

"I believe it also means 'swift'... which I think you beautifully demonstrated with your little knife trick," he added.

Little knife trick?

Her jaw clenched. The movement was so quick that she nearly bit her tongue and the barbed comments on the tip of it. She would happily oblige in demonstrating another one of her tricks if he would give her a blade. Perhaps making it disappear into his other side to balance out his scars.

"Tell me, Emer, is there another trait from your namesake that I am unaware of that aided you in jumping out of a window?"

Something sparked in her stare and she slowly turned to face him.

"Why don't you climb through yours and I'll tell you," she offered, utterly unaware that she had started to smile.

"Hello, Merrow." The smile he returned seemed to say.

"Flying lessons will have to wait," he remarked, reaching for one of the bowls he placed on the desk and extending it to her.

Emer scowled at him as she gingerly pulled at the blankets and worked to get herself to the edge of the bed, all while attempting to not further anger her wounds. Calder watched, knowing full well she would not ask him for help.

"You look pathetic," he chastised before walking to the fire and setting her bowl on one of the chairs, while sitting to enjoy his in the other.

A short time later, Emer extricated herself from the bed and just as carefully took her seat across from Calder, drinking in the fire's warmth and the strange sense of security she found within the walls of his room. She was sure she was one of the many secrets that they held and yet of all the questions she could conjure, her tired mind returned to those of a raven-haired boy.

Calder's stare repeatedly fell to Emer's hands as she ate. Her nails were torn from clawing at the tree, the beds still caked with blood. Scratches marred her fingers. A particularly nasty gouge on her left index finger trailed from the center to her fingertip, deep enough to scar. A reminder of her bravery or stupidity, he hadn't decided. Regardless of the merit associated, there was a good chance they were going to get infected. Calder entertained bashing his head against the nearest hard surface because he knew that meant he was going to need a favor from Banner. If there was one person he didn't like owing, it was him and now it seemed he owed him a drink and a favor.

They ate in the comfortable silence that settled between them.

"Thank you." Emer murmured, her expression mildly confused at her own sentiment.

"Be still, my heart! The Merrow has manners!" he shouted, clutching his chest in a stunning display of humor. It was then that she lost the fight against her eye roll.

"You are the barbarian in this relationship. Not me!" she barked, crossing her arms and wincing at the way the movement angered her shoulder.

"How forward you are. I think I like it," Calder returned with a roguish smirk.

"I didn't mean '*relationship.*' I meant that in this *situation*, you are the barbarian." She could tell by the glint in his eyes that her correction had not managed to reach his ears.

"There's no need to be coy now, Merrow," he chided.

"Are you drunk?" Emer spat.

"Why? Do you find me intoxicating?" he returned with a raised brow.

She turned to face him more fully, pinning him with a glare. "Since you are so confident in your ability to tell lies, I'll say it again." His eyes dropped reflexively to her throat. "In this *situation*, you are the barbarian." Her tone was slow and steady.

"True enough," he confirmed with a shrug. After a beat, he held her gaze once more. "You must know I do not wish to starve you, don't you?" he asked sincerely.

"Then let me go," her plea escaped, sounding far more vulnerable than she intended.

His eyes turned dark.

"Not until you tell me the truth."

The shift in his temperament made the space suddenly seem devoid of the warmth that had been there only a heartbeat before. Emer rose and made her way across the room to stare at the map above the desk. Her eyes traveled from the keep to her home isle, and finally, to where the Well was said to be located, high atop a mountain.

The truth did not just belong to her.

It belonged to the other men on the boat.

It belonged to Lachlan.

It belonged to her father.

The truth could damn all of them just as quickly as it could set her free. Was it faithless to fear the others had not survived and could, therefore, not succeed in saving her father in her absence? Was it selfish to save herself?

She could not answer his question when she had so many of her own. A paralyzing doubt gripped her throat, and she felt a burn begin to form. Whatever she chose—action or inaction—she would have to own the consequences.

"I don't trust you with the truth," she explained, holding his stare and searching his eyes for some evidence that she could.

Calder hung his head with a sigh and then let out an unamused chuckle.

"We finally found something we have in common then." His expression grew sardonic. "I don't trust you either."

She watched as his eyes grew more distant, no longer looking at her but rather looking through her. "I don't have much time. What can I do to prove that I am not a threat?" she asked urgently.

"You can come to your senses and understand that you are not in control here, *little* Merrow. You leave when I say you leave and if your time is so precious, I suggest you do it quickly," he remarked as he stood and made his way to the door.

The softness of his features from when he first entered the room was replaced with severe frustration. Frustration that she quickly matched, picking up the remaining boot and throwing it into the center of his back.

He stiffened, his head rolling between his shoulders as his muscles tensed. Emer froze, wondering if she had finally pushed him too far.

His head turned slightly and his gaze found hers over his shoulder. His pupils were dilated and the sight made pinpricks skate across her skin.

"I will be back before nightfall to ask you to reconsider your stubbornness or, at the very least, tempt your hunger. You may stay here for now while you... consider." He kicked the boot into the corner of the room where it collided with its mate and then left.

CHAPTER 9

The sound of fumbling at the door drew Emer's attention, and she positioned herself, ready to face her captor once more. The sound of metal scraping against metal heightened her alarm. There was a sharp hiss followed by something heavy clattering against the stone corridor. Her blood ran cold as a voice that was not Calder's growled and cursed under their breath.

Emer frantically searched the room for a weapon. Finding none, she quickly began to pull at the string that closed the neck of her tunic and leaped behind the door. She twisted the chord between her hands readying herself to throw it around the throat of the person currently trying to break in.

With a crack, the door opened, but the intruder did not enter.

Emer raised her hands, holding her breath and silently praying they would walk away because she was not sure if she had the physical or mental strength for what came next.

"Flower?" a male voice asked from the threshold. A voice Emer recalled slithering from beneath the shadows of a cloak.

There was another whispered curse just before a dark form entered the room.

Calder's profile came into view, though his eyes did not find

Emer, and instead, remained fixed on the hall. Without skipping a beat, his large hand clasped her wrists where she still held them above her head, clearing his throat to cover her surprised gasp.

Spooky Raven bastard.

Calder tilted his head and tsked at the unknown and unwelcomed body that remained just outside the room. "If you are here to proposition me, you are not my type, but I'm sure there is a sad soul somewhere looking to disappoint their parents."

"Fuck you, Cal," the intruder growled.

"So informal," he cooed back to the knife-wielding man before him.

Leaning his shoulder against the edge of the open door, he loosened his grip on Emer's wrist slightly. "Since we are forgoing formality, Dempsey, you would do well to remember who you are talking to," Calder commanded. "I'm curious. Have you lost your sense of direction or just your head?"

"Funny you should ask..." Dempsey chuckled. "It appears I am not the one who has lost something," he mocked, tipping his chin towards Emer's boots, visible in the corner of the room. "Or someone... a rather petite someone at that," he added.

Calder's thumb brushed lightly across Emer's racing pulse but gave no reaction that he was bothered by Dempsey's observation.

"You didn't answer me. Why the fuck are you in here?" Calder's voice rumbled.

"Perhaps I was passing by and found your door open. It would only be polite to investigate such a strange scene. Perhaps the intruder who left the door open was no intruder at all. Perhaps they are a guest, or perhaps they are a ghost, roaming the shadows during the night." Dempsey spun the tales in the same sickly charming tone he had spoken against Emer's skin the night before.

"Have the spine to accuse me of something or stop wasting my time," Calder growled.

"Something to hide, *sir*?" Dempsey asked with a grin.

"Whatever you think you have seen here... it will be nothing compared to what I know about the friends who provide you with the Aisling root."

Dempsey remained quiet.

"How do you think your superiors would feel about your familiarity with the Northerners... care to find out?" Calder challenged.

Emer could finally appreciate the superiority in his tone given that she was not on the receiving end.

Before Dempsey could offer a retort, Calder continued, "I feel I must warn you, though, you will have difficulty denying the aforementioned allegations if they come to light given your lack of tongue, which I will have forcibly removed from your skull." Calder paused. "With that knife," he said, dipping his gaze to the knife Dempsey continued to clutch.

Dempsey stepped back slightly, proving that Calder could, in fact, snatch it from his hand at any moment. "So, the crow has a secret. How interesting," he mused, attempting to maintain whatever pride might have remained.

Calder stole back the step, once again closing the space between them. "I think you will find I have many. In fact, there is an old saying among my clan. Secrets and those who learn them are like wishes... they belong at the bottom of a well."

Calder's lips curled wickedly.

Dempsey's facade faltered.

"Luckily for you, I have far more pressing things that require my attention and have no time to spare searching for one," Calder explained, moving back to the door and holding it open.

Boots scraped against the stones as Dempsey turned to leave.

"Dempsey..."

After a brief hesitation, the man paused and turned to Calder as if he had no choice. Leaning in with the slowness of a beast preparing to strike, Calder spoke in a low tone. "If you make it a habit of touching my things, I'll find time for that well after all."

He slammed the door with his free hand and turned to face Emer, whose arms he still held in place above her head.

"How did you know?" she asked.

"I could smell you," he explained, allowing his eyes to trail down the exposed skin between her breasts, courtesy of the open tunic. "The salve you put on your neck." He directed his attention up to the chord clutched between her hands. "Strangulation, Merrow? The things I continue to learn about you." He finished with a click of his tongue.

"What would he have done?" she asked, still not having attempted to remove her hands from his.

He tilted his head slightly before saying, "Trouble finds you alarmingly frequently, you know that?"

Glaring, she ripped her hands free from his and he smirked.

"Would he have killed me?" she repeated the question.

Calder looked away and something dark crossed his features. "I wasn't lying when I warned you against the dangers of the Isle. It has its fair share of beasts," he sighed.

"You are all beasts but him I like least" she breathed. Unspoken understanding passing between them that Dempsey was in fact the man from the shadows.

"Good thing you are not a helpless maiden then. Come," he said, motioning for Emer to separate herself from the wall.

"You don't need to fear him. Not if you stay near me," Calder assured, but she shook her head in disbelief. "You doubt me? I think I should be insulted."

"Doubt implies uncertainty, and I am very certain that you are wrong," Emer said plainly.

"I think my leniency has caused some confusion. You clearly are not aware of my reputation, or else you would know that I have done far worse to people who have done far less to me than you."

Emer's jaw slackened.

"Surely you didn't think I would let just anyone throw a boot at my face?" he asked with a tilt of his head.

Emer wanted to curse her heart for the sudden leap she felt. Certainly, the abnormal response resulted from the recent trauma or the fact that the man before her had saved her twice in as many days. It was absolutely not due to the fact that the rule-minded Sea Raven was admitting that she was an exception. Her body's reaction was unacceptable, yet it defied her a second time when the corner of his lips tipped up.

"I didn't throw it at your face... I hit you in the back," she corrected him.

"You are mistaken. The first boot you threw was, in fact, at my face, but it missed... the second is the one that hit me in the back." He stepped closer as he spoke, and her breath hitched. His smile widened. "Don't start pretending to be afraid of me now. Remember, I can tell when you lie." The tone in his voice fueled an entirely different type of flutter—one that bloomed in her chest and settled low in her stomach.

Dempsey's sinister nature was masked behind charming smiles, whereas Calder's wicked smiles suddenly felt far more dangerous. As she watched his gaze move to her neck, her eyes grew wider, and her lips parted. He leaned in closer, bringing their eyes level.

"You may not fear me... but he does... and that is what I find interesting, don't you, Emer?" The rumble in his voice as he said her name was like cold water cascading down her bare back.

"Now, any thoughts on how he knew where to find you?" Calder asked.

Emer's face twisted, knowing exactly how Dempsey knew where to look. The memory of her screaming Calder's name rang in her ears.

She swallowed, knowing the confession was going to cost her something and hoping sharing the knowledge would be worth it. "When he grabbed me, I called for help. Your help," she said the last words more quietly.

Calder blinked once. Twice. Then with a nod said, "Well, now I find many things interesting."

While neither of them acknowledged it, they both recognized that the dynamic between them had shifted.

Calder sought Emer when she tried to escape, and in the end, she sought him in return.

It was not until later that she wondered why she had returned to the keep rather than running into the night. It was not as simple as choosing a known evil over the unknown. In the brief moment she had to choose, she chose the Raven over the sea and the shadows. Soon, she would learn if that was wise.

"Are you worried he planned to look through your things? Seems to be quite interested in finding out all your dark secrets," she asked in an attempt to change the subject.

"Wouldn't matter," he responded with a shrug.

"You have letters and documents all over your desk." She paused as his eyebrow raised. "What!" she barked.

"Did you find anything particularly important when you... innocently browsed my desk?" he asked.

"That was not the same."

"Agree to disagree. You found nothing, and neither would he, and I think you know that," he said with a satisfied smile. She shook her head in annoyance, but the act left her dizzy. She began to stumble back, but his grip caught her arm.

He eyed her for a moment before sighing, "Get cozy, Merrow. I can't let you leave this room, not even to cross the hall, and while I am sure you will remain unimpressed, I do have important things to do," he explained, stepping forward.

Emer moved to retreat but her legs bent as their backs collided with the bed. Calder loomed over her as she glared, now seated on the bed.

"A chair will suit me fine," she argued.

"Your stubbornness serves no purpose other than to hurt you," he observed, and suddenly, it felt as if they were no longer speaking of the seating arrangement.

Emer smiled. "It also serves to piss you off and I find that a worthwhile endeavor."

"Oh, I can tell." Despite himself, Calder smiled. "Rest," he echoed the earlier command.

"I don't need to," she said stubbornly.

"Yeah. And I don't need a stiff drink," he said as he dipped his head down to her. "Always making me repeat myself."

Glaring, Emer backed across the bed until she was against the wall. She pulled her legs to her chest and scowled at his profile. With a blink, her neck felt stiff and her head felt heavy. She dropped her chin to rest on her folded knees. On the next blink, she realized it took more energy to be angry—energy she did not have—and her scowl quickly faded. A more extended blink made her internally reprimand herself for allowing her eyes to linger closed for longer than before. Her brow furrowed and she coaxed her eyes back open. A final blink.

Then nothing.

CHAPTER 10

Calder knew the moment she fell asleep. There was a shift in the air. It grew still. Quiet. Peaceful. He didn't think she often felt peace, the chaotic creature that she was. There always seemed to be a nervous hum that vibrated from her, causing even the air around her to grow agitated. It took more effort than he would like to admit to not turn and look at her. There was a strange curiosity to see what she looked like when she was relaxed... when she wasn't angry or suspicious.

Keeping Emer proved to be more problematic than he anticipated, and while he had managed it, his motivation for doing so began to grow murky. Did he keep her because of her secrets or because releasing her felt like letting go of something more?

He had run into so many dead ends in search of the truth of his mother's death that something vital in him cracked. Pieces of himself lost over time, leaving edges ragged and raw.

In the quiet, he could recognize that it was not Emer's secrets fueling his need to keep her, but his own. The sense that she was a lost piece, even if she did not realize it. Ravens know things and Calder knew that it was no coincidence.

Of all the found shores, of all the lost boys, of all the runaway girls... it was here, it was him, and then there was her.

If, however, she truly was not connected to the violence of the past nor there to cause violence in the present, then he needed to get her far away from the keep and Dempsey's attention.

Emer shifted and Calder looked over his shoulder, half expecting her to be poised to strike him over the head with a blunt object. Instead, she had slipped down the wall and her knees were curled into her chest as she slept.

"So tiny," he whispered incredulously.

Despite himself, he watched her for a moment.

She let out a contented sigh.

He quickly looked back to his papers.

It wasn't until he had almost finished his correspondences that he heard a sharp intake of breath.

Calder shuffled the parchment on the desk. "Nice of you to join the living. Things were peaceful for so long, I wondered for a moment if the Elders stole you in your sleep," he said without bothering to look at her.

Rubbing her face, Emer tried to orient herself back from the dream she escaped to. One that had been dipped in warm whiskey and wrapped in sea breeze. She eyed the covers she was cradling and pushed them away.

The room was lit by the soft glow of a fire, the light of day having slipped out of Emer's reach yet again. Silently, she mourned its passing.

When Calder turned to meet her gaze over his shoulder, he paused, watching her in silence for a long moment. Emer smoothed down her hair, her unruly locks seemingly bewitched to defy the natural law.

Calder cleared his throat and returned his attention back to his desk. "Another compromise?" he asked.

Emer's brow rose, but she did not answer.

"You get this." He slid a bowl across the desk to the side nearest to the bed. "As long as you are answering my questions."

Again, she would face the knight of Isle Basalt, but this time, with a ghost of a smile on her lips.

"I answer. I get to eat?" Her tone was an echo of Calder's own indifference. A tone that prompted him to spare her another slightly suspicious glance.

"Yes," he said the word almost as if it were a question.

"Delightful." Leaning forward, she snatched the bowl—a dish of meat and vegetables.

Since first meeting her, he came to expect many things from the girl who washed onto his shore. Finding trouble like a moth to a flame. Impulsivity, to be sure. Poor decisions, almost as a rule. What she was in this moment was pleased and *that* he had not expected.

Cheeks stretched with food, she smiled again. This time, in a way that made her nose crinkle.

What the actual fuck is happening?

"Why are you here?" he asked only to have Emer repeat the same answer she had given him before, that she was here for her family, though the words were muffled as she chewed this time.

She rocked side-to-side gleefully as she ate.

Calder pinched the bridge of his nose.

"But your family is not from here." It was a fact that he had already decided was true but required confirmation regardless.

She paused chewing. Her expression grew contemplative and then she shrugged. "Given that you did not present that as a question, I don't believe I have to answer. Based on your own rules, of course."

There it was... the reason for her smile. She only agreed to play the game because it was hers, not his.

Clever girl.

Calder fought against the baser instinct to simply terrify her.

In any other interrogation, that is what he would have done. That is the exact reason why none had ever gone this poorly. He would have thrown chairs against the wall, watching with satisfaction at the fear that bloomed into their eyes and answers poured from them like spring rain. Once, he hung someone out of one of the keep windows until they complied. But not with her. While that tactic worked on grown men with blood on their hands, she willingly jumped out of one of the very same windows.

He rolled his head between his shoulders, trying to clear it from the fog she seemed to cause.

"How did you get here?" he continued.

"I swam, couldn't you tell?"

A petulant sound left him. "Alright, where did you swim from?"

"Tír fo Thuinn," she cited the land from one of the fairy tales often told to children of Rest.

"Fucking fitting," he said with a hoarse chuckle that did not contain a thimble of humor. "The land beneath the sea. Surely not a lie," he said through gritted teeth.

At this, Emer's chewing slowed. She stared at him in open surprise—he should not have known that.

"Do I look like a patient man to you?" he asked dryly.

"No. But you are a man who appreciates order and rules. You only said I had to answer your questions. You never said with what detail or that you had to approve of my answer." She smirked before licking her spoon clean.

"You're a child," he hissed in frustration.

"And you're a sorry loser," she returned. "I am of no consequence to you. The longer you keep me, the more foolish you will feel for having overreacted so spectacularly. Save yourself the embarrassment and let me go."

"Your very presence is concerning. Your resistance is even more so. Your disregard for your own mortality is utterly alarming. You will have to accept that you are entirely unexpected and wholly chaotic," he listed and it was unclear if he was justifying her captivity to her or himself.

When she attempted to argue he raised his hand to pause her.

"It does appear that you have satisfied your end of the bargain," he said as he rose. "I will toast your little victory here while I am getting good and drunk. Something I would like to do expeditiously if you don't mind," he said as he raised an invisible glass and backed to the door.

He opened it, checked the corridor, and motioned for Emer to leave. Her cheeks warmed in embarrassment at the swift dismissal. She slipped from his bed, placed the bowl on his desk, and then retrieved her boots from the corner of the room. When she did not hear footsteps follow, she turned and found him leaning against the door.

"You have grown too comfortable for my liking, so that is no longer where you will be staying," he explained with a slight grin.

Pushing off the wall, he led her down the corridor. To Emer's relief, they stopped only a few paces down the hall. Unlocking the door, he motioned for her to enter.

The room was dark, but Calder removed a lantern from the corridor and placed it on the desk by the bed. It was almost identical to the one room she had been in before.

"Standard accommodations, of course. The only notable difference is the apparently *necessary* lack of trees outside of your window," he said with a wink.

Her grip tightened on her boots as if she debated throwing them at him once more.

"Now... if you could try not to spoil my plans by getting yourself into mortal danger, that would be much appreciated."

He punctuated his not-request with a bow as he backed towards the door, still bent forward. He paused at the door waiting for Emer's smart-ass rebuttal and frowned slightly when he was met with nothing. The room's silence was only broken by the rather pathetic sound of her boots dropping to the floor. The sight caused Calder's brow to furrow and he shook his head as if attempting to dislodge the scene as he backed out of the room and locked the door.

Nothing ale can't fix.

CHAPTER 11

With another night came a familiar nightmare. Recently, they began to take the shape of memories altered and corrupted by Emer's fears.

She was in her room, but it was not her room. It was painted in the gray of grief that seemed to wash out any true color. Whispered voices drifted down the hall, hoping to torment her.

Hushed conversations had become common since their father fell ill. Emer's mother tried to protect her and Finn from the harsh reality they found themselves in, leaving them to fill in the blanks left by the unheard words. Even though she knew they would only lead to heartbreak, she followed the whispers as they coaxed her from bed.

"We are losing him." Lachlan's words echoed until the walls began to wail and the house shook.

Emer clapped her hands over her ears as she crouched down, curling into herself. The shadows on the floor turned into a black fog that seeped over her bare feet. Soon, thick tendrils began to creep towards her hands and wrapped around her wrists. It wanted to pull her down into the darkness.

Ahead, she could see the inky black entity creeping through the open door to her parent's room. She fought against it as it strangled her limbs. When she reached the entrance, she pulled herself through and slammed the door closed.

Her heart broke before she even turned around.

Every time, the dream was the same. She would burst through the door to keep out the darkness, and he would be there.

Her father.

Every time, the dream devastated her because this part was the memory.

His features were pinched and wary. His skin had taken on a gray pallor, but it still possessed the telltale warmth of life. Even in sleep, she could tell he had no peace.

Like a child seeking comfort from the monsters chasing her in the night she stood at his bedside. Curling up on the hard floor beside the bed, as though the proximity to him could make the realm a little less terrifying, she reached up and took his hand in hers.

She could almost feel the faint burn in her shoulder from the position she held her arm. Even in her dreams, she knew the weight and warmth of his hand in hers. It was something she had tried to memorize just in case.

She squeezed it twice.

Once for love and once for luck, promising that she would do anything to save him.

Emer sat up with a gasp. The tears she had wept in her sleep were cold and tacky on her cheeks. Slowly, her eyes adjusted from the pale world of her dreams to the equally glum sight of another morning at the keep. It took her several moments to calm her heart and breath. The dull hum beneath her skin, the wrongness that vibrated in her blood was still present, but the emptiness in her chest that she had so often felt was strangely absent. Perhaps the sadness that overflowed within her left no more room for fear.

The sharp sound of metal colliding rang through the early

morning air. It was not the melody sung by a forge but rather the song of swords in battle. It was soon joined by a chorus of shouts that had Emer scrambling to look out her window. She was unsure which prospect was more terrifying, that the keep was under attack or that she allowed herself to hope Lachlan had survived and was there to rescue her.

Her eyes struggled to acclimate to the light. From her new vantage point, she could see directly into the courtyard. As the sunspots of her vision dissipated, she found it was not a siege on the keep nor a rescue attempt. The shouts and swords were wielded by the knights training in the space below.

Approximately, a dozen men formed a circle. Their boisterous shouts and attention were devoted to the two men who fought with short swords in the center. One with ink-black hair and the other with dark brown.

Each brutal strike was matched with raucous cheers, and every powerful guard with heckling. The man with brown hair was disarmed and replaced by another, and then another, and then another. The victor remained and continued.

He paused for a moment, running his hands through his hair and out of his eyes.

Calder.

Emer pushed off the windowsill, shrinking back as if he could have seen her. The thought was both fanciful and foolish. He would not be bothered to look up to her window, so she slowly leaned forward to peer out again.

The challenger approached and held two small axes to mirror Calder's own. The Sea Raven struck hard and fast. The muscles of his shoulders rolled and his forearms tensed from the movement, confirming what Emer had long suspected. The man before her had been made for and by weapons. Yet despite the power behind them, his movements were impossibly fluid and graceful.

After only a handful of moves, he had the man disarmed and bent on one knee.

Even with the great distance between them, the hunger in his eyes was unmistakable. There was no weapon he was not proficient in and it was clear why he had been chosen to train the men. Whether by ax, short-sword, or his own hand, whoever faced him would fall.

Nervous pacing in the courtyard caught Emer's attention. Dempsey circled Calder, watching and waiting. After two more opponents, Dempsey began pushing his way to the front of the crowd. The moment Calder made eye contact with him, his smile sharpened. He was the predator and Dempsey was a mere scavenger—only willing to approach once he thought his target grew tired.

Calder tossed away his ax and sword, challenging Dempsey hand-to-hand. They smiled, blatantly looking forward to whatever pain they were about to inflict on one another.

Dempsey was the first to strike and moved aggressively as he lunged forward. Calder moved inhumanly fast, dodging Dempsey's fist with an unwavering grin. The force behind Dempsey's movement caused him to stumble forward. Rather than moving to attack, Calder simply turned and waited for Dempsey to re-engage.

Dempsey's flared nostrils did little to hide how quickly Calder managed to fluster him. A feat that was particularly impressive given that he had yet to lift a hand against him.

It was unclear if Calder used his opponent's emotions against them or if he consumed them, fed from them to nourish his own savagery.

Dempsey thrust and threw his fists, each blocked by Calder's palm or forearm with just enough degradation to cause his next blow to falter.

After the next block, Calder struck and no one was more surprised by it than Dempsey. Emer was a close second.

The longer Emer watched, the clearer it became that, while she had fought Calder, he had not fought her. Possibly more sobering than the realization of what he was capable of was why he'd been distracted enough that day for her to get the upper hand.

With each blow to his face and upper body, Dempsey's anger became more evident in the decreasing strategy of his movements. Calder ducked low and swept the legs out from under his opponent in a swift motion. Dempsey stared up at Calder from his back. Rage, sweat, and blood poured from him.

Forgetting for a moment that the broken man on the ground was the same man who had her fighting for her breath, she allowed herself to feel the fleeting spark of sympathy. Something she was certain Calder did not possess. What he did feel was written across his face in a very intentional way—satisfaction.

Calder reached his hand out, confusing all who watched. He gripped Dempsey's hand firmly and held his stare as he grabbed his sleeve and pushed it up his forearm.

Something wicked deep within Calder preened at the evidence of Emer's ferocity written on Dempsey's skin. His eyes darkened, though his expression did not waver. When his gaze made the slow ascent back to Dempsey's, wide with shock, he ripped his arm back as he pulled down the fabric.

Emer didn't breathe.

Dempsey didn't move.

Calder didn't hesitate.

"Again!" he ordered so loud that Emer thought she actually heard the words rather than read his lips.

The men cheered, wholly unaware of the shift that had taken place among the fighters. Dempsey hesitated for a moment but then once again squared off.

If it was not apparent that the game being played had changed by the way the men regarded each other, the crowd should have been able to sense it in the way they fought. Calder no longer fought defensively; this time, he was the aggressor. His fist connected with Dempsey's chin, splitting open his lip. The spray of crimson blood as he spat was visible across the pale stones of the courtyard.

Dempsey charged.

Calder blocked the blows aimed at his face. Those that did land against his lower body did not seem to faze him. Instead, he took advantage of the position it left Dempsey in, bringing his elbow down against his shoulder. As Dempsey flinched, Calder brought his fist to connect to the other side of Dempsey's head. He reeled back, leaving himself open to the powerful kick that Calder landed on his chest. The impact threw him back against the ground so hard that the crowd no longer cheered.

Calder's chest heaved as he studied his victim, prostrated before him. He began to step forward, but a firm hand clapped down over his shoulder. Whether Calder was finished or not, the match was over. He looked at his keeper with a feral snarl. Banner's hold did not yield, instead, he gave him a supportive squeeze before tugging him away.

In the heat of the fight, Calder had been distracted by the need to feel Dempsey break beneath his fists, but now in the calm, he could feel them. Eerie cries reverberated off the keep's high stone walls as wraith-like shadows were cast on the ground. Low curses and sentiments of superstition slipped from the men. Several retrieved charms from their tunics, pressing them to their lips as they gazed above. Ravens had come.

Within moments, the beautiful and foreboding creatures found sanctuary on the limbs of the tree that Emer had once sought the same from. Perched along its branches like some terrible omen. All the knights of the keep began to murmur and point.

All except one.

Calder's expression remained neutral as he turned his back to Dempsey, leaving him on the ground. Without drawing attention to the act, Calder turned his gaze to the window of Emer's new chambers. Their eyes found each other amidst the chaos.

He kept watching her as he said, "I've got a job for you."

A sinister smile pulled at Banner's lips, and the pair left the courtyard together without another word.

CHAPTER 12

Outside, the bedlam persisted.

Inside, Emer paced anxiously.

Each croak that sounded frayed her nerves a little more. Ominous cackling, as if the birds were laughing at something she would find no humor in. These ravens did not feel like the white one she encountered on the shore.

Birds were supposed to bring songs, memories of morning, and warm sun. These creatures seemed more akin to dragons than birds, with their giant black forms, sweeping shadows, and piercing cries. She suspected they were the very things that gave birth to the concept of the giant winged beasts. Their presence felt equally odd and threatening; although she only caught a glimpse of Calder after the ravens arrived, she was confident by the set of his jaw that this was not a regular occurrence.

Were they here to serve as an omen or was their swift descent on the keep an answer to a call?

Emer turned to the door just as Calder placed two firm knocks against the wood—an announcement of his arrival rather than a request to enter.

His hand was visible first. Fingers, tacky with blood, gripped the door's edge as it opened. Darker stains marred the valleys between his veins and she quickly realized the shallow cuts that dusted his knuckles were the product of Dempsey's teeth.

As the rest of Calder's tall form entered the room, her eyes shot to his. She was unsure if she had stopped the gasp that formed or if her body betrayed her and let shock spill from her without permission.

Only the faintest remnants of the gaze she had come to know remained. His pupils were blown out, the black laying siege to the blue. With her focus trained on Calder, Emer failed to notice the second set of steps trailing him.

Banner cleared his throat, leaning against the door frame with an impatient smirk as if waiting for an invitation. The two men shared a look, and Banner proceeded into the room, closing the door behind him.

Once inside, his gaze alternated between Calder and Emer before he looked down, releasing a huff of a laugh.

Emer, puzzled by his reaction, took an uneasy step back.

Calder suspected he knew exactly why Banner was laughing and fully intended to discuss it with him later. Perhaps in the Den.

Lacking little in the way of confidence and roguish charm, Banner adjusted his satchel and moved across the room with an arm outstretched to Emer. A hand slammed into him, causing him to pause. Banner's smile curled into a slightly sharper version as he studied Calder's hand pressed against the center of his chest.

Eyes still on Emer, Calder tilted his head in that ever-familiar predatory fashion. After a moment, his glare dipped to the lantern on the chair behind her. The one her fingers were now possessively hooked over the handle of.

Calder tsked.

"Merrow, were you about to bludgeon poor Banner with that lantern?" His voice contained all the light that was absent from his eyes.

She was not entirely sure what she intended to do with the

opportunistic weapon, but she quickly learned that while Calder had boundaries he would not cross when it came to her, others in the keep did not. A heavy object to the head seemed a reasonable way to establish them.

A small and incriminating growl left her as she released the lantern. With her hands now in fists, she narrowed her eyes on the stranger.

"Well then," Banner said delightedly.

He appraised her once more, his eyes surveying her and pausing at her wounded hands and shoulder. After a moment, he nodded as if approving of the half-wild girl before him.

"Banner," he said, introducing himself.

When Emer did not take his hand, he pulled it back with a snap of his fingers. Her expression was unimpressed and highly suspicious. Seemingly immune to the blonde's charm.

"He's here as a favor, Merrow. Try to play nice," Calder said in an exasperated tone, his hands flexing at his sides. With the blood-lust beginning to simmer, the trauma he inflicted on his hands started to seep in.

"I don't need a nursemaid," she said with a scowl.

"Shame. I have great bedside manner," Banner cooed almost absentmindedly as he rummaged through his satchel.

Calder's hand swiftly connected with the back of Banner's head.

"Fuck'n shit!" he grunted, wincing from the impact.

Banner cracked his neck to the side. There was less levity in his voice when he explained, "What I meant was, I happen to be quite talented in my line of work. A connoisseur of concoctions, if you will."

Moving to the table near Emer, Banner began retrieving various herbs, cloths, and jars.

"Based on the one on your shoulder, Calder was right to be worried about the state of your wounds. Have you seen what happens when something like that gets infected?" he asked, tipping his head and acknowledging her wounds while he continued to gather his things.

Emer eyed Calder questioningly.

"Oh. Sorry, boss, was that a secret?" Banner flashed him a smile over his shoulder, proving that he may not have been able to strike Calder back, but there were other methods of cruelty in his arsenal.

Emer glanced at her hands, uncurling her fingers slightly to inspect the wounds. The salve Calder had given her helped, but they remained irritated. The deep gouge that ran down her index finger seemed redder than the others. While she was not particularly pleased to accept help from either of them, she could recognize the signs of infection. As much as she disliked the men, she was fond of her hands. So, she sighed and nodded in consent.

"Good," Calder said gruffly. "I am going to wash up. Stay with her until I return," he commanded before storming out of the room.

Emer's stomach dropped. She hadn't expected him to leave her alone, and she stared at the space he had vacated, swallowing the desire to call him back.

Banner shook his head, muttering something before looking back to her and smiling.

"Would you care to sit?" he asked, motioning to the chair.

"No," she responded curtly.

"A woman who knows what she wants. I respect that. Okay then... well, I'll just..." he motioned his intent to step closer to where she stood. "Parents were healers. Well, Ma is. Was. Pa ran the pub. I inherited a knack for the art. Along with a penchant for poisons."

She was struck by his nonchalance and eyed him suspiciously.

"You can guess which I get the most requests for but diversified skill sets are valuable," he said with a shrug. "May I?" he asked, holding out his hands.

Emer cautiously extended her hand, ensuring the lantern was still within reach.

"Elders' tits!" he exclaimed, which he quickly followed with an apology. "What exactly did you pick a fight with to earn those?" he asked, adding the contents of several of the bottles to a stone bowl.

"A tree," Emer muttered.

Banner made a noise that sounded suspiciously like a snort.

"Did you lose a bet or were you just gloriously drunk?" he asked.

Emer narrowed her eyes at him. The casual way he made conversation with her made her want to like him, and she had no intention of allowing that.

"I don't like you," she said flatly.

Banner shot her a grin before continuing his work.

"Give it time," he returned confidently.

Emer looked back to the door, rocking from foot to foot as she considered how long it had been since Calder left, and how long it would likely be before he returned.

"Did he really not tell you?" she asked, uneasy in the silence.

"I only learned you existed a few moments before we knocked on your door," he explained. There was a slight air of annoyance in his tone that caused her to wonder if he was bothered by the secret or her captivity.

"Is this so normal that you just came? No questions asked?" she pressed.

Another chuckle left him as he searched the satchel for additional additives. Pouring what looked like honey into the bowl, he began mixing the contents. "This is most definitely *not* normal. And when he tells you something... you listen. Well, perhaps not *you*... but the sane folk do. Or so I am told."

His brow jumped as he met her gaze like they were sharing a joke and Emer didn't know what to make of the gesture. It was warm and genuine.

The sweet smell of the dried flowers, subtle spices, and honey filled the air. As Banner applied the mixture to her wounds, all Emer could do was frown in confusion at the care he took as he did.

"Rub some on your shoulder and neck," he instructed.

Turning his attention to his satchel, Banner pulled out clean strips of cloth to wrap her hands. As he tied the cloth, Emer grimaced and he apologized, loosening the knot to relieve some of the pressure. Despite their appearance, the mixture made them feel better than they had in days.

"Are you magic?" Emer asked him with a relieved sigh.

"First, you try to beat me, and now sweet talking? You tryin' to seduce me, little monster?" Banner teased.

At Emer's shocked expression, he continued, "It's not magic, but I did learn a lot from witches."

Emer nodded, her lips a perfect "o".

Amused, Banner returned to his task. His hands were calloused, likely from swordplay and hard labor, but there was also an elegant fluidity to his movements. She leaned in closer, her gaze snagging on the dark half-moons of his nail beds.

"You can tell a lot about someone by their hands," he mused, not bothering to pause his work. "Smiths have burns. Bakers can never seem to clean off the flour. Artists have paint under their nails. Men whose medium is poison have small dark moons to match our cold little hearts," he explained with a grin.

She should have been disturbed, but with the care he continued to take in tending to her wounds, she found herself curious instead.

"What do mine say?" she asked.

At this, a thin line formed in his brow as he considered her hands, old and new injuries, the slight tremor against his steady grip. "That you love as fiercely as you fight and as deeply as you fear."

Unwelcomed emotion gnawed at her and she pulled her hand away, opting to finish tying off the final strip herself.

"I jumped out of the window," she said, reminding herself of how she came to be marked by this place more than she was explaining to Banner. She wanted to call back her anger in hopes that there would not be room for the sadness that began to pool behind her eyes and drip down her throat.

Banner's eyebrow raised in interest. Perhaps he would be willing to help her with more than just her cuts and scrapes. The thought made her feel dirty somehow, as though it were an act of betrayal. However, just because Calder punished Dempsey for wronging her, that did not absolve him of his own offenses.

"Your beloved Calder has kept me prisoner for three days. These were the result of my first escape attempt. I jumped out of a keep window and onto the tree in the courtyard," she explained, infusing the appropriate amount of despondence into her voice.

Banner's posture stiffened and he shifted his shoulders. When he turned and began tidying his things, Emer bit down her frustration at his lack of response. She opened her mouth to speak again but was interrupted.

"That is not quite the whole truth. Now, is it?" Calder's voice sounded from the door.

Banner's lip twitched as Emer glared.

"I think I touched on the most important parts," she spat back.

"I would argue that you stabbing me with my own sword was pretty important," he said, pointing to his side as if she needed the reminder.

"So, that horseshit explanation for why you've needed multiple jars of poultices was... *lies?*" Banner's tone indicated that he had not believed any of the excuses Calder gave him in the first place.

Leaning in closer to Emer, Banner whispered, "You really stab him?"

Emer growled.

Banner leaned back and turned to Calder, grinning. "She stabbed you?" he asked, pointing between the two of them.

When he nodded in confirmation, Banner released a low whistle. "I like her," he chuckled, and now it was Calder's turn to growl.

"Don't you have a perimeter to check?" he asked impatiently.

Banner shrugged and then began packing his items into his satchel.

"Thank you, Banner," Emer sighed, disappointed that she would most likely receive no further help from him.

He paused, his smile shifting and his features softening as he regarded her. He nodded before making his way to stand in front of Calder expectantly. Calder rolled his eyes.

"Thank you," he said through gritted teeth.

The resistance to offer gratitude seemed to only delight the man more, and he rocked on his heels.

The fact that Calder had not struck him unconscious demonstrated that the pair had some modicum of mutual respect for each other, and Emer wondered if perhaps the Sea Raven was not as broody as she once suspected.

Banner had just reached the door when Calder called his name. "Yes, sir... 'Disembowelment, slow painful death, picked clean by ravens'... I recall... I won't breathe a word. But just so you know, you owe me two drinks now," he said with a rakish smirk and a wink at Emer.

They remained silent as Banner exited the room, and when she turned back to Calder, she rolled her eyes.

Most definitely broody.

CHAPTER 13

Even with Banner's departure, the room felt smaller with Calder in it.

He shook his head subtly as he watched her, an answer to a conversation he had not bothered to include her in.

Emer's glare intensified.

When Calder grinned in response, there was an edge to it—more snarl than smile.

Finally, he said, "So, first you attempt to beat him with a lantern, and then... what? Pretend to be helpless in the hopes that he would be moved to help you escape?" he scoffed. "Believable, given that you jumped. Into. A. Tree."

His brow arched in challenge or disappointment, she couldn't tell. She was angry with him, but more than that, she was angry with herself for caring that he was angry.

Emer closed her eyes as she worked to calm the building thrum, her body growing heated from the storm of emotions and doubt. When she opened them she found Calder's obstinate glare pinning her down, plucking at her already frayed nerves as if it produced his favorite melody.

Perhaps the Raven wished to build a nest from them.

"Why would you care if I tried? Do you not trust your men?" she spat back. Something flashed in his eyes too quickly for her to track it.

He shook his head again.

"I thought you were smarter than this, Merrow. You may pretend to be a damsel, but Banner was the one who tricked you into thinking he had a heart to appeal to. Don't play with monsters, sweetheart. You won't win," he said with a sharp smile.

She wanted to throw things.

She wanted to rip her hair out.

No, she wanted to rip *his* hair out.

One of the ravens outside croaked, and this time, they both winced.

"Grab your cloak and follow me." His voice was tense and left no room for rebuttal. Emer, however, was as stubborn as she was petite.

"Why would I do that?" she asked, crossing her arms.

"Because thirteen ravens just descended on this keep. Because Death is not far behind them. But most obviously because I... fucking... said so." He punctuated the last words with a commanding step forward.

By the time he finished the statement, he had crossed the room.

"The Isle is hungry today, Merrow, don't offer yourself up so sweetly just to spite me."

Emer could feel how true his words were in the strange energy in the air. She could hear it in the incessant warning of the winged beasts outside the window and see it in the slightly wild look in Calder's eyes.

The Isle was hungry, and it had a taste for her.

"What do the ravens mean?" The trepidation in Emer's voice betrayed her.

"I will tell you *if* you put on your coat and come with me."

Understanding that she would be going with him either way,

she opted to make it easier for them both. She took her cloak from his grasp and followed him out of the room.

The cries of the ravens crawled down the corridors, clinging and sweeping across the stones like cobwebs.

Once outside the keep, Emer strained to keep up with Calder's determined footfalls. She had hoped that in his distraction, she might be able to create enough distance to make an escape, but the moment her steps slowed, he shot her a glare over his shoulder.

As they rounded to the back of the keep, Emer was struck speechless by the rocky cliff that appeared. The short journey resulted in their arrival to an entirely different realm. The landscape of Obanes looked as if kindness fell in love with violence. Her soft fields and whimsical trees wrapped themselves around the hardness of the rocks and sharp cliffs.

The whistle of the harsh wind against the rock face beckoned her to it, and Emer found herself walking to the edge without further thought.

Calder tensed as she reached the drop-off. He had not lied. Death was there and he had no way of knowing who it would claim.

The air around them was thick—almost sticky—and cold. Emer struggled against the hood that was obscuring her vision, the weight of it growing increasingly oppressive. She pulled it back, and the powerful wind immediately set free her hair. In its natural state, it fell to Emer's hip bones and usually warranted containment with a messy plait or unruly knot. At this moment, there was no containing it, the sunlight catching the streaks of copper and turning them to flames fed by the wind.

It was unclear if the roar of the sea had managed to drown out the emptiness in her chest or if it banished it altogether, but she relished the feeling. She turned to Calder, only to find him watching her.

"What did you mean?" she shouted into the wind, emboldened by its wildness. "About death and the ravens."

"Thirteen ravens is an omen. They mark the beginning of an end," he explained, his jaw tight and his eyes cold. It was not fear that ruled his features but a strange sort of determination and a level of indignation.

As if Calder would defy the Elders themselves because they used his own totem for something he had not personally sanctioned.

She felt the birth of a laugh as she contemplated the level of conceit that would require, but she felt the sensation die in her chest as she pondered the implications of what he had said.

"That could mean many things," she argued in a poor attempt at indifference.

"It *could*," he replied gruffly. "If I did not also feel Death growing closer."

Emer took a step away from him, forgetting that she was near the edge of the cliff, and Calder flinched when her feet paused just short of the cliffside. Tipping his head back, he stared at the sky unable to remain impassive with Emer so close to the edge.

"You feel it?" she asked, her voice lost somewhere between disbelief and denial.

"Sea Ravens sense it. Natural death feels like breathing in the winter air. Unnatural death makes our bones grow cold," he explained.

Before Emer could ask what it felt like now, a shiver racked through him.

Unnatural.

Calder straightened his spine, pulled his shoulders back, and rolled his head between his shoulders as if trying to keep his bones from seizing.

"Why are we here, Calder?" Her voice was unintentionally pleading and heavy with the weight of the last few days.

His gaze grew sharp in response to her petition. As she searched the storm within his eyes, the damp wind at her back reminded her of the cliff and a fear that had begun to take root bloomed violently.

If Death was searching for a soul to claim, would its Raven offer her as a trade?

Heat began to surge through her as if her body hoped to protect her from the ice his stare formed in her veins.

"I don't know," he breathed, and for a moment, they stared at each other.

The loud rasp of a raven soaring above them pulled her attention from Calder and to the sky. She knew it was a mistake to leave herself vulnerable, but Emer looked up anyway. To her surprise, she did not find a dark, ominous raven looming above but a glimpse of ethereal white.

Slightly off balance, she teetered back but Calder caught her arm and pulled her away from the cliff and into his chest. The wind stopped and the waves quieted as her attention focused entirely on how her body molded to the hard lines of his.

He was the cliffside and she was the ocean, liquid and chaotic.

"Hide," he growled.

"Wha—"

He pulled her past him and hurried her towards the edge of the keep. She could feel his stare burning her as she scrambled from the cliffside and to the wall, where she crouched amongst bushes covered in bursts of purple flowers. Almost as soon as she was concealed, she saw Dempsey emerge from around the corner and pause to stare viciously at Calder.

"You!" Dempsey's voice tore through the air in a roar.

Calder stared at Dempsey with the same bored expression he always seemed to wear. A mask, Emer now realized.

Dempsey resumed his unsteady stride forward—evidence that he thought ale was the best remedy for his wounds.

The split and swollen lip.

The marred ridge of his eyebrow.

The deep purple and black stain on his cheekbone from the

blood pooled beneath the surface. Those things were proof enough of the encounter with Calder, but it was the damaged look in his eyes that screamed of his defeat.

"How dare you!" he slurred as he stood in front of Calder, his voice guttural and harsh.

Calder raised a brow as he looked down at the man, admiring his work leisurely before meeting his eyes. "You chose to fight me," he drawled, taking a step forward and eating up the small space between them. "You have only your own pride and wandering hands to blame."

Dempsey threw his head back with a howl of a laugh.

"You're a self-righteous bastard, you know that?" he yelled. "Judging me all the while protecting a foreign whore," Dempsey barked, and the contortion of his face caused fresh blood to seep from his lip.

Calder tilted his head. "Protecting *her*? Based on the skills you displayed today, I suspect I would have been protecting you from her if you had laid a hand on her." His tone remained controlled, but something about Calder began to harden at the mention of Emer.

"Is that so?" Dempsey huffed. "I will be sure to bring someone along with me next time I look for her then."

Calder's expression shifted; he bent his head until it was a breath from Dempsey, whose feet remained unmoved but body bent back. "I said I'd cut out your tongue for talking about her. I will let you ponder what I will do to you if you touch her."

Even from a distance, Emer felt the grit in Calder's voice.

"Walk away," Calder warned.

He turned his back on Dempsey, who seethed at the dismissal.

Dempsey muttered parting words, but their meaning was lost in the howl of the wind against the cliff.

The relief Emer felt at the averted altercation would have surprised her if it were not quickly replaced by terror at the sight of the blade in Dempsey's hand. He stood motionless a few paces from Calder, staring down at the knife and contemplating its weight.

This was her chance.

Dempsey had not yet seen her and Calder would soon be too occupied to pursue her. The harsh thought caused her stomach to twist. Had the Isle made her so cold that she could turn her back without a thought for the man who stood admiring the waves?

Her lips moved in silent pleas for Dempsey to sheath his blade, for Calder to turn around, for the Elders to intervene.

Dempsey turned and began to walk back to Calder.

If Emer wanted this to stop, she would have to stop it.

"Calder!" she screamed as Dempsey raised his knife.

Calder had been poised for Dempsey to attack, but as he whirled around and looked towards Emer, it was clear in the wild look in his eyes that he had not expected her to call out for him. That moment of distraction allowed Dempsey to achieve something he never had before. Dempsey gained the upper hand against him.

Knocking Calder to the ground, Dempsey leaped on top of him. They fought for purchase of the knife that was suspended above Calder. Dempsey used his weight to aid in the descent of the blade, and Calder, muscles tired from the morning's sparring matches, fought to slow its path to his throat.

Calder turned from the blade, his eyes locking on Emer's as he mouthed a single word.

"*Run.*"

Dempsey followed Calder's gaze to Emer and smiled. It was a crooked smile, his lips shaking from the effort it took to maintain control over the knife. He leaned down, whispering something in Calder's ear.

Whether Dempsey's mind was dulled with drink or the prospect of long-awaited retribution, he seemed to be lost to everything else, including Emer's approaching footfalls.

Pain shot through her wrists and shoulders as she struck the large man, displacing him, and driving them both over Calder.

It was not until Emer stared down at the white waters of the waves crashing against the rocks beneath Dempsey's suspended body that Emer realized just how close they had been to the edge. With no air in her lungs to send it forward, her scream died in her throat.

Dempsey's grip on her wrist was a brand. He clung to her, dark eyes alight with fury and fear. If he was to meet this bitter fate, he would sweeten it by taking something of Calder's with him.

A sharp pain raced up one of her legs and then the other. Tears pricked her eyes and she snapped them shut, waiting for the moment she no longer felt the ground beneath her chest... but it never came. She was not falling, she was being ripped in half.

Emer's body jerked as Calder pulled, and Dempsey hissed curses and threats as he struggled to keep his hold on her bandaged hands, slick with Banner's concoctions and her own fear. Slowly, everything unraveled.

They slipped.

He slipped.

Time slipped.

CHAPTER 14

The only sound more haunting than Dempsey's scream was the abrupt silence when it stopped. A silence matched by the darkness behind the closed eyes Emer retreated to.

She felt her body slide across the ground and knew she was no longer suspended over the cliff when the wind could not reach her tear-burned cheeks.

Calder spoke to her as he pulled her back from the edge, but she could not distinguish his words.

He gripped her shoulders, but her eyes remained closed.

He shook her, and still, they remained shut.

His hand cupped her cheek and she stared up at him.

The lines of his profile were harsh against the soft sky behind him as he grimaced at the carnage on the rocks below. When his eyes returned to her, they were dark and worried. Despite not knowing what he was looking for, she wanted to hide as he searched her eyes.

The unraveled bandages now exposed her shaky, bare hands. Hands with new faint scratches on the backs that she would be able to see long after they healed. She clasped them over her mouth to prevent another scream.

Calder tried to sit her up, but she recoiled, rolling to the opposite side and vomiting. There was a ghost of a touch to her back that might have been comforting if she was not so incredibly numb. She rose to her knees, the acid still dripping from her lips as she turned to him. His mouth moved, but the ringing in her ears was too loud.

"I killed him."

The confession left her in a strangled whisper, but inside, it had been a scream.

"Eyes on me, Merrow."

His command went unmet as she continued to look towards the cliff. He knelt next to her and his hand clutched the back of her neck as he tried to make her meet his gaze.

It was as if she felt everything and nothing.

It was someone else's pain.

Someone else's body.

Someone else's neck, cradled by a strong hand.

Her body vibrated violently and without her permission. An impossible cold spread through her limbs. The tension that consumed her threatened to shatter her frozen bones until her body matched the crumpled mess of her soul. A single word managed to pierce the noise in her head.

Breathe.

She knew the voice was right, but somehow, the act of breathing seemed outside her realm of control. The thumb, which was pressed against the side of her neck, just at the edge of her jaw, began to move in soft strokes. She forced herself to take a breath, and the darkness at the edge of her vision started to recede.

Two words this time.

Good girl.

She fell to her hands and knees, watching as each tear darkened the earth below her. She dug her fingers into the ground to anchor herself and stop the slipping feeling that plagued her.

"We need to go." Calder's voice had grown more urgent, and the bite in it had her mind shifting.

Emer's glassy eyes snapped to his, unsure of what she would find. She had sworn she was not dangerous. Sworn that she meant no harm.

Not only was she a killer, but she was also a liar.

Would Calder tell them it was an accident? Did it matter?

He pulled on her once more, growling something incoherent. She rocked back onto her heels as he tugged at her, trying to coax her to stand, but she could tell his patience was waning. Regardless of whether she lived out her days in a cell or if she was executed, her father would be damned by her crime. With her chin tucked against her chest and warm tears streaming down her face, she caught the glint of something at her side.

Dempsey's blade.

When she watched her hand reach for the knife, she recognized the scars, but she did not feel in control of the act. It was as if the light that burned brightly inside her had reduced to a flickering candle. A soul so thoroughly broken, it surrendered to its baser instinct.

Survival.

It was not her survival that she was willing to fight for; but that of those she loved and because of the promise she made. She would do anything. Anything, she learned, meant scarring her body and staining her soul until she scarcely recognized herself.

Knife in hand, she looked at Calder, who watched her warily.

His eyes narrowed as he searched hers; he recognized the remorse, but it wasn't until the knife's pommel crashed against his temple that he realized what it was that he couldn't quite place.

Resolve.

She scrambled to her feet, disbelief and bile clogging her throat as she looked at the collapsed form of the man who had just saved her. She could not help but recall the day their paths crossed and whether or not she had looked so broken when he found her sprawled on the shore. She hesitated for a moment before turning and breaking into a run.

Her legs shook with each step she took and her skin prickled as if the eyes of the entire keep watched her escape. As she reached the wooded area beyond the clearing, she heard the troubled call of the white bird that haunted her. Throwing herself behind a tree, she fell to her knees and vomited again. Her throat and eyes burned, and she wanted nothing more than to curl into a ball and cry. Time for such things was a luxury that neither she nor her family had. Rising to her feet, she pressed her nails into her palms and ran.

Darting through the forest felt much like when she swam for the surface of the sea. Every muscle in her body was devoted to hurdling herself towards the unknown. The thought of the monsters that awaited her in the woods would pale compared to Calder's fury when he awoke, and *that* thought had her feet moving faster. She had not known the Sea Raven long, but she was certain he was not felled often nor easily. The only explanation for her ability to blindside him was that he had dropped his defenses as he held her; he did not expect her to strike. The moment he chose to trust her was the moment she chose to betray him. Despite her guilt, she would do it again if necessary because nothing would get in the way of keeping her promise, including a blue-eyed Raven.

Night fell quickly and though it did little to cover her deeds from the day, it did illuminate the consequences. Despite colliding with several trees, she was determined to gain ground. Her boot caught on another rogue root, sending her tumbling to the dirt. Groaning, she rolled herself on her back and mentally surveyed each of her limbs to determine if this latest incident was the one to finally shatter one or more of her bones. Satisfied that her limbs were whole and deciding it best they remain that way, she resigned herself to curl up next to the very root that had brought her to the ground. Pulling the cloak around her, she stared at the sky in the breaks between the trees. Several stars winked in and out and she could not help but scowl at the thought they were mocking her with a secret that only they knew. One they had no interest in revealing.

All the relief she felt when she managed to escape from the cliffside began to wane. Her legs ached, her stomach writhed, and her lips were turning blue. She was never supposed to do this alone. She was supposed to be with Lachlan. He had been to Isle Basalt before and said he could get her to Lunochy. They both agreed that she should be the one to make the request, that the Guardian would sense her love, feel her desperation, and recognize her belief. She may think the Elders were bastards, but she certainly believed. More than anything, she wished now she would have told her mother and Finn that she was leaving. She wished she would have said goodbye rather than slipped away in secret.

Her failures began almost the moment her boots left her homeland, and now she feared those who loved her would be left to wonder about her fate until they joined each other across the Array.

She had not been brave. She had been the desperate daughter of a dying man who thought she could be enough to fix things while slowly breaking herself. She clutched herself and wept over how wrong she had been.

The thunderous sound of men's boots on the deck and booming voices caused Emer to shake with dread.

In the chaos, she fell, her body sprawled out on the deck, and a boot quickly met her back from one of the men who continued his course as if he had kicked a sack of potatoes. The shouts continued to surround her. Emer curled into the ache as she fought to catch her breath. She opened her eyes and rolled onto her back. It was only then that she was able to truly appreciate how doomed they were. The boat was no longer a vessel but a mass pyre prepared to sail their burning bodies across the Array.

Ready or not.

Water surrounded them as far as the eye could see, which, in the dead of night, was not as far as it stretched, but the men struggled to douse the flames. Emer crawled away from the commotion, rising to her feet. It quickly became clear that it was not only the blaze that the men fought. More flames poured over the boat. Flames carried by arrows that pierced through the night sky like nefarious little beings eager to consume everything they touched.

The men's shouts were joined by the sound of splintering wood as the arrows embedded themselves deep into the boat's surfaces. The air was thick with smoke and fear. Rough and powerful hands clamped down on her shoulders and began to jostle her.

"Emer!" The voice and the hands of the man who held her demanded her attention, and it took what little strength remained to refocus on him.

"Lachlan... I..." Her focus was pulled to her right as more wood splintered nearby.

"Get to the Well," he growled.

His words still echoed through her as her eyes flew open and she gasped for air.

A dream. A memory. A little more of her heart broken.

"Get to the Well," she echoed through gritted teeth.

An oath to her father, an ode to Lachlan, and a command to herself. Emer did not sleep, instead she continued to recite her purpose like an incantation until the blue-gray of morning broke and she resumed her trek.

Not long before, she wouldn't have even dreamed of seeing this strange place. As she hiked through the darkened forests, her bones stiff and soul tired, she felt no gratitude for finding herself in it. Even the song of the morning birds sounded mournful, a dark and dire melody.

Her path swayed as she walked, moving beneath the light that filtered through the canopy, hoping she could steal a moment of warmth. Clouds soon began to gather and she stiffened her jaw as she attempted to ignore the despair taking root.

When the first raindrops slipped past the frame made by her hood, acute rage followed in its wake. Her hands balled into fists at her sides as she raised her gaze to the sky. Each drop of rain that slid down her skin felt like a slap in the face. Whether it was the Elders' cruelty or simply their indifference, she cursed them.

Soon, the rain began to pour in steady streams and her cloak was soaked through. The hem, having been designed for its much larger owner, dragged through the mud.

She had loved the rain once. She had loved so many things that now seemed to despise her. The sea, the stars, the rain. They had all turned on her, but she still felt safer with the elements than any of the Isle's inhabitants, so she stayed far from the main path. The benefit was that she would be less likely to encounter others on her journey, the danger being she could easily become lost in the woods. She was no explorer but knew the basics of navigation using the North Star and the path of the sun.

In the distance sat the remnants of a dilapidated cottage. It was a strange site this far off the path and she wondered what caused its residents to seek such isolation. The frame had long since been claimed by its surroundings—a sign that those who once called it home had not done so for some time. The interior was damp, although a vast improvement from the outside, and the air was heavy with the scent of loam. The rotted floor gave way in several places, allowing the flora another route to claim the space. Vines and cobwebs intermingled, forming a macabre chandelier with drops of rain slipping down and glistening like jewels. While furniture was sparse, a table and fallen chairs were located against one of the walls, with a crumbling hearth on the other. Even though there were dry items available to leverage as kindling, she lacked the knowledge needed to build a fire without the benefit of Ravenstone to provide the spark.

She carefully crossed the creaking floor to where an armoire was situated in the corner and studied the trinkets and jars. The labels on the jars were obscured by layers of thick dust. Many had been broken, their contents aged and indistinguishable. The pungent scent of the air gave way to something else, something sweet. As quickly as it had overwhelmed her, it was gone, and she was left unable to place it.

Having soaked up most of the sky, she removed her cloak and draped it over the nearby chair. Her tunic did not fare much better and had grown translucent where it hung on her shoulders. Gripping the fabric, she wrung it out as best as she could before slipping down the far wall and allowing herself a momentary reprieve from the downpour.

Emer's eyes closed, and her tired mind had the anxious thought that she had forgotten something important, but sleep claimed her before she could remember what it was.

She had forgotten to keep her eyes on him.

CHAPTER 15

The soft breeze tousled Calder's dark curls and tickled his forehead, urging him into semi-consciousness. It was far gentler than the shrill cry that broke the afternoon air.

The rhythmic crashing of the ocean against the rocky cliffside threatened to return him to sleep, but pain drew him back. His head pounded. His side ached. This time, when Alabaster called, it was fainter... farther away.

In time, with a thunderous clap of the ocean, Calder inhaled. The breath was painful and he curled into himself. One arm wrapped his abdomen while the other pressed into the ground. After a moment, he pushed himself off the carpet of clovers and grass, their luckless little forms crushed as his hands clenched into fists.

The motion of rising to his knees caused his surroundings to bend around him as the memories of how he found himself in this state slowly returned. The tender flesh around his split eyebrow throbbed. The pain was a lightning bolt, pulsing behind his eye and striking through his skull. He rocked back on his heels and brought his hand to his head, drawing fresh blood from the gash.

"Elders' damned man-eater," he stuttered out.

Each of his movements was labored and stiff from his time in the elements. He huffed a derisive laugh that Emer had managed to knock him out for so long.

He staggered on his feet, wiping the blood from his ruined brow before it could cloud his vision.

Merrow fucking indeed.

His frustration began to ebb as he recalled how her eyelids flickered from lack of air as she panicked. The horror that overtook her features as he tried to hold her together. He saw it in her eyes. She feared herself as much as she did him at that moment. They were all things he realized too late. A heartbeat before the flash of steel turned everything black.

He sighed.

Tipping his head back, he studied the sun, slowly slipping beneath the sea. The day might be coming to an end, but his hunt was just beginning. His gaze turned from the cliff to the forest. He did not hunt like other men. The white raven called out to him again.

"Yeah. I fuck'n hear you," he gritted out.

The mere sound of the creature formed tension that settled between the blades of his shoulders like an anchor. He closed both eyes and ignored the throbbing behind them.

Focus.

He pushed his vision away and felt the magic bleed over his eyes like cold water. When he opened them again, the blue was devoured by the deepest of onyx, and the view he had was no longer his own.

From the vantage of the white raven soaring overhead, he could see her path clearly. While Alabaster's eyes aided him with the vision, his tracking knowledge made sense of the scene as they soared.

The echo of her movements as she ran seemed to lift off of the earth, her small boot prints carved into the forest floor. The large puddle she had bounded through made his lip turn up, confident that she had hissed like a splashed cat in that moment. He could see where she became tangled in a group of yew saplings. More scars for her collection. His jaw worked as he found more evidence of her carelessness. She made no attempt to conceal which direction she had fled in.

Calder released a disapproving tsk.

He wondered if it was because she was too lost in visions of what happened at the cliff, too desperate to escape the keep, or if she did not have the instincts to hide her tracks. He would need to ask her once he found her.

And find her, he would.

The large white abomination in the sky cawed loudly, sounding almost proud at what he had to show the man who looked through his eyes. Calder usually found the creature tiresome, albeit convenient; he could not help but appreciate that the raven seemed to want to keep track of Emer as much as he did.

"Follow her," Calder demanded.

She needed time to come down from the shock and he needed time to hide the cause. They would be reunited soon enough, but until then, he wanted eyes on her. Either his or Alabaster's.

His back muscles rolled as he shifted, pulling his sight back. It took more effort than usual. Probably due to the head wound. Alabaster made a noise of dissent.

Judgmental asshole bird.

He'd have flipped the rat-with-wings off if he was a lesser man. With a rumbling growl of resentment, he turned from the tree line and faced the drop-off of the cliff.

The sea had hewn steps into the stone cliff as if his dear friend knew he would need them one day. Peering down, he could see where Dempsey lay broken on the rocks below, just out of reach of the high tide. Causing him problems even in death.

He descended the steps, his boots scratching upon the stones as he went. The constant spray of salt frosted the stairs, the rocks, and the cliff. Not even the brine in the air that rushed towards him could mask the iron tang of blood. The gore that met him as he reached the rocky outcrop at the base was equally as vibrant as the seascape around it. The few placid pools of seawater surrounding Dempsey were thick and shaded with crimson.

As he weighed his options, Calder ran his hands through his hair, damp from the wet breeze. Carrying dead weight up the narrow stairs would be harrowing even if his ribs weren't bruised and his head wasn't splitting. He had little interest in joining Dempsey like a broken doll at the base of the cliff. Rubbing his hand against his chest, he spared the corpse another long look. If the man had a soul, the Elder of the Sea would be able to collect him from the waves just as easily as one of the others could the shore.

Crouched over the body, Calder was preparing to drag him to the water when the sound of falling stones caught his attention. His eyes snapped up to the cliff edge to find Banner casually nudging rocks off the edge with his boot.

"You know," Banner spoke around the rolled skullcap lit between his lips. He pinched it between his fingers, inhaling deeply, before pulling it away.

"Shit like him floats," he said as he raised his brow conspiratorially.

Calder let out a snort and shook his head. When Banner returned his friend's smile, smoke curled from his lips.

Calder moved to the cliff's base and began collecting rocks. He stared up at Banner, who now sat with his legs dangling off the edge as he tipped his head back and exhaled a cloud of thick white smoke.

"You gonna help me?" Calder hollered.

"I did. I suggested the rocks. Besides, I am doing a perimeter check like the good little knight I am," Banner remarked with a wicked grin as he looked back down to Calder.

"And how are things looking?" Calder groaned as he made his way back to Dempsey.

Banner tilted his head and watched as Calder began stuffing Dempsey's clothes full of rocks.

"Fuck'n fantastic," he chuckled, making no attempts to hide his amusement.

Shallow streams from oncoming waves washed across Calder's boots as he pulled Dempsey's body to the edge of the rocky shelf. Weighed down and within reach of the sea, Calder stood, stretching his back and neck before taking one final look at the body.

"May what lurks in the dark find you before anyone else," he mumbled. Planting his foot against the body, Calder knocked it into the frothy surface and the sea greedily accepted the offering. Within moments, the body was lost from sight. He knelt down to one of the uncorrupted pools of water and submerged his hands, quickly turning the water murky. Then, in silence, he scaled the rough stone steps.

"So," Banner stretched the word as well as Calder's patience. "Care to share who fucked up your face because methinks it was not him," Banner asked, tipping his head to the open water.

Calder scowled, and it pulled on the fresh gash. Ignoring Banner, he continued his ascent.

"What did you want to do with this?" There was an air of mischief in Banner's voice.

Calder stopped mid-step, turning to see the bag he had not previously noticed, resting at Banner's feet and filled to bursting with Dempsey's things.

Calder gave him a questioning look before releasing a grunt of approval.

Banner assessed him in kind.

"You thought they were here for her?" he asked, biting back a slight smile when Calder rolled his eyes. "You're pretty shit at reading ravens," Banner added as if it was obvious Death had not been here to claim Emer.

Li had often remarked that Calder was, in fact, shit at reading ravens. It was hardly his fault the birds were so damn cryptic.

"Fuck off," he gritted out, staring off into the tree line.

Banner laughed.

"I'll just leave this on the beach then, where the Northerners last landed?" he offered without further commenting on Calder's evident concern for the green-eyed ghost that had been haunting the keep.

Banner slipped his boot through the bag's strap, bringing it into reach and slipping it over his shoulder.

Its weight drew his tunic away from his neck and revealed the dark ink of his tattoo. A raven immortalized on his chest, its wings stretching across his collar bones and curling over his shoulders.

While many did not make a note of the raven feather tucked into his braids, the tattoo was an unmistakable mark shared by many of the Sea Ravens.

Where Calder wore his wings on his back, Banner had a tally of the souls he sent across the Array. A number no one could be sure of. His companions never saw his back—if anyone else did, it was because they were already dead. Some just didn't know it yet.

Calder turned to him and nodded before heading back to the keep.

"Why do you never say bye? To your BEST FRIEND!" Banner called across the distance that Calder had quickly created.

Calder's head ticked to the side and Banner's dark chuckle carried on the wind.

Calder made his way to the keep's tenant-in-chief. Kadell was a ruddy-faced man who was one of the few who actually knew why

Calder remained at the keep. Calder's presence and the services he provided were entirely voluntary. Any debts he had to the Isle were paid long ago in the common currency of Sea Ravens—death.

Staying at the keep kept him on the coast, leaving only an ocean between him and the Isle of Rest, home to his mother's murderer.

While it was not ideal announcing to Kadell his intentions to depart at the same time as Dempsey's disappearance, Banner's efforts would sow doubt, and if that failed, Calder's temper would sow discord—two things Kadell very much disliked and would not be subjected to for the likes of Dempsey.

With a formal release in hand, Calder made his way back to his room, stopping only momentarily to glare at the tree line. The last bit of gold sky streaked over the green canopy. He paused, needing to blink away the memory of Emer's eyes. It was infuriating that she seemed to be able to distract him despite the distance.

Strange magic.

It took little time for him to collect his belongings. His possessions fit back into the bag he packed them into several years prior. Carefully filing papers into the pages of his books, he tucked the items in tightly and tied off the bag.

Rather than packing his weapons, he slipped into his battle leathers, straps that spread over his chest, back, and shoulders, and began donning his swords, knives, and ax. His body was braced for a fight, and at this point, it was one he welcomed.

The last item he grabbed was the small metal butterfly necklace that he moved from where it had rested amongst the books when he saw Emer toying with it. The pendant of polished iron shined up at him as it sat leaden in his palm. It made the center of his chest burn as it warmed to his own body heat. His mother loved this necklace. With a shake of his head, he stashed the jewelry into his pocket and made his way to the door.

He did not bother glancing back as he left the room. He did not say goodbye as he exited the keep. He was now between the shadow of Obanes and home. The realization that if he returned, he would do so without the answers he left in search of had his fingers searching for the pendant in his pocket once more. They traced over the lines and curves he knew as well as the night sky. If he did return, it wouldn't be empty-handed.

Not if he returned with *her*.

CHAPTER 16

Rainwater dripped from the ends of his damp curls, barely missing contact with Emer's skin. He was close enough that he could breathe in her scent. It was one that he could not name when he first noticed it but soon found it reminded him of forget-me-nots in the evening. Like the very rain that slowed her escape and allowed him to catch her. Like a storm.

Still crouched over her, he scanned the room. No traps. No trip wires. No way to know an intruder had entered the cabin. She hadn't even stirred when he approached, though he had not been quiet, and it was evident that she'd passed out from exhaustion rather than willfully disregarding safeguards and leaving herself vulnerable.

Calder wondered if she had walked all night or spent it outside. Her clothes were still damp from the brief storm that struck during the earlier hours of the morning, so he knew she hadn't been in the cottage then. As angry as he was to be caught in the downpour, he had smirked at the thought of her dripping wet and cursing each of the seven Elders by name.

Standing slowly, he backed away from her. Rain scattered from his hair as he ran his hands through it in thought. He moved to one of the nearby chairs and sat.

Calder knew what it was to be a killer, and of all the mysteries surrounding Emer, there was one thing he was certain of since the cliff... Emer was no killer.

There was a cost to seeing someone's life drain from their eyes, knowing that you had a hand in causing it. He was struck with sudden sympathy and guilt. He thought back to the first time he had taken a life. It was intentional, something he had been trained for, yet he could still recall the weight of the deed on his soul.

He wandered through the woods, the faint song of Li finding him through the trees as she collected wildflowers. He wished he found peace in the woods, joy in his sister's song, but he found the day lacked both. Sadness and anger were his only companions since his mother's death. He certainly did not have his father's presence for company. Their patriarch spent his time soaking his sorrows in the deep crimson of vengeance. A calling that could not be set aside even to celebrate his only daughter's day of birth.

So, today, Calder hunted wildflowers because it was what their mother would do. What their father should be doing.

He tilted his head back, catching a glimpse of the sky through the trees. Alabaster perched above and staring down at him affectionately. Calder despised the menace and mentally corrected himself. His constant companions were: sadness, anger, and Little Bastard.

His sister screamed.

Many had made the mistake of thinking that they would be easy prey with their father preoccupied, and there were few things more precious to Keithen and the Morvran clan than Li. But where his treasured daughter was, his ruthless son was not far behind.

Calder raced through the trees in the direction of her cry, sword in hand. When he found them, his sister had a sack over her head. One man held her arms and the other her feet as they fought to carry her through the woods. A third man shouted commands as the others tried to keep hold of his flailing sister.

Calder was glad they had covered her eyes. It made the next part much easier. He slipped the ax from his belt and its quiet whistle through the air was abruptly halted as it sank deep in the back of the man clearly in charge. He shouted as he collapsed, his ability to walk severed. He would not die, not yet.

Calder turned his attention to the other two as they nearly dropped her.

"Shit," one hissed.

"Fuck," the other agreed.

She was on her feet, hands bound and face still covered as the men pulled their weapons. One grabbed her by the arm and used her as a shield. Calder cocked his head as the man raised a knife in front of her throat. She went still. Not from fear but to listen.

"Do you know what the dancing raven loves?" she asked him, her voice saccharine and calm.

"Elderberries," Calder answered, her signal to drop.

His sister ducked low at the same moment that Calder pulled a knife from the sheath at his chest and embedded it in the man's throat.

Turning his attention to the last man standing, he closed the distance in a heartbeat and the sound of metal rang through the air.

"Leave it on, Li," Calder demanded.

Clang.

Grunt.

Thud.

The third man was pulling himself along the ground when Calder wrenched his ax from his back, evoking an inhuman wail.

"I'll release you if you tell me who sent you," he said with a coldness that a boy of sixteen should not have possessed. Pain made the man's words almost unintelligible, but eventually, their motive became clear.

Ransom.

He bent slowly and patted the man's cheek. "I'm a man of my word," he whispered just before he snapped his neck, releasing the man straight across the Array. He took his sister by the hand and led her from the woods, without taking off the sack.

He took his sister to pick wildflowers on her birthday.

One.

Two.

Three.

Like picking petals off those very same flowers, he suddenly had three bodies to his name. The first of many.

Perhaps he would be as lucky as the knights from storybooks who stumbled upon sleeping maidens in the woods.

Perhaps she would listen to what he had to say. Perhaps, for once, she would not run. Regardless, both of their souls would benefit from delaying their reunion. Hers could use the rest, and his could use the quiet.

CHAPTER 17

Although Emer had left the waking world alone, she was embraced by a foreign warmth that hinted that was no longer the case. Her eyes burst open with a gasp, and she found the familiar pale blue eyes looking back at her. If she had any doubts that the white raven was a co-conspirator in her suffering, they were gone now.

A silent sob parted her lips at the cruelty of it. Even with the price she paid for saving Calder, it was not enough to purchase her freedom from him.

She did not need to look around the room to know he was there. It was evident in the heaviness of the atmosphere. Emer continued to stare at the haunting, white harbinger perched on her boot, who watched her with an innocent curiosity as if he had not just damned her for the second time. When Calder remained silent, Emer slowly turned to where she knew he lurked.

Boots crossed at the ankles on the table, Calder leaned back casually in one of the chairs. "We need to talk. Also, good morning."

Anger pooled like molten metal in her chest. Hot and heavy.

"Has anyone ever told you that the gold flecks of your eyes

seem brighter when you are afraid?" There was a roughness to his voice that reminded her of the stones on the shore. Then he added, "Or is that anger?"

Each word cut across her skin and brought blood and indignation to the surface. Holding her breath, she assessed the likely outcomes that awaited her. She died slowly in three of the five that flashed across her mind. In the fourth, she died quickly. In one scenario, however, she at least made it out of the cottage.

Calder cocked his head as her muscles tensed in anticipation of her escape.

"It's rather adorable, you know," he cooed, drawing her attention back from the vine-covered window. "That you think you can run from me. It's delusional, of course. But, admittedly, adorable all the same."

The mirth in his voice caused nervous energy to thrum through her.

He was positioned in a way that made it difficult to escape through either the door or the window on the far wall, but another route was available that he would be unable to follow. Emer looked between the exits and then back to him.

"Please don't." He tipped his head back slightly. His expression pleading.

She turned away, her mouth pinched into a thin line as she dropped her head. The act, while it looked submissive, was anything but. Her eyes locked on the rotted floor of the cottage. Pushing off the wall, she dove towards the opening, unbothered by the veil of cobwebs and plant life. Calder darted up. The quiet cottage filled with his curses and the sound of the chair tumbling across the floor. No sooner had her fingers dug into the dirt below the boards did a firm arm wrap around her side and pull her back.

The impact of her spine against the floor was more shocking than painful, however, the surprise did little to discourage her resistance. Emer began to kick wildly but Calder thrust his thigh between her legs, pinning her body to the ground with his own.

Before the fist she raised to strike him could land, Calder had her wrist pinned above her head, rendering her defenseless.

Emer continued to writhe beneath him, but the more she fought, the further he pressed her to the floor, caging her with his body.

"What is your plan, huh? Keep running until you find something that finally kills you?" he grunted as she bucked her hips up, still attempting to dislodge herself. "Answer me, Emer!"

She felt his roar vibrate through his chest pressed against her own. His free hand now hooked around the side of her neck, his thumb pressed under her jaw, forcing her gaze to his.

"Anything could have found you in this cottage. Do you not understand that? If you need to fight something, fine. Fight me. But for fuck's sake, stop running."

Emer stilled beneath him. Her vision blurred with tears as she looked up into his dark eyes, greedily searching hers.

The room fell silent apart from their heavy collective breaths, which caused the small space between them to grow heated.

"I won't let you keep me," she said with finality.

Calder's head dipped to the crook of her neck, the ends of his hair tickling the sensitive skin. "I know," he murmured before lifting his head and returning his stare.

He released his hold and rolled off her, resting on his back at her side.

"I'm not here to hurt you. I never *wanted* to hurt you." There was raw honesty to his words, with the spaces between them woven with resentment. "And I'm not going to turn you in either."

Emer shook her head slowly from side to side. A sharp, broken laugh escaped her lips and he stared at her in surprise. As her slightly maniacal giggle persisted, his features twisted with concern. Sensing his confusion, she threw her hands up and then rubbed her face, muffling her hysterics.

"What is the point of all this then? Did you return for an apology... a thank you?" When she looked at him, her eyes were red and her expression was pained.

"I know you must be here out of duty to the family you love. Just as I kept you out of duty to mine. Depending on the story's telling, love can make someone the hero or the villain," Calder said in answer.

"Or just the monster," Emer whispered.

Had she struck something vital when she attacked him? It was the only explanation for his strange behavior and rambling thoughts.

"My mother was from the Isle of Rest."

His statement was brief but weighted in a way she could not appreciate at first. Her lips parted to speak, but paused, extending the silence as an offering.

"So was her murderer. They wrote to her asking for help. They preyed on her kindness."

She felt an inexplicable burning in her throat. Still, she fought against her need to provide words of sympathy, sensing that he had more to share. She was struck by the realization that she was also desperate to understand.

"It is no secret that I have hunted for her killer for years. When I saw you on the shore that day, I was confident you were there to taunt me. Somehow sent to mock my pain or possibly to tempt history to repeat itself. When she was smuggled back to Isle Basalt by the man she had fallen in love with, my father, they landed on that exact shore."

Her gaze remained fixed to the ceiling, fearful that even the slightest movement would banish whatever spell had been cast over them.

"I hated you. Hated you for how much you made me feel just by existing."

Emer replayed their interactions back in her mind in rapid succession. How she treated him when he found her. How she stabbed him with his own sword. The unsent letter. Each moment looked so different to her now. Every wound she inflicted against him was for the sake of her father's life and every punishment he imposed on her was retribution for his mother's death. Neither had been the hero or the villain. They were just two broken children.

"I'm here for my father." The confession left her before she consciously decided to tell him, but she pressed on. "He is dying."

He nodded solemnly.

"I was wrong to think you were my penance for failing my mother. I think you may actually be my redemption."

Emer turned her head sharply to find he was already looking at her and was instantly paralyzed. The suspicion that once resided in his eyes was now replaced by something different.

Sympathy.

Understanding.

But the change between them went beyond that, more profound and unseen.

"You... you want to help me?" her voice shook with uncertainty, and as soon as the words left her, she felt foolish.

"I do," he replied.

"But you don't even know what it is I'm meant to do," she remarked with a shake of her head.

"Now would be a good time to tell me then, don't you think?" he said smirking and drawing himself off the ground.

This time, he did not offer his dominant hand, the hand marked with the rune for death. Instead, he extended his left—a rune for peace resting in his palm.

Emer slipped her hand into his, and just as she began to smile, her expression fell.

"Dempsey."

It was as much of a confession as she would allow herself regarding what she had done.

"Such a shame really. Being labeled a deserter is punishable by death. Although a little bird told me that it is likely he was running from the Northerners, to whom he was known to owe quite a large sum." Calder's voice was steady and his gaze firm.

Emer's lips parted to protest, but Calder raised his hand slowly and placed the tips of his fingers just in front of her lips, not daring to touch her.

He allowed the moment to linger before adding more softly, "He will not be missed."

Though she could not deny the relief she felt at the realization that she would not be hunted as a murderess, a sickening ache formed in the pit of her stomach.

"Dempsey just disappeared. You left. And no one questioned you?" She could hardly believe that there would not be an inquest that would lead straight to them. Particularly after the condition in which he left the training drills earlier that day.

A familiar smirk appeared on his face, the fiendish smile he had when he first locked her in his room. "I said you did not need to fear me, not that I wasn't worthy of fear."

This caused her to wonder if no one questioned him because they truly believed the ruse he had crafted or if they simply feared his wrath.

"And what are the repercussions of displeasing the dreaded Calder?" she asked, partially in jest but primarily out of genuine curiosity.

"Be glad you will never know that horror."

Calder made his way over to the cottage corner and retrieved a satchel and two bedrolls.

Emer had cursed him, cut him, struck him, and he brought her a bed. She would have scoffed at his confidence in being able to find her if she wasn't trying to ignore the strange sensation in her chest at his kindness. She bit down on the inside of her cheek to distract from the unwelcome emotions.

He cautiously began his journey back, keeping his eyes on the distrusted floor, but paused when he looked back at her. "What's wrong?" he asked with a frown, a bedroll under each arm.

"Just tired," she said quickly.

He grunted in agreement, rolling out the covers. He dropped a satchel filled with provisions and motioned for her to sit.

"I'm exhausted and my back is fucked. I propose we rest for the day. You can tell me where we are headed and we'll start fresh in the morning," he suggested as he stretched himself out over the bedroll that was concerningly close to the other. She hesitated.

So much time had already lapsed and Emer was hardly any closer to reaching the Well, but her chances of getting there in one piece were far better with Calder and a clear head. She nodded and sat down on the bedroll at his side.

"Eat," he said gruffly as he tossed an apple at her and then began to tear at a piece of bread. Rolling the round fruit between her palms, she struggled to acclimate to the new roles they'd inherited.

"Are there a lot of you?" she asked.

"There is no one like me, Merrow," he said, turning his head towards her and giving a wink.

"A lot of *Ravens*?" she clarified with only a slight glare.

"There are enough," he answered vaguely.

"And you aren't just a Sea Raven, are you?" she asked, picking at the apple that now rested in her lap.

At this, Calder rose to his elbow, angling his chest towards her, watching her as he slowly chewed his last bite of bread. After a moment, he shook his head, unable to hide the smile that formed from watching her nervously fidget with her fruit.

Emer recalled his previous comments about those bowing to his command. All of the letters from people wanting... or rather needing his approval. How he could leave the keep without earning questions even if he had earned suspicion.

When she met his gaze, he watched her expectantly, and she was acutely aware that he had been waiting for this moment and that whatever she was about to learn was a secret only to her.

"Calder... Morvran?" she asked on the exhale. Amazed and

slightly embarrassed that it took her this long to see what he had been trying to show her.

He was not a member of the Morvran clan.

Calder was their leader.

"I can't decide which is more delicious. The look on your face or the sound of my name on your lips." He slid his tongue along his teeth, pressing it into his canine. "I feel as though I am at a disadvantage now...." He let his words trail off, leaving space for Emer's answer.

"Réaltaí."

"Emer Réaltaí, " he echoed.

The quiet reverence of his voice made her name sound like a secret, a poem, a spell of unknown magic that demanded it be spoken with care. For a moment, she found herself wondering what things would have been like if she had allowed him to speak it that day on the shore. Regaining her focus, she said, "You know, the men in my village tell stories about you and the terrible things you've done."

Calder's expression fell, but before he could defend himself against whatever the stories she'd heard were, she let out an amused chuckle, which then grew into a genuine laugh.

Emer looked at him carefully, trying to reconcile the monster she had heard tales of and the man sitting in front of her picking a fallen leaf from her sleeve.

"The Sea Raven who brings death on his wings." She repeated the phrase she once heard from a man who was surrounded by several empty mugs of ale.

"Well... that is totally inaccurate," he scoffed. "I prefer the *devilishly handsome* Sea Raven who brings death on his wings *and* monsters in his wake," he grinned. "Tell me more about these 'terrible things' I'm supposed to have done?" he asked, returning to his back like a child preparing for a bedtime story.

"I'm sure you have heard them," she remarked, finally taking a bite from her apple.

"I have not heard them from you," he pressed, pulling a wine-skin from his satchel. "An incentive," he explained, handing it to her.

She removed the stopper and breathed in the pleasant smell of mead. After taking a drink, she returned the stopper and steepled her hands beneath her chin as she thought.

"Burnt down a village?" she asked.

"True, but grossly lacking context," he said matter-of-factly.

"Drinks the blood of his enemies." Her nose wrinkled.

"Not intentionally," he responded with a slight smile as she gave a disturbed shake.

"Just accidentally when you were ripping people's throats out with your teeth?"

Calder laughed, pulling the wineskin from her lap and taking a long pull. He sucked his bottom lip between his teeth as he contemplated. "An interesting tactic. Care for a demonstration?" his words came out like a purr and she felt her eyes grow wide at the suggestion. When he leaned forward, she simply cleared her throat and changed the subject.

"Whores in every port?" she questioned and then watched his expression very carefully.

"I hardly think I've been to *every* port," he said with a sly grin.

Back and forth they went. Emer quickly found that the apple was no match for the mead as it went straight to her head. She grew sleepy, and when she closed her eyes, she saw a flash of the rocks below the cliff painted in red. Her eyes flew open again and she took another drink, thankful for the mead. Despite the fact that it was the Morvran she found as her company, she was grateful for that too.

Tap. Tap. Tap.

"Ask me, Merrow," he commanded.

"Do you regret any of the people you have killed?" she asked in a brittle voice.

"None," he said without hesitation.

Emer nodded thoughtfully.

"Do you?" He considered his question. "Let me ask it differently. Who would you rather be alive, me or Dempsey? If you knew only one of us was walking away from that cliff with you, would you have chosen me or Dempsey?"

Emer swallowed down her surprise at the slight shift in Calder's expression and the uncertainty in his eyes.

"You," she finally said in a whisper.

"Remind yourself that when you fight. It's either you, them, or someone you love. For me, it's not even a choice," he said more softly and Emer wondered how many times he had made that not-choice.

"Does that scare you?" he asked, the tension returning to his jaw.

Her eyes softened as she said, "Of the men who can be monsters and the beasts who masquerade as men, I'm only afraid of the latter."

"With a monster by your side, you have no need to fear beasts," he replied.

She blushed.

He grinned.

CHAPTER 18

There was a direct correlation between the level of animation in Emer's storytelling and the amount of mead consumed. Calder watched in unabashed amusement, due partially to the outlandish stories, but more by how Emer told them.

The nature of the conversation varied between tales of the Morvran's brutality—something he had both earned and inherited from his father—and more debaucherous themes. While Calder had not offered further comment on the latter, he did correct several details for the former. One such correction was that he did not, in fact, have a pet firedrake, to which Emer pouted for what seemed like a reasonable amount of time.

"Why didn't you tell me who you were?" she wondered aloud.

"What good would that have done?" he argued.

"I probably would have realized I didn't stand a chance when I tried to run the first time," she grumbled.

"See, no good would have come from it."

After the rain darkened the skies on and off throughout the day, the sun finally set, and the pair rested on their respective bedrolls.

"You never told me how you found yourself here?" It was not the first time Calder had asked the question, but it was the first time it seemed out of genuine curiosity rather than suspicion.

For a moment, Emer looked aghast. "Are you telling me you no longer believe that I swam? Here I thought that it was such a convincing lie," she said with a smirk.

He let out a deep chuckle before allowing the cottage to fall into a companionable silence. In the quiet, Emer's nervous tapping was a soft whisper of the secrets she kept and the turmoil they caused.

Calder waited.

"I was on a ship manned by a small crew and we were attacked in the middle of the night. One of my father's men is a friend of mine and he threw me overboard during the attack to protect me."

Calder snorted and she narrowed her eyes at him.

"I'm sorry, did you say someone threw you overboard to 'protect' you?" His eyebrow raised as he stared back at her.

"Well, yes... obviously, there was a lot happening. And you just had to be there. Lachlan didn't want me to be captured and one of us needed to get to shore," she explained.

Calder released a low whistle.

"Anyway." She continued glaring at him. "We were supposed to sail much further north. I was never supposed to be here."

He shook his head, laughing ruefully. "Based on yours and this *Lachlan's* questionable decision-making, I am surprised you made it off your isle."

"Oh, fuck off."

His expression lit up at the way she growled the curse. "Such language. You've clearly been in my company too long as it is, but I feel I should keep you a little longer and teach you how to sail since, clearly, no man in your life has done so properly," he remarked, his eyes full of a delighted heat.

"Firstly, we were *attacked*. We didn't sink. Secondly, I don't need your help getting to Lunochy." She was so angry that she did not realize how easily she let slip everything she tried to keep hidden.

"Lunochy!" he exclaimed. "Merrow, you aren't even on the correct side of the Bleeding Trees. Do you even know where Lunochy is? Or how much shit lies between you and there?" he asked, genuinely shocked to learn of her destination.

As her eyes began to grow glassy, he realized he had not considered why she would be traveling to that particular place.

"The Well?" he asked sorrowfully.

She swallowed hard. "I will lose my father if I don't." Her voice grew thin and her words seemed to get lost in the darkness of the cottage. "We've tried everything else. You may think I am naive for having hope or incapable of succeeding, but I would go to the ends of the realm to protect my family regardless of the personal risk or less than favorable odds." Taking another deep breath and lifting her chin higher, she added, "I would rather die chasing after hope than submit to hopelessness in safety."

The corner of his lips turned up, "She would have liked you."

At her clear confusion, he clarified, "My mother. She would have liked you."

Now it was Emer's turn to be silent.

They remained in the quiet until it slowly slipped into sleep. It was the first time Emer had slept soundly in recent memory.

When Emer woke the next morning, it was to chilled air and the scent of sea water filling her lungs. The fire had been smothered, and if it was not for the two cloaks that covered her, Emer's bones would have been far stiffer than they were.

The space Calder occupied the evening before was vacant, but the watchful bird perched on the back of the nearby chair meant that he had not gone far.

She found him a short time later just outside the cottage and standing beside two striking horses. They were black as night and intimidatingly large. Horses fit for a Raven.

"Do you ride?" he asked without turning to greet her.

"I don't leave my village, so no," she answered.

"Then this will be far more entertaining than I previously anticipated," he mused.

"W-why entertaining?" she asked, not doing a compelling job of hiding her concern.

"Because it's gonna be a long ride," he said with a chuckle as he stepped away from the horses and into the cottage to retrieve their things.

When he returned, he secured the remaining items to the horses and then led them to Emer, introducing them as Danu and Aven before dropping the reins of the latter into her hand.

Emer stared down at the strips of leather and then back up at the beast, her features pinched with contemplation.

"You can't mount him, can you?" he observed.

She shook her head and Calder hummed.

Dropping to one knee, he smacked the thigh of his bent leg and offered her his hand.

Emer, for the first time, stared down at him.

"Don't look so surprised. I am actually quite charming," he said.

Emer hesitated, reassessing the horse and the likelihood that she could climb the creature unassisted.

"You will stab me but you hesitate to step on me?" he said with a bored expression, wiggling the fingers of the hand that remained suspended between them.

"You were trying to hold me against my will! I think I was entitled to my reactions. Besides, I saw you fighting at the keep, I am surprised you didn't enjoy being stabbed!"

A wicked grin appeared on his face. "I never said I didn't, I was simply drawing a comparison for your benefit," he cooed. "Which reminds me."

He removed Dempsey's knife from the sheath at his hip and tapped it against her calf, urging her to bring her boot to his thigh. When she obeyed the silent command, he cast his gaze down, still smiling, and slipped the knife into her boot.

"To the victor," he said quietly and then brought his hand out to her once more. When he met her gaze, there was a slight glint. "Also, if my chivalry is particularly moving to you, I would happily accept any gratitude you see fit," he said with a wink.

Grinding her boot into his leg, she stepped up, gripped the saddle's pommel, and drew herself onto the horse. All without taking his hand.

Calder stared at her, hand still raised. After a moment, he cleared his throat, rising to his feet and dusting off his breeches.

Standing at his full height, Calder put into perspective just how large the beast beneath Emer was and knots quickly formed in her stomach as a result. As he mounted his own and strode forward, Emer could not quiet the yelps that escaped her as she swayed.

Calder slowed, allowing her to come beside him.

"Emer, you are making him nervous." His voice hinted at concern rather than reproach.

Her eyes were fixed on Aven's body beneath her, her jaw clenched tightly.

"May I?" he asked, moving in closer when she gave a tight nod.

Leaning from Danu, Calder placed his hand over Emer's. "Hold the reins loosely, just in front of the saddle until you need to direct his change in course."

She eased her grip.

"Let your legs do most of the work," he explained.

When her legs immediately tensed, he tapped her thigh. "Relax, Merrow."

Following his direction, Aven began to move forward. Emer turned to Calder excitedly, the pride in her expression mirrored in his own. She tensed briefly at the feel of his hand pressing against her lower back. The ease with which he managed to slip it beneath her cloak did little to discredit the tales of the "debaucherous and whoring pirate king."

"Relax," he repeated.

Her body began to rock along with Aven's strides.

"Good."

The knots in her stomach were replaced by an unfamiliar heat, one she thought might have seeped into her cheeks. She looked at Calder again, awaiting further instruction, but his gaze was still fixed on her lower body. It was her turn to clear her throat.

Eyes snapping away he said, "To stop, sink your weight down, and lean back. As you do, pull back gently."

When Aven obeyed, Emer let out a triumphant squeak.

The thought of whether Calder, clearly well-versed in training the mechanics of riding, had ever been this distracted while doing so brought Emer an inappropriate sense of satisfaction.

"Don't look down unless I tell you. While we are alone, you can keep your gaze between the horse's ears," he said curtly before pulling ahead.

Emer could not help but notice that despite his own advice, he looked rather stiff.

Out of the woods and back on the main road, Emer found the concern she felt about taking this route before had vanished. It was hard to imagine anyone more threatening than the Morvran at her side. Even if those they passed did not know him by name, there was little about him that invited opposition. As long as he was there, she was safe.

Finally free of the ever-present foreboding that had loomed over her since her arrival, Emer was able to appreciate the landscape for more than the threats it posed to her journey. The greens were greener, the mountains more prominent, and the sky was harsher. It was unlike the scenery she had come to know from home, where soft fields blurred into rolling hills beneath timid skies. This Isle was all dark shades and sharp lines. It was beautiful.

"How did your parents meet?" she asked absentmindedly, wondering how his mother acclimated to this new world, knowing it was a stark contrast to theirs.

It took Calder a moment to answer, like he needed to dust off the words, and when he spoke, they were brittle from disuse.

"They met on Rest. Do you know the Ash Wood?"

Emer nodded excitely at the mention of the forest on the eastern shore of her Isle.

"My father had been sent during the war. He was too young to be afraid of the fight and too proud to think they might lose. My mother was a midwife by trade, and despite the danger, volunteered to travel between towns. When she found him in the Ash Wood, he was barely clinging to life and she saved him. Even though he was her enemy."

"I've been there once," she admitted.

Calder gave her a smile that was more sorrowful than sweet. "Will you tell me about it?" he asked.

And so Emer recalled the day shortly before a winter solstice that had long since passed where she walked through the woods. The leaves had already fallen, painting the woods in vibrant yellows, deep reds, and bruised purples. She spoke of the creek through the center of it, the smooth stones that caused the water to rush through the land in a rippled and melodic stream.

When she finished, he simply nodded as if working to commit each word to memory. There was an equal measure of fondness and sadness when he spoke of his parents—although he had not said it, she was certain his father had joined his mother across the Array.

"How furious was your clan when your father went to war and returned with your mother?" she asked.

He huffed a breathy laugh and explained how his father had smuggled her back on one of his ships, knowing he would not have gotten permission to bring her back and not caring whether he would be forgiven for doing so. When his parents returned, the war had already ended, but there was still a fair amount of strife. To his father's dismay, his mother was not safe. The clan initially did not accept her and urged him to send her back. That was when he announced that they had already married—a significant break from tradition. Over time, they saw the way he loved her and how deeply she loved him in return and, eventually, they accepted her.

"My clan can be brutal, but what you likely are unaware of is that we fiercely protect what is ours. We believe that blood does not determine family, but rather who you would shed blood for. My father would burn entire villages to the ground for my mother. She loved her home and leaving it to come here was a great loss to her, but there was nothing she loved more than my father," he explained.

Emer had heard many tales of the Sea Ravens but never considered that their unstoppable nature and bloodthirsty character was driven by something as pure as the protection of others.

"If your mother found safety here, why do you insist I remain hidden?" she wondered.

The muscles in his jaw stiffened.

"You are not my wife and we are not in my village. Dempsey's response to you should be sufficient evidence that you would not be safe. I told you my father would burn villages to the ground to protect her; the reason she was safe was because he *did*."

Emer's breath caught. A love worth burning the realm down for sounded dangerous, but she could not help the envy she felt at the idea of being considered so precious. She would blame the romanticizing of violence on her recent trauma, physical and otherwise, because there was no denying that was exactly what she was doing.

"He sounds frightening," she confessed.

"A Morvran driven by anger will send many to their death, but a Morvran driven by love will become Death," he recited the words that had once been a promise but now felt like a tragic prophecy come to pass in the wake of his parents passing.

"Lina was put in charge of the village and I was sent to the ships to ensure that the Morvrans had a presence on the land and sea at all times," he explained.

Emer choked on her next breath.

Elders' tits. Lina!

How had she forgotten about Lina? About the letter. The discomfort at the recollection of their time together coupled with the thought that he might be promised to another was written across her features.

Calder caught the pinch in her expression and smirked. "Oh, I am sure I mentioned Lina. At the very least, you know about her from the letters you read."

"I do. She seems to worry about you." She swallowed hard.

He nodded, but this time, there was no smile. "Lina is..." his voice trailed off. "Lina likes to fix things. She always has. She deserves far more than a life of broken things," he continued.

"Perhaps it brings her joy to mend the things she cares for," Emer remarked. "Where is Lina now?" she asked, closing her eyes and cursing herself for continuing a conversation that was making her so uncomfortable that she practically itched.

"At home in our village."

Our village.

"I have never liked her to spend much time at the keep. As you can attest, the men do not have the best manners and I would rather not have to murder them for speaking to or laying a finger on my sister. It would be frowned upon, you see?"

"Your sister," Emer repeated and Calder didn't bother to hide his amusement as he nodded in confirmation.

"You would be terrible at dice," was all he said in return.

Emer knew her relief was painfully evident, but the way he smiled at her made it hard for her to care. It was a relief he did not mention and she thanked the Elders because she had no desire to study it any further.

Emer's mind drifted to Finn, the topic of siblings an acute reminder of his absence.

"I think the Elders must weave a special bond into the hearts of brothers and sisters. If you were to cut us open, you would find a matching thread that connects us. That is why we fret. Because if their hearts break, ours will follow," she observed, lost in thought and rambling for longer than she intended.

Rather than teasing her for her sentimental musing, Calder asked, "Is he who taught you to fight?"

"Yes. Finn is not a fighter by trade but he has a warrior's spirit. He is in charge of the village now. For now, I mean. Until our father recovers." She paused. "I know you don't particularly like anyone, but I think you would like him," she said with a smile.

Calder gave a noncommittal shrug.

"Do you cheat when you fight him too?" he challenged, pointing to the healing split in his brow.

"He taught me to not underestimate my enemy, so maybe you should take notes from him," she teased.

"Is that what we are, Emer? Enemies?" he asked.

"Once upon a time we were, but now I'm not so sure," she said thoughtfully because while Calder no longer felt like her enemy, lack of malice did not necessarily make one a friend either.

"Then what are we?" he questioned.

"Strangers," she replied.

Calder's brow furrowed and then his gaze swept over her face. It was clear that while he had not known the answer to his own question, hers was not one he expected. "Tell me something I don't know then... perhaps by the time we reach our destination, your answer will have changed."

To Emer's surprise, when she did, Calder offered her something about himself. They traded details back and forth, offering pieces of themselves equal to what the other had shared and removing their armor without leaving themselves unnecessarily bare.

Emer took each new thing she learned about Calder and wove it into the once bleak mental picture she had of him. A tapestry that was growing more colorful and complex. He was twenty-four, two years older than Emer, but his stories made it seem like he had lived multiple lifetimes. His sister was even younger still, only twenty, and he had been fiercely protective of her as they grew up. Emer hoped to learn more about his parents and their love story, but he was careful to avoid the topic. Their deaths still weighed on him heavily, and although fighting against that weight appeared to have become second nature, she wondered how long he had been carrying it.

By the time the town came into view, they approached it as acquaintances rather than strangers.

CHAPTER 19

Emer had proven to be reckless, unpredictable, and perfectly capable of all manner of chaos without the help of a crowd. The moment they entered town, the variables would increase exponentially, and with each stride, Calder grew noticeably stiffer.

He turned to look at Emer, her eyes alight with interest as she took in the unfamiliar sites. For a brief moment, he considered whether or not his mother had looked upon these villages in such a way. It was a look that would soon dull as Emer came to realize that while all wanderers, drifters, and all manner of the lost were welcomed in towns such as these, outsiders and interlopers were not.

"I mean it this time, Emer. No matter what happens. Eyes. Down," Calder said in a tone that would make the very sea itself still.

She began to lower her head but then paused briefly as if surprised by her own obedience. Danu came to Aven's side and Calder took her reins and began to lead them into town.

The ground beneath them transitioned from dirt and grass to a stone road. Before long, the sounds of their steps were joined by the distant murmurs of people.

Arborlynn's location made it a prime place for trade and merchants. Less ideal were its crowds and propensity for crime. Though its dense population and bustling street would typically be the perfect setting to blend in, with Emer the entire town was kindling, and she was an unruly spark.

Without seeing her surroundings, the cacophony of sounds quickly became overwhelming and she shifted uncomfortably in her saddle. The shout of a nearby vendor made her flinch and she began to press her nails into the palms of her hands fretfully. The assault extended beyond the sounds. Various tempting and revolting smells rose through the air to find them. Having grown stiff, she was startled when Calder adjusted their direction. Snapping her eyes shut and working in a calming breath, a sweet and familiar scent swept over her like a comforting blanket. For a moment, she was home. Baking in the hearth with her mother. Emer did not even realize her head had risen to seek out the source of the scent until a firm hand squeezed her thigh.

"Seriously! You'll risk being seen because some man is flashing his tarts," he scolded under his breath.

Certain that no one in the realm's history had ever made a more risqué statement regarding bread, Emer was forced to clap a hand over her mouth to stifle her laugh.

"Will make terrible choices for bread. Noted," he murmured.

"And potatoes," she added.

Calder let out a puff of air that sounded suspiciously like a snort.

"Keeping a list?" she asked quietly, smiling when he hummed in agreement.

Reaching the stables, Calder dismounted Danu and approached the young man to discuss the terms of boarding.

The stablehand shifted slightly, his eyes drifting repeatedly to Emer. Even with her features hidden under his old cloak, it was clear by her stature that she was a woman, and Calder found himself more inclined to violence with each stolen glance.

Calder stepped to the side, blocking the man's view, and dropped the agreed-upon sum into his open palm. Leaning in, he closed the man's fingers over the coins with enough force that joints cracked and the coins pressed hard into his skin. "I'm gonna need you to focus here, friend," he whispered, snapping with the fingers of his free hand.

The man groaned.

"Focused?"

A nod.

"Good. Good," Calder said with a wolfish grin.

"Am I going to have a problem with your eyes wandering in the future?" he asked, to which the man furiously shook his head.

Calder released his hand and the coins fell to the mud, bloody from where one with a rough edge broke through the skin.

Patting the man's cheek, he said, "Long may that continue."

When Calder turned away, his smirk immediately fell. Walking to the far side of Aven to ensure Emer's back remained to the stables, Calder tapped her thigh lightly.

As she dismounted, Calder's hands slipped beneath her cloak, catching the small of her back and slowing her descent.

It was not until Emer stood pinned between the horse and the Raven that they realized the wordless dance they had just completed. Neither acknowledged the ease with which they now interacted nor how abnormal it *should* have felt but didn't.

"What happened?" she asked quietly, gesturing towards where the stablehand had vacated.

Calder stepped back, removing his hands from her waist. "Just stay close and *behave*," he said firmly.

Emer dropped her head exaggeratedly. "What is it that you expect me to do exactly? Skip through the streets naked?"

Calder scoffed. "Don't be ridiculous. You aren't coordinated enough to skip."

As they walked, Calder explained that he had someone in town that he needed to speak to. Despite the fact that those around them spoke the common language, Emer knew her voice would likely stand out as much as Calder's first did to her and she fought the urge to ask questions about his appointment. He offered to help her but hadn't elaborated on what that help might entail. Perhaps this man was a merchant and able to provide the supplies needed for her journey. He had advised that this town was on the path towards the well, not that she knew enough about the landscape to confirm or discredit that. Her stomach felt hollow as she considered the man they were meeting might be Calder's means of pawning her off on someone else. He made no secret of how troublesome she was, and for the first time, the thought bothered her. The lump that formed in her throat suddenly made her more amiable to the silence.

The crowd and her intrusive thoughts made following him through the market substantially more challenging than the keep, and not a moment too soon, the pair reached the Alder Barrel.

The tavern was easily marked by the stumbling men and the general odor of poor choices. The air was filled with the sounds of men shouting, exchanging coins, and mugs slamming down on the wooden tables.

Feet sticking to the floor with each step, Emer followed Calder to the far corner of the room, which was heavy with the scent of yeast, sweat, and toxic masculinity. The further they descended into the chaos, the stronger Calder's headache and Emer's nausea.

He stopped at a corner table, pulling out the seat and motioning for Emer to sit. The legs of the chair proved themselves to be as wobbly as her constitution, tipping slightly as she took her seat.

Kneeling beside her, Calder spoke just loud enough for her to hear over the room. "The conversation I need to have is very important and being seen with you would complicate it—"

Emer did not let him finish explaining before turning her head slightly to scowl at him.

"Emer, you attempted to sail in the night with a group of armed men to make landfall undetected. That was and *is* problematic," he continued.

At the truth in his words, her scowl deepened.

"There is no record of the ship, the attack, or the men. But if any of them survived or if they were captured and there was any suspicion that you were associated with them—Em." He paused as he watched the horror on her face before saying, "I need to know if anyone knows to look for you."

"If they are and they find me, will they take me?" she asked, finally understanding the weight of the accusations that could be leveled against her.

"It is not worth the risk to find out. I'll come for you once I'm done. Just stay here and everything will be fine."

Emer's eyes darted around the room worriedly but were drawn back to the sound of Calder tsking. "You insult me, Merrow. You've seen me fight but doubt my ability to protect you from a couple of drunks? Everything will be fine," he repeated.

When Emer let out a huff in return, Calder pressed a hand into the table in front of her and leaned in closer, swallowing the space between them. "Don't tempt me to show off."

She could hear the smile in his voice. A dark promise rather than a threat.

"And keep your cloak closed," he said, pulling the panels together. "Or the brawl that ensues will not be caused by the lovely shade of your eyes."

The moment he left, she felt the loss of his grounding presence. A wave of anxiety crashed over her and she needed to fight the urge to search the crowd for him. She focused on the weight and shape of the knife in her boot to remind herself that, even without him, she was not helpless.

A woman's voice sounded from just behind her as if she materialized out of thin air. So startled that someone was talking to her, Emer had not even processed what the woman said. Why would she need company?

Eyes downcast, Emer shook her head at the woman's offer. A refusal that was quickly ignored as the woman began to run a finger over Emer's cloaked shoulders, causing her to flinch at the contact, fearing the woman would pull back her hood.

"I do not think this one is here for jinxes or jollies, woman. Leave them be," a melodic voice sang from a table nearby.

The woman's once sickly-sweet voice turned harsh as she muttered under her breath and stormed off.

Curious if Calder had been aware of the near disaster, Emer tilted her gaze up and found him several tables down talking to an older man, who had his back to her. He had a long braid and several weapons fastened to his body, though no one seemed particularly concerned by his arsenal.

The woman who propositioned Emer now floated behind Calder, languidly drawing a finger across his back as she moved. His posture straightened under her touch and he paused the mug he was bringing to his lips. She was stunning, wearing every curve with unparalleled confidence and no qualms about displaying them. Though her dark eyes were alluring and her full lips were painted crimson, most in the room seemed to be focused on how her jet-black curls fell over her large breasts.

As she reached Calder's other side, she bent down, resting her elbow on the table, providing him ample opportunity to appreciate the pale flesh spilling out of her corseted dress. When her eyes finally settled on her prey, she discovered that he was wholly predatory. Her eyes widened as he tilted his head towards her, appreciating his genuinely handsome appearance.

Emer quickly scanned the room and confirmed that Calder was, in fact, the most handsome of the group, and although she had not seen much of this Isle, she was fairly certain he would be the most handsome man in any room.

Calder pulled his bottom lip between his teeth, savoring the ale he had drank and possibly the woman before him.

The woman leaned in, using the noise of the room as an excuse to get closer.

Emer matched the movement, leaning in closer like a moth to a flame. Compelled to watch the fire dancing before her even though it hurt.

Hurt. Why the fuck did it hurt?

She ground her boot into the leg of her chair, the hilt of her knife pressing against the bone and offering a different kind of pain.

Whatever left Calder's lips next caused the woman's hopeful gaze to pinch. She stormed away, muttering what could have very well been *actual* curses on the tail of a second rejection. Without warning, Calder's gaze locked to Emer's through the crowd before she dropped her head, muttering her own curses.

Having no desire to be caught a second time, Emer kept her eyes down, counting the score marks in the table beneath her to distract herself from the look that had been in Calder's eyes when they ensnared hers. She felt the heat unfurl beneath her skin and was certain by the slight twitch of his lip that he had noticed it too.

Emer blinked the thought away, returning her attention to the wounds in the wood when something solid slammed into her back and pushed her into the table. The impact was quickly followed by a mug clattering across the wood. Its contents rapidly spread over the table and Emer, too stunned from the initial collision, was too slow in pushing back from the table to avoid its path.

Now standing, Emer held her arms out reflexively as she surveyed herself. The sticky and stale liquid soaked the sleeves and chest of her tunic; the material clung to the swell of her breasts, ruining the illusion she had been trying to maintain. Crossing her arms tightly, she searched the space to see if anyone had witnessed her mistake.

Across the room, Calder choked on his ale while his companion patted him on the back.

Shrinking into herself, Emer closed the panels of her cloak. The man who caused the incident, much like the other patrons, had not noticed she was a woman. Her shoulder ached from where she had received the man's apologetic slap and she wished he had been a bit less remorseful.

After tipping her chair to remove the remaining liquid, Emer reseated herself, sullen and soaked in the tepid ale that left her skin tacky and her mood sour. Her discontented groan was cut short by yet another unfortunate interaction and Emer began to dwell on the knife in her boot for an entirely different reason.

"Move," the presence at her side demanded harshly.

Emer held her breath, hoping that, by some chance, this command was not directed towards her. She did not linger in uncertainty for long.

"Eejit, I am talking to you!" the man growled as he slammed one hand against the table in front of her and gripped the back of her chair with the other.

Recoiling, Emer slid her hand into her boot and curled her fingers around her knife. While stabbing the man likely fell outside the realm of Calder's instructions, available options were quickly dwindling, and before she could conjure an alternative, she was being ripped from her chair.

Her feet barely touched the ground as the man held the fabric of her tunic and cloak in a tight fist, bringing them face to face. Instantly, she was hit with a boorish exhale of his ale-infused breath.

Surprise gave way to understanding as the man took in the face beneath the hood. The murderous look in his eyes shifted into a more threatening one of hunger. Tongue darting over his lips, he looked her up and down. Too distracted by her chest to register the knife poised against his.

"And here I thought it would be the ale keeping me warm tonight," he crooned.

Emer steeled herself, ready to plunge her knife to its hilt but paused at the sound of a familiar but notably more possessive voice.

"Remove your hand or I will be gifting it to her as a keepsake."

The man leaned back and squared off with Calder. For a moment, he looked between them as if debating whether she was worth the trouble that Calder's tone promised. It was a debate that took far longer than Emer would have liked, but eventually, the man set her on the ground. Emer adjusted her hood and quickly moved towards Calder.

"What business is it of yours, Raven?" the man challenged.

"If you know what I am, then you know we don't share. Walk away and don't look at her again unless you want her to be the last thing you see," Calder warned.

With a sneer, the man backed his way into the crowd.

Calder grabbed Emer's hand to lead her from the table, but stopped abruptly and raised it between them. His wicked grin glinted off the blade she still clutched.

"Merrow... were you about to steal my fun?" he asked, eyes delighted.

Emer raised the middle finger of the hand he held before ripping it free and stomping towards the exit.

After only a few steps, she came to regret the distance. Glass smashed nearby, and when she turned, she saw the man who had attacked her moments before crash face-first into a table. The wood cracked and split from the impact, leaving a large gash streaming with blood as he sank back to the floor.

Calder's features were frozen in a mirrored confusion. Then, sensing what was about to come, he turned and reached for her with urgency.

CHAPTER 20

A shout from somewhere else in the tavern tore through the air and Emer did not need to speak the native language to know that the throaty call was a command to fight. The moments that followed felt as if they happened underwater, slow and quiet. Emer's eyes snagged onto Calder's. Her limbs felt heavy as she moved to reach for him. Her fingers had just brushed his when suddenly everything was happening too fast. A wave of brawlers tore them apart and swallowed them into a sea of churning bodies.

There was no rhyme or reason to the violence, just men eagerly seizing the opportunity to draw blood from whoever was unfortunate enough to find themselves in the path of their blow. Those who did not intend to fight quickly fled to the door to avoid being caught in the madness. The tavern became a blur of flying limbs, drinks, and chairs.

Emer struggled to stay on her feet as she ricocheted off the other patrons. The cloak she had worn for her protection instantly became a hazard, the excess length becoming trapped beneath the brawlers' boots. She dug her fingers into the hood's fabric, fighting fiercely to keep it in place. Another large body pinned the cloak to the ground and the clasp dug into the sensitive skin of her throat as it ripped her back. Emer twisted but only managed to crack her hip against the corner of a table before crashing to the ground. White hot pain flashed across her knuckles as they grated against the rough floor, causing her grip on the knife to falter. She watched helplessly as it was kicked out of sight by the stampeding boots. Realizing that she would meet the same fate if she remained on the floor, she ignored the pain and scrambled to her feet.

Emer did not call for Calder, knowing her pleas would be lost amongst the fleshy sound of fists colliding with faces and the sea of profanity, and instead, began to carve through the crowd in search of him.

A blur from the corner of her eye had her turning just in time to see a chair being brought down over her. As she braced for impact, a tall, cloaked body appeared, and the chair splintered against his back. Of the two of them, however, it was Emer who flinched. The man merely cracked his head to the side in annoyance and, noticing her attention on him, turned.

While his features were partially hidden beneath his dark hood, she saw how his lips parted as if surprised, and it was unclear if it was because he had expected someone else or if it was because he had not expected someone like *her*.

"Merrow!"

The word roared from somewhere in the mass of limbs. The wariness she felt at turning from the stranger became moot when he calmly strode passed her. Seemingly bored of the bedlam unfolding around them, he disappeared into the crowd.

Emer set her focus on finding Calder and began scouring the tavern, only to find an equally familiar pair of eyes come back to haunt her. The shouts, the thundering of the pounding boots, and the cracking of the wooden chairs brought it all back.

It brought him back.

"Lachlan?" The word left her as a whisper, scarcely audible over the chaos.

His eyes were still filled with the terror she had seen aboard the ship as it burned around them. The same desperation as when the arrow pierced his back. Emer felt as if her body was cast back into the sea and her veins bathed in ice. She had grown instantly numb. Even her fear could not reach her in the strange place of unreality that she was suspended in. Perhaps the lack of fear was the most unambiguous indication that she had gone mad. When she blinked, the insanity that gripped her momentarily eased. No ghost remained, only monsters.

The crowd had lessened, but the bodies that littered the floor confirmed that those who stood were the exact ones she needed to avoid. Another body crashed against her, driving her onto a table. Its rough edge dug into her stomach, and she blindly kicked out her legs. Her foot connected with a shin. The weight of a large hand was the only warning before he gripped her shoulder like a vice and spun her. Her back bent over the table as he pushed her down and pinned her with his forearm over her throat, sealing off her air. The man loomed over her, his smile sharp as he eased from her throat, and instead, pressed his arm over her chest, ensuring she remained pinned.

In the struggle, it took Emer a moment to register the cool press of his blade against her jaw, and she gritted her teeth as she ceased struggling.

"What do we have here?" he asked, reeking of drink and perpetual disappointment.

Any remnants of fear were quickly incinerated by the rage that burned through her. She snarled every curse she had ever heard from Finn, stringing them together like the jewels of the vilest necklace. Even her assailant paused before smiling at her.

"Such a mouth you have," he chuckled as he leaned closer and took in a deep breath.

"I have no *fucking* idea where she gets it from," the cold calm in Calder's voice caused both Emer and her assailant to still.

He righted one of the toppled chairs and dragged it to the table, unconcerned with the brawl raging around them.

Emer watched her assailant's eyes track Calder as he eased himself into the chair at the side of the table where her head lay.

Elbow on the table, Calder assessed the man who seemed to think he could escape the Raven's sight through stillness. Calder dropped his hand to the side of Emer's head, lazily twirling loose strands of her hair in his fingers.

"It's rude to play with your food, Merrow."

Calder's calm and confident demeanor empowered Emer who lifted her chin, no longer fearful of the knife at her throat.

The man stared down at her, horrified, realizing he was woefully ill-equipped for the game he had become an unwilling participant in—a Raven's toy and a Merrow's snack.

Calder drove a knife into the table next to Emer's head, and while she did not flinch, her assailant did. Even though the chaos around them continued, the three occupied each other's space so thoroughly that she could taste Calder's whiskey-rich scent. The man's forearm remained pressing her down, but his knife trembled, and he leaned away from her and her threatening shadow.

Calder brought his lips to her ear and whispered, "All you have to do is ask." An offering to reduce the man before her to ribbons or support her doing it herself.

The man's eyes widened with fear.

Emer shook her head slightly, her skin hot where it touched Calder's lips.

Calder hummed.

"Make him bleed, sweetheart."

Before the man could retreat, she gripped the hand that wielded the knife at the wrist and, with her other, retrieved Calder's from the table. Beads of blood seeped from the slash she made across the man's cheek, running in a jagged diagonal line from his temple to the top of his lip. He stumbled but did not retreat. Neither did Emer, choosing to close the space between them instead.

The man snarled.

Emer dipped beneath the man's meaty fist as he swung it at her and used her new position to drive her heel into the back of his knee. He collapsed, and before he could recover, she rounded to his front. Grabbing his head, she drove it down as she brought her knee up. She released his greasy hair with a curse, allowing his now limp body to fall to the floor.

Looking over her shoulder, she found Calder standing, poised to step in. It wasn't until that moment that she looked at him properly. His thick black curls were disheveled and drawn across his forehead. His weapons were sheathed, but his knuckles were bloody, and he had a bruise forming on his cheek.

Stepping forward, Calder curled his arm around Emer's waist and shielded her as he led her away.

"Am I allowed to say that was ridiculously attractive?" His voice was an amused whisper amongst the chaos.

"Not the time," she groaned.

"Later then."

They held tightly to each other as they continued to push their way through the crowd, Calder using his elbows to carve out a path. Soon, they tumbled out of the Alder Barrel, along with a handful of others who did not share in the bloodlust intoxicating the crowd. It was unclear when her body had become molded to his, but as they escaped, Emer did not attempt to move away.

"I lost my knife," she announced somberly.

A line appeared between Calder's brow as he looked down at her tucked under his arm. His eyes narrowed on how her bottom lip was pushed out on the tail end of her mournful admission.

"Yeah, well. I almost lost my mind. So, let's just plan to not do that again, okay?" he grunted, urging her forward.

She pulled her hand from his to correct the hood she realized was still down, but he snatched it back a moment later as if, without it, she would slip from under his arm like smoke. There was no doubt that someone had seen Emer, and Calder eyed the crowd intently as they continued down the road. His features were not frantic but feral.

Once they had gained some distance from the rowdy crowd, he directed them down an alley. Emer closed her eyes, resting her head against the wall of a nearby structure. She brought her hand to her throat, testing the tender skin.

"Let me check you."

Her eyes flew open to find Calder already reaching for her cloak and she batted his hand away. "I rather think I can tell where I'm injured without your confirmation. Thanks."

He rolled his eyes like she was the unreasonable one.

"Is it really that scandalous to let me touch you?" he asked.

She brought her hand up to his chest to push him back, but the man was as solid as the wall behind her. "Despite the example set by your many companions, I do not make it a habit of letting men indiscriminately remove my clothes."

He grinned, trailing a finger down the inside of one of the cloak panels before placing his other hand against the wall and leaning closer.

"But it's so much fun," he taunted.

Emer slapped his hand. "Don't make me stab you."

Her threat only made his grin grow wider. He dipped his head, bringing them eye-to-eye. "With what knife?"

"Everything alright, miss?" The question came from an older man watching nervously from the mouth of the alley.

While the passerby had misconstrued the situation, it warmed Emer's heart that he was concerned for her, and she could not help but have a fondness for him. Giving Calder a withering glare out of the side of her eyes, she bit back a smile.

"As a matter of fact—"

Before she could finish, Calder pushed off the wall and straightened to his full height. The man took a startled step back, and whatever he saw in the Sea Raven's expression had him averting his gaze.

"Beg your pardon," he stuttered as he scurried away.

"Coward," she spat under her breath.

Calder turned his attention back to her with a raised brow. Her muscles tensed as she felt the heat of his body draw closer and the weight of his head as he dropped it to the crook of her neck.

"Tell me, little Merrow, do you need rescuing?"

She didn't realize he had unclasped her cloak until he was pulling it open and inspecting her bruise.

"Bastar—"

He hushed her curse.

"Endearments will get you nowhere" he said as his thumb moved under her jaw and gently tilted her head back.

Although he had warned her of the dangers of the Isle, there was something markedly different about seeing those dangers brought to life on her skin. Evidence that despite her strength and despite his efforts, she was crushable. She was killable. She could be taken.

With one hand holding her head still, he used his other to brush loose strands of hair from her face. "How many men did you scar tonight?" he asked as he cleaned her.

"Just the one," she said sulkily. "And you? Oh, great and violent Morvran?"

"Eight," he answered.

As he brushed his thumb over her cheek and watched the drops of blood smear over her once uncorrupted skin, he suddenly questioned the restraint he had shown. If those men wanted to paint things red, he was more than willing to oblige.

"Why haven't you asked me to go with you?" he asked.

Emer shifted, attempting to turn out of his hold, but he gripped her tighter. "Merrow," he said softly. "Ask me."

Swallowing hard, Emer spoke the words she had allowed to

sour within her for fear he would deny her. "Come with me," she said in a polite command rather than a question.

Calder grinned down at her.

"As if this would have gone any other way."

"Yeah?" she asked.

The thick black thread of anxiety loosened.

He hummed in acknowledgment.

"Besides, who would tend to your battle wounds if not me?"

"I strongly recall telling you that I did not need you for that," she returned, her own grin forming.

"For *other* things then," he remarked suggestively.

Emer shook her head, turning away to hide the emotions pricking at her eyes and focusing instead on the growing number of people passing the alley.

Calder stepped back and tugged at her hand, "Let's go get your Well, Merrow."

As they made their way further into the alley, a shadowy figure stepped out in front of them.

Chaos, it seemed, had gotten a taste of Emer, and now it was addicted.

CHAPTER 21

The scrape of boots against the stone behind them had Calder and Emer's heads snapping to find two other men approaching. One of them being the man from the Alder Barrel. His cut and bloodied face pulled into a snarl.

Although each was armed, it was not a weapon that caused a chill to lick Emer's spine, but rather the rope, small sack, and makeshift gag of cloth. Their intentions were clear, and Emer tucked herself close to Calder, running her hands over him in search of a concealed weapon to replace the one she lost.

"You don't want to fucking do this," Calder warned.

The men laughed, looking at each other and back to Emer. "You didn't mention she had a dog," the one in front of them said.

"Wrong animal," Calder growled under his breath.

Oblivious, the man from the tavern answered back, "Did you think I needed two of you for that little thing?" He punctuated his question by waving his sword at Emer.

She stepped towards him, shooting out her arm and brandishing the knife she had slipped from Calder's sheath.

"Your face tells me you would," she hissed.

"She wants to fight," one of the men said with a hoarse laugh.

"No one said anything about the condition she had to be in when delivered," said the man with the gag, licking his lips.

Death. Calder felt it chill his bones, and he closed his eyes, letting it cascade down his spine.

Alabaster croaked in the distance.

Calder leaned down and trailed his lips across Emer's ear as he asked, "I want him this time. Share with me?"

His words did something to her that was entirely inappropriate for the current situation, and it was unclear who was more shocked by the satisfied smile that curved at her lips—the three men before her or the Sea Raven who smiled back.

"I want that one," she said, pointing her knife at the man who called Calder a dog.

"Poor bastard," Calder laughed and nodded in agreement.

The complete disregard for the three would-be assailants had them exchanging concerned looks.

Calder crossed his arms in front of him and unsheathed the two swords at his hips. "Tha mi an dòchas gu bheil thu deiseil airson bàsachadh."

I hope you are ready to die.

The alley quickly became segmented by the two fights, Calder focusing on the two Emer had not claimed as her own. With his mind split, Calder allowed one of the opposing blades to kiss his arm and draw a feral sound from his throat. While Emer's presence was a distraction for Calder, his was a motivation for her. The snarl that left him moments before caused the rage pooling within her to overflow. Dodging her opponent's sword, she used the man's move against him and pivoted out of the blade's path. Emer gripped his wrist with one hand and spun into his now open chest, plunging her knife into his shoulder. He wailed as she pulled the knife free, warm blood spraying across her cheek. It ran down her neck and over her thundering pulse. Still holding the man's arm,

Emer spun herself from his grasp and then drove her knee into his elbow. His sword clattering against the stone was a melodic crescendo to their dance.

Bloodied and bitter, the man crouched low and lunged. As they fell, Emer threw her elbow into the side of his head—a final attempt to incapacitate him before she hit the ground. The impact left her vision spotting, and for a moment, she did not realize the weight on her had grown still. Shallow breaths rattled from her compressed chest as she pushed against the unconscious man, her other hand slipping against the stone now slick from his seeping wound.

She rose from the ground, a portrait of beauty and violence much like the cliffs by the keep, and just like the cliffside, she was now covered in blood.

When Calder caught sight of her, his eyes flared at how the dark parts of the man now tainted the parts of her that had been bright and clean.

Emer took a deep breath, set her jaw, and began to stalk towards where he fought; her knife gripped tight in her hand. Before she could draw too close, however, Calder waved her away. With her fight no longer distracting him, he could give his opponents his full attention and all the wrath that came with it.

He alternated defensive and offensive moves between the men, each intentional and powerful. As they began to tire, Calder devoured their struggles. He used a block to push the older man back, and his head hit the ground with a sickening crack that left him groaning in place.

Unfurling his fingers from the hilt of one of the swords, Calder crooked them and beckoned his remaining opponent forward. The man charged, bringing his weapon down with all his might. Calder blocked with one sword and lunged with his other, plunging it deep into the man's abdomen.

As children, Emer and Finn played with wooden swords and would cry out dramatically as they pretended to die. It was at that moment Emer learned that men don't cry out when they are stabbed through the chest. They grunt. A feeble noise, so muted compared to the sound made by the metal as it sliced through flesh.

Calder's nostrils flared as he stared into the man's eyes, driving the sword to the hilt.

Another grunt.

This time from Calder, straining from the force required to twist his blade.

Crack.

In one final act of aggression, he pushed back and kicked the man free of his blade.

Calder was prepared to see disgust when he looked at Emer. He expected to see terror in her eyes, possibly even for her to run. He was not prepared for the sigh of relief that swept through the now quiet alley nor the small arms that wrapped tightly around his middle.

"Thank you," she whispered against his chest.

He flinched.

Swords still in hand, he stood rigid in her embrace. Though his arms remained at his sides, he slowly lowered his head and allowed his chin to rest on her head.

Pressed against him, she opened her eyes to survey the carnage in the alley. The sun had just fallen, but not even the cover of night could hide the thick pool of darkness surrounding the one that met Calder's blade.

A hint of mourning swept through her heart. Not for the man who lay dead before her, but for herself. For the girl from the meadow who never reached the shore. The part of herself that drowned below those waves—the one that would have felt sorry.

Calder stepped back and moved down the alley behind her, returning a moment later and securing her cloak around her. He took her hand in his, and the blood on their skin further bound them together.

Pressing his lips to the top of her head, he spoke softly, "You did good, Merrow."

Another time, she could have gotten drunk off the pride that infused his voice, but just like whiskey, his words burnt all the way down. Throat tight, she remained silent as Calder led her into the night.

CHAPTER 22

The space of calm that immediately follows chaos is a strange one. A mercurial moment of intense emotions and nuanced realizations. Like the recognition that time moves like cool honey when you are afraid. Fear makes everything slow and thick. Moments of joy, however, are more like sugar. Small, precious, and easily scattered. That knowledge made the realm seem crueler, and the truth became painfully evident when Emer began to hear the growing sounds of the town. To them, there was not a body in the alley nearby.

Their day was measured in sugar.

Her nose scrunched under her hood at the scent of the blood still clinging to her. A wealth of gore concealed with a simple cloak.

Returning to the more populated streets, Emer tilted her head slightly and glared at those who passed from beneath her hood. The suspicious glint she had so often observed in Calder's eyes was now heavily reflected in her own. Shared features that resulted from the same lessons learned.

One: men grunt when they die.

Two: painful moments linger.

Her grip on Calder tightened. Once the monster she ran from, now the one who led her from harm. Calder squeezed her hand back.

"What?" she asked, blinking in confusion.

"I said you need to get on the horse," he repeated, his brow furrowed with concern.

"Horse?" she asked, only to realize that they were back at the stable.

Her thoughts were heavy and her movements slow. It was a weight Calder recognized and one that seemed to grow heavier every time he witnessed the darkness of the Isle attempting to blot out the light of the tender-hearted girl who did not belong there.

Impatience had him gripping her waist and hoisting her on a horse she soon realized was Danu rather than Aven. He quickly situated himself in the saddle behind her.

They did not acknowledge that their bodies suddenly made contact in more places than they did not. His chest pressed into her back, his thighs cradled hers, and his arms rested at her sides.

Calder looked down at the way his body caged her. Protective. Claiming.

The next thing that wanted her would have to pry her from his damn lap—the fucking Elders included. Perhaps not the sanest response, but he had learned if there was space between them, it would be exploited. The logical solution, then, would be to have no space. Even with a set of reins in either hand, he kept one arm wrapped around her.

When he drew in a tired breath, he pressed further against her, but she did not move, and he wondered if the contact was as grounding for her as it was for him. When her muscles relaxed and she nestled into him, he had his answer.

He drank in her rain-like scent mixed with the tang he knew all too well. Like forget-me-nots watered with blood.

"I won't run again," she said quietly.

"I will not give you a reason to run," he replied, voice flat but words warm.

The back of Emer's head rolled rhythmically with the horse's stride, and although her eyes were heavy, her mind would not allow her the peace she needed for sleep.

She tried to focus on how Calder's chest rose and fell against her back, counting his heartbeats. The more she focused on him, the more her body relaxed, and soon, she felt herself drifting off. She raised her hand to rub her eyes but paused to take in the blood coating her hands.

"I need to get this off," she confessed.

Calder flinched slightly as though her voice after the extended silence had caught him off guard. "It's the middle of the night and too cold for you to get wet," he protested.

Emer sat up, turning to look at him over her shoulder. The bare hint of moonlight caught her eyes, illuminating the melancholy that consumed them. Despite his better judgment, he steered them off the path and towards the trees until he heard the bubbling sounds of the creek.

After dismounting Danu, Calder tapped his hand against her thigh and held her waist as he brought her down in front of him. "Are you sure you are okay?" he asked with a subtle tilt of his head, his hands still gripping her tightly.

"Would you be disappointed in me if I said I wasn't sure?" she returned.

With a soft smile, he backed away. "Not something I am capable of, I'm afraid."

Kneeling before the stream, he cupped his hands and washed the blood from his face. He may not have the same conflicted feelings regarding the violent acts they had committed, but that didn't mean he wasn't exhausted.

From beneath the sound of trickling water, he heard Emer hiss as she knelt next to him, discovering one of the many new bruises she had earned from her fight. Her nose wrinkled and she felt the resistance of the blood that had dried on her face. Mercifully, when she leaned over the water, the night concealed the worst of it and revealed only a dark shape rippling with the water. It seemed she would not have to face herself tonight.

Reaching towards the stream, she frowned, finding the cleansing water was not within her grasp. A glare replaced her frown as she repositioned her body, digging her hip into the grass and stretching her legs out in the opposite direction of her arms to balance her weight. Her fingers danced over the water and she growled.

Calder paused to watch her.

"If you don't let me help you, I will be retrieving you from the water. *Again*," he chastised with a knowing smirk.

Even though she ignored his warning, she pressed a hand further into the grass to fight against the pull tipping her over the embankment.

Calder pushed himself up and moved to kneel behind her, pulling her up and rearranging her so that his arms were on either side of her. With his fingers around her wrists, he guided her hands under the water and meticulously washed them.

The realm grew quiet as she watched him work. The bloodlust still stirring in his veins made them thick and raised as they snaked up his wrist and disappeared under his rolled-up sleeves.

For a moment, Emer glimpsed a contentment she did not realize her nervous soul could experience and knew it could quickly become something she craved. The foreign sensation was quickly overshadowed by guilt. Her purpose remained the same, and while she was sinking into a man's embrace, her father was likely in bed an ocean away, sinking further away from them all.

She straightened her spine, and Calder pulled her back from the embankment, positioning her so they faced each other. Emer closed her eyes against the shiver that rolled through her as Calder worked to remove the blood from her face with gentle strokes.

"Still okay?" he asked.

"It could have been worse," Emer sighed, slumping forward slightly.

"That isn't what I asked. The threat of what could have been does not take away from the wounds of what was," he said sternly.

"What does it matter?" she asked him, exhaustion heavy in her voice.

Calder's hand hovered over her shoulder before ghosting across the skin of her collarbone, his hands eclipsing that of the man who left marks where his fingers had dug into her skin. "He bruised you. It matters."

Emer brought her hand up, covering his where it had settled. "They will fade. I will not," she vowed.

"Of all the men I have watched bleed, he may be my favorite," he spat, eyes darkening.

"Truth be told. I'm surprised you only killed the one," Emer confessed.

"If I thought we had time, I would have slaughtered all three," he gritted out.

A breathy sound had his eyes snapping at hers, and she let out a laugh that quickly smothered to a giggle.

"Not a joke," he spat.

Even dripping in vitriol and spoken so harshly, it was practically unintelligible, she only giggled harder.

"Do you intend to fight every beast from here to the Well?" she asked teasingly.

"If necessary," he answered, standing up and helping her to her feet. "You know," he said thoughtfully as he held her arm to the side and appraised her. She shifted on her feet as his eyes traveled from head to toe, taking in the ale, blood, and dirt. Her previously white tunic was now stained from various transgressions, but he studied the fabric as if looking at a fine dress. "You look more and more like a Morvran each day," he commented, satisfied with his surveying.

Emer looked down and grimaced at the unsavory colors, now bleeding together from the water like a gory watercolor. She had thought his affinity for all-black clothing related to his role as Sea Raven, but now she realized it was more practical.

"I look savage," she huffed.

"I believe that is what I said," he replied with a wolfish grin.

She pulled her hand from his and crossed her arms against the cold of the night air.

"We both know I will never look like a Morvran, no matter how blood-covered or sharply accessorized I am," she argued.

"Perhaps you are right. You blush far too easily," he said with a shrug, though Emer caught a glimpse of a smile as he turned.

"It's a shame you did not come to the Isle for recreation. Extended time with the Morvran clan would be quite *transformative*," he mused.

She could not help but feel a twinge of disappointment at his remark. Admittedly, she hadn't considered anything other than reaching the Well, including what would happen afterward—willfully ignoring that her plans required her to eventually say goodbye to the man who had been her constant companion.

"I suppose it is for the best. This place does not require long to dull bright things that don't belong here," he spoke in a faintly somber voice.

While she was confident any emotion in his words was related to his mother, she could not help but let the last of them linger.

Don't belong here.

It wasn't meant to wound her. It was simply the truth. He had witnessed firsthand what happened when a vibrant soul was brought to a dark place. His father coveted the light his mother brought here, and Calder would forever blame him for letting the shadows consume her. It was the vice of protectors that they believed they could guard what they coveted. It was also a fallacy.

Emer pulled at her tunic, attempting to distance the chilled fabric and her skin. She gritted her teeth from the chattering she felt emanating from her bones, but despite her efforts, Calder's eyes narrowed as he watched her.

"Cold?" His tone was accusatory.

Even wearing her cloak once more, she couldn't seem to find warmth in any part of her body.

"N-no," she stuttered.

"Yeah, okay," he said with a mocking nod. "Given we had to leave town before I could secure the rest of the supplies we needed. We are going to have to get creative," he explained.

"Creative?" she echoed warily.

"Steal. We are going to need to steal."

Emer stepped back and looked around as if the minnows in the creek would turn them in. "From who?"

Holding her stare, he answered.

"The Morvran clan."

CHAPTER 23

The closer to Murdoch they drew, the more distant Calder became. Securing his mask into place as the moon secured its place amongst the stars. A mask mirrored after his father—the mask of the Morvran.

Soon, storm clouds loomed overhead, darkening the sky with the same somber gray that seemed to be reflected in his eyes. Rain began to fall just as the loch came into view, and Emer turned over her shoulder, ready to share in the relief that their long ride was ending, but found he had stopped Danu and was several paces back. She called his name through the heavy sheet of rain, but his eyes remained fixed on the town beyond her.

"We can't take the main road," he bellowed once he reached her side.

The admission made her go slack, and a crack of lightning illuminated the confusion in her eyes.

"Don't look at me like that... I said stealing, didn't I?" he reminded with audible frustration. "We'll navigate through the wooded areas to where my cottage lies on the outskirts," he explained.

He held Emer's gaze, waiting for her to challenge him but

instead he saw the moment she understood that his search to find his mother's killer had been driven by more than revenge. He knew from the way her eyes softened that she understood how badly he wanted to return home and this was not how it was meant to happen.

She nodded and followed him off the trail and into the trees.

The shadowy forms that loomed in the distance took shape and revealed themselves to be the ships that called the loch home. Their rich wooden structures were at peace, nestled amongst each other.

Calder searched the once familiar landscape for some sign that it felt his absence, even if only marginally to how he felt it.

It looked the same.

"Why are there no guards preventing us from continuing? Strange that we would be able to arrive unnoticed," she asked, staring out into the silent and sleeping town.

Calder's breath formed tiny wisps in the cold night air as he responded, "Because it is highly unlikely that anyone would be insane enough to sneak into this village."

Holding up his clenched fist, he signaled to stop before dismounting and approaching Aven. The tap on Emer's thigh felt muted by the cold that invaded her muscles. Emer's boots sank into the mud and Calder firmly held her hand as he led her across the rugged terrain. Cautiously, they made their way closer to the structure that bordered the tree line, navigating through greedy limbs.

After removing the boards that covered the window, Calder motioned Emer to step forward so he could hoist her through the opening.

Inside the cottage and bathed in darkness, Emer's hand collided with something, knocking it to the floor and startling her. Firm hands gripped her sides as the breath of air she knocked from Calder crashed against her neck.

"Sorry," she whispered.

Calder cleared his throat before saying, "Do us both a favor and don't move."

She felt him pass her and move into the space he once called home. The telltale sound of Ravenstone being struck preceded a soft glow from the far side of the room. The modest flame then traveled slowly, forming a second. Candles in hand, Calder returned to where Emer stood, offering one to her and then motioning her further into the home. His home.

Though still largely in darkness, they began to take in the room now revealed by the candlelight. Furniture was sparse, aside from the necessities, and everything was coated in a thick layer of dust. As with the man who stood in the center, slowly and segment by segment, the larger picture began to take shape. The main living area led into two other smaller areas—a bathing room and a sleeping area.

Calder swept through the back room, collecting various items, casting enough light to show the unmade bed that looked like he had only left days ago rather than years. Intense exhaustion overwhelmed Emer, and she imagined what it would be like to lie on that bed. Blinking quickly, she looked away and began to survey the rest of the living area.

The Calder of before had not shied away from clutter and chaos. Maps, books, and bits of scrap parchment were littered throughout. Emer thumbed through stiff papers, maps, and port notes. Pulling out what looked to be a design for a ship.

"*The Ceasg,*" she read aloud.

Lost in thought, she had not noticed that he now loomed behind her. Moving his candle towards the parchment in her hand, he let the flame catch the corner, and they watched as the fire slowly ate at the thoughts and dreams of his former self. He pulled it from her hand before the flames could lick her skin and stomped out the ashes with his heavy boots. Looking over her shoulder, she searched for the Calder from those pages.

"There are enough ghosts here, Merrow. Don't search for more," he said, tipping his chin towards the window.

Calder exited first, setting down the sack of supplies before returning to Emer, who was already easing herself down from the sill. His hand found her hips, and he halted rather than slowed her descent. She remained suspended before him for a moment. His lips parted to speak, but all that left him was a pained grunt.

Stumbling forward, he dropped Emer, revealing the man who had struck him. Two others appeared from the shadows, grabbing his arms as he fought violently against them. A fourth reached for Emer.

"Don't *fucking* touch her," he snarled.

Calder drove his forehead into the nose of one man before pulling his arm free and throwing his fist into the jaw of the other.

"Stand down by order of the Morvran," he commanded, lunging towards Emer before he was once again restrained.

There was an audible sigh in the quiet that followed before one of the men said, "Wish we could, sir. But we have different orders."

Standing in the village center, Emer watched as the rain fell against her boots and the puddle beneath them grew murky with mud. The four men who detained them stood shoulder to shoulder at their backs—a wall of stone and steel. In the distance, two additional men led Aven and Danu away.

Ahead marched a petite woman who moved like smoke, so unbothered by the rain it was as if it didn't touch her. She wore leather leggings and a pale tunic cinched to her waist thanks to a dark leather corset and Emer wondered if she was afraid, envious, or in love.

"Hello, brother," Lina said icily.

CHAPTER 24

The sudden laugh that rumbled from beneath Calder's hood was in such contrast to his earlier demeanor that it was borderline maniacal. The somber Calder that Emer had entered the village with was someone he did not intend to share with anyone other than her.

"Detainment? Is that any way to welcome me home, sister?"

Lina tilted her head, proving that menace was a family trait.

"Let's not pretend you weren't going to sneak off into the night as if you were never here," she challenged.

It was not the warm homecoming one would hope for, nor was it even the reunion of siblings. The two that now faced off amidst the storm were orphans who only had each other, regardless of their anger.

Lina's gaze finally trailed to Emer before snapping back to Calder.

"You're all dismissed," Lina commanded, and the men who had stood guard nodded before dispersing into the shadows once more.

One of the guards clapped Calder on the shoulder and began

apologizing but quickly corrected himself at the sight of Calder's disdain directed toward the unwelcome limb on his person.

Lina stepped toward her brother and gave him a soft smile right before she punched him in the stomach. Bracing a hand on his knee, he chased the breath she had knocked from him.

"Welcome home, Cal," she offered.

"Missed you too," he rasped.

When he was upright again, she raised her brow with an unspoken question. One Calder answered by looking back to Emer, rain cascading down his face and shining in the sparse moonlight.

Closing the distance he said quietly, "It wasn't supposed to happen this way."

Unsure if his words were motivated by apology or regret Emer answered, "Yet, here we are."

He gave her an approving squeeze and led her forward. Once in front of Lina, he slid his hand up Emer's back to the base of her hood. Gripping the fabric, he tugged it down. Emer straightened as she felt the heat of his hand return to the back of her neck. His grip was light, and the contact of his skin against hers provided a welcomed anchor.

Emer had been many things—the damsel, the enemy, the shadow—but she was uncertain what exactly her role was here. As his thumb continued to brush slow strokes across her skin, she raised her chin, knowing whatever she was would not be hidden.

"Lina, I would like you to meet Emer," he said, sliding his hand down, applying pressure to her lower back, and urging her forward. "She saved my life, and she needs our help."

The following silence was interrupted by the sound of shutters tentatively opening and doors creaking. Proving the only thing swifter in this village than the guards was its gossip.

Lina nodded briefly before saying, "Let's take this conversation somewhere warmer, shall we?"

Emer and Calder followed Lina up the path she had come

from and passed more and more village members. Each new face played the same scene—surprise, elation, and confusion.

The cottage was a welcomed respite from both the rain and the stares. As was true of Lina, there was little pretense to the home. A roaring fire cast long shadows from the humble furniture present in the room. It contained several chairs, a table on the adjacent wall near the window, a plush rug, and three doors to adjoining rooms.

"As the Elders would have it, I had drawn some water for a bath. I imagine you would appreciate it far more than I," Lina offered, motioning Emer to follow her across the room.

Warm, damp air met them as they entered the dim space. A lantern hooked to the wall revealed a round tub in the corner and tendrils of luxurious steam rising from it.

"You look like you've fallen in love," Lina observed thoughtfully.

Emer's brow furrowed as she turned her attention to Lina, who wore a large grin.

"With the bath, I mean," she explained, walking over to a shelf and selecting a jar whose contents she then poured into the water.

A floral and woody aroma infused the steam.

"Heather. It will help you sleep," she mused.

"I wish I had more to offer than words of thanks," Emer replied.

"I suspect you are the only reason my brother is here, and while I may be furious with the bastard, I am thankful for you." Lina sighed as she left the room, closing the door behind her.

Having already filled a cup with ale, Calder sat with his elbows on his knees, staring into dark liquid as if it had the words his sister needed to hear.

Lina took the chair opposite to him and sat quietly for a moment, studying him like he were an ancient text that she knew the language of but was so out of practice that she had to pause for a moment before she could begin.

"You didn't drown her, right?" he asked.

Lina scoffed.

"The girl is safe. You, on the other hand..." she let her words trail off.

"I know you are angry—" he began to say.

"I'm a Morvran, Cal. When are we not angry?" she challenged.

Silence fell between them once more. It was weighted with resentment and grief.

"Would you have ever come home if it wasn't for her?" Lina asked flatly.

The ale in Calder's mouth turned to ash as he considered the answer he wanted to give her versus the truth: that their father had told him not to return until he found justice for his mother, saddling Calder with an impossible task simply because he did not want to face his failure. They both looked at their parents' love through the lens of a fairytale.

Lina saw an epic love story.

Calder saw the dragon who stole away the maiden.

If protecting Lina's version of the story meant also preserving the peace she had found to cope with their loss, Calder would continue to be the villain.

"Was it mom?" Lina asked softly.

"I found her unconscious on the shore by the keep in Obanes," he explained, and Lina let out a soft chuckle.

Rising to her feet, she went over to the almost depleted barrel of ale and drew herself a mug. "So, yes..." she answered, taking a drink.

Calder nodded, and when Lina returned to her chair, she dropped into it with a new heaviness.

"Well, fuck..." she breathed, shaking her head.

"Yeah," Calder confirmed, swallowing his ale hard.

"Cheers to Mamaí," Lina remarked quietly.

Including only the necessary details, Calder explained Emer's situation. When he concluded, Lina very gently sat down her ale, rose from her chair, and left the room without explanation. She returned with a bundle of clothes in her hands a short time later.

"I refuse to let poor Emer subject herself to the rags you dressed her in. Elders know she has been through enough," she explained, taking the clothes towards the bathing chambers. She paused, watching her brother over her shoulder. "There are other things we need to talk about, Cal. We'll have a nice long chat when you come back down the mountain. Deal?"

Making a deal with Lina was like doing so with a Fae, but despite his unease, Calder nodded.

Emer made her way out of the water, the cold air tensing her muscles and threatening to erase the relief they had found.

Assessing the clothes Lina provided, she held up the thin cotton dress and panicked at the thought of wearing nothing but that in front of her present company. She let the garment fall and instead searched for the sodden clothes she had been wearing, only to find they were no longer there.

Emer wrung out as much water from her hair as possible, leaving the long strands flowing down her back, and then, in nothing but the flimsy dress and woolen socks, re-entered the living area.

Taking a drink of ale as he turned, Calder looked at Emer only to turn away sharply, his body jerking in time with a faint choking sound. Composing himself, he gestured for her to take the vacant chair.

Emer shifted on her feet, acutely aware of how bare she was beneath the loose fabric, before reluctantly accepting the seat.

"I'm sorry, Lina, but my clothes?" Emer started, but Lina waved her away.

"Burned. And even that was too good of an end for them. I'll have new ones brought to you in the morning," she stated authoritatively.

Calder's head snapped to the hearth, where he could still make out the remnants of the clothes. Given that Emer would likely die of illness or mortification if she attempted to ride dressed as she was, it was clear Lina was not going to make their departure easy.

"So, my brother tells me you are family now," Lina commented, and it took a moment for Emer to interpret her words.

Family is who you are willing to shed blood for.

Her induction to the family had been the moment Dempsey disappeared from the cliff. The memory caused her to shiver slightly, but she forced a small smile as her fingers absentmindedly tapped her palms.

"You're okay," Calder soothed in a low voice.

He leaned forward, gifting Emer his mug of ale.

"Drink."

Although the word was presented as a command, his tone was comforting, and Emer took the drink before handing it back and offering a nod of gratitude.

Lina watched the exchange and spared Calder a single mischievous glance before setting her sights on Emer.

"I don't know, brother," Lina said wistfully as her eyes narrowed and she leaned closer. "She is quite a beauty... she may be Selkie after all. I bet hearts break all over the Isle of Rest with you gone."

Surprised by the comment, Emer swallowed her ale hard and shifted nervously before answering, "Not one."

"Well, if no one at home has your favor, I am sure the men here would be delighted to earn it," Lina said, motioning to the village beyond the cottage walls.

"Lina," Calder cautioned.

"Point taken, brother. I am sure the men *and* women would be delighted to..."

"Lina!" Calder barked, and she burst out laughing.

His glare lingered on her before he turned to Emer, waiting for her to remark on his sister's offer.

"With the exception of my brother, there are no hearts to break back home," she continued, and Lina seemed to immediately understand her meaning while Calder searched her expression.

"In that case, bones break just as well," Lina offered. "To women who look like flowers but draw blood like daggers," Lina toasted, frowning into her empty cup.

"Well, the ale is gone, and the rain has stopped... perhaps we call it a night. Calder, I've had wood and blankets brought to your cabin. Wouldn't want the Cold One to catch a chill."

"Cold One?" Emer echoed.

Lina grinned, "A story for the morning, I suspect."

"We will not have time to linger tomorrow, Li," Calder advised, drawing a sardonic smile from his sister.

"Of course," she replied coldly.

CHAPTER 25

Emer clutched the panels of her still-damp cloak around her as they walked. The sound of their boots carried through the night as they made their way to Calder's cottage, though they would enter through the door this time.

With a defeated thud, Calder dropped the sack of items they had come for just on the other side of the threshold. Whoever had been tasked with delivering the blankets and wood had also taken it upon themselves to light a fire and leave bread, apples, and dried meats on the nearby table. There was more apprehension in Calder's movements than when they had broken in.

Discarding her cold cloak and boots, Emer made her way over to the fire.

Calder remained leaning against the front door, reminding her so much of when they first entered his room at the keep. Only, this time, he was the uneasy one.

Emer cleared her throat before offering, "Your sister is lovely." Which came out more like a question than an observation.

Calder snorted and pushed off from the wall.

"So lovely that she not only stole your clothes so you would not be burdened with them anymore, but also... unpacked our horses," he ground out, staring into the corner of the room where their bedrolls and belongings were.

"At least she didn't hide the horses," she joked.

He paused and raised his brow. "Do you know where they are?"

Emer's face pinched because, no, she did not.

"Make no mistake, we are hostages," he advised.

"Seems to be a family tradition," she muttered to herself as he faded into the darkness of the back room.

Staring at the fire, Emer heard his heavy footfalls as he returned, and when he did not speak, she turned to find him watching her with his mouth set in a grim line.

"We should eat and then rest. You can take the bed," he offered.

Emer met him at the table and accepted the bread he had already torn free for her.

"You said there were no hearts to break at home," Calder observed.

Tiredly, Emer hummed in acknowledgment.

"Not even Lachlan's?" he continued, and Emer paused the bite of food she was about to take, the honey dripping from the bread and down her hand.

Calder reached forward, dragging his thumb up her wrist and collecting the honey before bringing it to his mouth. Something about the fact that Emer was in her socks made the gesture far more intimate than it was, and for a moment, she forgot what his question had been.

"No. Not Lachlan," she answered.

Calder quirked a brow.

"I cared for him, but not like that," she explained.

Calder's features relaxed slightly, and he let out a thoughtful hum.

"Why did you wait until we left Lina's to ask me that?"

His eyes flicked up to her briefly, and as he turned his attention back to his plate, the corner of his lip twitched.

"Maybe I just don't like when others get to see that pretty pink blush of yours," he replied, banishing any words Emer had prepared to strike back with.

She had no words and no wholesome thoughts. What Emer did have, was several very bad ideas, all related to the Sea Raven, who still wasn't meeting her eyes.

"It's late. We should sleep," he urged, and Emer nodded, still not trusting herself to speak.

Moving to the sleeping area, Emer carefully stepped over the bedrolls he had laid out for himself and sat on the edge of the bed.

"Did my sister say anything to you while you were in the other room?" he asked, removing his boots and kicking them into a corner.

"Oh, yes, she wanted confirmation regarding a myriad of scandalous rumors. Rest assured, I told her the tales of the bloodthirsty seducer of women were completely false, and you are as threatening as a kitten," she goaded, curious as to what Lina could say that would put him on edge.

Calder turned, the lantern light casting his features in a sinister glow. "False, huh?" he asked, his eyes trailing her as he stepped forward.

"Not bloodthirsty?" he asked.

Emer shook her head.

"Not seductive?" he asked, running his tongue over his teeth.

She shook her head but bit her cheek to hide her growing smile. He came to stand in front of her, leaning down and squinting. "Do the stars in your eyes make it hard to see, or have you just not been paying attention? Because I know you saw me bait and beat Dempsey in the courtyard that day. More than that. I know you *kept* watching."

"Why did you do it?" she asked.

"For the same reason you didn't turn away. He deserved it."

Emer slipped beneath the covers, watching with rapt attention as Calder dropped to his knees. When he laid back, long legs stretched out and fingers laced behind his head, the room instantly felt smaller. In the quiet of the cottage, she could hear only her heart and Calder's slow, steady breaths.

"Relax, Em. It is not like this is your first time falling asleep with me in the room."

Sitting up sharply and equipped with an even thornier retort, Emer startled when their eyes met, Calder having made no attempt to sleep.

"I know that," she said ruefully before laying back down. "Also, I was intoxicated one of those times and very tired the other," she continued, unsure why she felt the need to make excuses and feeling immediately foolish.

"Shall I go break into the Kinkaids' pub and steal some ale?" he teased in a honeyed tone.

"So you can choke on it?" she spat in an equally saccharine voice.

"You know what," he grunted as he stood. "I changed my mind. I want the bed."

"You're not serious!"

"Almost exclusively."

The room was plunged into darkness a moment later as he extinguished the lantern they had carried over from Lina's. Emer muttered obscenities under her breath as she moved to free herself from the covers with more drama than was necessary. A yelp escaped her as her leg collided with Calder, who now stood at the side of the bed. He loomed over her, and even in the dark, she could feel his stare. "I didn't say you had to get up."

Despite being under several blankets, she felt exposed.

"You are, however, on my side."

He slipped his arms under her back and legs, his calloused palms warm against her bare legs.

"Do you know what they call a group of ravens, Merrow?" he asked in a low voice.

One of Emer's hands gripped the front of his tunic, and she shook her head though he couldn't see it.

"An unkindness," he remarked as he tossed her to the other side of the bed.

Muffled curses radiated from under the layers of blankets as the bed dipped under his weight.

"Thank you for warming it up," he cooed.

She swiped furiously at the mess of hair covering her face.

"I can't believe you just did that!"

"So dramatic," he chuckled.

She tried to kick him, but the blankets confined her legs.

Calder snorted.

While sleep eluded them, the silence found them quickly. As her eyes adjusted to the dark, she could make out the silhouette of his back. She expected his breath to steady as he relaxed. It did not.

"Want to know something?" he asked in a hushed tone. His question was met with silence Emer forced herself to maintain.

"I know you are awake. You are doing the hand-tapping thing you do when you are nervous."

She made a petulant noise.

"You might be the most dangerous creature I have ever slept with."

"You are not sleeping with me. You are lying next to me."

"Semantics," he said, and she felt the bed shift as he shrugged.

"Am I allowed to comment on how attractive it was watching you fight at the tavern yet? Or..." his voice trailed off. Her lips parted, but shock prevented her words from forming. "Later then," he added for her.

A pause.

"Sweet dreams. I look forward to hearing the ones about me in the morning."

"Not a chance," she sneered.

"So many lies from you tonight," his voice sounded deeper in the darkness of the room.

Emer gaped and assured herself that lack of sleep would also account for the poor choices she was entertaining and her loss of control over her wandering mental faculties.

Sleep. She needed sleep.

But when she closed her eyes, she saw the men in the alley and heard the slick sound of blood.

"Calder?" she asked quietly.

"Yes, Merrow?"

"Tell me something good, for I should not like to face even a small death with a heavy heart," she asked, referring to the belief that one's time asleep is its own kind of temporary death when the soul is separated from the realm of the living but not quite joined with the realm of the dead.

So, he told her a story of his favorite good thing.

"My mother used to say…" It started and continued until Emer fell asleep.

CHAPTER 26

It was cold. So incredibly cold. There was no sunlight to warm her or illuminate her climb. The walls of the Well were damp and mossy.

Deep gouges were carved into her palms—a record of the many times she had slipped from the rough stone and plunged back into the dark water. Her father's waning heartbeat echoed and ricocheted all around her. Her mother cried from somewhere above, and Emer covered her ears against the assault.

Reaching for the stones again, she tried to climb, but again, she slipped, her fingernails peeling back as she fell. When she crashed into the water this time, she did not sink. Instead, she collided with something floating. It rolled as she pushed herself up and away.

The dead eyes of Lachlan peered back at her through the darkness. The only thing she could hear over her screams was Finn telling her that she had failed.

Emer tried to curl into herself and away from the horror of her nightmare, but she was met with resistance. The more she focused on the tangible sensation of the weight restraining her, the more the illusory surroundings of her dream began to fade. The macabre bled away, and the darkness eased, taking with them the chill that had gripped her skin, leaving her with the sensation of cascading warmth.

Unwilling to relinquish her contentment to the waking world, she permitted herself one more moment to keep her eyes closed and her soul quiet. One more deep breath before she faced the day. The scent that filled her lungs conjured thoughts of warm whiskey and ocean air.

Eyelids fluttering open, she watched dust dance in the air through beams of light filtering past boards over the window. A languid smile tugged at the corners of her mouth as her head rolled to the side, bringing her lips against something solid. Calder's palm pressed against her collarbone—his long fingers curved over her shoulder, holding her.

After several surprised blinks, Emer's gaze trailed down where his forearm draped over her chest, snagging on how it rose and fell with her breaths. The arm not currently swallowing her whole was propped under his head, face turned down and out of view.

Beneath his hold, she looked small, but not in a way that made her feel inconsequential or fragile. He held her like she was something precious worth coveting. Like she was his.

Emer shifted, becoming acutely aware that one of Calder's legs was nestled between hers. Her movement caused him to stir, but he did not wake. Instead, he pulled her closer, shifting so that the sunlight now brushed his pouted lips.

Calder's eyes flew open as if the weight of her attention had become a tangible caress. Unguarded and bathed in the morning sun, she learned that throughout the deep stormy blue of his gaze were thin lines of gray that crossed at sharp angles. The knowledge felt like a secret—something known only by those he allowed close enough.

He blinked hard, and his fingers twitched against the skin of her shoulder where they had slipped beneath the loose tunic.

"You had a nightmare," he said quickly, his voice rough with sleep.

"Oh, right." She nodded subtly, the nightmare forgotten. "Calder?"

"Yeah?" he asked with a swallow.

"Not having a nightmare anymore," she confirmed.

"Right," he echoed, pulling his arm away, only to realize his lower body was just as entangled.

Clearing his throat, he rolled to his back, adjusting the blanket over his hips. Emer shifted to her side, no longer hiding her grin.

"Don't," he groaned into his hands and rubbed them over his face.

Emer smirked, her delight growing the longer he avoided looking at her. Despite his efforts to present himself as annoyed, he was clearly flustered. An accomplishment she wanted to be passed down through oral tradition alongside all the other tales about the Morvran. Looking at him now, hair mussed and features boyish, she couldn't recall any others. She did know that none of them captured this version of him. Like the ley lines in his eyes, this Morvran was a secret.

"Don't what?" she asked.

He turned his head slightly, peeking at her from underneath the hands pressed into his face, and Emer caught the slightest color in his cheeks. Propping herself up, she tugged at his arm.

"Calder Morvran, are you... blushing?" she asked, pulling harder.

He snatched her wrist in his other hand, pulling her until her upper body was draped over him.

"One more word and I promise I will make your cheeks far redder," he warned.

"How?" she challenged.

There was a flicker of surprise in his eyes before he arched slightly and lifted his chin, bringing his nose to hers. When she didn't pull away, he angled his head, allowing his mouth to brush hers in the ghost of a kiss.

Emer's lips parted as she sucked in a sharp breath, which was quickly stolen by the feel of his smile.

"Sometimes." He turned his head from side to side, drawing their lips together and apart—a tempting tide she could drown in. "Like when you were standing by the fire last night, standing in my home, I let myself imagine it," he said dreamily, his mouth still coasting over hers.

"Imagine what?" she whispered back.

"Getting to keep you," he confessed.

The words were a spell that wove magic through her body, pulling her lower and into a vision of what that life would look like.

Another featherlight brush and he was gone.

"But I will not be my father, and you won't choose this place and all its horrors over yours, so we should get up, or else I will be too tempted to prove how quickly I can make us both forget that."

Emer's attention snapped back to him. She searched his eyes for something to grasp to halt the strange sensation of falling.

He brought his hands up to either side of her face, pulling her back down and placing a kiss on her forehead, letting his lips linger. When he pulled back, he gave her a soft smile.

"There's that blush," he said, stroking his thumb over her cheek. "We should go. The tide was on my side when it brought you, but time seems to hate us both."

The desire that had been warming her veins suddenly burned like shame with the knowledge he was right. Her father's life depended on her, and instead of being up before the sun, she was in his arms, thinking of all the ways she could forget.

Shifting her so he could sit up, he bent over to slip on his boots before standing and looking down at her. He studied her the same way he had when they first met but rather than devoting his intensity to puzzling out where she had come from, he seemed content to memorize her just where she was.

Still dazed, all Emer could do was stare back.

"I'm going to clean up. Your clothes should be here soon. If someone knocks, don't answer it. Wait until they leave to open the door," he advised, then left.

In the silence of his departure, Emer felt the acute ache of losing something she didn't even know she had held. It joined the ache of knowing all that she had the potential to lose, and she sucked a sharp breath because, in the stillness, she felt just how much she *hurt*.

Pressing her nails into her palms, Emer stood from the bed and made her way into the living area, where she proceeded to pace and spare brief glances at the door of the bathing room until a sharp impact against the door drew her attention. Per Calder's instructions, she waited several moments before opening the door, and when she did, she found a neatly stacked bundle of clothes.

As she began to close the door, a piece of parchment nailed to it caught her eye. "*To friendship*" was scrolled elegantly on the note, and from the nail hung a thin strip of leather that threaded through one of the several naturally occurring holes of a pale stone.

Emer ripped the note free and clutched the necklace with a smile, savoring the weight of the gift and the sense of belonging that accompanied it.

Back in Calder's room, she quickly donned the light, fitted tunic and dark breeches. Slipping on the corset, she tightened the laces so it hugged her waist and hips. Lastly, she retrieved the necklace, tying the leather around her neck and letting the weight of the stone slip beneath her tunic to rest between her breasts.

Reaching for the door, she paused at the sound of hushed arguing from the other room. When the voices fell silent, she exited with more noise than necessary. Calder loomed in the doorway of the main entry, staring at the male caller in a way that would have most individuals backing away slowly. Hearing her arrival, he turned to acknowledge her.

When the stranger attempted to peer past him, Calder gripped the door and pulled it closer, blocking the man's view. The sun caught on the signet ring and various heirlooms that now adorned Calder's hand. Though, by the standards of Isle Basalt, he was no royal—in this town, he was king, and that thought caused the traitorous flutter of Emer's heart to make an appearance. The jewelry was not the only change. While his dark stubble remained, his thick onyx hair was now free from the grime of the journey and curled at his brow. The fresh black tunic and breeches he wore were darker, but even these were well-worn.

Calder assessed Emer in kind. When his eyes lingered on her corset, she wondered if he was once again allowing himself to imagine.

A throat cleared from the other side of the door, and Calder stepped back, closing it entirely before making his way to his belongings resting in the corner of the room.

"It appears my sister is not quite finished with her... *hospitality*. I need a moment with her this morning before we leave," Calder explained.

The heaviness of their earlier conversation caused her shoulders to fall, and despite the added disappointment of this latest news, she nodded.

Calder's movements were clipped as he slid into an array of leather straps and fixed his various weapons to his person. He had an ax at his waist, a knife on his thigh, and two short swords at his hips. Those, combined with the tension in his jaw, had her fearing for the safety of the man she could hear pacing just outside.

Unsheathing one of the knives, he flipped it so he was holding it by the blade and tapped Emer playfully on the nose with the hilt. "What if I promise you a honey cake and give you my blessing to stab the messenger?" Calder asked, offering her the knife to replace the one she had lost, nodding towards the door.

Snatching the blade, she shot him a disapproving look and slipped it into her boot.

"I wager before we leave, your fingers will be itching to inflict *at least* a flesh wound," he swore.

With a sigh and a crack of his neck, Calder opened the door and gestured for Emer to follow. The man, who had ceased his pacing, turned on his heels. He let out a relieved breath as if he expected Calder to sneak out the back window, which, given how they had arrived, was not entirely unfounded. With an outstretched arm, he moved past Calder and towards Emer. "I was sad to hear I missed your arrival last night. I'm Ewan. *Dia duit.*"

The butchery of her native greeting almost caused her to sneer, but she quickly found herself more concerned by how he was raising her hand to his lips.

Calder's hand clamped down on his shoulder, pulling him hard enough to turn him away from Emer. "Keep to task, Ewan," he demanded, gesturing him on.

"Of course," Ewan responded stiffly.

The lane they walked was cast in shadows by the surrounding pine and yew trees, revealing glimpses of the loch between them. Ewan quickly proved he could fill the silence with various anecdotes of the village, which, by all accounts, was well-established and home to many skilled workers, warriors, and artisans. Emer soon realized she could not let her gaze linger on anything too long lest it invite further commentary.

"Ewan." Calder paused, giving the man time to shift his attention from Emer. "Is there a reason you are giving me a tour of my village?"

"I just thought the lady—" Ewan began.

"The *lady* does not care about the native flowers. If you want to impress her, pick something more violent or magical. Or both... like Aggie," Calder said with a wave of his hand.

"Aggie?" Emer asked, speaking for the first time since they left the cottage.

Calder leaned towards her and, in a conspiratorial voice, answered, "Our witch."

He spared Ewan a smug sideward glance before returning his attention to the path ahead.

"I'm sorry... what?" Emer balked.

"Oh, she is harmless. Unless you try to play her in a game of chance, then she is most definitely a witch," Ewan explained.

A statement that caused Calder to let out a derisive snort because, while Sea Ravens were gifted with magical talents, witches could draw upon the magic, possess it—wield it. This not only made Aggie one of the most interesting residents, but also one of the most formidable.

Emer's thoughts were cast back to childhood, hiding beneath the sheets from the noonday witches said to hunt disobedient children. But witches were not just simply stories designed to scare young ones. When unexplained things occurred in her village or one of its neighbors, there would often be talks of Fae or the Old Wives—powerful witches older than the tomes that held their secrets. Whispers of the influence of the Maidens of the Moon would sweep through the night when celestial bodies grew strange. It was often said that those who did not heed the cautionary tales learned quickly that *one does not cross a witch more than once.*

Ewan gestured to one of the cottages across the village square and, as if conjured by the mention, an older woman appeared at one of the open windows. She removed a candle nearing the end of its life and replaced it with a fresh one, already burning. An act that was particularly strange given that the sun was high in the sky and would be for some time. She then proceed to riffle through a stack of cards before placing several in the sill and studying them with a furrowed brow.

"Why the candle?" Emer asked, tilting her head.

"Oh, Aggie calls it her sentry. Something about blue flames warning of the presence of an evil spirit. She has a candle burning in that window morning, noon, and night. Seems like such a waste, but who am I to tell a witch what to do with her candles?" Ewan said with a shrug.

"Who, indeed," Calder muttered as he paused and urged Emer towards one of the structures.

"Of my two promises this morning... which one are you finding more appealing?" Calder asked with a sly grin.

Emer glared at him. "Honey. Cakes," she said slowly, and Calder shrugged.

"Slight change of plans, Ewan. The Merrow requires sweets, and I would be loath to tempt her hunger if I were you," Calder explained, a glint in his eye suggesting he might hope the man did just that.

Ewan hesitated momentarily, his gaze darting around as if expecting Lina to appear out of thin air and reprimand him for the detour.

Before the man could speak, Calder turned. "I wasn't asking, Cunningham," he called back, leading Emer towards the bakery.

Warm air carrying the scent of baked goods and all things saccharine greeted them as they opened the door, followed quickly by Calder barking, "Oh, what the fuck!"

Surprise flickered over Banner's features before he schooled them into cool indifference and pushed from the counter where he had been leaning.

"Has Lina recruited you in her schemes to keep us here?" Calder asked harshly.

"I just arrived. Coincidentally, *her* schemes are not what called me away from the keep. I was asked to look into Dempsey's disappearance. I think I'm on to something," he replied.

Emer would have been concerned by the mention of Dempsey's name if not for the knowing grin Banner shot her as he spoke. He paused for a moment, taking her in. Gone was the broken girl he had wrapped with bandages. "Looking good, little monster. The Isle suits you."

Something about the approval in Banner's expression made

Emer preen because though his words were often dripping in flirtation, his regard seemed far harder to win.

"So, you were looking into a crime you had a hand in covering up... and?" Calder let his question trail off.

"*And*. Given I know precisely where the fucker is, I decided to use this time to come home and water my plants. Obviously."

"Which fucker?" Lina asked from where she stood, leaning in the door frame.

Calder pinched the bridge of his nose.

"Mornin', Li. A dead fucker," Banner answered before turning his attention back to Calder. "What are you doing here?"

"We experienced a complication," Calder said.

Lina snorted.

Banner straightened. "Did you kill those people in Arborlynn?"

"Person!" Calder corrected. "I killed *a* person in Arborlynn."

"Really? Because the overly chatty man I passed early this morning said three. In fact, he talked about it so much that he almost joined them," Banner said with a roll of his eyes.

"That could have been unrelated. Did he say where they were found?" Calder asked.

"In the alley near the tavern," Banner advised, confirming Calder's fear that something else was hunting that night. The question was whether or not they caught what they were looking for. He glanced at Emer, and Banner tracked the movement.

"Either the Elders don't like you, or their beasts just really do," Banner observed, and there was something unsettlingly true in his words.

Sensing her unease, Calder stroked his knuckles down her spine, and the thread of dread tugging at her began to ease.

"Depending on the day, sometimes I think it's both," she sighed.

Calder led Emer to the fountain's edge outside the bakery, where she sat contently with her dandelion tea and honey cake.

She trailed her fingers over the soft purple buds of the heather that sprouted through the stones at the base.

"Lina!" shouted a man in the distance as he weaved through various passersby and crossed the square.

"Okir, if you are here to win back your coin, you have a better chance of Emer here agreeing to ride a horse through the village naked," she greeted.

"That's not happening," Calder interjected.

"You heard the man," Lina said, crossing her arms with a smirk.

Okir, a man with kind features colored tan from extensive time at sea, shook his head. "Elders, Lina. The scribe needs to speak to you about one of the recent raids. They've gotten worse these last few days. Ideally, both of you." He gestured to Calder.

"Nice to see you too, Okir," Banner chimed in.

The man shot Banner an incredulous look. "I'll be sure to call for you if we need anyone dead."

"Rude," Banner barked. "I have good ideas," he muttered into his tea.

The siblings shared a brief glance, and it was clear that while many things between them remained unresolved, they were a united front when it came to their village.

"Enjoy the morning and wait for me. I'll be right back," Calder instructed Emer as he leaned forward and took a bite of her honey cake before darting away.

As the pair left, Lina said faintly, "You really are the worst."

"As much as I would love to stay and see what kind of trouble you can stir up, I actually do need to water my plants," Banner said with a bow.

"Poisonous ones?" Emer called out as he walked away.

Banner turned on his heels, walking backward and smiling at her so alluring and sharp that she was sure it had made more than one heart bleed.

"You know how I like pretty, murderous things," he answered with a wink before turning and striding into the stream of people.

With the butter and sugar melting in her mouth and the tea warming her belly, Emer stared down at her reflection in the fountain. Her eyes were not focused on her own features but on the way the sky and edges of the town were captured on the surface. The longer she stared, the more she seemed to be able to see.

A murky figure took shape in the reflection, a soft smile on their face, made slightly crooked by a thick scar running through their upper lip. When she turned, she found a face free of scars but wrinkled with age. Emer, startled at the elderly woman's unexpected nearness, knocked over her tea.

"Didn't mean to scare you! I was just curious what you saw," the old woman said with a smirk.

"Nothing. Just a little jumpy is all," Emer advised, lifting her hand dripping with tea and giving it a shake.

The woman raised a brow.

"The constellations in your eyes would lead me to believe otherwise," the woman observed, reaching out to take Emer's nearly empty teacup.

"It's Aggie, right?" Emer asked.

The woman hummed in acknowledgment, swirling the remaining tea in the cup several times before allowing the liquid to fall to the stones. Eyes narrowing, Aggie's brow furrowed as she studied the cup. Leaning forward, Emer stared down at the bits of tea coating the inside and then back to the woman whose face was now pinched in concern.

"Elders, what is it now?" Emer asked with evident exasperation.

The woman's eyes snapped up to hers, wide and worried.

"What did you see?" Emer asked again, more urgently.

"Drowning," the woman answered quietly.

Saltwater coated Emer's tongue, and a shiver rolled down her spine as she recalled slipping beneath the waves.

"I'll be keeping my boots on the ground for some time then," she remarked, shifting slightly away from the offending cup.

"There are different types of drowning, child. It is unclear if it is your body or your spirit that cannot breathe," the woman said softly.

Emer swallowed—the honey cake in her stomach soured.

"Why would my spirit not be able to breathe?" she asked warily.

Aggie's eyes turned apologetic, and Emer knew the answer before the woman spoke.

Grief.

CHAPTER 27

Emer didn't have a destination in mind as she rose and excused herself, only the deep need to escape the prediction and the doubt that coiled around her heart, strangling the fragile hope she had been guarding there.

"Take care of our Sea Raven, starling," Aggie called after her.

Pressing her palms into her eyes, Emer mentally clawed and pushed at the words, trying to change their shape to fit a different story. She tried to rationalize that the grief could have been about Lachlan, but she shook it away as soon as she had the thought. Losing him hurt, but it was not the kind of hurt that had someone gasping for breath.

Emer yelped as her body crashed against another.

"Careful now, love."

Ewan's voice grated against her already raw temper, as did his hands now firmly fixed to her waist from their collision. "Sorry, Ewan, I didn't see you. Are you okay?" she asked, attempting to push back from him.

He grinned at her, his hands tightening slightly as he said, "I think my pride may have taken most of the impact."

A different unease replaced Emer's previous panic as his gaze raked over her. She bent back, testing to see if she could reach the knife in her boot, and thinking about Calder's earlier promise. She pushed against his shoulder once more, and the moment his grip eased, she stepped back.

"Are you so unaccustomed to someone trying to care for you that you assume I mean you harm?" Ewan asked, cocking his head to the side.

The interest in his eyes was suddenly replaced with something that caused her rage to burn even hotter than before. Pity.

"I feel I need to have a stern talk with my friend. A delicate flower such as yourself needs to be tended to."

The thought of Ewan demanding anything of Calder caused her to laugh. It was a dark and humorless laugh that she was certain the Cold One himself would have been proud of. Given Ewan's shit-eating grin, she was certain he attributed her laughter to his charm rather than fantasizing about causing him physical harm.

"I told you. She's not impressed by flowers."

Immediately, Ewan's body went rigid.

Calder stood tall as he approached, his chin held high and his eyes sharp. The hand that wore the death rune opened and closed at his side.

"He touched you," Calder said in Emer's native tongue.

Struck speechless, Emer did not immediately give meaning to the words.

Still speaking the language of Rest, Calder echoed the words he had spoken at the Alder Barrel.

All you have to do is ask.

It was different hearing them now. They were not the poor imitation of a man seeking to impress. They were not simply words memorized and stored in his mind for occasional use.

Calder sounded like home.

If she traced the words back through the air, they would lead straight to his heart, in the space he had carved out for his mother.

Those words, Emer realized, were not just of *her* people. Calder was his mother's son, and the words he spoke belonged just as much to him as they did to Emer.

Calder's muscles grew tense as he waited for Emer's answer. Although Ewan did not know precisely what Calder had asked, his expression gave a fairly good indication.

Finally, Emer answered, savoring how the familiar words felt on her tongue as she told him she was fine.

Calder did not acknowledge how breathless she sounded.

Emer did not acknowledge his smirk.

"Luck seems to be in your favor, Ewan. Had Emer seen you as a threat, she most likely would have stabbed you. She has a nasty little habit of turning her blade on those who take liberties with their proximity," Calder mused casually.

Ewan Cunningham had the color of someone who had spent time in the shadow of others for so long that even though the heat would surely burn him, the prospect of time in the light was too alluring to resist. While he demonstrated a level of deference for Lina, it was clear in how his eyes narrowed on Calder that it did not translate to both of the Morvran siblings.

"Tell me, Morvran. Does that knowledge come from experience?" There was a triumphant defiance in Ewan's tone.

Emer turned, expecting to see Calder's familiar glower, but found something far more startling. Calder was *smiling*.

A smile that was genuinely pleased in a hungry sort of way—all teeth.

"If you are asking if I have taken liberties with my proximity to her. Yes, enthusiastically and frequently. Have I been stabbed?" Calder dragged his gaze to Emer. "Only once."

Further proving his point, Calder took her hand, intertwined their fingers, and pulled her away. "Always a pleasure, Ewan," he called.

"The storm grew violent last night. Surely you would not risk her safety by leaving without knowing the road's condition." Ewan challenged.

His expression was smug as his eyes darted to Emer like he expected her to appreciate his concern for her safety by pointing out a perceived oversight on Calder's part.

Calder glanced at him out of the corner of his eye.

Tsk. Tsk. Tsk.

The sharp and mocking click of Calder's tongue cut through the quiet. Each one was a blow meant for Ewan, but Emer felt the warning roll down her spine—bone by bone.

When he flicked his eyes back to hers, she saw the glint of mischief flash just before he blinked them closed. When they reopened, the ice blue and streaks of gray were being swallowed by onyx. The darkness spread from the center of his eyes and bled into the white like ink washing over parchment. Before long, his gaze was consumed entirely, a void of darkness staring back at her. Not at her, through her, and Emer had the sudden thought that perhaps she should be afraid. Instead, she leaned forward, captive to the pools of nothingness before her. She did not move. She did not speak. She did not glance at Ewan, who seemed entirely unsurprised by the strange turn of events.

Calder's jaw worked momentarily, and then a satisfied hum rumbled from his throat.

"Wouldn't you know, a fine ride indeed," Calder corrected.

A blink and the darkness had receded. His shoulders stretched back as he lifted his chin and drank in Emer's shock.

If Ewan had given a parting comment, she did not hear it. In truth, all she could hear was her heartbeat in time with Calder's heavy footfalls against the cobblestone. She gaped at him unabashedly, but her companion continued on as if he had not just transformed into a creature of myth before her very eyes.

It was Calder who spoke first.

"Raven got your tongue, Merrow?" he asked wryly.

She just blinked. Her mind worked to organize the details of what she'd seen. When he spoke of Sea Ravens' talents, she had not expected for his body to transform into something not quite mortal.

Magic. The singular thought ricocheted in her mind.

Calder was a little bit magic.

"What... what was that, Calder?" she asked, the faintest hint of awe in her voice.

"Me proving a point since apparently you riding into town at my side, on my horse, in my clothes was not sufficient."

She shot him a glare.

"Ah," he remarked insincerely. "It is my talent— the ability to project my consciousness into ravens. I can see what they see, hear what they hear, and guide their direction," he explained. "Careful, if you keep looking at me like that, I might think you are impressed."

"And Lina's?" Emer asked.

"My sister has a very different type of sight. She is a War Weaver, but I believe you would be more familiar with the term Seer."

Emer's mind conjured Aggie's words once more.

"She can see the future?"

"It is not like how I see you now. She told me once it is like coming up from beneath water. Too bright and slightly out of focus. I think that's because the vision precedes the actual event. It's blurry because it can change," he advised.

He explained how those with sight didn't have complete control over their visions but that they could see those nearing death and strategize accordingly, weaving a different future in battle.

Emer's steps halted, and the resistance of his hand in hers stopped him as she thought of what he had said earlier about his talent. She considered all the times she'd run. She recalled the raven's cry that distracted Dempsey and how Calder's eyes looked when he first found her that night. She had never truly been his shadow—he had been hers.

"I was never going to escape you, was I?" The words left her with a slight chuckle.

A wicked grin pulled at his lips.

"Not a chance," he confirmed.

CHAPTER 28

Securing her satchel to Aven's saddle, she brought the flap down, turning to see Calder exchanging hushed words with his sister. She had stared at his back enough from her days hidden beneath a hood to know he was not particularly pleased with the direction their conversation was going in.

Whatever the distressing topic had been was no longer being discussed by the time Emer approached. Lina greeted her with a smile that stopped short of her eyes.

"As sorry as I am for the cause of your journey, I am grateful that it brought you here. Even if it was not for as long as I would have liked," she offered.

"Earlier, Calder told me about your talent, that you can see those nearing death in battle." Emer's eyes filled with a silent plea, and before she could answer, Lina nodded in understanding.

"When my mother died, I had not seen it. It felt like my chest was being ripped open. I had no evidence as to why I believed something happened to her... I just knew. I sent a raven to Calder, and he immediately began searching for her."

Lina's hands found Emer's.

"If your father was gone, I think you would know. Raven or not," Lina advised with another firm squeeze.

Emer closed her eyes, thinking of her father. She imagined the place in her heart that warmed in his presence, the place that swelled when she made him proud, the place that ached when he became ill and she faced the potential of losing him. The place she was certain would be cut from her the moment she lost him.

Lina was right.

A daughter knows, Raven or not.

Aggie's words crept back in, and Emer pressed a hand into her chest, each beat a grain of sand falling through the glass. They were running out of time.

Lina stepped away to address her brother.

"I've requested your cottage be prepared for your stay upon your return. Perhaps you will consider keeping our lovely friend here until after Samhain."

Calder watched her through accusatory eyes—something wordless and heated passing between them. Unfazed by her brother's fury, Lina added, "She could light the bonfire. That was always Mamaí's favorite part. She would want Emer to do it."

Gone was the boy Emer had watched in bed just that morning—this Calder was made of frost-covered stone. A thick tension settled, filling the quiet and cut only by the sharpness of Calder's tone when he finally answered.

"No."

A single word with an edge so sharp that Emer wanted to reel back to avoid its bite and a sting that would last disproportionately longer than it took to speak.

"Are we done?" he asked, and for a moment, it looked like Lina was going to argue, but instead, she dropped her head and stepped forward, hugging him stiffly.

"May the road rise up to meet you, brother," Lina offered.

Hugging Emer next, Lina whispered softly, "Bring him back to us, okay?"

Emer did not think Lina meant just from the Well, and another corner of her heart—an uncharted place not belonging to her family—ached.

Aggie's words still lingered heavily as dusk fell over the realm and the darkness of the landscape matched that of Emer's thoughts. Crestfallen, she tilted her head back, looking up at the moon and willing the tears she felt burning her eyes to not fall. As she blinked away the moisture, she could have sworn the clouds sharpened and shifted in the moonlight.

It was not uncommon for her imagination to paint the landscape with her anxiety, much the same way children saw monsters under their beds in the dead of night. However, this time, the monsters were not under her bed... they were in the sky, falling like cast-out stars.

"Calder?" she breathed at the exact moment he cursed, and Alabaster cried.

Looking around frantically, he shouted, "The trees. Get to the trees!"

Leaving the main path, Emer urged her horse into a full gallop. Calder steered Danu to Aven's flank, racing alongside Emer and guiding her toward where the trees bowed to each other over the path, their union producing a shadowy fortress of limbs and leaves.

When Emer dared a look, dark forms with large wings dropped from the sky. "What are those!" she shrieked over the pounding of hooves and her heart.

"Sluagh," Calder bellowed, his knuckles white against the reins.

"Sluagh! Aren't they attracted to dying things? We are not dying things!" Emer reasoned, panic lacing her voice.

"They are here for me."

Calder's words almost stopped her in her tracks. Her head

whipped to the side as she watched him through her wind-blown hair.

"But you... you're not..." Emer stuttered.

"Little Bastard, Alabaster, isn't a pet raven, Merrow. He is an intimus. The mark of a fractured soul," he confessed, proving that his mother's death had caused grief so profound that it attracted not only a creature meant to mend the damage but also the beasts that wanted to lap at the wounds.

Once inside the trees, Calder turned to Emer, whose blood was pounding in her ears and muting his voice.

"Merrow, listen to me. We need to separate. You ride down the tunnel, and I will lead them away," he explained hurriedly.

Emer shook her head, fear so tight around her throat that she couldn't speak her protest. Calder reached out and tugged on her reins, pulling her closer.

"Breathe," he demanded, and she listened.

"I may hate Little Bastard with every bone in my fucking body for being a daily reminder of my grief, but the Sluagh cannot take my soul while he is watching over me. They can, however, hurt you. I will find you again, I promise," he said firmly.

Before she could argue, Calder smacked Aven, sending them racing down the tunnel. She looked back just in time to see Calder breaking into the trees.

Peering into the darkness and waiting for her eyes to adjust, it felt as though the shadows peered back. Aven's ears twitched and Emer had to fight to stay mounted as the horse began to rear and shift nervously. Large bodies flew overhead, searching for entry through the canopy. A terrible screeching from above cut through the gaps in the trees. Emer's veins seized with ice at the realization that Calder had been wrong. They hadn't come for him. It was her sadness they craved.

Deeper in the forest, where the trees were dense, Emer paused, listening for the sound of their wings and snarls. Instead, she heard a faint chime ring through the air, sharp and quick. In the distance, was the soft glow of what appeared to be a lantern illuminating someone lounging on their back across one of the lower branches that stretched over the path.

Although details of his features were obscured, reducing him to a lithe silhouette, it was clear his form was too large to be a woman and too elegant to be a Sluagh. One leg lazily hung from the branch, swinging along with the tune he was humming.

Above him, his long fingers idly curled and swept through the air as if playing an instrument, and the other hand absentmindedly flicked a coin into the air. A chime rang out each time he caught it.

Below him, the light was cast to the ground in beautiful shapes and a kaleidoscope of otherworldly colors. Emer was transfixed as the shapes swayed and moved over the ground.

The humming stopped.

Looking back at the man, his shadowy form now faced her, both legs hanging from the branches. He stared down with a predatory tilt of his head. Slowly, he leaned forward, allowing his youthful face to catch the lantern light. His angular features softened as he looked down and an amused smile tugged at his thin lips. Decidedly not monstrous, yet something in her soul trembled.

She had been so captivated by his unnatural eyes, the color of purple heather, and the mischief within them that it took her several long moments to take in the rest of his person. His skin was pale. It was not pale in the way that some look when ill but like moonlight, possessing a soft glow. His hair was silvery-white, falling over his forehead to his straight brow. While he looked only in his twenties, something about his gaze and the stories it seemed to hold made Emer wonder if he was much older.

What was most shocking about the stranger was not how utterly unique he was. It was not his striking beauty or how out of place he seemed amongst the branches. It was that he was no stranger at all.

The man who stared down at her was the same man who had taken the blow from the chair in the Alder Barrel, but before she could acknowledge the recognition, another shriek tore through the air. The Sluagh were getting closer.

Emer flinched at the sound, her breath catching in her lungs, and Aven again reared, almost throwing her off. The man reached his hand down to her, and without thinking, she accepted it, standing on Aven's saddle before allowing him to pull her up on the branch and back towards the heart of the tree.

He urged her down and crouched before her, bringing the lantern between them. Finger to his lips, he breathed a *shhh*, blowing out the candle.

The branches shook as several Sluagh landed on the limbs higher up. The next scream caused even the darkness to shudder.

Emer let out a whimper, and the man's hand covered her mouth. The smell of smoke tickled her senses like the warm ash-covered stones of a hearth. It was mingled with a familiar sweetness that conjured memories of the wine she would enjoy during solstice celebrations. It reminded her of the warmth it left in her belly and the pink it brought to her cheeks. They were memories that wrapped her like a blanket—content and safe. She closed her eyes and willed those memories of the past to block out the present.

Warm air stirred violently, whipping around them. The trees creaked, and the leaves rustled so loudly that it almost drowned out the cries of the Sluagh. The panic coursing through Emer had sweat dripping from her brow, and even the stone around her neck felt hot.

Then, as quickly as it started, everything stopped. The wind died down, and the night grew still. The hand over her mouth slowly pulled away, and through the darkness, he asked, "How do you hide it?"

At the furrow between her brow, he clarified, "How very sad you are."

Emer sucked in a sharp breath but did not answer him.

After a few moments, when she remained silent, the lantern sparked again.

"They are gone. They cannot take you anymore," he said solemnly, and Emer nodded, taking his hand and making their way out of the sanctuary of the tree.

Emer's legs still felt unsteady as she jumped down, looking in the immediate vicinity for the horse that was most certainly not there.

The sound of a rider barreling through the tunnel drew their attention, and soon, Calder emerged from the darkness. Relief flooded his eyes, seeing Emer safe and whole, but quickly shifted to something more violent as he took in the stranger beside her and unsheathed his sword.

"Well, that's just rude," the stranger huffed.

"Calder!" Emer barked. "Put your sword away. He protected me!"

Calder's eyes narrowed, suspicion joining the existing menace.

"In case you are wondering why dear *Calder* is looking at me like he wants to eat me..." the man spoke to Emer, his eyes narrowing. "I think it's because he does not like my kind much."

Something behind the man twitched, and for the first time, she noticed the long, gossamer wings. When her eyes snapped back up to his, he winked.

"You're Fae," Emer remarked in wonderment.

Releasing the lantern, now suspended in the air, the Fae slipped his hands into his pockets and rocked on his heels.

"Keane," he introduced. "I enjoy long walks through heather fields, wine, the harp, and mushrooms... not the kind for soup," he punctuated his speech with a wide grin. "And you?"

"Absolutely not," Calder scolded, which earned a bristle from the newcomer.

"If you think I am the kind of common trickster who needs to con someone into revealing their true name, then I am offended," Keane scoffed.

"I think you are Fae, full stop. She has no interest in your stories, secrets, or anything else you have to offer," Calder gritted between his teeth.

Before, the coldness of his voice would have scraped like ice against Emer's spine, but instead, she felt the swift heat of resentment flood her veins.

As if sensing it, Keane turned to her with a sly grin, "Darling, didn't your mother ever warn you about controlling men? Sure, he is dark and brooding... but you are a strong, independent woman. Let us rid ourselves of his suffocating masculinity."

He extended his hand, and there was familiarity in the offering and fondness in his eyes. A fondness that remained despite the fact that Emer did not return the gesture.

Calder dismounted Danu, rolling his wrist and twisting his sword as he drew closer.

Keane tilted his head and smiled, "I rather think that is not a game you want to play with me."

The wind heated and stirred once more, and although Keane's hands remained in his pockets, it was clear that he had also drawn his weapon.

Calder glared and Keane responded with a shrug.

"I'm going to give you a pass just this once as it's hard to believe a boyishly charming face like mine could end you without lifting a finger. But I will remind you that the Sluagh feared me. Why do you think that is?" Keane asked cockily.

"Because, as I was saying, you are dangerous. Hence the fucking sword," Calder said curtly.

"And again, I say, rude. Do you see me just whipping it out every time I see a Sea Raven? No, because, unlike *your* kind, I can be civil," he remarked, crossing his arms in offense.

"Your kind doesn't know the meaning of civil," Calder countered.

Keane rolled his eyes and gazed absently at the canopy above. "Yes, because fighting and fucking your way across the Isle is oh-so-civil," he purred. "Shall I regale your lovely companion with the tales of your pious people?"

"We have no time for your ravings," Calder sneered.

"Oh... but, Raven, ravings are for madmen, and man, I am not," he retorted smugly.

Emer inserted herself into the break in their verbal sparring.

"Calder, if he wanted to hurt me, he could have more than once."

Calder's eyes widened slightly before saying, "What is that supposed to mean."

Emer recounted the events that took place the night of the brawl as succinctly as possible, pointing to each respective party when applicable, pausing periodically to allow Keane to confirm or deny her account where it concerned him. However, aside from raising his hand and clarifying that he had not interfered but acted as a supportive presence, he did not interrupt or deny any of what she'd said.

Calder crossed his arms at his wrists, sword still in hand. While his gaze had not strayed as Emer spoke, it was evident by the sharpening of his features that his thoughts had already shifted.

"I think I would have remembered seeing you," he argued.

Not one to balk at a challenge, Keane clicked his tongue and tapped one long finger against his chin.

"Well, you were on the other side of the pub staring at a rather large set of breasts if I recall."

Unlike with the previous verbal strikes, at this one, Calder's lips pulled back into a cruel smile, "And you were busy staring at *her*."

It was not a question but an accusation.

"If you think you can take her, you are mistaken," Calder threatened.

All mirth vanished from Keane's expression as he said, "If you think you can protect her, so are you."

Emer stepped back.

"If either of you think that you can continue to speak about me like I am not here. Then fuck you both." She scoffed before stomping into the darkness.

After shooting Keane a withering glare, Calder snatched Danu's reins and followed her. Rolling his head between his shoulders, Keane turned on his heels and joined them.

"I missed the part where I said you could come with us," Calder spat with clenched teeth.

"I am surprised that with your astute observation skills, you also missed the part where I didn't ask," Keane returned from where he casually trailed behind them.

Something large shifted in the trees to Emer's right, and she paused, dropping low and retrieving the knife from her boot. Before she stood, Calder and Keane were at either side of her. They released a collective sigh at the sight of Aven trotting out of the shadows.

Still shaken, he nuzzled apologetically against Emer, who took his reins and walked him through the remainder of the tunnel.

Emer paid little attention to the two men who continued to follow her or their hushed arguing. Even after they left the tunnel and Emer and Calder once more mounted their horses, the pace was slow, and Keane walked steadily at their sides.

"Still following?" Calder groaned, looking at Keane out of the corner of his eyes.

"Still breathing?" Keane shot back.

"You must have been following her for a while if you managed to protect her during the brawl in addition to the Sluagh," Calder observed.

Keane's hand flexed around the coin in his pocket.

"Am I to believe your intentions are purely altruistic when you have been stalking her?"

Keane let out a snort. "More so than yours," he challenged.

"Why?" Calder's voice was cold and calm.

Emer, having heard the exchange, stopped Aven and turned expectantly.

"Would you believe I'm here for jinx and jollies," Keane offered coyly.

When his answer received unamused stares, he dropped his shoulders and nodded. Pulling the coin from his pocket, he held it up for their appraisal. It was only about the size of a silver piece, but rather than solid metal, it was gold on the edges and vibrant green glass in the center with flecks of gold suspended in the green.

Calder's eyes shot up to Keane's.

"Centuries ago, I made a bet with an Elder, and this came with my prize. Tell me I am wrong. Tell me it is not the exact likeness of her eyes," Keane challenged.

CHAPTER 29

The trio remained silent as they stared at the trinket glinting in the sparse moonlight. There was no denying the similarities in its creation to that of Emer's.

"I have watched this Isle and its people turn on her at every corner. You may be able to get her to the Well, but I will be able to get her back from it."

Calder's expression hardened, but the faintest traces of fear haunting his eyes left from when he had raced to find Emer lent truth to Keane's assertion.

"I have your word you will not harm her?" Calder asked, finally shifting his gaze from the coin to Keane.

"I swear it."

Without another word, Calder sliced his palm and extended his hand to seal the bargain. Keane slipped his hand beneath one of his wings, freeing a hidden blade, and mirrored the act.

When their hands met, Keane's eyes closed while Emer's widened. Calder had made a bargain for her safety but made no mention of his own.

Keane released Calder's hand with a sigh, turned to Emer with a soft smile, and said, "Now, why don't you tell me who you angered to warrant all this unfortunate attention."

Emer deflated slightly before shrugging. "The Elders?"

Keane hummed, "Same, darling, same."

"Why wasn't your deal that you wouldn't harm *either* of us?" Emer asked.

"Because he is not excluded from the list of things that can hurt you," Keane said, causing Calder to chuckle darkly.

"If I am so dangerous, then why do you seem so invested in royally pissing me off?" Calder asked.

"Oh, because I very much don't like you." Keane said with little levity and a bat of his lashes.

"There is something I've been wondering about, actually. The man who attacked me in the tavern... did you have something to do with his face smashing into the table?"

Eyes glinting, he gave a short nod.

"So, it was your fault that the brawl broke out in the first place," Calder said flatly.

Keane glowered. "I can't control how people behave! But at least I gave aid," he said defensively, his shoulder rolling as if he could still feel the crack of the wood as it shattered on impact.

Emer shook her head, sighing, "I thought you two were going to play nice."

"Oh no, darling. We agreed to protect you. *Anything* that becomes a threat will be... dealt with," Keane said with a saccharine smile.

"So, you will work together if and only if there is a threat, and will be at each other's throats any other time. All the while secretly hoping the other does something that can be construed as violating the terms of your deal so that you can cause them bodily harm?" she clarified, speaking more slowly than necessary.

Both men nodded.

"Great," she sighed.

After a few thoughtful moments, Emer relented.

They both watched her. Calder with exasperation and Keane with anticipation—hands poised as if to clap.

"No stabbing," she commanded with narrowed eyes.

They declined in unison.

Emer glowered.

"No stabbing *each other*," she amended, and both men rolled their eyes in tandem before agreeing.

"No tricks." This she directed at Keane.

Though it was common for mortals to carry certain elements to combat the magic of others who inhabited the Isle, Keane still scoffed at Calder, who waved his be-ringed hand, drawing particular attention to the iron ring on his middle finger.

"That is like asking me not to breathe. However, this day, I swear that, henceforth, no trickery or magic will be used to willfully deceive, or at the expense of, our travel party."

Their back and forth grew into haggling and continued until Emer was sure she had considered any factors that could prove problematic. She paused, looking at the two dangerous beings before her, surprised for the first time that she did not feel the thread of her anxiety tugging against her choice.

"Now that we have worked out all the kinks—"

"Hardly," Keane muttered.

"This is a terrible idea," Calder remarked flatly.

"That means we shall have wondrous stories by the end of this," Keane sang, clapping excitedly. "Now that we have established our boundaries like the healthy adults we are... shall we greet each other properly?"

Emer began to introduce herself, but Keane waved her away.

"I was just kidding, Emmy, love! That one has only been shouting your name from sun up to sun down since I met you! I was just trying to prove a point," he said with a pointed look at Calder.

"That's not her name," Calder corrected.

"You literally named her after a semi-murderous—albeit

alluring—sea creature. Your thoughts on the matter are invalid. But while we are on the topic... I believe I will call you lord of the pirates as a rule and pirate whore when I'm feeling spicy," Keane said to no one in particular.

"Already picking out pet names—you'll be fast friends indeed," Emer chuckled nervously as she gave Calder a pleading look.

"I rather lack the fondness for magic beings to consider befriending one," Calder said.

"Well, you are not exactly my cup of tea either," Keane remarked.

"In my experience, magical creatures at sea have a nasty habit of trying to steal your soul or wear your flesh. Neither of which tickle my fancy," Calder sighed.

Emer rubbed her temple and forced a smile as she looked at Keane, who had moved from crossing his arms to stroking his chin as he listened. "He has a point... but, hey, who am I to judge."

"Do you have any intention of stealing souls or wearing flesh?" she asked dryly.

"Have you seen this face?" Keane asked, pointing to his own.

"Darling, that would be a crime against the realm. Also, souls are rather heavy, and I tend to travel with a lot of wine. Speaking of which... if we don't leave soon, the pubs will be closed by the time we get to town," he said urgently while motioning Emer to her horse.

"How the *fuck* do you even know where we are going?" Calder growled as he strode towards Aven.

"Don't insult me," Keane remarked with a scowl.

Emer smiled faintly despite herself.

Keane was not the magic her naive heart had dreamed of as a child, he was the beautiful nightmare her reality needed because she was searching for powerful magic, and now she knew it was *real*.

"Don't mind me," he advised as he perched himself on Emer's

horse, his legs hanging off the back and his smirk on full display for Calder, who glared intensely. He set his shoulders, mounted Danu, and once again, they were off.

"Emmy, would you be a dear and grab my refreshments from the satchel?" Keane requested, resting his finger delicately on his throat to signal his distress. "That one... yep, there. Yeah, that one," he directed, waving his hands as she explored the various compartments.

Her finger brushed against a small bottle and cloth pouch, and she paused. With a pinched brow, she handed the wine and cheese that she was certain she had not packed to Keane, who accepted them with delight.

"If you are wondering if I just made this quest classier, the answer is yes, I did, and you're welcome," he said as he devoured a piece of cheese while offering her another.

Emer declined.

Still twisted in the saddle, she could see how delicately Keane's wings draped down his back, looking almost as if they were an adornment to his jacket rather than a part of his person. They were sheer when not catching the light and almost perfect, save for a jagged tear through the center of one like a petal caught by another's thorn. Emer righted herself, remembering what Calder had said about scars, and wondering what stories Keane's might have.

CHAPTER 30

When Emer came to the Isle, she was in search of many impossible things—the last of which she thought would be the watchful eye of a Raven, the protection of a Fae, and the quiet her normally chaotic soul had found alongside them.

Keane, not one for quiet of any kind, passed the time sharing harrowing stories and retelling ancient tales. The accounts of which stood up against Calder's scrutiny time and time again. Emer drank them in, allowing them to fill the spaces within her she had long reserved for worry. By the time Keane began to spin prose about Mian Loch, Calder only hummed or grunted in response to the narrative.

Much like Emer's own story, it began with a well. However, this story was a cautionary tale about an arrogant man who asked for the love of a woman who had denied him. The Elders and their magic do not interfere with matters of the heart, and when the man's request was rejected, he began to kick the well and tear at its bricks. Water overflowed, creating the loch and releasing the Guardian who had lived within it—a Merrow. Thinking the beautiful woman in the water was his prize for besting the well, he went to her. When he took her hand in his, the same melodic voice that had denied him began to sing, and she continued to sing as he drowned. What he thought was his reward was, in fact, his reckoning.

"The moral of the story obviously being no means no," Keane summarized.

Calder offered another approving grunt. Emer, however, wore a pensive expression and her mouth twisted into a frown.

"Was the well destroyed when the loch was formed?" she asked.

For a moment Keane just stared at her thoughtfully, "I have told this story many times and that is the first time anyone has asked me that."

This only made Emer's frown deepened and Keane gave her a soft smile.

"The magic of the well overflowed to allow its Guardian to protect not only the well, but the maiden the vile man had been demanding. The legend says that the Merrow will now hear the pleas of those hoping to wish at the well at the edge of the loch. It also says she has developed a taste for prideful men."

Emer smiled, relieved that the wretched man was not able to destroy such a beautiful thing solely to appease his fragile pride. "Maybe I should invite Ewan there for a picnic," she mused under her breath.

"I don't think you would need any assistance from a fellow Merrow to deal with him," Calder retorted. It was the first time he'd deigned to speak for some time, and Emer turned to find him still watching her.

"Speaking of which. Be ready to show those fangs where we are going."

There was a wariness in his eyes that could have been caused by the trouble they'd faced before or a sign of the trouble waiting for them in the town beyond, but Emer found herself desperate to assuage it. She pressed her tongue against one of her canines, something she had seen him do many times, and tested its sharpness.

His eyes fell to her mouth, and then he shook his head, but even as he turned away, she caught the twitch of his lip.

When Invengarry finally came into view, Emer's body screamed in relief. The town had been settled out of necessity as a respite for those traveling north, and she quickly learned that her definition of "necessity" was vastly different from the founders of this particular pit.

Aside from a modest inn and stables, the other structures appeared to be dedicated to drink and other forms of pleasure. There was not a merchant to be found—no stalls of goods or sweet breads. She had not thought she would miss the town that she'd been attacked in, but she now romanticized it in comparison.

Though she would never have considered herself timid, Emer was almost immediately scandalized by the sights and sounds that greeted them. Averting her gaze, she attempted to swallow her embarrassment. Instead she choked at the sight of Calder watching her from the corner of his eyes, smirking.

Mercifully, they reached the inn without incident. Keane and Calder dismounted their respective horses at the same moment, bringing them almost nose to nose. Keane wiggled his brows while Calder looked up, seemingly searching for his lost patience before turning and making his way to the inn.

Though trust was scarce, in a realm of magic, bargains were far more common, and their terms were clear. Keane could not harm Emer, take her, or play any part in others doing so.

Halfway to the worn wooden door, Calder hesitated and turned back. Ignoring Keane's questioning stare, he tapped Emer's thigh and raised his arms to her in offering. She smiled down at him warmly, accepting his aid, while Keane watched on.

Once her feet hit the ground, he turned to make his way back to the inn. "I need to see about the room. Stay out of trouble, yeah?"

"Did you say *room*?" Keane stepped back, placing his fingers delicately against his chest to emphasize his disgust.

Calder stared at him, entirely unamused.

"Aren't you seafarer-type wealthy? Certainly, you can afford more than *one* room, man whore," Keane chastised.

"We already discussed the arrangement. Not that it's any of your business."

Keane, still displeased by said arrangement, glowered.

"Just take that guy's room," he said, shifting his weight and pointing to a man leaning against the wall by the inn's door.

Emer gaped.

"We can't just take his room!" she scolded.

"Why? He isn't going to need it," he said, bored with her protest.

"Of course, he is going to need it... that is precisely why he is here!" She pinched the space above her nose, but Keane merely rolled his eyes.

"Do you see that big black dog with him?" he asked calmly. Emer quirked a brow and then looked back to the man who was most definitely sans dog.

"No?" she answered tentatively.

"Exactly... because you aren't going to die. He is," he explained, tossing his head in the man's direction. "And hopefully, he will do us the courtesy of doing it before he occupies a perfectly good room."

Emer's eyes widened as she looked at the man and then back to Keane.

"Emmy, please! I'm not a monster. I planned to drink to his memory and toast his chivalrous sacrifice." Keane tilted his head sweetly.

"Do you need a reason to drink?" Calder scoffed, not acknowledging any of the other, arguably more pertinent, details of the discussion.

"I wasn't talking to you," Keane remarked over his shoulder. He turned to Emer, who was now visibly annoyed.

"Fineeee... but thank the Elders I am here to chaperone," he relented, turning his nose up at Calder as he did.

"Chaperone? I thought you were here waiting for me to fuck up so you could snatch her away. How is the view from your ridiculous moral high ground?" Calder shouted as he disappeared into the inn.

Emer absentmindedly toyed with the stone of her necklace as she considered what might motivate Keane to guard her so fiercely from Calder. The solid press of it against her palm provided a grounding sensation.

The corner of Keane's lips curled mischievously, revealing his gleaming white teeth. "Something on your mind, love?" he asked.

Before she could answer, a gruff voice drew her attention.

"You must be a daft, treacherous lass to have the gall to walk around here alone!" he snarled.

Emer reeled back, shocked by the outburst. The man who had been leaning against the inn stalked towards her, hate lighting his eyes. It was a reminder that the experience she enjoyed in Calder's village was the exception—this was the rule. A rule she had allowed herself to forget.

"What a peach... still broken up about him," Keane asked, sliding a finger across his throat with a single click of his tongue.

Emer's eyes darted between the two of them, waiting for the man to react, and when he didn't, Emer threw Keane an accusatory look.

"Oh, yeah. He can't see me," Keane said nonchalantly as he picked an invisible piece of lint off the shoulder of his jacket.

"Some chaperone," she hissed.

Disgust simmered in the man's features as he closed the distance between them, undeterred when Emer reached down to retrieve her knife.

"You're all the same. Here to light this town on fire too?" he bellowed, pulling back his fist.

Keane effortlessly swept to his side, grinning when the man bumped into him.

"Halt," he whispered, his voice like a sweet melody.

The man froze, his arm still pulled back and ready to strike. The hatefulness of the cruel man's features was as distant as the foggy look that now consumed his gaze.

"Apologize," Keane commanded, and although the man fumbled with his words, he complied with the request.

"To make up for your despicable behavior towards my lady, you will hand over your key. Now." Keane's lips upturned as he spared a glance to Emer.

The man shuddered as the words coursed through him, forcing the movement in his limbs. He reached into his pocket, removed his key, and held it out.

"Emmy, please accept his apology so he can go spend what is left of his miserable afternoon in the pub. Or, if you like, I can expedite his departure." The calm in Keane's voice led her to believe he was quite pleased with the opportunity to display his power over mortals. Mortals like Calder. Like her.

Still holding her knife, she reached out with her free hand and snatched the key. The man's arm remained suspended, unaware or uncaring that the key was no longer in his possession.

Keane leaned in, whispering to the man, and then patted him on the shoulder. The contact seemed to draw him from his stupor, and he blinked wildly for a moment. When he looked at Emer, there was no recognition. He simply righted his jacket and then left without a word.

"'Some chaperone' indeed," Keane said, his voice smug and free of the compulsive melody.

"Proud of yourself?" she questioned.

"If I'm not, then no one would be, and I am far too wondrous for that to be the case," he sang back.

She frowned at the comment.

Keane shifted uncomfortably at her sympathetic expression.

"Was that really necessary, though?" she groaned, fiddling with the heavy metal key.

Keane wilted slightly.

"As I said before. The man had no use for the room. His time will be up before the sun fully sets. Also, while I have complete confidence you could have gutted the poor bastard, that would be quite an unnecessary mess. More selfishly, if I don't use my... abilities... I tend to get... itchy," he explained.

Emer's lip tugged.

"I figured you would be more accepting of me using them on that sad excuse for a male rather than an unsuspecting fool... like dear Clader."

"Calder."

"Whatever." He waved away her correction.

As if summoned, Calder appeared and narrowed his eyes on the knife still in Emer's grip. "Why is it that whenever I leave you, I return to your unsheathed knife?" he asked.

Keane crossed his arms haughtily. "Does our girl make a habit of pulling knives on men?" he asked.

Emer pushed past both of them and made her way to the room that corresponded to the characters stamped on the key.

In the distance, she heard Calder snarl, "What did you do?"

To which Keane responded, "Aside from providing stimulating conversation and general merriment, I secured her a private room. What is it that you've done today, knight?"

CHAPTER 31

"I need a drink," Calder announced.

With a pointed glare aimed at Keane, he rubbed a hand over his chest, willing the tension away that seemed to have seeped into his bones since they departed Murdoch.

Devious pale-purple eyes found his. "We could follow our new friend to the pub and take bets on when the Elder of Endings collects. Loser buys the lot."

"Fine by me," Calder answered.

At the same time Emer, having overheard the exchange, barked, "Absolutely not!"

She returned to Calder with wide eyes, and he shrugged. This offense was not even in the hierarchy of his darkest deeds, and he was fairly certain she knew that.

Keane clapped delightedly, pleased by either Calder's agreement or the way his agreement made Emer glare at the Sea Raven.

Likely both.

Emer tossed the key she received from the stranger to Calder and ripped the one he had returned with from his hands. Crossing the short distance to where the horses were boarded, she retrieved her satchels and threw them over her shoulder.

Calder smirked at the sight.

"Shouldn't you help her?" Keane criticized, and Calder glared at him out of the corner of his eyes.

"You go over there, tell her you think she needs help, and let me know how that goes," Calder challenged.

He knew better than to expect her to ask for help—he also knew better than to doubt what she was capable of.

"She's just... so tiny," Keane observed quietly as she drew closer.

"Say that to my fucked eyebrow," Calder argued, pointing to the wound Emer had gifted him, not bothering to mention the much larger one that decorated his ribs. Keane looked at him with suspicion.

"I'm going to put my things in my room. You two do what you want with the other." Her voice strained from the weight she carried but she remained fairly steady as she marched away from where they both stood watching her.

"Is the dog still here?" she asked.

Keane pointed to where the unseen creature sat. His onyx-black fur and yellow eyes were visible to no one else aside from the Fae.

"It will linger in the area until it is time to escort a soul across the Array and to the Elder of Endings," Keane explained.

Emer reached into her satchel and grabbed one of the bits of stale bread and cheese that had remained. Giving a sharp whistle, she tossed the items in the general direction of the seemingly empty space Keane indicated. The offering appeared to be accepted as it never hit the ground.

"It's not like anyone else is going to think to feed an invisible dog!" she barked, turning back and into the inn.

"Fuck us, right?" Calder remarked, to which Keane nodded in agreement.

When Emer returned to the front of the inn, she found Calder leaning against the structure, glowering, and Keane busy stroking Alabaster, who seemed all too happy to be spoiled.

Keane begrudgingly released the white raven, and the trio made their way to the pub on foot. Upon their arrival, the sights and smells of which were as deplorable as Emer had expected, Keane eagerly scanned the dimly lit room for the man marked by the hound.

"There's our man!" he said excitedly.

As if on cue, the dead-man-walking grabbed his chest and collapsed to the floor. The barkeep leaned over the counter to stare down at the now deceased man—a sight that earned only a slightly raised brow. With a roll of his eyes, he snapped his fingers and pointed to the body, signaling for someone to come and collect it, which seemed to be deemed a mere tripping hazard. Hardly anyone else appeared to notice, and Emer could not help but grimace at how terribly sad it was.

"Well, shit," Keane pouted. "Either of you bet on 'he'd die as soon as we got here'?"

They shook their heads.

"Just as well... neither of you could afford my tab."

Keane led the way through the small space to a table whose occupants quickly removed themselves. Their expressions were blank as they wandered out the door, ales still in hand.

"Where did you send them?" Emer asked, tugging on the sleeve of his jacket.

For a moment, he looked pensive. "Where do you suppose people go when one tells them to fuck off?" he asked thoughtfully.

Emer turned sharply, horrified.

"I'm sure it's fine," he said, waving away her worry like it was a bug that could be batted away.

Emer dropped into one of the newly vacated seats, shaking her head. Returning from the barkeep, Calder set down three large ales. The contents of which splashed across the already stained wood.

Gripping a mug in both hands, Emer brought it to hover before her lips, pausing as her eyes snagged on the sight before her. A Sea Raven with a raised brow and a Fae with a smile filled with glee. Not for the first time, she found herself wondering if she had drowned that day and everything happening now was simply the magic of her dreams leading her across the Array. She could see her heart crafting someone as brave as Calder, and her spirit someone as wild as Keane. They embodied the cautionary tales she grew up with, passed down like recipes throughout the generations. However, compared to the men before her, the stories were made with inferior ingredients, resulting in a version paler than the real thing.

Emer closed her eyes and drank the dark liquid to the dregs, not pausing to allow the muddy taste to linger on her tongue. When her gaze met her companions once more, she received an approving nod from Calder and a disgusted look from Keane.

"Elders bed me sideways! You have been in the company of this barbarian too long!" Keane scolded.

Emer shrugged.

Keane's chagrin shifted to his beverage. He dipped his lips to the liquid and then swiftly retreated.

"No. Nope. Absolutely not. I respect myself too much," he said, shaking his head in protest.

Returning the mug to the center, he snapped his fingers and conjured a beautiful chalice filled with sweet red liquid. "Hello there, gorgeous," he said wistfully before sipping.

"Why did you let me waste coins on ale if you could just conjure your own drink?" Calder challenged.

"Because I enjoy your misery. I'm sorry if that wasn't obvious," Keane returned with an expression of genuine concern. Calder glared, studying his features with predatory intensity.

"What?" Keane spat before taking a sip from his chalice.

"You're Wraithnocti," he observed.

Keane straightened his shoulders before pinning Calder with

his stare. Calder tilted his head slightly. "I was under the impression Wraithnocti can't walk in the daylight."

"And?" Keane remarked, tilting his chin up.

Calder looked around and then threw out his hands to emphasize the time of day.

"Do I need to explain to you how magic works? Because, if so, I have deep concerns," Keane answered.

"I've never heard of such magic," Calder returned, causing Keane to grin widely.

Leaning back in his chair, Keane swirled the chalice lazily. "You can be impressed. It's okay... I won't tell," he said with a wink.

Emer, already feeling the effects of the ale, let her head fall back and snickered.

The moment her hood slipped from her head, her companions sat straighter. Calder's hand dropped to one of his knives at the exact moment the air around them warmed. Calder turned sharply to Keane to find him already scanning the crowd. When Keane's gaze drifted past Calder, his attention snagged.

"You truly just want to protect her, don't you?" Calder asked him quietly.

Keane gave a single sharp nod, which Calder returned.

Sensing their unease, Emer began to fidget until Keane smiled warmly at her. "Since our earlier game was ruined, how about we try for another?"

"What kind of game?" she asked with a grin.

"Traditionally, in an establishment as fine as this one, one would play either dice, daggers, or drinks."

"Fuck no. We are not playing dice," Calder said firmly.

"Why?" Emer asked, slightly vexed by the prompt dismissal.

Calder leaned back and crossed his arms as he said, "Tell her the rules."

Although Keane bristled at the order, he complied.

"We take turns proposing a task, and then we roll dice. The lowest roll must then complete the task," he explained casually.

"By *tasks*, he means a dare. As in, he can dare us to do whatever he wants and to further my previous 'fuck-no', agreements with Fae are binding, so we would have to do whatever Elders' forsaken atrocious thing he pleases," Calder said with a sneer.

"Okay, what about drinks?" Emer inquired.

"Rather than dares, drinks relies on truths. We state an act, and those who have not engaged in it must admit their plainness and not drink. Those who have get to toast themselves," Keane said with a sideward glance to Calder.

Emer tapped a finger against her lips.

"So, if I were to say something like, 'lived to celebrate my 300th birthday,' I couldn't drink, but you..." she said, raising her brow in question.

Keane laughed. The warmth and sincerity of it seeming to surprise even him.

"Emmy, darling, you may have a little Fae in those veins of yours. As a reward for your devious demonstration, yes, I would have indeed needed to drink."

"How old are you?" she barked in bewilderment.

"Old enough to have thought of the best comeback the other day, only to have found out the person it was intended for died 200 years earlier," he sighed. "Time flies when you're drunk. Anyway, let's play a round. One turn each."

Emer nodded enthusiastically while Calder devolved back into annoyed grunts.

"Normally, I would say ladies first, but I suspect it would be best to start the bar low. Raven?" Keane prompted, earning him a sharp glare.

"Stabbed a man," Calder said threateningly before turning his eyes on Emer. "Drink up, sweetheart," he added, sparing Emer a heated glance.

Keane assessed her with a raised brow as she drank.

"Let's revisit *that* another time," he remarked, bringing his grinning lips to the rim of his chalice. Reminding her that beneath the whimsy and charm, he was still something to fear.

"All part of the job, love, I promise," he said with a wink.

They watched Emer expectantly, and she worried her lip in thought. As far as life experiences go, it seemed the ones worth sharing had happened only in recent days, and almost from the moment she had washed ashore, Calder was there for them.

So, she chose the event that preceded it all. "Survived a shipwreck," she said proudly.

Calder smirked as he mirrored her movement and lifted his ale. Catching the wonder in her eyes, he tipped back his chin and tapped the scar under his jaw that he had earned from that particular dalliance with the sea. Only when Emer began to feel an ache in her cheeks did she realize how widely she was grinning at him.

"Been in love."

Emer's attention snapped back to Keane, who watched her thoughtfully, taking a sip from his chalice. The sound of the tavern around them rushed away like a retreating wave. Warmth slithered through her veins and left tingles across her skin. Emer realized Keane's magic was demanding an answer she was not sure she knew.

Reflexively, she looked to Calder, who watched her with equal measure. She felt the phantom brush of his lips against hers, haunting and taunting her.

"Emmy." Keane's faint and worried voice preceded the sharp bite of the magic that had the heat arcing through her bones like tiny streaks of lightning. Punishment for not obeying the rules.

Emer hissed.

Calder winced.

But fear and a tiny sliver of pride kept them both still as statues.

"There are many kinds of love. Surely, you have both loved in *some* capacity. Just drink and be done with this. I can't keep my magic from forcing you, and whatever pain you are feeling is nothing compared to what it can be. Just drink," Keane pleaded.

They drank, chests heaving in relief as the magic released them.

With a slight cough, Emer quickly shifted the attention.

"Who were they?" she asked Keane.

He gave her a sad smile.

"I have a nasty habit of loving things that are bad for me, and I am a collector of many vices."

"Any *current* vices?" Emer asked, trying to understand the wistful look in Keane's eyes.

"My most recent paramour and I are on a break," he offered with a casual nod as if his explanation were commonplace.

"A break?" she echoed.

"Well, yes, I didn't actually risk my life to return and let them know that things were over... so, technically, we are *still* on a break."

His explanation received a suspiciously understanding noise from Calder, and Emer could not help the laugh that burst free from her. While the sound initially drew smiles from the two men before her, it also drew attention from those around her. Several patrons leaned in and began to whisper. While others openly glared, malice and resentment stark in their eyes.

Keane sucked his bottom lip between his teeth as he scanned the faces, pausing on a man who sat alone and allowed his gaze to linger on Emer for too long. Leaning back in his seat, he conjured his dice into his palm to busy his hands.

Calder leaned towards Keane. "Why don't you take Emer outside for daggers while I talk to our large friend over there."

Without taking his eyes off the man, Keane nodded.

Standing, he reached out his hand to Emer. "Another game before we call it a night. This time, the winner gets a prize."

CHAPTER 32

The cold steel slipped from Emer's fingers, embedding deep into the empty barrel outside the tavern. She began to jump up and down excitedly, pleased that even intoxicated, she was still an ace with a throwing knife.

Keane threw up his hands with an exasperated groan. "You wicked little trickster. You could have at least mentioned you were good at this."

"And where would the fun in that be," Calder remarked, moving towards them with two fresh mugs of ale.

Emer moved to retrieve the knife, and Keane leaned against the side of the tavern next to Calder.

"So?" Keane asked quietly.

Calder raised his mug of ale and took a long drink. "Our curious friend managed to disappear into the crowd before I got to introduce myself. He didn't seem interested in her anymore, and I didn't want to get too far," Calder explained.

"I bet you didn't," Keane observed. "Any theories as to why the Isle seems particularly interested in our girl? I mean, I am a believer in eternal grudges and all, but this can't be just because she is from Rest. This feels... different."

Calder glared at him out of the corner of his eyes for a moment before letting out a slow exhale.

"You were in Arborlynn with us, yes?" Calder asked, and Keane nodded. "What do you know of the men who died in the alley?"

"They didn't die. They were slaughtered. The alley reeked of blood, magic, and Emer. Originally, I thought you had done it, which is why I kept following, but then the Sluagh came for her."

Calder cursed under his breath. "We just need to keep her safe and get her home," he said, eyes still fixed on a returning Emer and unaware of Keane's deepening scowl.

"Look at you two bonding!" Emer said, clapping happily.

"We found a common interest," Calder remarked.

Emer extended the knife to Keane, which he accepted less enthusiastically than he had moments before. Reaching for Calder's ale, she gave a wobbly bow when he relinquished it.

There was a loud crack followed by metal clattering onto stone. Keane cursed, and Emer ran forward, retrieving her knife to examine its condition. The blade was fine, but she frowned at the scratch that now marred the handle.

"Sorry, darling, I think the thing is cursed or something," Keane said, rubbing his neck bashfully.

Calder kicked off from the wall to where Emer stood, holding the knife in both her hands and staring down at it as if it were a wounded bird. Slipping his fingers under her chin, he lifted her face and found her lip held in a pout she only seemed to wear when she was drunk. He tapped her lip and surprise flickered over her features.

"Don't fret, Merrow. It gives it character. Something to remind you of the adventure."

For a heartbeat, he got lost in the way she looked at him and the way it made him feel. His thumb stroked the line of her jaw.

"When we get home, can I get a knife of my own? Not that I don't want to keep yours."

Calder's thumb stilled, and his muscles tensed.

Home.

He fought the urge to correct her, to remind her that she did not belong and that, despite the hopeful look in her eyes, she never would. It wasn't a reminder she needed at that very moment and he stroked her jaw once more, letting himself imagine it was possible too. Forcing a smile, he nodded.

Emer grinned and danced away to collect her winnings from the Fae she had just hustled.

"What do I win? A wish?"

"You always set the terms of your deals before you win. Not after," Keane explained, spinning the coin he always seemed to be fidgeting with and sending a familiar chime through the air.

"What about that?" Emer motioned to the coin.

"Even if I could give this to you, which I can't, you would not want it, lovie." He sighed and flipped the coin towards her.

Emer snatched it out of the air, clasping it to her chest.

"Not so fast. Put it in your pocket," Keane instructed.

Emer followed his command and then watched him expectantly. He slipped his hand into his pocket and, to her surprise, pulled out the very same coin. She quickly searched her own pocket only to find the coin was gone.

Emer frowned.

"How about a secret instead?" Keane offered.

Emer nodded in agreement, and he crooked his fingers at her, beckoning her closer. Fae secrets were prized possessions that were never offered up freely. Keane's secrets were heavy, and he had many, but besides that, he knew she would cherish it even if she did not understand its value.

"The bargain I made with the Elder came with more than this coin."

She pulled back from him slightly, pure awe dancing in her eyes. Her expression began to fall as she noted his smile was not the one she had seen from him previously. It was soft but didn't reach his eyes, the sparkle that typically danced in them absent.

"What did you win?" she asked, her voice thinner.

Calder paused his drinking, attention settling on the coin in Keane's hand.

"I thought I was clever," Keane huffed a derisive laugh, "I had made bargains for favors and relics, deals for power, all so I would never be as weak as I once felt. And one day, someone offered me something that meant I could keep everything I had collected—immortality," he sighed. "If I won, they would grant me immortality in exchange for a single favor, but I couldn't know the favor in advance."

Keane began clutching the coin so tightly that it dug into his skin, and Emer reached over, placing her hand on his. He shook his head as if he hoped to free himself of the melancholy that the memory gripped him with.

"Anyways. I won. Damned myself in the process. Hindsight and all that," he said with a shrug.

Beneath the attempt at nonchalance, tension still tugged at his features. Behind his mischievous glint and wicked grins, there was a well of sadness compounded by his lifetimes.

"If you made the bargain to get immortality, perhaps you can make one to get out of it?" she said encouragingly, though it seemed a strange thing to be hopeful for.

Keane laughed.

"Shockingly... not many seem interested in helping me die. I suppose I am just too charming."

After several more rounds of game and alcohol, the decision was made to return to the inn before Emer curled up on the ground or

Keane tried to lure passersby into a fairy ring for a more entertaining target.

With unsteady feet, Emer walked with her arms hooked around each of the males' elbows. Occasionally, Keane attempted to incorporate some fancy footwork, but Emer was too drunk and Calder too sober.

As they stumbled down the road, the merriment that hung in the air was replaced by an oily dread. It slipped down Emer's throat, halting her breathing and stealing her speech. Searching for the cause of her unease, her attention snagged on a hooded figure with an eye of coal and one of gold. The question of whether or not he was staring back at her was answered when he tilted his head expectantly.

Emer tripped, and strong arms grabbed her from either side, causing them to become a tangle of limbs and stumbling boots. When she was no longer in imminent danger of crashing into the ground, her head snapped up, searching for the man who was nowhere to be found.

The amused expressions worn by Keane and Calder as they righted her shifted as they took in her worry and she felt a pang of guilt for depriving them of the brief respite from worry.

With a self-deprecating rub of her head and a pained smile she explained, "I'm fine. The ale just went to my head."

Calder was not comfortable with her returning to her room alone in her current state; Keane was not comfortable with her returning to her room with Calder, so the three of them made their way down the narrow hall of the inn—one of them kicking or bumping something, the other two hissing a hush louder than whatever the original offense was.

Once in the room, Keane almost immediately took residence at the foot of the bed as one would imagine a pet would—a loaf of bread affectionately cradled in his arms.

"I knew I liked you," Emer said through a grin.

She curled up on the top half of the bed. A soft humming blanketed her just before the spinning darkness consumed her.

CHAPTER 33

She was back on the ship.

Arrows narrowly missed her, and the hungry night devoured her screams. Lachlan held her tightly, shaking her with nothing but rage in his cold, dead eyes.

"Get ashore."

"Get to the Well."

Words that were loud and quiet at the same time as if she were already under the water. Then she was weightless, thrown from the ship and hurtling towards the black water.

Drowning.

Emer startled awake with a shout, finding herself back in their dimly lit room at the inn.

Calder sat up from where he slept on the floor at the side of the bed. "It's okay, Merrow, it was just a dream," he soothed, eyes barely open.

Emer balled her hands into fists, sucking in a deep breath. Her slow exhale rattled as it escaped her. Drowsily, Calder leaned his forehead against the mattress and threaded his fingers through hers.

"I'm here. You're safe," he whispered, swaying slightly as he tried to remain sitting.

When her grip on his hand eased and her breathing slowed, Emer settled back into the covers. Calder, in turn, laid back down on the floor. After a moment, he reached up and pulled her hand down, intertwining their fingers once more.

Emotion clogged her throat as she recalled holding her father's hand in the exact same manner. The memory flashed in her mind of the night she promised him that she would do anything to save him. The last time she had seen him.

"Safe," he whispered again, slipping back into sleep.

She continued to stare at their hands until her eyelids grew heavy. Without thinking, she gently squeezed his hand.

Once.

Twice.

As sleep returned to claim her, the anchor of his grasp kept her from being swept away by the nightmares.

When Emer attempted to stretch the sleep from her muscles and stress from her bones the next morning, she kicked something heavy and solid. Keane remained curled at her feet, the only difference from the night being that half his loaf of bread was now gone.

As the three of them woke, it was a day that felt different from all those that had come before it. There was a shift—something both nameless and inherently right. The surprise and relief of finding something you had not realized had been missing.

Perhaps it was *because* they'd been strangers—some more recently than others—that they were able to share their secrets so freely.

Despite all their differences, they were united by the broken pieces they so often hid. Jagged edges that fit together, making each of them whole.

As Emer's consciousness formed, she became increasingly aware of the consequences of their game. Her stomach was sour, and there was an ache behind her eyes. Any other morning, she would have welcomed the warm greeting of the sun that slithered between the shutters, but today, its shine scolded her like a disappointed parent.

Her thoughts moved from the aches and pains throughout her body to another sensation. A weight that continued to tug on her arm, twined fingers, and the subtle twitches of someone caught between the realms of waking and sleeping.

Peering over the side of the bed, she found Calder sleeping on his side, one hand still holding hers while using his other arm as a pillow.

Cold One, indeed.

Although his eyes were slow to open, a soft smile appeared.

His voice was still harsh from sea shanties and sleep when he said good morning.

"Good morning," she returned, her attention trailing back to their hands.

He gave a brief squeeze before he released it and sat up. The change in position brought them to eye level.

"What did you dream of?" he asked, worry furrowing his brow.

"*I* dreamt I lived in a magical world where people didn't talk this early," Keane grumbled in a low voice.

Emer chuckled, but the vibration threatened to fracture her skull, and she winced.

"I'm dying," Keane moaned.

"I'm not that lucky," Calder said, rolling his neck and stretching his shoulders.

Despite a night on the floor, he was in far better humor than his companions.

"No loud noises," Emer begged.

She pressed her palms into her eyes, willing the stabbing away.

Calder leaned in close, his breath warm against her skin as he asked, "Would you prefer if I whispered?"

Her body reacted to his proximity despite the fact that she was even less inclined to entertain his teasing than usual.

"How is it exactly that you are not plagued with the same blight as us?" she whined.

His soft chuckle tickled the hair near her ear. "Debaucherous pirate, remember?" he grinned.

"Who cares? Keane is not even mortal!" she shot back, turning her head and meeting his gaze from behind her hands.

Calder pulled back, eyeing Keane meaningfully.

"She has a point. How is it exactly that you have lived all this time and yet are still this sloppy when drunk?" he taunted.

"Because... ass... I was drinking Fae wine rather than subjecting myself to your piss-poor mortal ale. As with *all things* Fae, it is stronger." His threatening tone did not match his curled-up form.

"Indeed. You both are the picture of strength and self-respect," Calder mocked.

The pair growled back but didn't have the energy or the sobriety to produce any further bite.

"I'll see if I can't find some raw eel and bitter almonds for you sorry excuses for travelers," he sighed.

At the mention of raw eel, Emer leaped up, Keane cursing as she jostled the bed in an attempt to escape the covers. Once free, she flung herself through the shutters of the nearby window. After making a noise reminiscent of a cat hissing, Keane took advantage of the vacant space in the bed, slowly crawling to the center and under the covers. The fabric did little to provide a barrier from the sounds of Emer emptying her stomach. Wiping her mouth on the back of her hand, Emer collapsed on the windowsill, her body dangling on either side.

"Sorry, Em. Eel and bitter almonds are a sworn remedy—"

"For fuck's sake! Enough about the eels. If you want to be useful, go and see if you can secure any peppermint, lemon balm, or valerian, you monster," Keane rebuked.

"I don't think you are in a position to give orders right now," Calder retorted.

A hand slid out from under the covers just long enough to form a vulgar gesture before disappearing back under the blanket.

Carefully, Calder gathered Emer into his arms and back over to the bed, where she took the spot Keane previously occupied.

"We are wasting daylight. Can't you conjure some sort of elixir or potion to cure yourselves?" he asked impatiently.

"I'm flattered, but I can't just conjure an elixir I do not know the components of, and potions are for witches," Keane grumbled.

"Then what *can* you do?" Calder challenged.

"Channel magic. Stop a heart. Compel mortals. Conjure flames. Leap through space. Useful shit," Keane barked, his form under the blankets tensing as if the outburst caused him pain.

Calder sighed, "I'll check the field out back."

Magic stirred the air and the shutters closed, blocking out the harsh level of light. The soft snick of the door signaled Calder's departure, and in the silence, Emer's mind returned to what Keane had said a moment before.

"Darling, if you let thoughts rattle around in your skull in your current condition, it is likely to cause permanent damage," he remarked from beneath the covers.

"Can all Fae do those things?" she asked.

Sliding the fabric down, he met her stare with a snort.

At Emer's earnest expression, he straightened. Isle Basalt was so rich with magic that it was easy to forget that it was a land more of myth than truth to others. In those lands, he had been treated like divinity. Keane smiled, seeing the same wonder in her eyes that he had recalled seeing lifetimes earlier. Unlike in his youth, he did not feel the addictive pull to flaunt his abilities and receive her worship. Instead, he felt a fierce protectiveness over her innocence.

"Not many, if any. I mentioned before I made many deals to become who I am. Some of those deals were not good, in which case, my magic feels more like a shackle than a gift," he said with a feather of his jaw.

Emer frowned as she asked, "Why?"

"Because, lovie, when the terms of a bargain are in opposition to what I want, I become my own worst enemy, and I am not an enemy anyone would want to have."

She gave him a sweet smile, grasping his hand in hers.

"Good thing we are friends then," she cooed.

"Calder would be jealous to hear you say that." Raising her hand, he softly kissed it. "Say it again when he gets back," he teased.

Emer fought against a laugh, and Keane smiled as his eyes tracked over her features.

"What are you thinking?" Emer asked, and the question jarred him for a moment.

His expression was a pensive one or waring emotions. "You feel so very familiar to me, and it is a foreign feeling I find myself tempted to covet," he confessed.

Emer's brow pinched. "How long have you been alone?"

An empty and defeated look flashed in his eyes.

"Long enough to think your friendship resulted from an Elder's mistake or a plan to punish me further. Both options terrify me."

"Do the Elders make mistakes?" Emer asked, not wanting to comment on her presence somehow being a punishment.

"I hope so, or else they are far crueler than I want to believe," he said, proving his scars went far beyond the jagged tear in his wing.

"What of your family?" she inquired.

"They maintained a regular Fae lifespan, living substantially longer than mortals. All of those most dear to me have long since passed beyond the Array," he sighed.

"Keane."

His name was a whispered, somber note in the quiet morning, barely louder than the song of the birds ringing in the day.

"Some centuries are lonelier than others. I'm growing quite fond of this one," he said, forcing a smile more for her benefit than anything.

"If finding each other was a mistake, it is one I am thankful for," Emer said warmly.

Keane nodded slowly but did not meet her eyes.

The door opened and the pair turned their attention to Calder, who was substantially muddier than before.

"Are any of these what you wanted?" he asked, tossing what looked like half the highland on the bed.

Slipping back into his carefree demeanor, Keane sifted through the various herbs and flowers. "Thank the Elders. Chew on this, Emmy, and all will be well," he explained as he popped one of the flowers into his mouth.

It tasted like citrus and fresh rainfall. Almost immediately, her stomach settled and the headache ceased.

"You really are magic!" she said, giving Keane a nudge.

"This realm is blessed with many plants and flowers with curing abilities. In fact, their healing properties have caused some to be nicknamed 'fairy herbs', although many other beings have discovered their uses. Witches are more well known for their use of deadly ones like foxglove, but it was a witch that taught me the wonders of lemon balm to cure a nasty night of drinking."

As soon as the color had fully returned to Emer's face and they were certain Keane could remain upright, Calder began delegating tasks for their departure. Leaving Invengarry meant saying farewell to the last suitable town until the Well. As they packed their belongings and the new provisions Calder had secured, they did so in preparation for sleeping under the stars. Although the ride ahead would be long, exhaustion almost guaranteed they would sleep with little issue.

A track in the mud just outside the inn caught Emer's atten-tion, and she paused, smiling down at the sight of the very large paw print. With a silent prayer that she would not encounter its owner again any time soon, they left.

CHAPTER 34

The only foil to a restless mind is an exhausted body. As soon as camp was set, Emer closed her eyes and embraced the stillness that so often eluded her.

For Calder, however, the quiet forest was too loud. It was a quiet that made him think of Death, a sound he knew well, and the accompanying sensation of balancing on the edge of a blade.

Death and the Morvran were partners locked in a timeless dance—some years, it took from him; some years, it walked beside him. With the Elder of Endings having granted Sea Ravens their talents, whether Calder liked it or not, Death was his kin and, therefore, never far.

Rubbing his thumb into the palm of his other hand, Calder watched Emer's chest rise and fall where she lay next to him. Her ability to sleep soundly with a monster on either side of her warmed a long-since neglected space in his cold chest.

He told himself that he wanted to preserve the lack of fear she had come to have, but he could hear his own lies in the quiet—he wanted her to believe that he could protect her. Regardless of what lurked in the shadows, it was no match for the indignation that lurked within him, and he was ready for a fight.

Whatever transpired, Keane and Calder agreed that it would remain between them and the stars that watched. Emer deserved her peace, or at least the possibility to hold on to it for as long as she could. Much like his mother before her, Emer seemed to earn people's aggression simply by existing, and just like before, the Raven would protect his redheaded girl.

Calder's eyes went black as he called upon Alabaster, who soared high above the canopy and it did not take him long to find evidence of the uninvited guest following them. This was the second time someone had come for her. He hadn't bothered to interrogate the men from the alley, but this new stranger would satiate his need for blood and answers.

He sat up, and Keane, who'd been lying opposite Emer, halted the coin he had been rolling along his knuckles.

"Someone is coming for her."

There was no need for Calder to elaborate further for Keane also noticed the man who paid too much attention to Emer in Invengarry.

While Calder silently rose from the bedding, securing his weapons, Keane began to pace. Subduing his magic as he had been so far went against his nature, and every part of him was humming at the potential for release. He cracked his neck and flexed his hands as his magic gnawed deep in his bones. Although his power could be dispelled by other means, violent outlets were his favorite and the ones he and his magic were most adept in. Keane *needed* to fight.

There were many nights when the energy stirring within him and the restlessness that accompanied it caused him to question the deals he made and the power he amassed. Tonight was not one of them. Violent thoughts had Keane's magic purring, and he rolled his shoulders in response, his cold expression curling into an even deadlier smile.

"Shall we draw lots to see who plays first?" The Fae's tone was low and sadistic.

Calder shook his head and let out an amused huff, Keane's sharp smile reminding him so much of Banner.

After securing the space, the men nodded to each other and made their way through the tree line and into the woods.

Since Emer had come into their lives, both had fought their baser tendencies for violence, and in the light of morning, they would gladly return to the men who drew smiles and laughter from her lips. Tonight, however, under the cover of darkness and at a distance great enough that the screams would not find her, they would become every bit of the monsters they were.

CHAPTER 35

Emer startled awake. Unlike the nights before when she had woken in a panic, it was not a nightmare that had her chest tight with fear. The unease that reached for her in the depths of sleep pooled heavily in the pit of her stomach at the sight of the two empty bedrolls on either side of her. Hoping to quell the rising panic, Emer slowly slid her hands over the material, searching for the telltale warmth of a body having been there.

Just like the bedding, everything was suddenly cold.

Peering over the fire into the darkness ahead, Emer waited for them to emerge from the shadows. Moments passed, but they didn't appear.

Only the occasional crackle of the fire broke the eerie quiet. Then, in the distance, a sleepy, dreamy sound in the wind took the shape of the word.

"Emer."

As she reached for her knife, she noted that their weapons were also missing. Wherever they had gone, they were armed, and Emer couldn't decide if that knowledge brought her comfort or fueled her concern.

The familiar hum beneath her skin began to pulse. A warmer

wind blew in beyond the trees, beckoning her closer until she could make out a faint glow in the distance. Carefully, she stepped over tree roots and fallen leaves as she made her way closer and discovered it to be the fire of a neighboring encampment. There was a body curled up next to it, sleeping, though she couldn't make out anything more due to the cloak they used as a makeshift blanket. If the dreamer did not know what happened to her friends, surely the large form crouched at the tree line watching them did.

Emer held her breath until she was certain she had not been noticed. Eyes closed, she willed the hum in her veins to quiet long enough for her to approach. As soon as she reached the shadow, their shoulders began to straighten. Emer lunged forward, knocking them off balance, and brought a knife to their throat as they fell.

Calder's stark black eyes stared up at her, his nostrils flaring. With a slight snarl, he repeatedly cracked his head against the ground in frustration.

"Oh, Merrow, you will be the death of me," he said in a hoarse voice.

Emer's chest heaved in preparation to yell a variety of obscenities, but they were captured by Calder's hand firmly pressed over her mouth. Her eyes blazed with anger while his remained distant.

"You can stab me later, but right now, you need to be quiet," he whispered.

He dropped his hand and placed a finger to his lips, pleading for her silence. Tipping his head, he drew her attention back to the individual by the fire. Emer didn't understand what game Calder was playing at. She turned back down to him with an unamused glare.

"As much as I regret saying this... you are going to need to get off of me."

She had not realized how he held her until she felt the increased pressure of his palms over her hips. An act that felt in stark contrast to his command. He slid his hand down her thighs, drawing attention to the fact that she was straddling him, and tapped the sides of her legs. While the dark of night hid the rosy hue of her cheeks, it did little to conceal the hitch in her breath. Emer startled as she returned to her senses, leaning to one side and un-caging him from her legs.

Calder rolled to his stomach and she mirrored the position.

They both remained low, shoulders pressed against each other, and their eyes focused on the clearing ahead.

"Why are you hiding? Or better yet, who are you stalking?" she scolded in a hushed tone.

"You are supposed to be asleep," he observed.

"You cannot be serious right now," Emer groaned.

"*You* cannot be serious," he echoed with such severity that it made Emer pause.

Even when they fought on the beach, his tone had never been so feral. It took her a moment, lost in the onyx of his eyes, but when she regained her composure, she set her jaw and let out a frustrated exhale. The sound caused a muscle in his jaw to tick.

"Should I remind you of the monsters you are likely to find in the dark?" he asked ominously, but Emer felt herself questioning whether it was a threat or a promise.

"*You* left me alone—"

He interrupted her with a hush.

"Momentarily. You weren't supposed to wake up before we finished," he began to explain, but his tone was unsure and his voice trailed off.

"Were you... am I interrupting some weird midnight tryst with some random woman in the woods? Because if so, I hope she makes your coc—"

"Is that a serious question?"

His voice was like gravel as he turned his still-black eyes to hers. Leaning in slowly, he brought his nose a feather's width from hers. Salt and whiskey coated her tongue as she breathed him in.

"Ask me. That. Again," he dared, and Emer's heart stuttered.

Her mind became devoid of thought as she felt the heat of his breath against her lips. Calder blinked, his eyes shifting back and burning into hers.

"Later. We will be talking about this later."

His hand slipped to his chest, unsheathing his knife and placing it against his lips, demanding her silence. She followed Calder's gaze just as a man emerged on the other side of the clearing.

His tall form stalked out of the shadows like a giant stepping out of the pages of myth. His eyes and hair were like charcoal, their darkness mirrored in the leathers that adorned his muscled frame. If Death had knights, he would be one of them.

A soft whimper spilled from her lips as the man unsheathed a short sword from his back. Calder's hand slid to hers and he squeezed it, pleading with her not to make another sound. She tugged in return, begging him to say something... to do something.

"We've got it under control," he reassured her, and Emer swiftly turned her gaze back to the giant and the one he lumbered over. The one she now realized was Keane.

The man kicked the sleeping form over, and surprise flashed in his features a moment before he plunged his sword down. A scream was building and ready to burst free from Emer, but it halted in awe as Keane darted out of the sword's path. The man stared in shock at his would-be victim, who now crouched on one knee several paces away.

Still kneeling with one hand pressed into the dirt, Keane's head rose, revealing a wicked smile. His magic was already crackling through the air as he closed his eyes and took in a deep and pleased breath.

"You," Keane hissed, releasing the clasp of the cloak he had borrowed from Emer. He straightened his jacket and froze. Leaning to the side, he examined the tear the man's sword had left in his jacket.

"These aren't made in periwinkle anymore, asshole," he snarled.

Sparks arched as Keane reached his hands behind his back and jerked free the twin curved blades concealed beneath his wings. The ornate designs woven into the gold handle of the knives made them look as if they were merely extensions of him—beautiful and deadly.

Keane surveyed the man, whose surprise had been replaced by a murderous glower. The flames of the campfire began to dance as a warm wind, sweet with Keane's magic, stirred the area like a goading entity counting down to their first strike.

The man gripped the hilt of his blade with both hands as he swung it down in a large arc. Keane brought one blade up and knocked his opponent's blade away. With the next strike, Keane spun to the side out of the weapon's path. His wings, which had been tucked tightly to his back, caught the firelight and cast an iridescent glow. The man shrank back, wearing a distasteful expression.

"Fae," he cursed before spitting.

"Nothing gets past you, does it, big guy?" Keane punctuated his mocking with a flawless wink.

Keane tossed his blade up, catching the knife so the sharp edge curved away from him. The man charged, but Keane *vanished*, becoming nothing more than a haunting chuckle carried on the wind.

Reappearing at the man's side, he left a shallow slice on one arm before repeating his vanishing act to leave a mirrored wound on the other side.

The man hissed, his sword swinging wildly but too slow to be effective.

Keane appeared once more in front of him, and the series of beats that followed rang sharp through the air. The men's bodies blurred into a sequence of thrusts, slices, and guards. Keane controlled his movements and shifted his weight with exquisite grace. Soon, he had locked the man's sword between his blades, knocking him back with an unforgiving kick to his abdomen and a forceful break. The man's next thrust was desperate. Keane gripped his wrist and slid the blade tucked along his forearm effortlessly across his opponent's chest, grinning at the melodic sound of the roar the act evoked.

All teeth and wicked delight. He stepped back to admire his work. This was the Keane that Calder was wary of—the Wraithnocti, the trickster, the killer.

"Aren't you going to help him?" Emer pleaded.

"Of course not, we drew lots to see who got to be bait... and besides, he doesn't appear to need any help, and I am in charge of standing watch in case there's more," Calder explained, remaining entirely focused on the clearing and the men that barreled across it.

Another roar sounded, and the man stumbled back, staring down at the large cut that now ran down his shoulder. Keane danced around, waiting for the man to collect himself.

"What a disappointing date you have turned out to be," Keane sighed before he tipped his chin up. "But have no fear. The night is young, and it's not time to die just yet."

Keane's magic slithered between them, coiling around the man's arm before cracking the bone to an unnatural angle. Moving forward with lightning speed, Keane gripped him by the back of the neck. "Although, I will make you bleed until you wish it was," he promised, driving his blade into his opponent's side.

Fire reflected off the unforgiving curve and drips of crimson dotting the ground as Keane moved to where the man's sword had fallen. He picked up the blade and tossed it into the distance before returning and cleaning his own on the man's shoulder. An act that had the previously indomitable man flinching.

Calder let out a deep breath and then pulled Emer to her feet. "You weren't supposed to be here," he said once more as his features turned distant and cold.

He freed his hand from hers as he moved into the clearing,

clapping. Keane, dripping in hubris, gave a bow. The pride slipped from his face as he noticed Emer following behind. Blood streaked down his harsh features, and even if she had not been there for the fight, the evidence of his brutality was tacky on his skin. The warm, sweet wind died in an instant, and only the iron-rich scent of violence remained as all Keane's attention fell to Emer.

Calder's steps were calculated as he descended on their victim like a feral beast. He grasped the man by the hair and ripped his head back to meet his gaze. "Did somebody send you?" his guttural and fierce voice was unrecognizable.

The man swallowed hard and grunted as he held his bleeding wound tighter.

Calder bent closer to his face, teeth exposed and movements more animal than man. "Who sent you!" he roared, but the man remained resolute in his silence.

"As much as I don't like you, I am going to give you a bit of advice. Talk to me, and I will kill you quickly. He won't," Calder explained, motioning to Keane.

Eye still fixed on Emer, Keane said, "He's right. I won't."

"Either you are here for him, which would make you a madman. You are here for me, which would make you a fool. Or..." His words trailed off as he again tilted his head and studied him. "You are here for her, which makes you a dead man."

Something in the man's eyes must have given him away. Calder released his head with a shove, leaving him collapsed at his feet. He groaned and turned his eyes to Emer. The pain in his gaze was gone, overtaken by something that looked strikingly like betrayal. Calder pressed his boot into the man's wound.

"Do. Not. Look at her," he commanded, pushing harder with each word.

Emer winced at the cry that filled the air. Before she could plead with Calder to stop, a familiar voice whispering in her ear had her breath catch in her throat.

"Hurry while they're distracted."

The words made Emer's body seize like the unforgiving hands of winter had gripped her very bones. She turned over her shoulder, expecting to see a ghost, but instead, found a very alive Lachlan.

Emer gasped, and Lachlan's eyes darted to where Keane and Calder still interrogated their captive.

"We have to go," he urged.

Ignoring his urgent commands, she wrapped her arms around him. Lachlan did not return her embrace. Instead, her disobedience caused his chest to vibrate in a frustrated growl. Lachlan gripped her arms tightly and moved to pull her into the shadows of the tree line. She needed him to understand—she needed to explain. Too late, she realized the space had gone quiet.

The heat of Calder's body pressed against her back, and his tattooed hand snaked around her hip, pulling her into his chest. Instinctively, Emer moved to grab his other hand, but Calder already held a blade under Lachlan's jaw. Wrapping her hands around Calder's forearm, Emer pulled with all her strength as she cried, "It's Lachlan. It's just Lachlan."

Calder's expression did not soften with her pleas, and he remained like stone beneath her grip. When he did move, it was not to pull away but rather to allow his knife to bite further into Lachlan's throat. "Right. The *friend* who threw you off your ship."

The corner of Lachlan's mouth tipped up at how Calder spat the word 'friend'. Emer pushed against Lachlan's chest in an attempt to force him back, but one of his hands moved to cover hers. A gesture that was far too intimate and caused that thread of anxiety spun through her spine to tighten.

"Good. You know who I am then. Thank you for keeping my girl safe, but I can take it from here."

Emer's eyes widened.

Calder's narrowed.

"Yours?" Calder challenged, tilting his head and twisting his blade enough to draw a small bead of blood.

Finally, Lachlan released Emer's hand, raising his as he stepped back and surveyed the way Calder held her. He let out a derisive snort and shook his head, evident disgust in his features.

"Elders, Em. Did you even try to get to the Well, or did you forsake it immediately just because you got a little attention?" Lachlan accused.

Emer sucked in a shocked breath.

"What the fuck did you just say to *our* girl?" Keane barked, straining as if something was physically preventing him from charging forward.

Lachlan's features quickly shifted, taking on the fond expression she was familiar with seeing. "I'm sorry, Em. I didn't mean it. It's just that I have been looking everywhere. I thought you were dead, and now here you are. We can talk about all this later, I just need you to come with me," he urged, offering his hand and pleading for her to follow.

Calder guided Emer several steps back, his hand still splayed over her lower belly. "Anything you want to keep should stay far away from her," he warned.

Leaning down, Calder collared his hand lightly around Emer's throat. He did not exert any pressure—instead, he used his grip to keep her attention on Lachlan as he brought his mouth to her ear. "Tell me what you see?" he asked.

For the first time, Emer allowed herself to take in her friend. His appearance was more unkempt than she had ever seen him before, which was understandable given the circumstances. However, his loose-hanging tunic revealed strange symbols inked into his skin. Symbols that, if he were properly dressed, would be hidden entirely. They snaked up from beneath his tunic and to just below his neck.

Having calmed slightly, Keane stood shoulder to shoulder with Calder. He drew in a deep breath and hissed, "Magic."

"Magic?" Emer questioned.

"You see those markings, sweetheart?" Calder asked in a rough whisper. "Your Lachlan plays with a very dark kind of magic."

His lips brushed her ear as she shook her head in denial.

"Calder," Keane said sternly. There was a weight in his voice that hadn't been there before—one that curved the word into a question.

"It doesn't look like Keane trusts you much, Lachlan. If I were you, I would work real hard at convincing him. I'd start with explaining why, if your destination was Lunochy, you were attacked while on an entirely different course," Calder challenged.

Lachlan let out an amused huff before he turned his eyes back to Emer's with an arched brow as if the question were unreasonable. It was a familiar expression, and suddenly, Emer realized how often she had seen it when she'd questioned something.

"Emer?" Lachlan beseeched.

The longer Emer looked into his eyes, the less she recognized him. When she saw him in the tavern, she never considered he was actually there because of the way his dead eyes had watched her, absent of all warmth, but it had been him. As Lachlan's eyes darted to Keane, Emer realized the reason he had not come for her then was the very reason why he tried to escape with her now. She had protection, and he was something to be protected from.

Watching as the firelight danced in the milky sheen of Lachlan's gaze, she wondered how she had ever seen anything else—because in her bones, she knew this was how they'd always been, but she was so busy painting pretty lies of her own, she hadn't seen his.

"Your eyes," she whispered.

A hum vibrated deep in Lachlan's throat, and he hung his head briefly.

"Calder is right. Keane gets bored quickly, and you still haven't convinced him," Emer said calmly.

Lachlan ground his teeth. "I need you to trust me." He echoed the words he used when he told her they needed to sneak off the Isle for the Well. When he told her, she needed to leave with him.

Emer's gaze dropped and everything around her fell silent. She no longer had to wonder if she could trust her old friend. She found her answer in the very hand he held out to her. It came in the form of tiny dark moons on Lachlan's nail beds. The acute anguish the knowledge brought had her sucking in a sharp gasp.

"You did this." The words were laced with so much pain that they carved and cut her throat, burning her as she spoke.

Lachlan pulled his hand back, balling it into a fist as if she would forget the sight. The evidence that he had been in contact with poison. Poison, she was now certain, ran through her father's veins.

She would tear into this man until he looked as raw as she felt. Emer gripped Calder at her back and, with a feral sound, relieved him of one of his daggers and threw it.

Lachlan staggered back slightly, gripping the hilt of the blade and pulling it free from his shoulder with a hiss. Darkness leaked from the wound and slipped free from the symbols on his skin like smoke, bleeding across the ground. It decayed fallen leaves and turned stray branches into dust.

Lachlan *was* poison.

Calder grabbed for Emer, and Keane appeared in front of them, a barrier between them and the ravenous smoke that crept toward them.

With each of Keane's footfalls, the smoke dispersed as if it were merely fog. Extending his sword directly in front of him, Keane snarled, "Tell whoever you borrowed your magic from that it lacks heart."

Lachlan's gaze darted over them before once again settling on

Emer. "He never would have let you leave with me and if you stayed. You would be dead."

"You're lying," Emer screamed, pushing against the restraint of Calder's arm.

"The men who died in the alley. Tell me, Raven, do you know what killed them?" Lachlan asked. "I do, and you are no match for them. If you want her to leave this Isle alive. Let her leave with me."

"Calder, get her out of here," Keane demanded.

But it was Emer who responded. "Not until I know why. Not until he is dead!"

Keane turned to Calder.

"We protect her from *anything*, remember?"

"I'm sorry," Calder whispered the moment before he lifted Emer, kicking and screaming, and fled into the shadows.

Calder kept a firm grip on Emer's wrist as they tore through the camp, collecting what he could with his free hand. A task made insurmountably more difficult with Emer fighting him every step. With as much as he could manage loaded onto Aven, he lifted Emer onto Danu and then situated himself behind her.

"You're a bastard," she said. Her voice was hoarse from protesting, although the rasp did little to hide the way it still shook with emotion.

Pressing his lips to the back of her head, Calder closed his eyes.

"I know."

CHAPTER 36

Despite the speed at which they raced through the night, Emer could not escape the thoughts that had sunk their claws into her mind in the clearing.

Lachlan had poisoned her father.

In addition to coping with all that his betrayal meant, Emer had the added fear that the Well may no longer be the cure she fought so hard for. Her panic was a thick film over her thoughts, and until she felt Calder shifting behind her to dismount, she hadn't even realized they stopped riding, nor was she sure how much time had passed. Looking down at him, her anger was stoked anew, and she leaped from Danu without assistance. Her legs buckled slightly upon impact, and Calder reached for her.

"You had no right!" she snarled, pushing against his chest.

Calder's nostrils flared as he took a step back. Emer matched it, bringing her fist down again. His eyes remained locked to hers as she hit him, absorbing her anger because he could do nothing to take away her sadness. Chest heaving, Emer took a step back and shook her head before turning sharply towards Aven. Calder's hand lashed out, grabbing her wrists and tugging her back.

"I can't let you go," he said regretfully.

"I'm not asking, Calder."

Without another word, he pulled her into his chest, wrapping his arms tightly around her. Emer struggled, and Calder dipped his head down, nuzzling it into the side of her neck and caging her body until she grew still.

Slowly, Calder shifted their weight, rocking ever so gently from side to side. Emer closed her eyes and twin tears streamed down her cheeks. The fear had numbed. Her anger ebbed, and finally, painfully, the sadness came.

When her breaths stuttered, he held her tighter.

Emer searched for the place inside her, the one Lina had said would feel her father's absence, and while every part of her felt fractured and bruised, she still felt him there. Collecting herself, she released a slow exhale and leaned away.

"Why?" she asked. When he lifted his head and searched her eyes, she clarified. "Why won't you let me go back?"

"Because he could have killed you," he replied.

Though nothing about Emer outwardly changed, her voice was more brittle when she spoke next, and suddenly, she felt so much smaller.

"You made it clear I am not welcome to stay when this is all over, so why would you care what happens?"

Calder's eyes heated.

"You know why," he said, releasing her and creating distance.

But Emer shook her head. Everything she thought she had known, everything she had once believed to be true, all seemed to be wrong. "I don't believe you," she said softly. Once again mistrusting everything, including herself.

Calder ran his hand through his hair. "Don't, Emer. We are not doing this now. You are understandably upset—"

"And you are afraid," she interjected in a hoarse shout.

Calder ate the space between them, taking her face into his hands. "Fucking terrified," he agreed the moment before his mouth crashed against hers.

There was no gentleness in the way he kissed her. Only the desperate need to breathe her in until his lungs burst and she filled the hollow pit that formed when he saw her in Lachlan's grasp.

The sigh Emer released when Calder parted her lips was lost beneath his answering groan. The sound vibrated down her spine, scraping across the thread of anxiety like a blade. She sank into the kiss like it was her own personal well of healing.

Grabbing his tunic, Emer pulled their bodies flush.

Calder slipped a hand into her hair, angling her head.

She kissed him until they were breathless; until the tension had melted from their muscles; until their anger and sadness had dulled.

He kissed her until he could no longer taste the tears on her lips, and then deepened the kiss, swallowing the tears she had yet to shed.

Dragging his mouth from hers, he kissed and bit along her jaw and down her neck. Drinking in each gasp, his mouth elicited. Kissing his way back up the column of her throat, he brought his lips to her ear and whispered, "Believe me now, sweetheart?

Emer opened her eyes to find Calder looking down at her through heavy lids. "You were right about him. I can't believe I didn't see it."

"There is no way you could have known what he was."

Emer scoffed.

"You did!" She brought her hands to rub her face in frustration. "You questioned me about him from the very start, and I defended him."

He took her hand, kissing the small cut on her palm she received while hitting him. "I hated him for the mere fact that he mattered to you, and that was before. Now," he paused, leaning in close and kissing her neck gently. "I hate that I didn't get to rip his throat out with my teeth."

"If he somehow manages to survive Keane, I promise I'll let

you try next." Her voice was listless, and she swayed slightly as the night's events claimed the last of her energy.

Grabbing the single bedroll he managed to retrieve in their escape, he began clearing the ground of the larger rocks and sticks.

Despite the fact that her lips were still swollen from their kiss, she arched her brow when he laid down and gestured for her to join him.

"No fires tonight. We will have to leverage the more interesting ways of keeping warm," he said with a coy smile.

Laying next to him, she followed his gaze to the stars burning brightly overhead. Since leaving home, Emer often found comfort when she looked up at the stars, knowing her family was beneath the same sky. Even though, at times, it seemed like the stars were mocking her with their secrets.

Sighing, she asked, "What do you feel when you look at the stars?"

After a moment, he answered, "Am I meant to feel something?"

She frowned.

"If you don't, then why do you look at them the way that you do?" she countered.

"Because when you know what they mean, you can read them like stories," he explained.

She sat up slightly and turned her attention fully to the sky, her face scrunching as she tried to make out any discernible shapes.

"Do you know the story of the Rivals?" he asked in a low tone, causing Emer to shake her head.

"Come here," he said so quietly that she almost missed it. When she turned, she found the arm that was not tucked behind his head extended. She settled into the crook of his shoulder and he brought his hand up, guiding her gaze to a specific cluster of stars.

"The Rivals were said to have fought in a tournament to win the heart of the Gray Witch."

Despite looking, her eyes failed to locate the two forms he

described. Slipping his arm from behind his head, he brought his fingers to her chin and aligned her gaze to where he had been pointing, and then resumed his relaxed posture.

"There," he whispered.

Trailing her gaze up his forearm and to the tip of his finger, she saw them. Two large bodies locked in battle. Pulsing stars around them seemed to mirror a spark as their swords clashed.

"When her love died, the Gray Witch cast him into the sky along with her own heart. Every night she looked upon him, told him she loved him, and swore that her heart would always be his and that she would find a way to bring him back. And every day, she sought revenge against those who separated them."

Emer's eyes remained fixed on the unique star pulsing a pale red in the center of one of the figures chest —right where his heart would be.

"I suppose that is fairly romantic," Emer remarked, trying to stave off the ache she felt for the lovers who had lost each other.

"No, Merrow. The story is a cautionary tale," he continued. "When you take the light of someone's life, they will become the monster that will drag you into the dark." His tone was grave.

Emer thought of his parents and the consuming love they shared. The kind of love that left its mark, even on the stars. "Well, that just made it sound even more romantic," she said with a sniff, and he could not help but smile.

"So violent," he murmured as he rested his head on hers.

"Calder?"

"Yes, Merrow?"

"You said you hated Lachlan before you knew what he was. Did you put your knife to his throat before or after you saw the symbols?" she asked.

His stubble caught in her hair as he pressed his curved lips to the top of her head.

"I think you already know the answer to that."

"So, you pulled a knife on him because I cared about him?"

Calder hummed, and the sound was full of humor and menace. "Tell me more about how much you care for him." His grip found her thigh, pulling it across his lap until it was hooked over his hip. "Go ahead, really. I would *love* to hear how much you care about dear old Lachlan."

There was a challenge in his eyes that was at odds with the tenderness in the hand that trailed idly from her knee to her hip.

"*Cared*," she corrected.

"Clearly," he returned, smirking slightly as she melted into him.

He did not move the hand that held her leg around him. She did not move the arm that was draped over his chest. Sooner than either of them would have liked, a dreamless sleep claimed them.

CHAPTER 37

Calder awoke to a warm wind tousling his hair.

Keane sat perched on a fallen tree nearby, staring at him with a petulant expression. It was then that Calder recognized the weight of Emer's body wrapped around him, his own hand laying scandalous claim to her as she slept.

"I should find a witch to make your dick fall off," Keane said flatly.

"And yet, you didn't wake me when you arrived," Calder asserted.

Keane conjured his chalice, taking a large drink before turning and spitting it out in an attempt to remove the taste of the rotten magic that had clung to Lachlan and still coated the back of his throat. True magic—Keane's magic—was sweet.

"Emmy looked peaceful. After what happened last night, I wouldn't risk waking her up. Besides, *if* she is fond of you, then she will stay. So, against all odds, I am actually rooting for you."

Calder's throat tightened as he realized the ache he would feel at the loss of her warmth when she woke would pale in comparison to the pain of her leaving for good. If his soul had been fractured before, he was certain the moment he lost sight of her on the horizon, he would lose it entirely.

Strange and *wicked* magic.

With Keane back, there was too much they needed to discuss, and he forced himself to run his hand up and down Emer's spine, waking her.

"Morning," he said.

"Good morning," she responded.

"Debatable," Keane drawled.

Emer sat up quickly, looking at Keane. He, in turn, cast his eyes to the ground and made no attempt to move closer. His posture was no longer proud or certain. Even his wings seemed to fall lower than usual. Both men remained silent as Emer rose, waiting for her to decide the terms of what came next.

They had left her alone, they had brutalized someone in front of her, they had protected her, but they had not listened to her. The fear at the truth of all those things was evident in the remorseful heather-colored eyes that stared back at her. Waiting to learn if she would scream at them, admonish them, or fear them.

Keane and Calder were no strangers to monstrous deeds, but it was clear that having her witness them was what made them feel like true monsters and the pieces of her heart that each of them had stolen broke.

Misunderstanding her sadness, Keane began to try to explain. "You were safe, Emmy," Keane said in a low voice. "We carved protection runes into the surrounding trees and..."

Keane rubbed his thumb over the faint pink line on his palm, the only sign of the already healing cut. Runes without magic were nothing more than symbolic but Calder's runes activated with the magic in Keane's blood held power.

Keane moved closer, eyes pleading, and it became evident that the cut on his palm was not the only injury he'd sustained. His clothes were torn and dirty. There was a large tear down one side and a healed cut through his right eyebrow.

She raced forward, wrapping her arm around Keane. "I'm still mad at you, but I'm so glad you are okay."

Keane shuddered briefly before returning the gesture tenfold, squeezing her tightly as he pressed a kiss on the top of her head.

"I'm so fucking sorry," he swore.

Without fully releasing him, Emer held out her hand towards Calder and smiled to herself as she felt his strong hand close over hers only a heartbeat later.

Held tightly between them, she murmured, "Thank you for protecting me."

Emer backed away, watching them through red-rimmed eyes. "You are both idiots, by the way. I was afraid *for* you, not *of* you."

Their shoulders dropped, her words releasing the weight that had shackled them both, one that had been there long before her but, somehow, only she could remove. Something *good* that accepted them, monsters that they were.

"Are you ready to talk about it?" Keane asked gently.

Emer nodded.

Unlike his typical method of relaying information, Keane kept strictly to the facts—how Lachlan had hired Ubel to take Emer, though, in reality, he was merely a distraction; how they had drawn lots to determine who would go into the clearing versus who would stand to watch.

"I won," Keane said proudly. "I took your cloak to disguise my scent and waited for him to strike."

"Why did you let him strike before reacting?" she asked, giving Keane a scolding look.

"Emmy, love. I am immortal, remember?" he reminded her softly as he tapped her on the nose.

She whirled to face Calder.

"You *aren't*. And you still drew lots. What if it had been you?" she pressed.

"Then I would have gladly taken my position next to the fire and even more enthusiastically worn that bastard's blood," he remarked with no hesitation.

Keane cleared his throat, shifting on his feet uncomfortably. "He did have a condition in coming for her outside of payment."

"Condition?" Calder echoed.

"He wanted a lock of Emmy's hair," Keane sneered.

"He died slowly, yes?" Calder's voice was sharp and cold.

"I took breaks to hydrate." Keane smiled at Calder before turning back to Emer with a fretful expression. "I'm sorry, Emmy. Do you want me to go back and get you a lock of his hair?" he asked.

Emer declined.

"And Lachlan?" Calder asked.

Keane looked down briefly before answering.

"I expect he has succumbed to his wounds," Keane explained, running his hands through his hair. "He fled into the woods, and I tracked him most of the night, but there was another scent, different magic, that made it impossible to locate. I lost him, Emmy."

Lachlan had gotten away.

Recognizing the Sea Raven's sense of urgency and deep contemplation, Keane's eyes narrowed. "You know we cannot travel through the Bleeding Trees," he said sternly.

Calder's expression was hostile, but Keane stood firm.

"The new moon is a day away."

"I am aware," Calder growled, the unified facade from earlier burnt to ash as they glared at the other. "What if he tries again?" he bit out.

"Then we will fucking handle it, Calder. We are not going through the woods."

"What's wrong with the woods?" Emer interjected.

Keane sharpened his glare at Calder momentarily. "The Women of the Woods. They are the residents and protectors of the Bleeding Trees. They care for them and, in turn, draw power from the forest," he explained casually to the astonished mortal before him.

The woods themselves stretched across the length of the Isle, rendering it almost impassable. Those who dared to traverse the landscape risked their lives to do so. However, a great fire ravaged the woods several centuries earlier and resulted in a narrow clearing that has since allowed travelers to cross free from the reach of the Women.

When Emer asked Keane what made the inhabitants so dangerous, she saw the slightest twitch in his wings.

"They have a nasty habit of bloodletting travelers who can be lured across or near the tree line," he said with a sigh. "To make matters worse, they and the others who call the woods home are particularly excitable during the new moon and you smell as sweet as honeysuckle. While they would not harm you, we would not receive the same hospitality, and that would leave you vulnerable," he said flatly.

Emer balked, "I what?"

She had not realized that Calder began to stride past her. He paused momentarily, his breath causing the hair on the back of her neck to stir.

"He said... you smell like *dessert*."

She drew in a sharp breath at the deep sound and the mental images of his mouth that it conjured.

"Oh," she remarked, turning slightly to look at him over her shoulder, Keane's pacing and muttering still present in the distance.

Calder studied her for a moment, his hands balling at his sides. "Yeah. *Oh*," he echoed darkly before continuing his stride past her.

After thoroughly discussing the risks, the three agreed to navigate to Belwarie and proceed through the clearing.

Emer excused herself to prepare for the next leg of their journey, leaving Calder and Keane alone.

"We have to send her back," Calder said. Even as he spoke the words, he could taste how false they were on his tongue.

With sudden clarity, Calder realized that it was not his father's pride and belief that he could protect his mother—it was his fear of separating from her that fueled his inability to leave her, and he was acutely aware of how easily he could become the very thing he despised so much in his father and no longer trusted himself to be able to let her go. When he took a deep breath, Emer's scent flooded his lungs from where it had woven itself into his tunic.

"I'm sorry, Lachlan must have hit me harder than I thought. Can you please repeat that?" The use of the word 'please' did little to weaken the venom in Keane's voice.

"If I try to keep her, you will take her away."

Keane's eyes flared wide with anger. "I don't take orders from Ravens," he countered.

"It's not an order. It's a fact. You and I made a bargain. Protect her from *anything*. Including ourselves. If I ask her to stay, she is in danger here, and your magic knows that. If I ask her to stay, it will force you to take her."

Calder's eyes were cold as he held Keane's, which burnt with a riotous hatred. Keane's magic began to hum and stretch beneath his skin in agreement.

"I hate you," he ground out as he fought the instinct stirring inside him. "You are going to *regret* this. You are going to want her! You already want her, and you are going to make her hate me."

Calder just nodded.

"You better fucking hope it doesn't come to that. I was fine with being your enemy, but there is no corner of this vile land where you will be able to hide from me if you make me hers." The anger in Keane's voice had ebbed into something that sounded almost desperate—he resigned himself to the truth that when any of them told this story in the coming years, there would be no happy endings.

"I want her to stay," Keane confessed.

Calder closed his eyes and tipped back his head, fighting the sickening weight that had already settled into his bones.

"That's the problem. So do I."

CHAPTER 38

The town of Belwarie was unlike the villages they visited before. No bustling locals or rowdy taverns were painting the night in debauchery; the lack of noise—lack of life—was unsettling. Each breath drew in the stale air and coated the back of their throats with an acrid taste. Belwarie was more than just the Isle Basalt of myths. It was a town of nightmares.

Not even the sun wanted to linger longer than it had to, and darkness settled quickly, leaving only a sliver of moon to guide their way, and despite Calder's best efforts, they were unable to reach the clearing before the sunlight began to draw back from the land. If there was one thing that could make the town less appealing, it was facing it at night. Unwilling to enter the town blind, Calder separated from the group briefly to collect materials for a torch, which Keane lit with ease.

Those who had settled the town after the great fire had done so out of greed, knowing others in need of safe passage would be desperate enough to pay whatever toll the inhabitants wished to press upon them. They had sown the foundation of their town with corruption, unaware of the dark things that would be drawn to it. Now, rather than a symbol of prosperity, it was a beacon of broken dreams and neglect.

The homes they passed were dark monoliths, with no light filtering through the shutters or under doors to indicate the presence of inhabitants and there was a stillness of growing discontent rather than peace.

Calder had pulled ahead slightly, his knuckles white around the torch he used to light their way and Danu's reins. Keane took to walking alongside Emer. When facing a threat, it was them against the realm, and with the Bleeding Trees bordering either side of the town, there was no shortage of threats.

The ghost of a giggle carried through the night air and had all but Keane turning to the shadowy space between the trees on their left. Keane's jaw worked as he continued to look ahead.

"Where is everyone?" Emer was the first to speak, her words a whisper easily heard in the eerie silence. It was not late enough for the entire village to be asleep, and even if it were, one would expect to see the occasional drunkard.

"The lore of those who pass through this town is that a great beast is dead and buried here," Calder explained as he scanned the vicinity.

A shiver rocked Emer as her attention turned to the woods in the distance and the bloodthirsty inhabitants lurking unseen.

"The lore is wrong. It is alive and well," Keane said without a thimble of humor.

"How do you know?" Emer's voice shook.

"Do you hear the animals? Even they know better than to draw its attention. The bastard demolished the dairy production of this town a few centuries ago, and I had to drink sans cheese when passing through this pit," he scoffed.

Emer wished the lack of snacks was the only thing she feared for them during this venture, but the cold licking up the back of her neck told her better.

"Do you make it a habit to insult creatures that have entire towns in hiding?" Calder whispered as he continued to scan their surroundings.

"Do you make it a habit to be dreadfully dull?" Keane scoffed back.

"I am not dull. I am just trying not to get killed in this shit-hole," Calder spat back.

"Everybody needs to stop insulting the town!" Emer hissed.

"Relax. I have not actually heard of him attacking anyone... the creature feeds off fear, and this town is lousy with it, thanks to the Women of the Woods," Keane explained as he reached up and began to soothe Alabaster, still perched on his shoulder.

"Why would anyone choose to live in such a... here? Why live here?" The words came out hushed, even though she was not sure what it was that she might offend.

"The monster you know is less terrifying than the one you don't," Calder answered.

As if sensing the presence of a challenging predator, Keane and Calder's attention turned at the exact moment fog began to pour from the tree line. Thick, milky mist rolled across the clearing until it pooled across the path. The atmosphere shifted, causing Aven and Danu to grow restive. The moment the fog reached them, the horses reared to their hind legs and cried out in protest.

Unprepared for their outburst, Emer was thrown free, grasping at the air as she fell. A hard squeak escaped her as she braced for the impact against the stone road, but it never came. Keane's arms wrapped around her and pulled her tightly against him. She felt his chest sink with a sigh, but the sound was drowned out by what was either Alabaster cheering or objecting to the rescue, digging his talons into Keane's shoulder.

While Aven had already fled, Calder continued to fight to gain control of Danu. A battle he was quickly losing as the fog rose and the horse grew more agitated.

"My coin is on the horse... you?" Keane wagered.

"Why are your bets always surrounded by grave injury?" she growled as he set her down.

"I am not understanding the question. Do your bets *not* surround someone getting gravely injured?" he asked, genuinely confused.

She shook her head and he looked utterly offended.

"How very mortal." His musing was more curious than dismissive, but Calder soon interrupted it by hitting the ground in front of them. They both flinched at the fleshy sound of Calder's impact as he disappeared under the thick fog that had now reached their knees.

"Fuck'n shit!" he cursed from beneath the clouded sea.

The crack of hooves against the path grew quiet, signaling that their transportation and supplies were long gone.

"Well, that was unfortunate..." Keane sighed. "Aye, right, you good?" he called into the fog at their feet as he leaned closer and peered down his nose.

A low groan sounded from the fog shortly before Calder re-emerged, its tendrils dancing around him. "Thanks for the help," he sneered as he slowly hauled himself to his feet.

His expression stiffened as he rolled his shoulder and hissed through his teeth.

"Excuse me, did you ask for assistance?" Keane scoffed, placing both his hands delicately against his chest as if he were shocked by Calder's annoyance.

"I didn't hear Em yelling for you, and you still caught her!" Calder protested.

"I didn't catch her. My body just so happened to get between her and the ground. Also... what are you, the Bailiffs? What's with all the questions?" he argued with an exasperated toss of his hands.

Emer mouthed an apology, but Calder was too busy glaring distastefully at being compared to those appointed to keep order between mortals and those with magic. He rubbed the back of his head furiously as he tipped it back and winced. The moment his sigh left his lips, it formed a cloud in the suddenly frigid air, and they all paused at the sight.

Before anyone could comment on the strange drop in temperature, the hair on their necks rose. The three turned in unison, having all felt the strange energy stirring to their backs. Peering into the darkness, they found what appeared to be two floating candles fashioned to look like horns. A flickering blue flame danced at the end of each.

"No warmth can be found near a blue flame," Keane recalled the ancient warning.

As if in agreement, Calder's own torch began to writhe like liquid azure.

Spinning Emer around by her shoulders, Keane gripped her firmly and held her eyes. "I have avoided the need to run for literally centuries, so you need to take what I am about to do very seriously. No matter what... do. Not. Let. Go."

He held his hand out to her and Emer clung to him.

As they ran, an inhuman screech came from behind them.

"What is that!" Calder yelled over the rumbling and screeching that seemed to be surrounding them from every direction.

"Fewer questions, more running... but if we survive this, we really need to fucking talk about why literally everything is trying to kill us!" Keane hollered back.

"You can't die!" Calder growled in return.

"Yeah, well, almost dying hurts like a—" Keane's words were drowned out by a sound that almost stopped Emer in her tracks.

Look at us.

The voice—cold and hoarse like a howling wind over the midnight sea—whispered in her ear.

Emer's chest began to ache as if the tendrils of fog that slipped down her throat had grown into fingers and were now strangling the beat of her heart. Spots began to form in her vision as the moment her heart should have beat passed her by.

"I can hear them," she gasped, unable to draw in sufficient breath.

"Don't look, Emmy!" Keane yelled as they continued to barrel down the road.

"Eyes on me. Only me," Calder demanded.

Salt coated her tongue as beads of either tears, perspiration, or a combination of both slipped into her mouth. She closed her eyes and her whole body trembled as she felt lips press against her skin. They echoed the path Calder had taken the day before, but rather than heat, it left a trail of frost. She strained her face in the opposite direction as she took in a sharp breath.

"It's so close," she choked.

With a roar, Calder pulled her forward and moved to run at her back, using the torch he retrieved like a sword. The creature hissed.

"Why is it only attacking her?" Calder bellowed.

"I don't know, Cal, why don't you stop to ask it?"

Emer's steps began to slow and her body began to list.

The uneven stones sent pulses of pain with each step, but the men showed no signs of slowing.

"I can't," she gasped as her legs once again began to buckle.

"If you stop, we stop!" Calder howled, and Keane squeezed her hand in agreement.

She caught the edge of her lip as she gritted her teeth, ignoring the metallic taste of blood that filled her mouth.

"Keane..." Calder growled.

"I know!" Keane barked again.

"Take her. Do something!" Calder shouted, and the muscles in Keane's back twitched, sending a shudder through his wings.

"If this doesn't work. Guard her like your life depends on it. Because it quite literally does," Keane commanded before he disappeared in a swirl of muted colors.

Emer's now empty hand tingled faintly where Keane's had been.

"He'll be back," Calder assured.

Emer's legs began to give, and Calder moved back to her side, his fingers now intertwined with hers. Again, she could hear the whispers building, the cold breath leaving pinpricks along her neck.

"Calder..." Her voice was resigned and unsure of what to say or what she hoped to hear in return.

"Tell me later, Merrow." He paused. "We'll have later," he vowed.

She felt the creature stir at her side, and her blood ran cold. Closing her eyes, she squeezed Calder's hand twice before releasing it and bracing for the shadows to take her.

A low growl escaped the Sea Raven as he held her hand even more fiercely than before. The smell of smoke and sweet wine wrapped her.

"Sorry, darling."

When Keane's eyes met Emer's, she could tell whatever plan he'd had failed, and the pain from his desperate desire to save her was all that remained.

They were always trying to save her and she knew they meant their oath. If she stopped, they would stop, and she would not allow them to be taken from each other without a fight.

"Your chalice," she said breathlessly, and Keane stiffened.

"Calder, what did she say?" he shouted.

"Your chalice!" Calder echoed impatiently.

Keane conjured the chalice, and Emer released his hand and accepted it. Tossing her head back, she allowed the burning liquid to fill her mouth. Once, Keane entertained her by lighting the liquid and manipulating the flame into a small dancing form.

Tonight, she did not need a delicate dancer.

Tonight, she needed a dragon.

With her free hand shaking, she motioned to Calder for the torch. The moment she felt the bite of the wood against her palm, she fixed her feet to the path and turned.

Keane and Calder were unable to stop their momentum and stumbled as they attempted to reach back and keep hold of her.

Bringing the torch up to her mouth, she released the wine in a fine spray, sending forth a ravenous flame. The unnatural body caught, writhing and burning. If her eyes had been open, she would have seen how her reflection glowed like a star in the pitch-black night of the beast's eyes.

Blinded by the violent flash of blue flames, Keane and Calder struggled to advance. Their own shouts vying to be heard over the high-pitched screams of the disintegrating beast.

Swaying slightly, Emer's eyes remained closed until the last of the burning light faded. With no breath left in her lungs, her lips parted and red rivulets dripped down her chin. As everything went dark, she opened her eyes to find nothing but an empty lane. She released a relieved breath and then collapsed like a doll liberated from its strings.

Calder lunged forward. His body splayed across the cobblestones and his hands pinned under Emer's head, he stared at her panting. With a sigh, his body molded to the path as every muscle sagged in relief.

Keane knelt at his side and patted him on the back with a low whistle. "I still can't stand you. But good catch." A pause. "I'll deny it happened until the day I die."

Calder nodded, his sweat-slicked forehead pressed against the stone. He struggled to right himself and pulled Emer into his lap. Her chest rose and fell with deep breaths, and he brushed the remnants of wine from her chin, the rough pad of his thumb stroking her bottom lip.

"She saved *us*," he whispered, staring at her in disbelief.

"I am certain the Elders wove in her nervousness for fear of facing her without it." Keane's voice was warm with affection.

Emer's fire would not have killed the beast—it merely banished it and forced it to reform. In order to be safe, they would need to cross the running water of the creek at the border of town, and yet Calder could not move.

He didn't want to let her go.

He.

Didn't.

Want.

To.

Let.

Her.

Go.

The thought caught in his mind, tearing until he felt the burn in his eyes.

"Shit. Shit. Shit," he cursed rapidly under his breath, the full weight of his mistake crashing into him. He'd made Keane promise to take her from him if he tried to keep her on the Isle, and in that moment, he could not even stomach having her taken from his arms. His eyes shot up to Keane—his regret clear.

"I hate you, you know that?" Keane growled, the anger he had felt when they spoke at the camp renewed.

"Not even a day!" Keane bellowed into the night, pacing around them and tugging his hands through his hair. "If you could have just set aside your own arrogance for a moment, you would have seen she didn't need us. We needed her!" he fumed.

Calder looked down at Emer, the sound of Keane's strides growing dull as he watched her. He could not ask her to stay, but that didn't mean he couldn't try to get her to *choose to* stay—to choose him. Without a word, Calder gathered Emer into his arms and began to walk in the direction the horses had fled. Keane cracked his neck to the side in frustration.

"Fucking figure this out, Raven. If I have to take her away... remember that I will be coming back, and I will be pissed," Keane demanded before walking ahead.

They found the horses just on the other side of the bridge as if the animals could sense it was outside of the beast's reach.

Still unwilling to relinquish her, Calder rode Danu with Emer in his arms. Keane rode Aven, his posture rigid with tension and resentment.

Lines had been drawn, unwavering like the space where the sky meets the sea. Somewhere in between is where Emer floated in a dreamless sleep. The cold water of the sea and warm wind gravitating towards her until their joined energies became a storm.

CHAPTER 39

I sle Basalt taught Emer many things.

One: men grunt when they die.

Two: painful moments linger.

Three: she had been right the first time—death was cold.

The warmth that surrounded her now was the first sign that the beast of Belwarie hadn't managed to kill her. More than that, she'd saved the others from it.

She was coaxed from sleep by a gentle swaying and the awareness of strong arms around her. Taking a deep breath, she was blanketed by whiskey and salt water.

She smiled.

Waking in Calder's arms had become more familiar than it should have been, but Emer could no longer deny that she welcomed it. She tried to open her eyes, but exhaustion held her as tightly as he did, and they fluttered closed after catching sight of his silhouette framed in the morning light.

"You called my name..." Calder's words trailed off.

At that, she opened her eyes. The intensity of his stare caused any remarks on her part to catch in her throat.

"When you collapsed, you called my name," he explained, and there was a combination of surprise and reverence in his tone.

Before she could respond, she heard Keane make clipped remarks from where he rode atop Aven. Her eyes darted between the two of them; their normally soft smiles had sharpened, leaving her balancing on an edge.

The muscles of Calder's chest tensed beneath her hand as she attempted to right herself. His heartbeat set a pace that mirrored her own, and she jerked away, feeling as though she had stolen a secret. The gracelessness of the movement caused her to crash back against him.

"We need to stop so I can gather herbs to counter the effects of the attack. She isn't well, Raven," Keane commanded.

Calder's jaw worked, but he nodded.

"What happened?" Emer whispered, trying to make sense of the strange tension that settled heavily over their group.

"What happened, Merrow, is you stopped." There was a heat in Calder's tone that was not entirely disapproving but not completely proud either.

"I did." Her lips curled in a sleepy smile. "You're welcome."

"It... changed things," he continued.

"What things?" she asked, matching his hushed tone and searching his eyes for an answer.

He crooked his fingers towards her and gave her a conspiratorial look. Leaning in, she tilted her head to better hear him. "*Secret* things," he whispered before taking her ear between his teeth with a sharp nip.

Emer gasped, reeling back and smacking his chest, which shook with silent laughter.

"I'm serious," she hissed, the pink staining her skin making the green of her eyes even brighter.

"So am I," he said in earnest.

"I think this is a good time to *stop*," Keane remarked louder than necessary.

He led the party off the path and into the tall grass. There was barely a breath before Keane dismounted and stood next to Danu, holding his hand out to Emer. Calder's grip on her tightened briefly before relaxing and releasing her.

"Emmy and I will look for the herbs. You can... go find us water or something," Keane said impatiently.

The crease between Emer's brows deepened when Calder did not balk at the demand.

As Keane led her away, she looked over her shoulder to find that while Calder had dismounted, he hadn't moved. He stood by the horses, his arms crossed over his chest, and winked. She thought she'd imagined it for a moment, but then he smirked as he began backing his way toward the tree line.

"Is everything okay?" she asked, placing her hand on Keane's arm.

"Of course," he replied with a stiff smile. "I am sorry I couldn't protect you. You know that is all I am trying to do, right? Keep you safe."

There was a vulnerability in his eyes that had not been there before, along with what might have been fear. Emer stopped, tugging at Keane's arm until he looked at her.

"I know," she said, embracing him in a tight hug.

Fear had him stiff in her embrace. He rested his chin on her head, kissing her hair softly.

"Besides. Now I can brag that I saved you," she spoke into his chest.

Hearing the smile in her voice eased some of the tension in his muscles.

"Too right."

When Keane found what he was looking for, he removed his jacket and laid it down in the grass to hold the various delicate plants he'd begun collecting.

There was something ethereal about the sight of him in a simple tunic as his long fingers reverently selected stems and leaves.

Satisfied with their harvest, he sat cross-legged before his jacket and began braiding strands of the herbs together. His rolled up sleeves revealed ornate gold markings that swept up the lean muscles of his forearms. They caught the sunlight and the art scrawled across his skin was suddenly ignited as if painted with luminous strokes.

"How did you get those markings?" Emer asked as she watched him prepare the herbs.

Keane's hands stuttered briefly. Clearing his throat, he asked, "What?"

Recognizing that it was perhaps rude to ask a Fae such a question, she stumbled over herself as she attempted to clarify.

"I'm sorry, was it rude to ask? I think they are beautiful and I—"

"No, Emmy. It's just... I suppose the question just caught me by surprise." His lips parted as if he intended to say more but his brow furrowed and he refocused on his task.

"What do you mean? What are they?" she asked.

"It is magic beneath my skin. Magic that is not comprehensible to mortals. So much so that they typically cannot even see it right in front of them."

Looking at him more closely, she could see that the marks were not just on his arms; they disappeared under his tunic and reappeared in wisps over his collarbones and the sides of his neck. They crept up his body like vines, some bare, whereas small flowers adorned others.

"What do they mean?" she asked again.

He shifted uncomfortably at her question, nervously rubbing at the back of one of his hands and distorting the gold five-petaled flower painted on his skin.

"They are bargains," he explained, gaze downcast.

There was a reason why people were warned against making bargains with the Fae, yet Emer could see with her own eyes the many who had not heeded them.

When Keane finally looked up, there was remorse in his eyes, and she wondered how many of the marks on his body weighed on him like the coin in his pocket. With a life as long as his, there were sure to be regrets. In comparison, Emer's life had been a blink and yet she already regretted plenty. Leaning forward, she placed her hand on his and squeezed it twice.

"Always twice," he observed out loud, and Emer smiled.

"Once for love, and once for luck," she explained.

Of all the obscure things Keane knew, of all the secrets he had closely guarded, he was certain that this knowledge would be what he coveted most.

"Keane?" Her voice was quiet.

"Yes, lovie?" he asked, already knowing the question.

"Why can I see them?"

His gaze rose slowly to hers, but he did not answer. Not right away. His brow furrowed as his eyes held hers.

"It is not common for Fae to become so attached to mortals, you know. For most, mortals are a source of entertainment or bargains. If, however, a Fae were to take a mortal as a mate, they would be woven into our world and be granted sight."

Emer watched him with wide eyes, blinking as her thoughts swirled like smoke between the shape of his words and trying to fill the gaps in her comprehension.

"But I am not your entertainment, nor am I your mate," Emer stated.

"No," he let out a chuckle. "No, you are not. You are, however, my dear friend. A mortal I protect and care for without gaining something in return. Some might say that is more powerful than romantic love," he continued, a soft smile appearing on his face.

His words seemed to have an almost immediate calming effect and Emer nodded in agreement. The way they can cut and wound, one might see words as solid things but after centuries of bending and twisting them into pleasing shapes, Keane knew better. Words could be a balm as easily as they could be a blade.

"I fell in love with your eyes first, I think. I knew you were special the moment I saw them. Love is a lot like magic in how it can make us feel both powerful and desperately powerless," he mused.

"So, I can see the marks. Because you love me... as a friend?" she asked with a tilt of her head and furrow in her brow.

Keane gave her a tight smile.

"More or less, darling."

Holding up the chorded herbs, Keane lit it with his magic and a gentle smoke scented with juniper drifted from it. Rising to his knees, he stood over Emer and twirled the smoke around her.

She closed her eyes, breathing deep and filling her lungs. It smelled like wishes and warm solstice wind—a salve for her tired muscles and soul.

Slowly, she felt the grip of exhaustion release her and the fog in her mind clear. When she opened her eyes again, Keane sat back on his heels in front of her, the morning sun wrapping him in a halo of light. Her eyes lit with wonder and he smiled a genuine and bright smile.

"Do you have a mark from your bargain with Calder to protect me?" Her voice was dreamy as she relaxed into the calm settling over her.

"I do," he acknowledged, tilting his head and brushing back his hair to reveal the feather marked behind his slightly pointed ear.

Emer grinned.

"How long will you have it?" she asked, running her finger over it and causing him to flinch away from the ticklish sensation.

"We did not stipulate a timeframe. So, I will have it until he dies or breaks our deal."

"Will you have one from this? From helping me?" she asked, her voice carrying a note of wariness.

"Not all bargains are selfish, Emer." His brow pinched in frustration. "Some bargains are meant to help. But no, I can take care of you without it indebting you in any way."

The relief in her features was a dull knife in his chest and the pain was evidence that at least once upon a time he had a heart. His long life had given him unmatched tolerance, and the hurt never reached his eyes even as he felt his soul blacken a little more.

CHAPTER 40

They walked back to the horses, arm in arm. Keane donning a flower crown Emer had made him and fully prepared to punch Calder in the face at the first twitch of his lip. To both their surprise, however, Calder was nowhere to be found.

"Is it too much to hope some kind of unknown creature devoured him?" Keane muttered, eyes scanning the area.

"You two have been at each other since the woods. Is everything alright?" she asked, still scanning the space.

"Peachy... everything is just peachy, love."

After how he greeted her when she woke up, Emer was eager to find Calder. While Keane seemed in no hurry and, after making a half-hearted comment about taking the horses and leaving, was content to lay out on a blanket and let Emer search.

As she eyed the tree line, debating where to begin, a raven black as night touched down on the limb of a nearby tree. It watched her, and Emer tilted her head and studied the creature. The bird returned the gesture and as Emer approached her attention caught on a piece of parchment it seemed to be ferrying. As if sensing her hesitation, the bird gave a slow bow. Cautiously, Emer worked the note free.

One monster down, one to go. Come find me.

Emer's heart seemed to stutter and everything around her faded as her vision narrowed to the thick black letters scrawled in front of her. Her original purpose for locating him was lost in the spaces between the beats.

"Did you find him? I don't hear any growling, so I doubt it," Keane hollered from over by the horses. Hiding the note, Emer cleared her throat.

"Not yet! Can you watch the horses?"

While the note gave no indication as to why Calder wanted her to find him, the anticipation tore through her like a meadow on fire. She did not wait for Keane's response. When the bird took flight, she followed.

With her eyes on her guide in the sky, her boots caught on various obstacles littering the forest floor and she struggled to keep pace. The raven adjusted its course sharply and she froze. Turning in place, she searched for it but dropped her gaze, frowning at its sudden choice to abandon her.

A branch cracked and she was acutely aware of how ridiculously stupid she had been to venture into the woods alone. Ripping the note free from her pocket, she scanned it again and her stomach sank at the realization that it was unsigned. She assumed it was Calder, but what if she was wrong?

Despite the ordeal from the night before, fear invigorated her once-tired muscles and her feet pounded across the uneven terrain. Sweat began to streak down the nape of her neck and her hair clung to her skin. Calder stepped out from behind a tree, sucking his bottom lip between his teeth as he smiled. Her breath caught as their eyes met. Pools of ink, black as the raven he had used to find her.

Relief crashed into her as his powerful arm wrapped around her waist, pulling her from the ground. Using her momentum, he spun her through the air, settled her in front of him, and pressed her back against the tree. Arm still around her waist, he slid his other hand to her throat, his index finger and thumb resting on either side of her jaw.

"What has you running scared, little Merrow?" he asked, a finger slowly sliding down over her pulse.

"I wasn't scared," she panted.

"Liar." His voice was all teeth as he dragged the words across the shell of her ear.

"Haven't learned your lesson about running from me? I told you. There is nowhere you can go where I will not find my way back to you." It was a truth he had proven many times over, but this time, when he said it, it felt like an oath rather than a threat, and it caused her chest to swell.

"Can you see me?" she asked, the darkness of his stare reflecting back her own surprised face.

He nodded slowly.

"Not as you see me. But yes, I can."

He tipped his head to the sky and she followed his gaze through the trees to see the dark raven had returned. She suspected his talent had not been isolated to Alabaster, but wondered why he chose another for this task. The bird began to dive through the trees with ease and grace.

"Do they go where you tell them?" Before the question had fully left her lips, a rush of wind crashed into her face and the large black bird perched itself on his shoulder.

"They do," he remarked as she muffled her gasp with her hands.

At such an intimate distance, she could see that the raven's feathers were not a mournful black but rather iridescent. Painted delicately with purples, blues, and greens. Dark and ominous at a distance. Alluring and memorizing once close.

It watched her the way it had earlier, the way Calder had many times before. She slowly raised her hand, intending to stroke its beautiful black feathers, but paused to look at Calder. He dipped his chin in approval. Carefully, she brushed her knuckles down its chest and smiled widely as the raven leaned into her touch. Looking back at Calder excitedly, she was surprised to see his affectionate blue and gray gaze staring back at her.

"Careful, Merrow, we wouldn't want either of the ravens before you to get jealous."

He dismissed the raven with a glance.

"Now, where were we?" he asked as he shifted the hand behind her head, wrapping her braid around his fist before settling it between her and the tree once more.

The corner of his lip curled as he used his grip to tilt her head. "Oh, right... there is something we need to discuss." The words rumbled deep from his chest as he nipped at her jaw before dragging his lips over her neck.

Emer tried to reel back, but she had little space to move. "Are you... are you angry with me?"

"And why would I be angry with you?" he asked.

"I don't know, which is why I'm asking," she huffed.

"No?" He placed his hand against the rough bark next to her head and leaned in as if to kiss her.

Emer closed her eyes as she drew in a breath.

"You were saying goodbye."

She felt the heat of his words against her lips. Startled, her eyes flew open to find his fixed to her mouth.

"What?"

"When you thought the beast was going to take you, you tried to let go," he accused, his eyes flickering up to hers.

"I wasn't..." she began to argue, but the lie died on her tongue. Because she had let go of his hand and she had expected to be taken.

He leaned in closer.

"Let me be very clear. The only way you will be leaving my side is by choice. Nothing and *no one* will take you from me."

Whether because of the heat in his words or his stare, her bones felt liquid. For the first time, it felt like the Well was not the end of something but the beginning.

Emboldened by his actions, she slid her fingers along his jaw and cupped his cheek. After a heartbeat, he closed his eyes and permitted himself to lean into her touch.

"I'm sorry. Can we be done being angry now?" she asked softly.

His chest vibrated with silent laughter and she felt a wicked smile form against her hand. He laid his hand over hers, turning slightly to kiss her palm.

"Are you feeling better?" he asked, eyes sweeping over her.

She nodded. "Good as new."

"Good."

Rational thought eddied from her mind at the first soft stroke of his lips on her neck. The sensation was quickly replaced by the scrape of his teeth, which drew a yelp from her. He chuckled darkly before she felt the languid slide of his tongue trace over the small hurt left by his canines. It was warm and wet and made up of all things tempting and wicked.

Her hands closed around his shoulders, the muscles tense and unmoving as her fingers pressed into them. He hummed his approval against her skin before drawing it into his mouth. The sound that escaped her was all the encouragement needed to fill the small space left between them. He slid his other hand down and gripped her thigh, lifting her from the ground completely. His movements were urgent and hungry, making up for all the times he had not touched her before and all the times he feared he might not get to in the future.

Emer wrapped her legs around Calder's hips. The act received an approving groan as his grip on her thigh tightened. For a moment, she thought he was going to pull away, but instead, he leaned back and stared down, committing the sight of her clinging to him to memory.

With a multitude of forbidden words dancing on his tongue, he kissed her forehead. Speaking everything he could not say directly against her skin.

Stay.

He pressed another kiss to her nose.

Stay.

And finally, her lips.

Stay.

His breath filled her lungs and stopped her heart. He tilted his head, deepening the kiss, the claiming stroke of his tongue eliciting a whimper that she would have been embarrassed by if he had not groaned in response.

The wind began to whip around them and his grip tightened. Emer protested as he pulled back, his forehead pressing against hers. As the branches shook and the fallen leaves stirred around them, they both knew the cause of the agitation. Her head dropped back as she searched for her breath.

"Keane is worried," she laughed.

Calder smiled, pressing a gentle kiss to the hollow of her throat.

"Your chaperone should be *horrified*."

An overwhelming calm settled deep into Emer's bones, chasing away the worries that had long since resided there. There was a lightness in her spirit—a drunkenness in her soul.

"Strange magic," she whispered.

The peace they found felt tenuous and fleeting— a moment that was measured in sugar and hard to hold onto. So, they held onto each other instead.

"After the Well," he paused, selecting his words carefully. "Lina was right. You should return for Samhain. There are things we need to discuss."

Emer nodded in agreement but there was one topic that she did not think could wait.

"I am not ready to let go," she confessed as she buried her face into his shirt, breathing in his scent.

He wrapped his arms around her, shifting to sit on the forest floor, and pulling her into his lap. "I have no intention to," he said into her hair.

"Have you ever known a mortal with Fae sight?" she murmured against his chest.

The intensity of Calder's stare shifted and he frowned. "Why are you asking me that?"

"Keane was saying there are different ways a mortal can receive it and I was just curious if you knew anyone else—"

"Anyone *else*?"

She didn't move.

He didn't blink.

Calder stood abruptly, startling her as she clung to his shoulders. The gentleness with which he set her down starkly contrasted with the fury of his expression.

"I'm going to kill him," he vowed quietly.

Before she could even attempt to ease his temper, they were moving swiftly through the trees. Her words and feet stumbled as she tried to keep up. Even Alabaster could sense his shift in mood, calling out to him from somewhere in the distance.

"I'm not his mate!" she shouted, hoping that piece of information would calm him enough to discuss it rationally.

He looked at her over his shoulder with a wild gleam in his eyes.

"You bet the fuck you aren't," he growled, clearly not finding solace in that information.

"Start explaining!" he roared as soon as the horses came into view.

Keane's hysterical laughter filled the air as he fell back onto the blanket he'd laid out.

"You aren't helping!" Emer shouted.

"We both know I never intended to, lovie," he sang back.

"What did you do!" Calder bellowed as they reached Keane.

"Perhaps my magic is simply fond of her," he offered, turning to Emer with a smile.

As soon as his eyes found her, his features grew severe and his attention snapped back to Calder's.

"Did you *bite* her!" he snarled.

It was Calder's turn to smile. His lips began to curl into a feral grin. A primal look flashed in his eyes as he admired the mark. Emer's hand flew to her neck and her skin grew hot with embarrassment.

"We need to get a salve on that, you have no idea where that mouth has been," Keane said as he sat up and began to rummage through his satchel, which rested next to him.

"I can tell you where it would have been," Calder provoked, meeting Keane's stare.

White hot anger coursed through Keane. Though his magic did not speak in words, he could hear it urging him to act. It slithered up his spine, wrapped around his neck, and whispered in his ears.

Take. Protect.

Keane clenched his hands into fists. If Calder had not asked her to stay... then he technically had not made himself a threat. He repeated the logic until the grip of his magic eased.

He opened his eyes and narrowed them back on Calder. Though his magic would not force his hand, the protective friend in him still wanted retribution.

"Can we please change the subject?" Emer barked as the rosy hue continued to spread over her pale skin.

"I quite like this subject," Calder argued, his tongue trailing under his canine, and it was unclear if it was reminiscent of the bite he left on her skin or his desire to tear into Keane.

"Yes... let's keep talking about this... it's inspiring new brutal ways to torture him and even I am becoming impressed with my creativity," Keane remarked humorlessly as he rose to his feet and began to crack his knuckles.

"Why are you trying to rile him up!" Emer groaned, fighting the urge to stomp her feet and match their childishness.

"I would much rather play with you, but he is intent on preventing that which means he has volunteered himself," Calder cooed.

Keane stalked forward with violence in his eyes. "That mouth is going to get you in trouble," he sneered.

"It's like he was there, huh, sweetheart?" Calder winked.

Emer's jaw went slack.

Suddenly, the wind whipped up around them. Calder's gaze turned black and sharp croaks pierced the air.

"Enough!"

Everything went still and quiet in the wake of Emer's command. The unbridled rage in their eyes ebbed away as they watched her.

"Don't diminish what we almost lost last night because you are afraid of what we have to lose. You are not angry with each other. You are just angry and I..." She paused. "Am too tired."

CHAPTER 41

With their minds occupied with questions whose answers either eluded or displeased them, the group was quiet as they resumed their ride.

Emer's thoughts were a series of repeating facts with one overarching theme. Everything was about to change. She would plead for her father's life, but the Guardian could still turn her away. The weight of a lifetime spent feeling insufficient was a daunting thing when her task was to climb a mountain and prove she was worthy. If the Guardian could be persuaded, with the revelation of Lachlan's hand in her father's condition, there was a chance that the magic could fail her. If the Well did work and her purpose was complete, could she return home knowing what she was leaving behind?

Things in her meadow had been so simple. Perhaps the problem was that she had come to discover she did not like simple things.

Mount Fiú loomed before them like a sentinel in the center of an otherwise desolate valley—they had made it to Lunochy.

It was almost cruel how badly Emer's body wanted to crumble in relief when she still needed to make the climb. When she studied the map at the keep and the expanse that stood between her and her destination, it seemed insurmountable. She closed her eyes, visualizing the thick black lines, faded spaces, and symbols. Symbols that she now understood because she had seen the roads, drank from the creeks, climbed the mountains, and slept beneath the trees. They were no longer faded spaces. Now, they were filled with memories.

When they reached the base, they found the terrain was steep and rocky. Unable to safely traverse it on horseback, they dismounted and gathered only necessities in preparation to continue on foot. With more than half the day gone, they would need to push hard to make it to the top of the mountain before nightfall. Beholding the mountain felt like looking at the last page of a book. Emer held her breath, ready to turn the final page and silently praying that she would find the happy ending she so desperately hoped for. She let out a shaky exhale and began to make the ascent.

Keane grabbed her wrist and pulled her into a bruising hug. "You were always more than jinx and jollies, Emmy. We will face this together," he vowed, his lips pressed into the top of her head.

With a perplexing sadness glittering in his gaze, he gave Emer a thin smile and then stepped back to stand next to Calder. Both straightened like men ready to follow her into battle. Despite the fact that only the one making the request would be allowed into the grove where the Well was found, they would make the climb together.

She had faced an ocean, an ambush, a Sea Raven, a Fae, a mercenary, and a monster.

She faced her fears, her failures, and herself.

She would and could face this mountain and whatever came after.

With each step, a piece of armor she had donned to survive the journey was removed—heavy things that no longer served her.

It was not long before her muscles began to burn, spreading

until her whole body screamed. When the voices of worry and doubt shouted at her, the men at her back shouted louder.

"We rest tomorrow, Merrow. Keep going!"

Emer welcomed the cold wind that swept over the mountain as it licked the sweat that rolled from her brow. Her leg buckled, sending small rocks skittering down the mountain.

"Just a little longer, Emmy, love," Keane called out.

Another step.

Exhausted and unable to look back for fear of falling, their voices felt more like phantoms in her own mind. Guardians of her imaginings who fueled her strength and hope. Despite their efforts, they sounded as spent as she did. When she thought she could not move any further, she once again pictured her family... her home... her father's favorite chair. Even when thinking of home, though, she found it felt incomplete without a set of stormy eyes and the familiar chime of Keane's coin.

She reached the last of the incline and grabbed the rocks above to pull herself up, ignoring how the rough surface bit into her palms.

"Calder!" Keane shouted.

Calder caged her body with his, allowing her to press her boots to his thighs and push herself the last of the way. Once at the top, she fell to her knees, and Calder followed shortly behind, collapsing at her side. His outstretched arm fell to her leg, and he squeezed her thigh once—a silent encouragement as he worked to catch his breath.

Keane was at her other side and despite the fact that the magic in his veins had made the climb far less arduous, even he seemed drained. He placed a gentle hand on her shoulder, and Emer lifted her head, taking in the rows of lanterns that lit the path ahead.

She slid her legs out from under her and began to tug at the laces of her boots, humbling and grounding herself as she prepared to pay respect to the Well and the sacred ground on which it sat.

"I won't be running off any time soon."

She smiled as she handed her boots to Calder. With his other hand, he searched his pocket for the iron butterfly hidden there. He ran his thumb over it for the last time before pulling it free and pressing it into Emer's palm.

Pulling it to her chest as she searched for words she knew she would not find.

"Go and get your Well, Merrow." Calder's voice was a low rumble and filled with unspoken promises. As she began to walk away, he spoke again, "But please don't be long."

While the base of the valley had already been bathed in darkness, the mountaintop still basked in a fading gold. An ethereal state where it was not still day and not yet night under a sky of deep blues and vibrant hues of orange. Some might say it looked like a bruise, but Emer always thought it looked like the ocean dancing with a flame.

She followed the path of lanterns; the stones beneath her feet were still warm from the day. Pale trees lined the path, standing witness to the promenade of broken souls to have walked the same steps that she walked now. There was an expectant stillness to the air that stirred a nervousness in her chest. Her breath caught as the path of trees opened into a clearing. In the center of it, the Well.

A burn bloomed in her throat and rose to her eyes at the overwhelming sight of the surrounding willows. Each branch was adorned with cloths of varying sizes, colors, and states of wear. Each one a request, a desperate plea, a broken heart, a loved one.

Her finger fumbled with the flap of her pouch, retrieving the thin strip of white from her father's tunic. She pressed it to her lips as she closed the final distance to the Well, muttering into the fabric.

"We did it."

"We did it."

"I did it."

With shaky legs, sore feet, and a weary soul, she began to make the three rotations around the Well, mirroring the path of the sun. Once complete, she approached the Well's edge and began coaxing the bucket from the darkness below. The rough and cold stone pressed into her forearms as she reached across the Well's cavernous mouth and retrieved the rope from where it fell from the arch. Chilled air rushed up from its depths, carrying the scent of fresh rain and damp earth. Although she could not see her progress as she hoisted the bucket's weight, she could hear the sound of water trickling from it as it ascended. Soon, her desperate eyes, glassy with tears, reflected in the sacred water. With trembling hands, she pulled the bucket to the edge, every part of her being fearful that the precious liquid would somehow slip through her hands before she could fulfill her task.

Her chest ached from the violent way her heart beat against it. She submerged the cloth, only faintly aware of the way her raw hands stung as the water washed over them. Pulling the cloth free, Emer stumbled to a nearby willow and reverently tied it to one of the branches as so many had done before her. In her heart, she knew she could return in a hundred years and still know which one belonged to her father.

Her lips moved silently as she recited the prayer while stepping back. Once back at the Well, she clutched the iron butterfly that she had removed from her neck—her token to the Guardian.

Each moment that passed that the Well remained silent, she felt herself growing colder. Her eyes pinched closed, sealing off her tears as she felt the familiar sense of falling begin to overcome her.

A comforting hand fell to her shoulder, and the wind swept the scent of smoke over her. Keane's eyes took in her devastation, and for a moment, she thought his heart might have broken too.

"Why won't the Guardian come?" she whispered, certain the pity in his eyes was confirmation of her failure.

He sucked in a deep breath as he knelt down to her.

"Why am I not worthy?" The words came out in broken sobs, and Keane threw his arms around her and began to stroke her hair.

"You are worthy, Emer. You are worthy, and you are too good for the monsters of this realm."

The fabric of his jacket grew damp against her cheek, and after a moment, she pulled back. She had been wrong. It was not pity she saw in his eyes. It was regret.

"Why did the Guardian not come, Keane?" she asked again.

This time, her voice was more insistent.

This time, she was questioning him about much more than before.

"Because... I came to you."

Despite how softly he spoke his confession, the impact had Emer leaning away—the ever-present wonder she held for him drowned by the weight of his deceit. A sight Keane averted his gaze from.

When no verbal or physical blows were thrown, he chanced another glance toward Emer and found her shaking her head, unwilling to let the truth she now knew settle and take root in her mind.

Jinx and jollies.

Emer's stomach turned violently, and she swallowed the acidic burn of the bile creeping up her throat as she recalled what he had said at the base of the mountain—he promised that she had been more. She blinked slowly, calming her racing heart and mind.

"Tell me the story then."

She could not hide the pain in her voice, and Keane's wings fell slightly.

"If someone on the soil of Isle Basalt speaks of the Well, the Guardian is summoned to weigh their merit before they know they are being watched. That is where the legends get it wrong. It never happens once they reach the Well," he explained, fidgeting under her attention.

"I tried to leave you. After I first found you. And I did... I left, but I didn't stay away for long."

Keane pulled his coin from his pocket, affectionately running his thumb over it despite the bargain it represented.

"I have looked at this trinket for 400 years, and when I saw your eyes at the Alder Barrel during the brawl, I lost control of my magic. You were never supposed to see me." He paused, holding up the coin and then looking past it to Emer. "It matched your eyes so perfectly, so impossibly, that I knew you were important. The more time I spent with you, the more important you became to me."

Shock and confusion coursed through her as she stared at the object in his hand. She could sense his conviction, feel his urgency, but she did not understand how it was possible.

"The magic forbade me from telling you I was the Guardian," he said, rubbing his hands down his face and dropping to his knees at her side. "But... I didn't want you to be alone."

Loneliness had been the prize for his fateful bargain. The inability to die while having nothing to live for. It was pain. It was hopelessness. It was his curse. It was also the one thing he could protect her from.

She considered the fight at the Alder Barrel... how he had stepped into the path of the chair instead of pulling her out of its way. She considered the inn... how he had not attempted to intervene until the man bumped into *him*. He had waited for Ubel to strike him before he reacted. He had made Calder repeat her request for the chalice when she asked for it because he could not have given it to her at her own request. It was a constant dance to find a way to help through indirect means.

"You are worthy. It is I who am not," he sighed, holding out his now empty palm for her. She hesitantly handed him the pendant. The *iron* pendant. Emer's eyes snapped to Keane.

He gave a sheepish half-grin. "That is another thing the legends get wrong. Iron does not hurt all Fae folk. I didn't have the heart to tell you, and it seemed to pacify the Raven," he said, not meeting her eyes as he held out his hand and helped her stand.

Keane brought his hand over the mouth of the Well, pausing to look at her. "I am so proud of you, Emmy," he praised.

Still holding her gaze, he opened his hand and released the pendant.

Every tear she had fought... every fear she had shaken off came flooding into her, and her soul ached with relief. Emer choked as she heard the sweet sound of the token hitting the water below. It echoed through her, and her tired body fell against Keane.

It was done.

CHAPTER 42

They had never discussed the *after*, Calder realized the moment he lost sight of Emer. When the ritual was complete, would she return down the path she had used to leave? Was he meant to follow after the appropriate amount of time? What was the appropriate amount of time?

His own uncertainty, combined with the fact that Keane was uncharacteristically anxious, left Calder pacing along the mountainside. It was not until the wind began to stir and he met Keane's eyes as he disappeared that Calder understood.

He cursed the Fae for his deception.

He cursed himself for not having seen the obvious.

He cursed the Elders for their games.

If Calder had been thinking clearly, he would have called upon Alabaster to search the clearing, but instead, he raced down the path.

At the base of the Well, he found Emer, whose shoulders were shaking as she spoke something into Keane's chest. A growl began to claw its way up Calder's throat at the sight, but when she pulled away, he could see she was laughing. Her cheeks were flushed, her eyes rimmed with red, and her lids heavy, but she was smiling, and every murderous thought he'd been entertaining ebbed from his mind. She was happy. He smiled as he made his way from the entrance to where they stood.

"Still with the bedroom eyes, then?" Keane sighed loudly.

"How about you don't fucking push me right now," Calder warned, and Keane nodded in understanding.

Emer hiccuped, still struggling to regulate the breadth of emotions that were flooding her.

"Deep breaths, lovie," Keane soothed.

Fear has claws that dig in deep and the scars that it leaves once you are freed from its grip still manage to sting at the faintest touch. Emer felt like her whole body was a wound.

"How do we know it worked? What if I was already too late?" she asked, looking to Keane and Calder to invalidate her worry.

Their silence was deafening.

"Emmy." Keane contemplated his words. "The Well accepted your request, but it is a Well of healing... its magic cannot reverse death. Bargains like that are a much darker thing."

"Is there nothing we can do? I don't think I will survive not knowing," she pleaded.

Calder offered to send Alabaster with a note, but it would still take nearly five days if he left straight away.

Keane, no longer bound by the rules of the Well that had prevented him from helping her before, said, "I can go. I can go and bring you news of what I find. Whatever that is, we will face it together. I promise."

He explained that the bargain that tied him to the Well put significant strain on his magic if he attempted to leave the Isle, and while he would return as soon as he could in his weakened state, it would likely not be until just before sunrise.

For her part, Emer did her best to explain the layout of her village and landmarks or visuals that would help him locate her home.

Physically and emotionally depleted, the group agreed it

would be unsafe to make the journey back down the mountain. Emer and Calder would find a suitable place to camp a respectable distance away from the sacred clearing and await Keane's return.

"Try not to get into trouble without me!" Keane winked as he vanished into swirls of colors, mostly periwinkle.

For a long moment, Emer stood looking at the ethereal mist as it slowly dissipated. Her nails rhythmically tapped against her palms as her body protested the stillness. She had been fighting, running, and searching for so long that she forgot what it was like to be still.

Lost in thought, she had not felt Calder come up behind her until he was wrapping his arms around her middle. He pulled her against his chest, taking much of her weight as she collapsed back into him.

"Can we be done running now, sweetheart?" he asked, bringing his head down to press his cheek against hers.

She closed her eyes and nodded.

"Come," he urged with a gentle tug.

They sat side-by-side against the Well. Calder raised her hand to press a soft kiss in the center of her palm before pulling back and staring at it thoughtfully. Aside from some of her oldest injuries, many of the marks that had marred it were gone. He rubbed his thumb over her palm and let out a soft chuckle.

"The Well must be fond of you," he remarked, turning her palm up so she could see her healed hand and the few faint pink scars.

"Well, that makes one thing on this Isle," she said in a huff.

Calder gave her an exasperated look, "I dare say a certain magical being is *quite* fond of you."

"Jealous?" she teased as she rested her head back against the Well.

"You think I'm the jealous type? Even though I said nothing when he shared your bed?" he asked with a raised brow.

She looked at him out of the corner of her eyes, surprised by his comment.

"I wouldn't consider *that* 'sharing' a bed. He slept the night curled at my feet," she corrected.

"I would have happily taken his post," Calder interjected.

"So, you admit you are jealous?" she pressed.

"If it is not clear by now that I would prefer to be the one to keep you warm at night, I would be happy to rectify that."

Despite his exhaustion from the climb, the heat had returned to his eyes.

"Even then?" she smiled.

"Even then," he said, pulling her hand towards him once more, but this time, placing a kiss against her wrist.

"You want to know something else?" he spoke against her skin. "I have never known someone to spend so much time barefoot."

Calder shifted to kneel in front of her. Retrieving the wineskin that had long since been filled with water, he began to clean away the grime. Using his tunic, he dried her feet before sliding them into woolen slips and replacing her boots. With unsure fingers, he began to tug and tie her laces; Emer felt it deep inside her, each movement unweaving the fear running through her until she felt the final knot loosen and the tension go slack.

Emer realized then that perhaps the most terrifying thing she had found on this Isle was how thoroughly she loved the man before her. It was the kind of love that felt like madness but she would gladly accept the madness as long as it meant having him.

Before she could say as much, a whisper in the wind caught her attention. Searching the clearing for the source, she found nothing but Calder's confused stare. She brought her hand up to her head and rubbed her temple, wondering if she had spoken too soon about accepting insanity. The wind tugged at her hair, and Alabaster cried.

"*Run.*"

Every flame in the surrounding lanterns burned blue in warning. Calder hurtled to his feet and unsheathed the swords. The hands that were fumbling with Emer's laces were now as steady as the steel of the blades they wielded.

Backing towards the Well, they scanned the clearing for the cause of the lanterns' shift, prepared for all manner of monsters. What neither could have expected was the relief in Lachlan's eyes as he ran into the clearing and saw Emer.

"You need to come with me. Bring your Raven. They will be here soon," Lachlan urged, extending a hand to her and motioning for her to close the distance.

"Big fucking mistake," Calder growled, positioning himself between them.

Scrubbing his hand down his face, Lachlan cursed, and this time, when he gestured for Emer to follow, there was a desperation in his eyes that was too raw to be false.

"I will explain everything. Please—"

"Must you be so dramatic?" A feminine voice sang from behind Lachlan, cutting off his plea.

Lachlan turned sharply on his heels and backed away to reveal more new arrivals.

Three forms now stood at the entrance to the Well. Everything about them was like stone and gave nothing away, but there was an undeniable sense of wrongness that accompanied their presence. There was no weariness to indicate that they had just scaled the mountain—no rapid breath or beads of sweat. They were the picture of calm and so beautiful it was almost painful. Their features were sharp and unforgiving, so similar that there was little doubt they were siblings—two brothers and a sister who would be identical if it were not for their eyes.

The woman who stood prominently in front had eyes blacker than night, no whites or light to be found. They were a stark contrast to the brother at her back with bright eyes of golden honey. The third, a synthesis of his siblings, had an eye of black and one of gold.

"Lachlan... not dead, I see," the woman greeted.

"No thanks to you, Neamhní," Lachlan said accusatorially.

She gave a playful shrug before turning to look over her shoulder to her brothers. "Yes, well, dear Teárlach has a flair for theatrics. This time, I will make sure there is no room for error," she cooed, looking towards the one with honey-colored eyes.

The movement revealed a strange mark that began on her neck, trailed under her jaw, and below her ear—a symbol of three joined spirals. Unlike the similarly designed symbol that represented life, light, and peace, the spirals of this mark were inverted, with spirals curling in the wrong direction.

A mark the brothers also bore.

Lachlan moved as if to stand at Emer's side and against the new threat, but Calder quickly stepped into his path, demonstrating he had no allies on their side of the clearing.

Holding Lachlan's desperate gaze, Calder snarled to no one in particular, "What do you want?"

Neamhní sighed.

"Such a complicated question. Don't you think, Bás?" she asked, and the man with gold and black eyes to her left raised his brow. "See, Lachlan intends to take your little friend because someone has it in their mind that she is 'special'," she said mockingly. "Well, that's not entirely true. It's her blood he needs, and the silly man doesn't know how much. Just that it has to be *fresh*," she clarified.

Numbly, Emer turned her gaze to Lachlan. For the crimes he had committed against her family, he was already beyond redemption, and yet she waited for him to deny this latest betrayal. Lachlan looked away, and Emer's shoulders sank.

"I wish you were dead," Emer said in a whisper.

"Trust me, I have been *trying*. See, you were actually why

Lachlan and I had our little falling out. We don't want him to get your blood," Neamhní said with a serene smile.

It was a smile that Emer felt like a bite, and with startling clarity, she realized the answer to why it had felt as if the shadows were intent on either keeping or killing her since the moment she arrived.

"Because you want me dead," Emer finished.

Neamhní's bottomless eyes seemed to shimmer as she said, "Very much so."

"You won't touch her," Calder growled.

"Oh, little bird, you couldn't save her from my beast... what makes you think you can protect her from me?" Neamhní chimed.

Calder spun his swords at the wrist, shaking off the chill that had begun to grip his bones. There was not a drop of hubris in his movement, only the promise of blood if they moved toward them. Lachlan, too, kept his weapon trained on the triplets.

"Lachlan, you really are the charmer. I am astonished you convinced the Sea Raven to fight at your side. Given that you had a hand in his mother's murder and all." The black-eyed beauty's words were a killing blow, and Calder swayed slightly from their impact.

Calder's body shook with the force it took to resist looking at Lachlan for confirmation.

"You lie," he hissed through gritted teeth.

"Am I? Your mother, a midwife from a long line of midwives, knew a *secret.* One about a baby that had been hidden on Rest. A baby whose blood was passed down to its descendants. Imagine Lachlan's shock when he learned what he had been looking for was right under his nose the whole time. He was quite disappointed if I recall."

Every word was like a stab through his heart, and Calder could feel the tired, tattered muscle begin to stutter. His mother had been a midwife, as was her mother and her mother's mother. She had been lured away and tortured by someone he later learned was from the Isle of Rest. Tortured, he now knew, in an attempt to determine the bloodline of the missing baby.

To find Emer.

Calder's vision warped with the effort to keep his fury contained. Protecting Emer while getting the revenge he craved was an impossibility, and the waring needs had him splitting the seams he'd roughly hewn throughout the years.

"Raven?" Lachlan said tentatively. "I have done many terrible things, and I did write Muireann requesting to meet, but by the time I got there, she was... not that, I didn't do that," he swore, denying for the first time one of the offenses leveled against him.

At the mention of his mother's name, Calder's grip tightened in preparation to strike, but the haunted tone of Lachlan's voice—so much like Keane's when he had spoken of the carnage in the alley—made him pause. Calder's attention snapped back to Neamhní.

"Such a clever little bird you are. Fine, so I *am* lying. Late Mother Morvran would be so proud."

Calder turned to the triplets fully, not protesting when Lachlan came to stand at his side. Though their motives differed greatly, they were in agreement that Emer needed to remain alive, and for now, that was enough.

"Just so we are clear. After they are dead, I am going to fucking tear you apart," Calder warned, sparing Lachlan a sharp look.

Lachlan nodded.

"A threat we will both need to be alive for, so I shall worry when the time comes."

CHAPTER 43

The triplets stalked towards their respective targets—Neamhní closing in on Lachlan, Teárlach advancing on Calder, and Bás casually striding towards Emer.

Bás spun a sword in one hand while his other was shoved arrogantly into the pocket of his breeches. The wide arcs of the swords became too perilous for Emer to remain near Calder, and given she could do little to aid him with only her knife, she attempted to use the Well as a barrier.

Bás lazily drew his hand out of his pocket, resting it on the edge of the Well as he studied her before pulling himself onto it in one fluid motion. Gripping the wooden arch above him with his free hand, he leaned over the mouth of the Well, entirely unconcerned by the dark abyss below. He looked down at her with an expression that was equally cruel and curious—like a little boy staring at a dragonfly the moment before he pulls off its wings.

Emer looked past him to where the others fought, but Bás, still leaning against the arch, shifted to the side to block her view. Emer gripped the edge of the Well, her blade scraping against the stone and reminding her of her disadvantage in this fight. Her knife meant she needed to get close, and his sword meant she needed the element of surprise in order not to be cut in half once she did.

"I saw you that day in the crowd. You didn't hurt me then. You don't have to now," Emer pleaded.

If she had not been looking into his eyes, she would have missed the way they slightly widened—the color in one writhing like molten metal. His lip twitched and then he lunged.

By the time Bás landed on the ground, Emer had already broken into a run toward the trees. When she risked a glance behind her and saw she was alone, she ducked behind one of the thick trunks.

Though her mind was hyper-alert, carefully listening for the sounds of her pursuer, her body had grown numb from fear, unable to feel the branches of the tree behind her biting into her shoulders through the thin fabric of her tunic. Her violent pulse shook her bones as she listened and waited for her moment to strike.

Although he was light on his feet, Emer still heard the faint crack of nature beneath his footfalls as if it, too, sensed that he did not belong there and wanted to warn all that did.

He released a haunting and melodic whistle as he stalked her— a taunt. A subtle shift in his tune signaled that he had turned away, and Emer slipped from behind the tree as Calder had done to her. She gripped the cold steel of the blade between her fingers and held her breath.

When Bás turned back to her, she hurled the knife through the air, embedding it in his chest. Thick crimson began to spread as he fell to his knees. The blade made a slick sound as he pulled it from his heart and threw it to the ground.

"We will dance together soon." His words, spoken in a voice that was like winter air and apples picked too soon, slipped between her parted lips and tightened her throat.

His eyelashes flickered and he collapsed.

Emer retrieved her knife and his sword and raced back to the clearing, praying she was not too late.

The sound of the fight that still raged brought her a strange relief. If there were still swords clashing, that meant they were still alive.

Calder fought Teárlach in the distance while Neamhní sat on the edge of the Well, pleased to use them as entertainment. Emer raced forward but tripped over something solid as she made her way into the clearing.

She crawled away from Lachlan's body. There was no blood or gore, but he was unmistakably still, and his eyes unblinking. He had betrayed her. He had poisoned her father. He had sought to use her. Yet, seeing the shell of the man she had once known caused a painful twisting sensation in her chest. She had mourned him once. Perhaps one day she would mourn him again.

Neamhní smiled cruelly, and with a snap of her fingers, Teárlach lowered his sword and backed away from Calder, turning his attention to his sister.

Calder stumbled slightly at the sudden absence of his opponent. His hair was sweat-slicked, his shoulders heaved from his shallow breaths, and blood pooled at the corner of his mouth. He looked exhausted, but he still held his swords ready to continue the fight.

Emer prepared to advance on Neamhní when a rough hand slipped around her throat and pulled her back against a hard chest.

"Miss me?" Bás whispered, his lips pressed against the shell of her ear.

Calder charged forward, but Neamhní hopped off the Well and intercepted him.

"None of that, little bird. Be still." Magic imbued her voice, and to Calder's horror, his body halted.

Looking at Emer, he found the same fear reflected in her eyes, and he wanted badly to tell her it would be alright, that he would protect her, but his lips wouldn't even form the lie.

"It's a shame Mother doesn't allow us pets. If she did, I would be tempted to keep you. I would have to break your wings, of course." Neamhní circled him, running her finger over his shoulders as she did. "Brothers, should we make him kill her or make him watch?" she asked coolly.

Calder fought against her magic, but even as she came to stand before him, he could not raise his sword.

"It's always more fun to let them fight, only to lose in the end. The hope makes the failure that much more delectable," she explained.

After tapping Calder playfully on the nose, Neamhní began to back away.

Teárlach snatched Emer from his brother and her boots scratched against the stone as he dragged her to the Well. She clawed at his hand, finding no relief from the crushing pressure. Darkness began to creep into the corners of her vision, but she could still make out Calder standing just a few paces away. The veins in his neck and forearms were raised and dark.

It hurt. The way she could feel his soul screaming to hers. Emer did not have the air to speak, but her lips formed the three soundless words.

Close your eyes.

The cold stone of the Well collided with her back as they forced her to bend over its edge. Despite the blur in her vision and the stone scratching against her spine, she kept her eyes on Calder.

"You should have stayed in your meadow, sweet Emer," Neamhní whispered before placing a soft kiss on her cheek.

She didn't need to see the sword—she saw the fear widen Calder's eyes as the blade plunged through the center of her breastbone.

Faintly, Emer realized Neamhní must have released at least some of her compulsion over Calder because she could hear him screaming. A slow warmth spread over her, but it quickly grew cold. The faint tickle of blood as it spread over her throat, now free of Teárlach's vice-like grip.

Drip.

Drip.

Drip

She was mesmerized by the echoing sound of the persistent trickle of liquid. However, with each drop, it seemed further and further away. She was so tired. Her eyes grew heavy and she lost the battle to keep them open—a small kindness as now she could no longer see the siblings as they watched the life drain from her.

Instead, she saw Calder. She saw Keane. Singing sea shanties at the pub. Lounging in the field. She saw them shielding her as they outran the beast, and finally, she saw Calder's smile.

The thought gave her comfort as her body grew weightless. Embraced by the nothingness as she fell into the Well. The last thing she heard was the piercing cry of a single raven before she once again found peace beneath the quiet cold of dark water.

One: men *and women* grunt when they die.

Two: painful moments linger.

Three: death *is* cold.

Four: despite it all, she was glad she left the meadow.

CHAPTER 44

The moment the ether dissipated and Keane felt the ground beneath his boots solidify, excruciating pain still racking his body, he collapsed. This was his bargain. His curse. His gift from the Elders themselves. His mistake.

If he ever tried to leave Isle Basalt, every drop of power that he had coveted would turn against him, and for better or worse, Keane had a lot of power. They'd allowed him to obtain more and more, only to weave it into the very noose that tied him to the Isle — to the Well.

No one defied the Elders.

He lay in the clearing where he had left Emer and Calder, wiping the blood from his lips as his body began to repair itself. Even as he felt his curse dissipating, there was an ache in his chest, an ache that he had felt when on the Isle of Rest that was unlike any pain he had known—like his very soul had been carved out with a dull blade.

He parted his lips to shout but found he was breathing shallow, rapid breaths and could not muster the sound. Everything was quiet. Everything was wrong. The air was thick and had an acrid scent. One of dark magic mixed with something else—something metallic. The lanterns that had been lit were now extinguished. Keane's magic stirred with panic and fury, lighting the lanterns with a fierce flame and illuminating the space with a harsh glow. But the light didn't chase away the darkness, it only cast shadows. A dark red stain streaked down the side of the Well, the source of the scent that Keane had wanted to deny.

Blood.

The realm became deafening and utterly still all at once. He stretched his hand toward the dark stain, but for the first time in his long life, his fingers trembled. If he could not cross the Array, he hoped the void forming in his chest would swallow him whole. Reduce him to nothingness. Stop the pain. If he could just cease to exist, then he would not have to endure what would come next.

His legs buckled without his permission, and he fell into the edge of the Well. Once he knew there would be no unknowing, it would be real. She would be gone, and he would be alone. Again.

He would endure it for her. He would know, he would remember, and he would utterly brutalize whoever did this. His fingers dipped into the blood, now cold and thick, and he knew.

He knew how she was betrayed.

He knew how she fought.

He knew how she called for help.

He knew how she died.

He knew how he failed.

Even though he hadn't understood it at the time, he had felt her go.

"Give. Her. Back," he spat.

The wind whipped through the clearing as his magic stirred and pressed against that of the Well. The willows shook as his rage filled the space.

"I will not leave her down there. So, you can give her back or I will take her back myself!" he roared, becoming every bit the monster he never wanted her to see.

He curled his fingers around the edge, the stone fissuring

beneath his grip. The image of Emer's sad expression as he told her the story of Mian Loch flashed in his mind. She had asked him if the beauty of the Well was lost as a result of one male's fragile pride. Shame washed over him, causing the wind to die. He pressed his forehead against the stone.

"Please," he whispered. "Let me take her home."

The wind whispered through the clearing, and a much softer magic drifted through the space. He waited with his eyes closed and breath held until he heard the faint trickle of water as the Well began to weep. It overflowed, washing away the gore that had painted its edges. The stream increased and the water rushed out to meet the wall of willows.

Soon, Keane was on his knees in a shallow pool. He could not be bothered by the water soaking through his clothes, not when a form began to emerge. Keane let out a ragged breath when he saw Calder and thought perhaps his vision had been a cruel trick, but then he saw what was in Calder's arms—who was in Calder's arms.

Emer looked asleep, cradled like that, her head pressed tightly to his chest, while one of his hands stroked her hair. There was a slight tremor in his movements that one might have suspected was from the cold, but the distant look in Calder's eyes spoke of something else.

As they began to drift over the edge, Keane lurched forward and braced their descent. The three of them collapsed on the ground and Keane reached for Emer, his hands hovering over her as if touching her would confirm what his eyes already knew to be true. Incoherent questions poured from him as he took her in. Rather than trying to pry her from Calder, he cupped her face in his hands.

She was so cold.

"Your father... he's okay, lovie. Everything will be okay. You just need to wake up, and we will all be okay."

There was no answer, and Calder shook more violently as he

dropped his head. It was as if he had held hope that Keane could have brought her back, and now he knew that she was truly gone.

Keane's eyes drifted down to the space just next to Calder's head, the jagged wound from where the sword tore through her. When he looked back at her face, his own tears streamed down her cheeks.

They stayed like that for a long while, clinging to her in silence. She had been alive that morning. Keane had sat with her in a field of flowers beneath the morning sun. Calder had kissed her under the afternoon sky. Now, they held her lifeless body between them beneath the midnight stars, and they could not imagine the sun ever rising again.

A soft murmuring broke the silence as Calder whispered apologies and promises to Emer, who would never hear them. Keane's fists clenched, furious he ever trusted him with her.

"Just so we are clear... if she didn't love you, I would have already killed you for failing to protect her," Keane said coldly.

Calder sat back.

"I'll give you my sword to do it. Just let me kill them first."

Calder's voice was rough from screaming, Keane realized, but his eyes were vacant of whatever emotion had torn through him.

"You may love her differently, but you do not love her more. If I have to live with the knowledge that I failed her, then so do you," Keane hissed.

He did not care if it was wrong to say. He did not care if he was cruel. If he was forced to place her on a pyre. He would burn it all down with her.

They did not stop on their journey back to Murdoch aside from giving breaks to the horses. They did not sleep. They did not eat. They did not speak.

This time, when he entered the town, Lina was already waiting for him in the village square with Banner at her side. The rest of the village made themselves scarce. Given the body in Calder's arms and the madness in his eyes, he was certain they had chosen to observe his return through cracks in doors and between shutters.

Lina looked like she hadn't slept in days, whether because she felt Emer die or simply heard her brother's screams as he watched her soul be cut from her body.

Banner, too, looked grieved as his gaze fell to the form Calder cradled—the girl who wound up on an Isle of monsters, only to have stolen the hearts they didn't know they had.

Calder released Emer to dismount Danu, and even then, it was only for a moment and only to Keane.

They remained silent, forgoing the nonsensical apologies that some tended to offer in response to someone's loss.

"We have a ship prepared to take her home," Lina explained, holding her arms out as if she meant to take Emer.

"No."

Calder's answer was clipped, his voice hoarse like he'd swallowed shards of broken glass as he pulled Emer tighter against his chest. He refused to let her go in every sense of the word and Lina's expression fell at the despair in his eyes.

"She's gone, Cal. We need to get her home," she sighed.

"She isn't!" he snapped.

Lina's gaze grew wide.

"I'm not mad, Lina," Calder said, shaking his head.

"I am. So... keep that in mind if you try to take her again," Keane chimed in sharply. His eyes met Banner's, and when he did not look away, Keane's lips pulled into a snarl. Banner lifted his chin in challenge.

"Calder," Lina said softly.

"I rode with her in my arms for days, Lina! She is not wasting away," he roared at a volume that he'd never taken with his sister. A commanding and terrifying tone, steeped in anguish. "She is not stiff or rotted... she is soft and whole and..." He trailed off. "I am not a stranger to death, Lina, but I can feel her. She is still here."

EPILOGUE

The stones beneath her dug offensively into Emer's body. They pressed against her knees, hips, shoulders, and face. The hissing waves lapped at her feet like angry serpents, but she could not be bothered to move. She was so tired.

Something tugged at her memories, though, something important that she could not quite recall. The next tug she felt was not metaphorical. It was not hypothetical. It was a gentle tug on her braid.

A curious set of eyes stared back at her. A young boy with shocking white hair stared down at her, grinning. His pale blue eyes searched hers, looking for what she realized was recognition.

"Alabaster?"

The word came out as a choked sob, and his answer was to smile at her wider.

"It's Coal, actually," he corrected. "I am sorry you died, Miss Emer. Would you like a hug?"

Emer gasped as the memories flooded back to her, along with the realization that her once-feathered friend had kept his word. She had died and he had waited.

She pushed herself up and rocked back on her knees. Coal,

taking that as acceptance of his offer, wrapped his arms around her middle. His tiny body held her tightly as if he could see all the slivers of her ready to break apart.

For a moment, though, her grief was eclipsed by her surprise. Alabaster, Calder's intimus, the being sent to heal his soul, was a boy of no more than eight, and he was hugging her because she was dead.

"Raven or Fae?" a deep voice asked.

Emer's eyes shot to those of the Elder looming over her.

"Which do you think will come for you? My coin has always been on Keane."

To be continued...

Acknowledgments

I can't believe the time has come to write these. You would think that after 140k words—there was a lot of editing down—I would have a more eloquent approach, but big feelings are hard. If my characters taught us anything it is how to use humor to balance them out.

To God - Who sent us a fair share of miracles without me having to climb a mountain in Scotland searching for a magic well.

To my family - You are the heart and soul of this book. For most readers - it's a tale of magic, monsters, and creative applications of the f-word. You, however, can see all the unwritten words between the lines where our lives met the fairy tale. You know the moments we laughed, the times we cried, and the monsters we faced. I tell people this is a love story, but not in the way they might think because it is the love story of us.

This is my love letter to you.

A special thank you to my beautiful sister for pointing out my dangling participles and then continuing to give me feedback even after I made an inappropriate joke in return.

To my husband - I would have given up on this dream a million times over if not for you. Thank you for keeping me fed, hydrated, and caffeinated (within reason). Thank you for squishing me when my oxytocin was low and the urge to run away to the woods was high. Thank you for reading each iteration of this book and finding something new to tell me you loved each time. You are my happily ever after.

To Jes - Who has been reading, writing and dreaming by my side since we were in single digits. You were the first person to read this. You were the first person who told me I could do this and I published this book on the 13th because that is my lucky number - the day the world got you.

To my alpha readers - Brittany, Jes, Vanessa, Katie, Z, Ashlee, Cris, and Mel. Your feedback and support during the roughest drafts were invaluable. Thank you for all the emojis, all caps comments, and +1s that kept me motivated as I refined and rewrote... and rewrote... and rewrote.

To TGC - You are my people, my safe space, my source of PAILS of serotonin. I'm regularly in awe of you all and so thankful to be a part of such a special group of beautiful souls. I love you forever and always my tated mates.

To the BookMasters - It has been an honor to watch each of you publish and thrive. You are the best writing partners, cheerleaders, and de-escalation negotiators there are! This road can be a hard one, and I am so glad I am walking it with you.

To Katie - For formatting this book, talking me off the ledge, and recharging my soul. Thank you for loving this book, especially on the days when I didn't.

To Jemma - Who is the closest thing I have found in this world to magic. Like Keane, you came into my life bringing so much color and adventure. I truly don't think this book would have happened if it weren't for you, because you were the one who taught me I could leave the meadow.

To my uncles, Tom and Chris - Thank you for being so excited for me that even on the days I wanted to quit, I knew I couldn't.

Lastly BTS - The reason why I have *seven* Elders. Apobangpo.

ABOUT THE AUTHOR

Readers can find CW Wren's writing at the crossroads of myths, magic, and mystery. Her background in Psychology, emphasizing behavioral neuroscience, shines through as she takes readers on explorations of grief loss and resilience.

Her debut dark fantasy novel, The Quiet Beyond the Well, demonstrates her talent for intertwining intricate world-building, relatable characters, and intriguing plot lines that leave readers asking for more.

Outside of writing, Wren finds joy in the tranquility of the ocean, exploring new destinations, losing herself in a good book, and cherishing moments with her loved ones.